BERKLEY TITLES BY ABBI WAXMAN

The Garden of Small Beginnings
Other People's Houses
The Bookish Life of Nina Hill
I Was Told It Would Get Easier
Adult Assembly Required
Christa Comes Out of Her Shell

VIOLET SEA SNAIL
JANTHINA JANTHINA

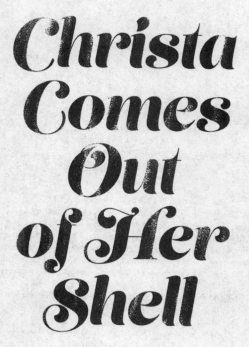

Christa Comes Out of Her Shell

Abbi Waxman

BERKLEY

NEW YORK

BERKLEY
An imprint of Penguin Random House LLC
penguinrandomhouse.com

Library of Congress Cataloging-in-Publication Data

Names: Waxman, Abbi, author.
Title: Christa comes out of her shell / Abbi Waxman.
Description: First edition. | New York: Berkley, 2024.
Identifiers: LCCN 2023026677 (print) | LCCN 2023026678 (ebook) |
ISBN 9780593198780 (trade paperback) | ISBN 9780593198797 (ebook)
Subjects: LCGFT: Novels.
Classification: LCC PS3623.A8936 C47 2024 (print) |
LCC PS3623.A8936 (ebook) | DDC 813/.6—dc23/eng/20230616
LC record available at https://lccn.loc.gov/2023026677
LC ebook record available at https://lccn.loc.gov/2023026678

First Edition: April 2024

Printed in the United States of America
1st Printing

Book design by Daniel Brount
Interior illustrations by Julia Waxman

*This novel is dedicated to the real Christabel Liddle, a reader
who carried a copy of* The Bookish Life of Nina Hill
*around her city to show me Nina enjoying various
attractions. Proof that no good deed goes unpunished.*

*Further, it is dedicated to readers everywhere,
without whom writers would be so lonely. We send
out stories like messages in bottles, hoping to be found.
Without you guys, we'd just be flotsam. Thank you.*

*And to families of all kinds, especially those
separated by distance and circumstance.
Love is a lion, powerful even at rest.*

"I am not an angel," I asserted; "and I will not be one till I die: I will be myself. . . ."

—CHARLOTTE BRONTË, *JANE EYRE*

Invisible threads are the strongest ties.

—FRIEDRICH NIETZSCHE

AUTHOR'S NOTE

Sadly, the island of Violetta is entirely fictional.

Christa Comes Out of Her Shell

1

SOOTY TERN
ONYCHOPRION FUSCATUS

So, I'm going to kick off by making one thing very clear: None of this was my fault. I was part of it, sure, but only like a flea is part of a cat. I was carried along, contributing my own pain-in-the-ass factor, no argument there, but I was not, in any sense, driving the bus. Let's not forget that when this story starts, I was literally on an island in the middle of nowhere. Hands full, head busy, heart well guarded. Safe as houses, baby.

Wait, that's not completely accurate. The island of Violetta isn't in the middle of nowhere; it's slightly to the right of Africa, many hundreds of miles into the Indian Ocean. It's a geographical, political and sociological anomaly. It's also home to a frozen vodka drink called the Barrier Island, *beyond which no man may safely travel*, but that's a sidenote. It lies two days' sail from a large

French-speaking island more than five hundred miles off the east African coast, which is probably why the French didn't bother to claim it. It was ignored by the Mauritians, because they thought the French already nabbed it, and blithely disregarded by the British, who had no idea who owned it, but had no reason to think it was them.

No one paid much attention to it at all until the 1950s, when an enterprising young Violettan by the name of Agnes Bottlebrush did a school project on the even younger United Nations and then quietly applied for membership for Violetta (Agnes was an overachiever with time on her hands). As the result of a series of fortunate and slightly comedic events, Violetta became the smallest member of the United Nations, and Agnes received a rapid promotion to Head Girl. Then she walked around to everyone's houses and handed them a copy of the UN Charter and gathered suggestions for what to put on the flag.

Agnes's successful endeavors attracted the notice of the BBC, and they sent a camera crew, along with a reporter who'd been the quickest to raise his hand when asked, "Who wants to spend two weeks on a sunny island in the middle of nowhere?" (In a strange but not wholly unprecedented turn of events,[1] that journalist's son married Agnes Bottlebrush's daughter several decades later, proving something about destiny, or karma, or the importance of follow-up when it comes to good journalism.) Bear with me; there may be a test later.[2]

---

1. Liza Minnelli (daughter of Dorothy in the movie version of *The Wizard of Oz*) married Jack Haley, Jr. (son of the Tin Man). I'm sure there are others, life being the romantic recidivist it is.

2. There won't be.

The capital of Violetta, such as it is, is also called Violetta, and has a population of around two thousand, of which several hundred are visiting scientists of all kinds. Why, you may ask, are so many drawn so far for so little? Well, it all goes back to the island's anomalous nature and fortuitous location.

Geographically, the island is too far from the coast to be readily reached by casual travelers, too inhospitable to be easily settled and too daunting from a distance (cliffs on most sides and a whacking great volcano in the middle). This peaceful lack of interruption for millennia gave rise to flora and fauna that aren't seen anywhere else, which in modern times brings a steady stream of scientists to the yard.

I've been here longer than most because I've spent the last four years studying the impact of the Indian Ocean Dipole on bubble raft snails. (I'm sure you know this, but the IOD is a phenomenon wherein the western Indian Ocean gets hotter than the eastern part, in a fairly cyclical way, which causes all manner of problems, climate-wise.) The dipole is only one of numerous challenges the little buggers face in the course of their intensely private lives; they're really fascinating creatures.[3]

I spend some of my time in the water, in a shallow-drafted boat loosely anchored about five hundred yards offshore, looking for my little bubbly colleagues, fishing them out, checking their data and putting them back in again. Much of the rest of my time is spent at the fishing dock, wallowing in bycatch, which is everything the fishermen caught and don't want. You wouldn't believe the things I've discovered, but you wouldn't be interested either, so trust me

---

3. No, not just to me. Lots of people like them, I'm sure.

when I say I'm blowing the doors off the pelagic snail community. Dr. Christa Barnet, queen of the seas.

On any other dock in the world, someone asking to rummage through a stinking pile of dead creatures would at least raise an eyebrow. Fortunately for me, the inhabitants of Violetta have grown accustomed to strange behavior, weird questions and odd interests. At any given moment, half the population of the island is enrolled in some kind of scientific study, and the other half is taking a rest and refusing to fill out any more daft questionnaires. Agnes Bottlebrush has a lot to answer for. However, if you're going to be invaded by a small army, it's much better to get an army dedicated to protecting and maintaining your ecosystem, rather than pillaging your natural resources, destroying your culture and pointing out your inadequacies.

On this particular day, the sun was a high, creamy disk in the cornflower blue sky as I was pottering around in my boat, doing science. The boat was loosely tethered about thirty feet out so I could take shore water samples, and I was leaning over the edge and scooping while breathing somewhat heavily. I'm not a very big person, and I basically needed to hinge over the edge of the boat to reach the water. It may have been ungainly, but I wasn't expecting company, so when pebbles started hitting me in the ass, I was pretty quick to turn around. A little kid was hopping about on the shore. Not only was he lobbing pebbles, he was also clearly trying to convey something important, because his lips were making a series of wide, round shapes. As I was listening to '90s hits at a pretty decent volume, I couldn't hear a word.

I yanked out my earbuds and held up my hand. "Simon! Stop, I had my music on." I shook my earbuds like sad mini castanets, but

Simon, who is the ten-year-old son of my landlady, kept hopping and yelling. Either he thought he had the voice of a god or I had the ears of a bat, possibly both. I scrambled around and started hand-over-handing the anchor rope, hauling closer to shore. It was only once I was much, much closer that I could make out even a single sentence. Unfortunately, the sentence I heard was "smash it with a hammer," which probably wasn't the best entry point.

"Mom says your phone keeps ringing," he said, which did explain the haste. Simon's mom, Miranda, runs the best boarding-house on the island. Her cooking is legendary—and I've gained both weight and inner peace under the influence of her sauces—but so are her temper and caprice. Noise isn't tolerated, contracts are verbal and nonbinding, and I swallowed because now I was in trouble and Miranda scared the applesauce out of me.

"Is she mad?" I asked.

Simon shrugged. "She said to tell you it's rung seven times and if it rings again she's going to smash it with a hammer." This was obviously a quote, and he tried to soften it with a smile. "You know—for her, not so mad."

"Crap," I said. "Let's hurry."

The way back from the beach is through narrow, high-sided dune canyons filled with the island's signature scent: dried salt and volcanic dust. The dunes are always in shadow, and you can feel the heat of the sun being snatched away the minute you step inside. They haven't been underwater for centuries, so the sand is not only cool but soft and deeply dry. Simon loves to run halfway up one side, his little light-up sandals pushing sand falls onto the path, then slide down and run up the other. I followed more sedately, marveling at his daring combination of growing limbs and reckless disregard for the laws of physics.

A denim blue butterfly (*Junonia rhadama*) chased across the path ahead of us, her patterned wings looking like the world's smallest tie-dyed blouse. A rustle to my left made me jump, and I spotted a sooty tern (*Onychoprion fuscatus*) flinging himself into the undergrowth, his flash of black and white reminding me of James Bond evading snipers. I fell in love with Violetta at first sight from the bow of the ferry, and I'm still completely crushed out. The humans are less appealing than the wildlife, despite the fact many of them share my field of interest. Humans talk so much and look at you expectantly, as if you'd been paying attention. Fools.

My landlady, Miranda, was sitting outside her house, as usual, drinking iced tea and gossiping with her sister, who owned another boardinghouse across the street. They looked up and watched me coming toward them, doing everything I could to express my regret and apology from the minute they laid eyes on me; I crouched a little, I raised my shoulders, I held up both my hands and I essentially sprinted up the street, with a triumphant Simon trotting behind like a greyhound with the rabbit in its teeth. The best approach with Miranda was extensive flattery, a mutual but unspoken agreement that the fault always lay with the tenant, and simple staying power. I was her oldest tenant, in terms of time served, so I had a little leeway. Not a lot, you understand.

"It's still ringing!" she said, with (probably) mock ferocity. She narrowed her eyes, which missed nothing. "Take it with you or turn it off, I don't care which." I nodded apologetically and sped past her to go up to my room. She added, "Don't make me move you."

I screeched to a halt, literally raising a tiny cloud of dust, and backed up.

"Please don't," I said. "I promise it won't happen again." Distantly, but clearly, the damnable phone started ringing again. Miranda slowly started raising her eyebrows, which is the beginning of an expression most tenants only get to see once, so I booked it up the stairs two or three at a time. I heard her laughing with her sister, so hopefully that means she won't gut me like a fish later on.

I finally have the best room in the place, and it's taken me all four years to get it. With great power, as you know, usually comes great responsibility, but Miranda has great power and a total disinterest in being responsible for anything. When tenants came to the end of their research, or they ran out of funding, whichever happened first, they were responsible for finding a new tenant for their room. Miranda's ideal tenant was one who paid the rent on time and came to her on their last day and said, *Thanks for everything, this is Professor Binglebangle, she's a geologist, she'll be taking over my room.* People already living in the house got priority, which means people are nice to their housemates and offer blandishments and sometimes outright bribes to get better rooms.

In the course of my four years on the island, I'd charmed my way up to the top floor, and earlier this year had only one move left before I reached Room Twelve, my ultimate dream destination. I'd visited someone in that room in my first week or two and decided on the spot it would be mine. (I love An Objective.) It has a balcony bigger than the room itself, with two sets of arched French doors onto it, and a view of the volcano that means you'll be the first to know if the world is about to end. The sun fills the room, you can hear the ocean, it has two ceiling fans and yellow shutters and is my favorite place in the whole world. As luck would have it, a week or so after I attained the top floor, the tenant of Room Twelve (an easily distracted entomologist from Leiden University) somehow let his study subjects escape and the whole house had to be fumigated. I have no idea how it happened, but one plausible theory is he left a lid open one time when his door was unlocked.[4] I helped pack up all the food before the fumigators arrived and was rewarded with his room.

However, the stairs up were no joke, and I was seeing stars by the time I flung the door open and started hunting for the phone, which of course stopped ringing the minute I put my hand on it.

Dammit. I looked at it: twelve missed calls in the last two hours, all of them from Mom. My mother being the force of nature she was, it could be about literally anything, but it was unlikely to be good if it mattered this much. I flicked to messages and saw I had numerous texts from her and both my sisters. Every text, from all three of them, said, **Call me**, which is honestly the most annoying text in the history of communication. Tell me more, and maybe I will. But order me to call you and my answer is going to be **Make me**. Besides, deductive reasoning indicated we were looking at some kind of family-wide issue, which meant I was now fighting the impulse to throw the phone out the window and hide under the bed. There was simply no way everyone needing to talk to me at once could be anything but bad news.

I glanced up from the phone screen and caught sight of myself in the mirror. With thoughts of my mother in my head, I straight-

---

4. Fortune favors the prepared mind, that's all I'm saying.

ened up and took a look. As always, I was wearing pieces from what she refers to as my "forest floor collection." It makes my life easier to wear khaki, green, olive or sand, because all of my clothes end up coated with seawater, salt lines and general beach muck. I researched and found the perfect pair of shorts, I researched and found the softest, most durable T-shirt, then bought four sets of both and never wear much else. Honestly, when Einstein did it, he was an eccentric genius; when Steve Jobs did it, he was a genius emulating an eccentric; and when I do it, I'm not making enough of an effort. Patriarchal bullshit; those are quality shorts.

I sighed at my reflection. I had a single strand of seaweed wrapped around my glasses and pulled it off to take a look. Not seaweed, but eelgrass, *Zostera capensis. You're a long way from home, baby*, I said to the plant (not out loud) and looked at myself again. To be honest, I looked like someone wearing a "geeky scientist" Halloween costume. However, while my clothes are shades of green and fawn, my hair is colorful and so are my tattoos, because those things are literally part of me, and for that I make an effort.

I took a deep breath and was about to hit *call back* when the phone rang again. I sat on the edge of the bed, just in case, and answered.

"Thank GOD," said my mom. "I hope you're sitting down." No *hello*, no *how are you*, no nothing, just straight into a warning.

I knew it. I clutched my eelgrass, which serves a huge variety of functions both natural and man-made, and was now pinch-hitting as an emotional support frond. "Yes, I'm sitting down."

Mom took a deep breath. "They've found your father."

My mouth literally fell open. I felt a rush of overwhelming emotion I couldn't identify, and when I said, "Where?" I was whispering. I couldn't get enough air for volume.

"Alaska," replied Mom, "but that's not the surprising part."

Thank God I was sitting down. "What's the surprising part?"

There was a hesitation, as if my mother couldn't quite believe it herself.

"He's alive."

FROM *PEOPLE* MAGAZINE, FEBRUARY 1999

It's been more than two years since Jasper Liddle disappeared, and his three little girls are still waiting for him to come home.

"My daddy's very clever," says Eleanor Liddle, the middle child of the family, who was eight when Jasper Liddle boarded his beloved Pilatus PC-12 in 1997, on his way to film a new season of *Liddle's Great Big World*. As the world knows, he never arrived. Lennie, as her mother calls her, resembles her father, his firm chin and famously blue eyes very much in evidence. "He's probably fine," she says, filling in the pieces of a puzzle. Her older sister, Amelia, reads quietly in the corner, while Christabel, a toddler when her father disappeared, runs around outside. Their mother, Denise, who's been forced to take an increasingly active role in the nature conservancy her late husband cared so much about, smiles shyly at her daughters. "They're all a little like him," she says, her voice soft but convincing. "He would be so proud of them."

Hopes for Liddle's survival stayed strong for several weeks after the crash site was found, deep in the Alaskan wilderness. The TV personality was an experienced explorer, naturalist and wilderness expert, who'd been carrying supplies (most of which were found on the plane). However, after six weeks of searching, the Alaska National Guard declared him officially lost. His widow, Denny, says she still can't quite believe it.

"He was so tough," she says, pointing to a photo on the wall of Liddle on the summit of Denali, a mountain he scaled during their honeymoon many years earlier. "But I guess no one's immortal." She shakes her head. "I still wouldn't be surprised to see him walk through the door."

Over the last two years, Denny Liddle has had to deal with repeated "sightings" of her late husband, competing theories about his demise (Bears? Aliens?) and continued media interest in his mysterious disappearance. And, of course, the increasing popularity of his iconic TV show.

"That's what he would be most pleased about," she says. "That the show lives on, and people continue to be inspired by the natural world he loved so much." She gazes toward the ocean. "The fact that he's almost as famous for the way he died as he was for the way he lived would irritate him to no end."

2

BUSH SUNFLOWER
ENCELIA CALIFORNICA

Meanwhile, in Present-Day Beverly Hills . . .

Agents representing entertainment professionals live lives illuminated by reflection. When their clients do well, they do well, and some cycles are virtuous and some are vicious. One fortunate feather in an agency's cap is a celebrity who DWF— died while famous. All famous people die, but most do not die famous. Most simply die old, like everyone else.

When they do kick off at their peak, their agency inherits an icon. It's an annuity, kind of, or like money in a mattress. Somebody benefits from the fact that Jimi Hendrix (for example) isn't a happily retired guitar player growing tomatoes in Seattle, though that would have been a better outcome in every other way.

Davis Reed was the CEO of such an agency. He himself had been Jasper's personal agent back when the TV show was first on the air and both men were in their twenties. Jasper had been a young graduate student who'd answered an ad for an on-air nature expert (no pay, plus a high probability of getting peed on), and Davis had been a junior agent for precisely three hours when they met. Davis's boss laughingly said, *He's your first client*, and somehow it stuck. Weeks later, Jasper and Davis had both fallen silent when Denny walked into the room, but she'd only ever looked at Jasper.

Now, decades later, Davis was sitting at his vintage Steelcase desk, musing idly on various subjects, when his assistant literally ran into the door. As it was a glass door, Davis had noticed his approach at the last minute and looked up in time to see the assistant overshoot and smoosh against it. At that exact moment, he'd also felt his smartwatch and connected ring both buzz, got three notifications at once on his laptop and two on his phone and reluctantly got ready to handle whatever fresh ration of bullshit this was. Something was obviously breaking big, and for whatever it was, an in-person download would be the most efficient way to get the news. Davis was nothing if not efficient.

His assistant was blessed with the kind of complexion occasionally called pellucid, and his face was swinging between celery and ballerina pink. Davis would have been concerned had he been a normal human being, but he wasn't.

"Spit it out," he hissed at his assistant, whose name he pretended never to remember.

"Jasper Liddle is alive."

"In what sense?"

"Living and breathing. He turned himself in."

Immediately, Davis pinched his eyebrows and the assistant felt his balls retract inside his body.

"'Turned himself in'? He's not a criminal; he's a client who's been lost, legally dead, and missing for twenty-five years." He looked down his nose at the assistant. "There's a group of Liddle's Ladies in Saskatchewan who've lit a candle every single night . . . which you should already know."

The assistant, whose name was Jordan, had made the conscious choice that he preferred the lecture he got for not knowing all the agency clients to the one he got for being late. If he dawdled for two minutes to read background on the subject of a message, he'd get the "being two minutes late cost me Tom Hanks" speech that he hated.[1] When Davis scolded Jordan for not knowing about three obsessive fans in Canada, he also got to demonstrate his ridiculous memory for facts, which put him in a better mood, overall.

Jordan, at age twenty-four, was at the top end of Gen Z. As an anxious and introverted teen, he'd gone to therapy and realized his pressing need for order was a massive strength. He majored in business and found a job organizing someone powerful and capricious because it scratched his itch for imposing structure while providing exposure therapy for sudden change. He thought of it as a growth period, and his therapist agreed. He settled his features into the "listening while chastened" expression he used more than any other.

---

1. And that also wasn't true. Yes, Davis had been slated to sit next to a very young Tom Hanks at some event and could theoretically have signed him as a client, but the "two minutes" was actually two hours, and Mr. Hanks had left an hour before Davis even walked in the door. But Davis never lets the facts get in the way of a teachable moment, especially if he's schooling someone who can't tell him to stuff himself.

But in this case, Davis didn't waste too much time. "And where exactly is he now?"

"Alaska."

"Alaska's a big fucking state and not an exact answer. In this order: Pinpoint his location, pull his file and check his contract. Book me a flight to Anchorage and whatever combination of helicopter, dogsled or trained orca it takes to get me to Jasper Liddle's side." He raised his finger. "Then draft one press release that says he's in New York, another that says he's in Madrid and one more that says . . . uh . . . Copenhagen. Then leak them to various parts of the Internet and hope it keeps the competition busy." He steepled his fingers for a moment, then added, "Track down all three of those whack-job Liddle sisters and see what they're up to." He hesitated. "I'll contact his widow myself." Another pause, just fractional. "I'll call Denny."

Jordan started to frown but decided instead to focus on the work while remaining divorced from the outcome, as his therapist had instructed. He turned and went to do the things.

As the door whispered closed behind Jordan, Davis flipped open his laptop. He'd made up the Liddle's Ladies thing on the spot, just to mess with Jordan, whose ability to roll with the punches was secretly very impressive to him. He started digging through folders, and ten minutes later he reached for his personal cell phone. *Time to play ball*, he thought to himself, dialing an unfamiliar number.

IN THE NEWS . . .

AP WIRE: (Breaking) Renowned naturalist Jasper Liddle found alive in Alaskan wilderness after twenty-five years.

VARIETY.COM: (Breaking) TV naturalist Jasper Liddle is alive! Founded longest-running public access nature show, valuable toy company, licensing.

BBC.COM: (Breaking) TV presenter Jasper Liddle walks out of the woods after a quarter of a century— someone get that man a cup of tea!

LE MONDE: Dernières nouvelles! Liddle est vivant!

SNOPES.COM: Is Jasper Liddle actually alive?

3

EUROPEAN STARLING
STURNUS VULGARIS

've never enjoyed returning to Los Angeles. The journey makes me cranky, and I'm no Suzy Sunshine to start with. First you have to get to Réunion, which takes a day, assuming you can find someone to take you if it's not a ferry day. Then you fly to Paris, because Réunion is a French island, and then to Los Angeles. It was agonizingly long, and I felt even twitchier and more snappish than usual. Everyone was talking about my dad. I saw headlines on newspapers, talking heads on airport bar TVs, and overheard conversations in several languages. It wasn't like Elvis had walked into a McDonald's and asked for a peanut butter and banana sandwich (which would have been sad, because they don't have those), but it was still an excellent distraction from the usual scandal and disaster. Nobody knew it had anything to do with me, the scruffy and scowling woman in the Dodgers cap, but I knew, and it was . . . uncomfortable.

Wait, no, I'm not being honest. *Uncomfortable* is the understatement of a lifetime: I was freaking the fuck out. I have no personal memories of him, but my dad has been a constant source of trial and tribulation my whole life *without even being physically present.* God only knows what was going to happen now that he was a) an actual living person, and b) the biggest story on the planet, at least right now.

When Dad disappeared, it affected all of us differently, and none of us well.

My eldest sister, Amelia, was ten when he disappeared, and immediately appointed herself Mom's protector. This would have been bad enough, too much parentification for any kid, but sadly, my mom didn't even notice, so Amelia felt both responsible and unequal to the task. Imagine getting a sudden promotion to a job no one saw you doing and that terrified you.

Lennie (a nickname that evolved from the way Amelia said Eleanor) was eight, and I think she just thought it was all very exciting, and then felt guilty in a little-kid magical-thinking kind of way and started acting out. She was volatile from birth, or at least that's the family trope about her, but she really leaned into it after Dad disappeared. I didn't see much of this, obviously, being only two at the time, but I've heard stories. Lennie has a prodigious temper, even now, and I won't lie . . . she scares the crap out of me.

Then there's my mom. The public story is that she was in Jasper's shadow and emerged once he was gone. The truth is more layered and nuanced than that. She'd been a producer on his show, and provided more than enough energy and light by herself, regardless of my dad's higher-profile wattage. His disappearance might have thrust her into the spotlight, but she hadn't been hiding before.

And finally there was me, the youngest and least directly affected, right? Well, when I was little I noticed people cried sometimes when they talked about my dad, when I was bigger I realized people were interested in my family because of my dad, and when I was bigger still I knew they were interested in me *only* because of my dad. Things had gone pretty poorly for me in my teens, and the light reflecting off my dad's halo didn't leave much unexposed. In the end, comparison with him was the scaffold they hung me on, so you'll excuse me if I'm a little reluctant to hail the returning hero. And yes, I realize none of that had anything to do with him personally, as he was theoretically dead at the time, but nonetheless, I'm going to cling to my irrational resentment, and good luck prying it from my sweaty, trembling hands.

The point I'm trying to make is that someone doesn't need to be physically present to have an impact—far from it. In fact, and this is borne out by the billions of people who adhere to messianic world religions, sometimes being completely dead is helpful, if what you're looking for is unassailable reputation. But I digress. Dad had been gone, presumed dead, my whole life, and now he was back, very much alive, and I wasn't confident it was going to be an improvement.

So far the press had been running the same photo: a man hunched on a seat in what was presumably an Alaskan hospital, rumpled, exhausted, a blanket draped around his shoulders. They took it from a distance, and he didn't know they were taking it. His hands covered most of his face, and a beard covered the rest, so for all I know it's Jimmy Hoffa or the king of Prussia. However, they were also running that shot everyone loves, the one with the ring-tailed lemur. Dad's looking handsome and grinning at the tiny primate, who appears to be up for it, though possibly it was just scared and planning to rip off his ear. Lemurs purr, you know; every home should have one.[1]

Anyway, there are a few photos like that, ones that pop up immediately when you search his name online. I'm so sick of the one with his shirt off, where he's holding his camera over his head as he crosses some murky river. Looking for shots of "hot dead celebrities"? That one's bound to show up. The one I really hate is the one where Dad is kissing Mom just before he got into the plane that then unhelpfully crashed. That one tops lists of "photos taken moments before tragedy," because there is no limit to people's love of the unsettling and intrusive.

I've always assumed people look at my dad, see how adorably my mom was looking up at him, and think *Aww, what a tragic romance.* And *Oh, the children. What a loss.* In the photo, Lennie was mugging for the cameras, already enjoying the attention. She was, and is, highly photogenic. Amelia is staring into the airplane cockpit, pissed off under her smile that she wasn't going on this trip after all. It had been planned. It had been discussed. And then, just a few days earlier, Dad had changed his mind.

"Next time," he'd said to her.

And me? I was standing just behind my mother, holding on to her coat. For me, that coat is the star of the photo, because I remember it so well. She wore it for years after that, the pocket always holding crumpled tissues, the sleeve where I pressed against it smelling of the hall closet, of sneakers and buttons. I can tell Amelia's angry with Dad and Lennie knows she's pretty, and Mom can't

---

1. No, of course not. Be realistic.

wait to leave. I've seen this photo so many times it's not upsetting. Like the photos of Marilyn holding her skirt down, or those guys eating lunch on a girder high above New York, they aren't people anymore. They're just pixels.

Despite the fact I have no memories of my father, I completely understand he means something special to other folks. To be fair, we're all influenced by people we've never met, often more than people we meet every day.[2] For some, my dad is genuinely significant, and once they discover who I am, you can rest assured they'll tell me about it. Sometimes they tear up. Sometimes I tear up. It's like two people from different countries, talking about a third country neither has visited. *Your father made me care about nature, your father made me less afraid of spiders/snakes/sharks* . . . Jasper Liddle meant wonderful things to lots of people.

Just not to me.

～

Los Angeles International Airport smells of yesterday's coffee and those pads they polish shiny floors with. The big round ones. I was musing about this as I stood in baggage claim, waiting for my backpack to clonk and squabble its way down onto the carousel. A small commotion at the chute told me my backpack was causing trouble again. It's not even very big; it's just somewhat . . . overpacked. Sure enough, it was wedged in the chute in mute protest, resentment straining its every seam. I stepped onto the edge of the carousel and leaned over to give it a tug at the same moment someone from the depths of the luggage system spotted the issue. With

---

2. See previous comment re: messianic religions. See also K-pop boy bands, astrologers and international media conglomerates. You get my point.

what was clearly a working day's worth of pent-up frustrations, they shoved it with an implement specifically designed for shoving. With a sudden pop and an audible rip, my backpack tumbled end over end and nearly took me out like a bowling pin. I jumped off the ledge just in time, although not without saying, involuntarily and extremely loudly, "Holy Mary, Mother of God," which came from nowhere and surprised everyone, including me.

Once everyone stopped staring, I bent to pick it up and felt a final pair of eyes on me. A small child sidled into my field of vision. She was wearing pajama pants under a dress that was clearly too small but had a horsey on it. Around her neck was a travel pillow, but she wore it with the gravity of an Elizabethan queen. She was momentarily floating untethered through baggage claim, as presumably the servants were locating her valise, and she watched with unselfconscious focus as I swung the backpack up and on. I may have staggered a bit, and I shot the little critic a look. *Give me a break,* I thought defensively. *I've been sitting on a plane for twelve hours and no one gave me a Peppa Pig neck pillow.* Having had this uncharitable thought, I felt pretty shitty when she caught my eye once I had my balance and smiled and gave me a very small thumbs-up.

Hang in there, I told myself. *Even this speck of humanity thinks you've got this.* I smiled back and turned to leave baggage claim. *Repeat after me: I am a celestial being of light, filled with calm energy and the ability to handle anything. I will not give in to stabbiness, regardless of provocation.*

The double doors swished open, and I took a deep breath and turned right to head up the ramp into International Arrivals. As soon as I cleared the corner, I started looking around for where they'd hidden the taxis, and saw a very good-looking man holding a sign with my name on it. As this was a major improvement on

LAX's usual ground transportation, I grinned and headed in his direction. I guess Mom decided to be both lazy and fancy, which is very her.

I won't lie: The driver was gorgeous, and damn if his eyes didn't light up when he saw me.

"Christabel!" he said happily, his voice carrying across the terminal. "Your mom said I wouldn't know you, but she was dead wrong." He stepped forward to take my bag and opened his arms to give me a hug. "I would have known you anywhere, regardless of your hair color." He grinned. "Colors."

I frowned and stepped back. "I'm sorry?" I looked again and suddenly recognized him. "Nathan Donovan?" If it's possible to blush all the way down to your DNA, I did it. Nate was a family friend I'd known all my life. I hadn't seen him in a decade, but that last meeting had been so mind-blowingly embarrassing you'd think his face would have been seared into permanent memory. I thought it had been.

He laughed. "None other," he said. He wrinkled his nose and the years fell away. "Now can I give you a hug?"

I nodded, still reeling from the fact that I'd failed to recognize the guy I'd had a pretty major tween-crush on. I guess the news about Dad had thrown me for a loopier loop than I'd thought. He was the same age as Amelia, but had been much nicer to the ten-year-old me than either of my sisters had been. He taught me to play chess, for crying out loud. And backgammon. And cribbage. And here he was, grinning at me with about a thousand watts of pure sex appeal, giving me a hug that lifted me off my feet. Normally, this is something I despise (just because I'm small it doesn't mean I'm portable), but I was too mortified and flustered to complain. I'll get him back later.

4

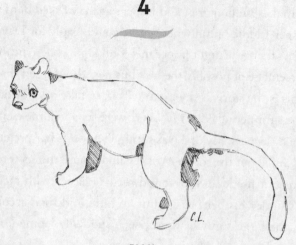

FOSSA
CRYPTOPROCTA FEROX

Alright, let me take a step back and fill you in a bit. In addition to being a famous TV naturalist, explorer and all-around badass, my dad, Jasper Liddle, was one of those people upon whom fortune generously smiled. You may be one of those people yourself, or you may resent one of those people, but either way, you know what I mean.

A good example would be the Liddle's Liddles. (Bear with me, we'll circle back to Nathan Donovan in a second.) In the early '90s, Jasper's show, *Liddle's Great Big World*, was doing very well, having secured a spot on national public TV. The show was the perfect blend of fascinating information, adorable animals and the occasional whiff of danger. Snakes. Sharks. Those fish with the things hanging off their heads. There were hip little animations explaining things, there were fun guests, it was a great show and the children of America lapped it up with ladles. However, public television rarely makes millionaires, and Jasper's agent worked hard to build the Jasper Liddle brand wherever he could. Sadly for Davis Reed, he wasn't there the night Jasper met John Donovan, so he didn't get his percentage of possibly the best business deal forged that year.

This is the story as my mom tells it, so take it for what it is. It was the summer of 1994. My sisters were six and almost eight, and not good sleepers. My dad was sitting in a sports bar pretending to give a shit about the soccer World Cup because things weren't going great at home and he found reentry easier with a couple of drinks under his belt. According to him, and then according to Mom, the largest guy he'd ever seen suddenly loomed over him and said, "I've been stalking you for two days."

At this point Mom would laugh, because Jasper immediately invited the guy to sit down and have a drink. "Here's the thing about your dad," she would say. "If he was in the mood to talk to people, he'd do it for days, and talk to anyone. If he wasn't in the mood, forget it. John Donovan got lucky."

It's possible it was good timing, but Donovan also made his own luck by saying, as soon as he'd sat down, "I have an idea that will make us both very rich."

Long story short: In the mid-'90s, a very clever man understuffed small animal toys so they could sit in a more "realistic" fashion. They took off. Beanie Babies were a cultural phenomenon and frequently unavailable. This is where the genius of John Donovan came into play: He realized disappointed children and their panic-stricken parents were going to be a substantial market. He and my dad formed Donco (Lidco sounded like a Tupperware subsidiary, Donlidco sounded like a town in Ireland, so Donco was where they ended up) and created Liddle's Liddles. They were cute, palm-sized wild animals, a teeny bit fluffier than Beanie Babies, with actual scientific facts on their tags. Jasper had the idea to pick unusual animals, like the fossa, which looks like a fashion-forward, sport model dog/cat/puma thing, but is actually none of those.[1] Parents snapped up Frankie Fossa and his friends hand over fist, and they were sufficiently cute to develop a cult following of their own. They're still made, they're avidly collected, and those little bags of pellets paid for my education and much else besides. Nathan Donovan is, obviously, John Donovan's son. I told you we'd get back there. Thanks for hanging in.

Anyway, the toys helped the show, the show helped the toys, and *Liddle's Great Big World* started selling all over the, well, great big world. Davis Reed was working his magic and everything was coming up roses and dollar signs and eco-friendly T-shirts when my dad crashed his plane and disappeared into the wilderness.

Fast-forward twenty-five years, and the heirs of both John Donovan and Jasper Liddle were heading out of Arrivals, with at least half of them feeling incredibly awkward. I heard my name being called. Christa *Barnet*, not Liddle, so someone who actually knew me. I looked around and felt my body flush again, this time for different reasons.

Alex Dutton, investigative journalist and professional thorn in my personal side, was standing close enough to be heard but sadly not close enough to be walloped. He raised his arm and grinned at me like we were old friends. Un. Be. Fucking. Lievable.

---

1. It's actually in the Eupleridae family, endemic to Madagascar and most closely related to a mongoose or a civet, something like that. Go look it up, I'll wait, totally worth the interruption.

Nate came through the doors behind me and slowed down. "Old friend?"

See what I mean? *So* aggravating.

"Christa!" Alex Dutton called again, and flashed what he probably would have described as a roguish smile, the hack. He's British, and has one of those nonthreateningly handsome English faces, if you know what I mean. He has a charming, persuasive smile, and uses it a lot. It's an excellent disguise for what he really is, which is a soul-sucking demonic fiend in human form. If this were a movie, the only way to kill him for certain would be to impale him.

"Alex!" I replied, matching his jaunty tone. "I'm incredibly sorry you're still alive."

"Ah," said Nathan, from close behind me. "Not a friend, then."

The journalist took a step or two closer, keeping one eye on my hands. "Have you spoken to your father yet? Alaska Airlines has no passenger of his name traveling anytime in the last week—is he too sick to travel?"

I had no intention of answering him, of course, but looking around, I saw he had a camera operator with him, and behind her were a few interested observers who'd noticed the camera and were ready for novelty. Too much of an audience to punch him in the face. "Come on, Nathan, don't even look at him."

"Got it," replied Nate, speeding up. "Let me know if you need any help."

"You're good," I said. "I do my own stunts." I looked over my shoulder. The journalist was still following, his cameraperson dodging nimbly between the luggage trolleys.

He started to fall behind and resorted to yelling. "Is it true Jasper Liddle is here in Los Angeles?"

Heads started to turn. I pursed my lips and sped up.

He raised his voice even more. "Now your dad's returned from the dead, has he called your mother? Your sisters? Has he called you?"

I stopped suddenly and turned to face him. "Mr. Dutton, I have nothing to say to you. How did you even know where to find me?"

Alex Dutton grinned, hoping to impress me with his commitment to journalistic excellence. "I knew where you were, so when the news broke, I started meeting flights from Paris that had taken connections from Réunion." He stopped a few feet away from us and gestured to his photographer to start setting up the shot. "There aren't that many of them."

Nathan looked at him and raised an eyebrow. "Stalking's illegal in California, you know."

"Hey." I shot him a quelling glance. "I got this." I lowered my voice but spoke very clearly. "Mr. Dutton. Something has given you the impression that you and I are friends, which could not be further from the truth. Please fuck all the way off." I turned on my heel and hoped Nathan's car wasn't too far away. My head was starting to hurt.

Alex Dutton was persistent. As we got into an elevator in the parking building, he did his best to join us.

"Why has your father come home now? Was the whole thing just for publicity?" He was holding the doors, and I was just about to reverse my non-punching decision when Nathan leaned forward and said, "Dude, your fly is down." Dutton immediately let go of the doors, and they slid shut on him checking his fly, which was, of course, closed.

For a moment, we rode up in silence. Then I said, "That was quick thinking."

"Not just a hat rack," said Nathan, tapping his head. The elevator opened and he led the way to the car. "You can throw your stuff in the back," he said, swinging open the door.

I just stood and stared. "Wait . . . Is that . . . You have your dad's car?"

He grinned at me. "Yeah . . . wanna drive?"

"Fuck yeah."

He laughed and tossed me the keys.

The Mercedes-Benz 500E is rightly considered one of the most formidable luxury cars of the '90s, and as I turned the key and heard the engine, I couldn't help grinning. I had always loved and coveted this car, and I wanted to go fast after so many hours of stationary travel. I'm not good at patient stillness, which is why I study snails and not anything that needs to be crept up on.

After Jasper disappeared, Nate's father, John Donovan, had kind of stepped in as a sort-of-dad, some of the time, if you can parse that much diffidence. My mother is a handful, so he was careful not to step on her toes when it came to systems of governance. But he was king of the day trip, and I have many happy early memories of sitting in the back seat of this car, wedged between Nate and my sisters, my mom sitting up front and laughing with John. Nate's mom, who I barely remember, only very rarely came.

I turned to Nate. "The engine sounds great!"

He nodded. "I could rattle on at length about this car, but I won't."

"You know it was a joint effort with Porsche, right?"

He grinned. "And apparently I don't need to." He looked at me and raised an eyebrow. "You're a little unexpected, I'll be honest."

He plucked the parking ticket from the visor and swung out of the car and over to the pay machine.

I frowned. *Unexpected* was a word people had used about me before, and I didn't really like it. If they didn't know me, how on earth could they know what to expect? They're basically saying, *Huh, the opinion I'd formed of you based on zero experience is turning out to be wrong. That must be your fault.*

Nate was standing at the pay machine, rocking back and forth on his toes. I am a highly trained scientific observer, so I observed. I can't help it; don't leap to any conclusions. I noticed, for example, that unlike his father, Nate was not a giant. Technically, I would put his height around five feet ten. He probably thought he was short, but as a shrimp myself (look, I can call myself a shrimp, you just can't call me a shrimp), I thought he looked plenty tall enough. Not sure for what, precisely, but I thought it. He clearly took after his mother, who I didn't remember as well as his dad, largely because they were already divorced by the time I was old enough to understand anything. She'd been a ballerina with the San Francisco Ballet, as opposite a physical type from her husband as was possible and, from what my mom has said over the years, a delicate flower who'd found both Los Angeles and sexual fidelity overwhelming.

I tried to evaluate Nate's body, again, purely empirically, but he was wearing jeans and sneakers, a pretty battered T-shirt and a flannel shirt that might have been as old as the car. It was hard to tell anything, but he looked like someone who would be good at dancing, if you know what I mean. I looked at his face as he headed back. Definitely good-looking, with a combination of wide cheekbones and an easy smile. I will add to the record that when he got back in the car and handed me the ticket, I confirmed he'd inherited his dad's deeply blue eyes.

He grinned at me. "Try not to get a speeding ticket on the way home." The right side of his mouth went up a fraction higher than the left side, which I shouldn't have noticed but did. His dimple on that side was deeper too. And while I was taking inventory, his upper lip dipped in the middle like the umbo[2] of, say, *Spisula solida*, or some other bivalve. What can I say? I'm a scientist, I was science-ing.

"I promise nothing," I said, swinging the big car around and onto the exit ramp. That grin, though. I felt a little hitch in my chest, which must have been related to air travel. I probably should have worn compression socks.

He smelled good too. For the record.

As I joined the flow of traffic back to the city, I suddenly remembered bitterly there was no point in developing an attraction to Nate Donovan. There was no way he would ever be interested in me, having seen everything he'd seen all those years earlier. Some things are just too hard to forget.

---

2. It's the softly rounded curve at the dorsal point of the shell, where it hinges. Obviously, it's more prominent in some species than others, but *Spisula solida* has a particularly pretty one. Intelligent people can agree to differ.

IN THE NEWS . . .

AP ONLINE: Following the incredible news of Jasper Liddle's reappearance, his family is gathering in Los Angeles to await his return. His daughter, Dr. Christabel Barnet, a research scientist, was photographed arriving at LAX today, following a hurried flight from Paris. Jasper Liddle's wife has not been seen in public since the news broke across the world, prompting concerns about her health. Liddle's current whereabouts are unknown, but reliable sources say he's been seen in Madrid.

Related: <u>Jasper Liddle archive</u>
Related: <u>Jasper Liddle: Twenty-five years later, what do we know?</u>
Related: <u>Donco trades higher (NYSE: DNCO)</u>
Related: <u>Dr. C. Barnet LinkedIn</u>

5

MONARCH BUTTERFLY
DANAUS PLEXIPPUS

As we drove through the airport, I spotted Alex Dutton conferring with his camera operator and resisted the temptation to mow him down. I knew he wouldn't be the last member of the press to have interest, and I could feel my temper rising in anticipation.

Nathan started talking, but I held up my hand and concentrated on trying to escape the gravitational field of the airport. I swear the traffic system at LAX is a test implemented by an alien intelligence to measure the limits of human patience. It will come as no surprise that I failed the test. Still, I could be the reason they choose not to invade and harvest our fingertips as a salad garnish, in which case, you're welcome.

Once I got out of the airport, I turned to apologize. "Sorry, what did you want to say?"

He grinned at me. "That's fine, I can survive a shushing. It wasn't important."

The speedometer was creeping ever upward, so I took my foot off the accelerator. I could feel Nate looking at me. He was definitely looking at me.

"Why are you looking at me?" I asked, more curious than anything else. Also, his constant looking at me was preventing me from looking at him, which I really, really wanted to do.

I sensed his shrug. "Like I said, you're a surprise."

I shot him a look. "Explain."

"Watch the traffic," he said mildly.

"Watch your mouth," I replied instantly. Seriously, it's a terrible habit, snapping back before engaging my brain.

He laughed again, easy. "Keep your hair on. I just meant the last time I saw you . . ."

"A decade ago," I reminded him. I could not *believe* he was going there. If I had seen someone at potentially their lowest moment, I might wait a bit before bringing it up in an enclosed space.

"Yeah, a decade ago, I wasn't sure you were going to pull it together."

Ouch. I shot him a look and found he was smiling. I frowned and turned back to the traffic. His smile was doing something to my breathing, and I was wondering if maybe I should pull over and let him drive because I was clearly jet-lagged. The angle of his jawline, the outline of his eyelashes . . . yup, definitely having some kind of emotional episode. I determinedly kept my eyes on the road.

He was still talking. "But here you are, totally gorgeous, clearly a badass, fighting off the British and driving away in the coolest car." He laughed. "I'm just a little shook. I haven't seen any of you except your mom in years, and in the last twenty-four hours, both Amelia and Lennie flew in, and now you. You guys are individually a lot, and collectively . . . I'm not sure anyone is ready."

I felt my shoulders start to relax. "My sisters came by broom, presumably?"

He mock-frowned at me. "Be nice." Then he smiled. "Although now you mention it, they did just kind of show up."

I laughed and lowered the windows. The warm-flowers-and-gasoline breeze blew my tension away *and* deposited particulate matter on my hair. He'd said I was gorgeous. He'd said I was a badass. Mind you, he'd also made it clear he remembered 2012 just as well as I did.

Better, probably. Most of my memory is a blur.

Sorry, let me back up again. I'll try to be quick.

So, my dad—let's call him Jasper, it'll be easier—disappeared in 1997 and I barely remember it. I was two years old. People think his plane crash is this big inciting incident in my childhood, this archvillain backstory, but actually, I have virtually no memories of him. My sisters have many more than I do, not that we sit around swapping tales.

Then, a few months after the search for Jasper was abandoned, there was a memorial service of sorts, at the Natural History Museum, or rather in the rose garden behind it. I don't remember it, but you might, because it was at that service that I wandered away for a moment and was caught by a photographer with a butterfly on my nose. You've probably seen it a million times: framed by flowers, my irritating little face turned up to the sun, a perfect yellow-and-black butterfly balanced on the tip of my stupid little nose, me laughing in that nauseating way that makes old ladies pat their bosoms and sigh over the innocence of little children. As my mother herself would say, it was enough to make a grown man yak. To this day, the pose and sickly sentiment are memed and mocked on the regular. *Butterfly Baby.* You would not believe the things that have been photoshopped onto that button nose. Or maybe you would; you probably have a better imagination than I do.

To make it worse, after my mom started the Liddle Foundation (which takes a chunk of the Liddle's Liddles profits and plows it into wildlife sanctuaries all over the world), she began appearing occasionally on talk shows, just as my dad had, bringing strange and photogenic animals to alarm the host and promote the charity. Part of my mom's reaction to losing Jasper and dealing with my older sisters was an inclination to take me everywhere with her. Including on TV. I don't remember which host first jokingly said *the liddlest Liddle*, but it stuck and trailed after me wherever I went. There is a mortifyingly large number of pictures of little-kid me holding various animals on national television. Let me be clear: I wasn't famous; none of us were famous. But we were *known*, in the sense that anyone who met me and discovered who I was (I dropped my last name and started using Barnet in college) would inevitably say, *Wait . . . you're the Liddlest Liddle? Your dad died in a plane crash, wow. That's you with the butterfly, right? Hey, I heard you once . . .* It's very weird. They think they know who you are, so you never get a clean slate—you carry baggage someone else packed for you. Imagine meeting a total stranger and they're like, *Oh, hey, I know you! Didn't your mom die of cancer? And your brother calls you Blimpy?* It's not being attacked with a shovel, but it's unsettling.

In 2002, Jasper was declared legally dead, and by then Mom was the story anyway, the brave widow soldiering on with the work of her late husband, her little girl by her side. (In case you're wondering, my older sisters refused point-blank to take part in anything, and my mom never enters a battle she can't win.) As I already said, this wasn't a very accurate story from the outset: My mom had a career before Jasper, during Jasper, and after, but the media likes to boil down a story until only the simplest syrup remains.

Then, as social media and the entertainment side of the Internet started growing exponentially, gagging for content, media interest became an irritating background hum. Like an air conditioner with a casual attitude to functionality, the story would unexpectedly break the surface three or four times a year, usually at the worst time. Maybe the Foundation would be in the news, or someone would think they'd seen Jasper in Uzbekistan, or I'd been on TV holding a marmot and there would be photographers at the house again. I tried to ignore it, because it wasn't that bad, but it still made me feel very observed.

Then I hit fifteen.

After the cute Butterfly Baby phase, I'd been a fairly plain and awkward child, thick glasses, a little too much hyper-focus in certain areas and not great at social cues. The other kids mostly ignored me, unless they were making fun of me. Overnight, my boobs came in, I shot up four inches (still short, just taller short) and suddenly I was interesting to my peers. From pariah to princess is a head-turning journey. I started going out, started drinking, started smoking pot, doing club drugs, partying with guys. My mom was busy, my older sisters were away at college and grad school, and I got very good at looking great while feeling terrible. It felt like everyone was watching me, and being hammered made that acceptable, maybe even fun. If they're already looking, you might as well do something worth talking about.

By the time I was seventeen, I'd been arrested several times for disorderly conduct, thrown out of bars and clubs on a regular basis, and was a favorite subject of the gossip websites. *Butterfly Babe Bares Buns in Beverly Hills* was a memorable if overly alliterative headline.

A familiar street sign went by, and I realized we were nearly home.

6

MARCEL
CANIS MARCELLUS

My mom never left the house my sisters and I grew up in, a row house on one of Venice's "walk streets." There is a more famous set of them in Venice proper, with celebrities, but ours is right on the border between Venice and Marina del Rey. The houses face each other across their front yards, with the garages accessed from alleys behind them. This creates a shady oasis of trees a literal stone's throw from Venice Beach. It's gorgeous, don't tell anyone.

As we pulled in and the garage door escalatored closed behind us, I swear I could still see my first wet suit hanging next to seventeen others. My older sisters and Nate had been big surfers and sailors, and eventually I'd been allowed to join them. By the time

I'd surpassed them in skills, they'd already left for college. I'd spent a lot of time alone in this house.

You can hear the garage door open from everywhere inside, so I wasn't surprised to hear my mother's familiar, high-heeled walk approaching the back door. However, there was also one hundred percent the sound of a small dog's claws skittering along, unless she had finally harnessed the rats to do her bidding.

I turned to Nate, who was getting my backpack out of the trunk. I stepped forward. "I can take that. Since when did Mom get a dog?"

He grinned. "Oh, you're in for a treat."

The door swung open, and I had two thoughts almost simultaneously: *How does Mom get younger with the passage of time?* and *Wow, that dog really hates me.* It was a miniature dachshund, as glossy as a racehorse, and apparently its default setting was "repel all invaders."

Denise Liddle (née Barnet), my mom, had been a beauty in her youth, and in her late fifties was still very attractive. She also gives the impression that whether or not you find her attractive could not be less important to her, which may be where I get it. When she opened the door, she was wearing a long wrap dress with a Japanese crane pattern, her dark hair twisted up into a complicated chignon, her makeup subtle but immaculate. For a second she stood there, taking me in, her chin tipped up. Then she grinned broadly, held her arms open and said, "Can you fucking believe this shit?" and in a rush I felt all the tension leave me.

After a moment, Mom stepped back. "Only your father could ruin my life by disappearing and then ruin it again by reappearing." She scanned me up and down. "I see Nordstrom still didn't come to the island." Her voice was notably deep and smooth, and she'd gotten into TV production by way of voice-over work. She could have been a movie star, maybe, if she'd had one iota of interest in it.

"No one comes to the island," I said, ignoring the mild insult.

Mom turned to walk back into the house. I followed, noticing her shoes, her jewelry. She didn't understand why I liked geckos, and I didn't understand why she liked Gucci, but both of us were entirely comfortable with our life choices.

The dog was propped on her shoulder, regarding me coldly.

I asked, "Who's the little guy?"

"His name is Marcel."

"He despises me," I said.

"He's incapable of it," said Mom. "He is a perfect chocolate button, filled with love."

The chocolate button narrowed his eyes at me as we entered the kitchen. "When did you get a dog?"

"When you abandoned me."

Oh, please. I was just about to open my mouth and retort when I spotted another good-looking guy walking across the kitchen toward us, holding out a plate of . . . mini pizzas. Dream combination (for me, that is; you might prefer triplets with cheesecake or Boromir with pretzels—I don't know your life). I smiled in a friendly way and took three, popping one in my mouth and grabbing the others for rapid replenishment. "I have no idea who you are, but thank you very much for the small pizzas." I looked at my mom and raised my eyebrows. "We haven't been introduced."

The man was tall, wearing a T-shirt, jeans and no shoes. He had one of those muscular bodies that look super casual yet probably take years of effort, and a face like a model for an outdoor-clothing company. He turned and looked at my mom too. Apparently, we were both raised in Regency England and needed a formal introduction.

"That," said Nathan, from right behind me, "is Leo." Then he added, "Sorry, I thought you heard me coming."

I peeled myself off the ceiling. "No worries."

My mother wandered over to the guy and booped him on the nose, an insult he responded to by biting her finger. I noted absently that putting someone else's finger in your mouth made it pretty clear you were intimate.

"Leo is my chef," said Denny. "Personal chef."

"And her trainer," said Leo, leaning forward and shaking my hand. This seemed formal considering he'd just bitten my mother's finger, but I went with it.

Mom turned a little, showing off her figure. "I have so much more energy."

I looked at Leo, who was gazing at my mother with a genuine expression of amusement and affection. *Hmm.*

"I will say in your father's defense," Mom continued, putting down the dog so she could pour herself a glass of wine, "that he did manage to achieve something I haven't, which is to gather all my kids under my roof at one time." She smiled at Leo, then at Nate and me. "It hasn't happened for far too long, and if someone needed to come back from the dead to achieve it, fair enough." She raised her glass. "To unintended consequences."

Nate handed me a glass of wine, and I was about to raise it when Marcel suddenly went for my ankles. I shoved him aside with enough force to lift him a little off the ground, and he retired to a safe distance to reconsider. Time to establish some basic rules of engagement.

"I can't believe you just kicked the dog." A voice, deep like my mother's but with far less kindness in it. "And you, such an animal lover."

I took a breath and chugged my wine. My sisters were here.

7

HIPPOPOTAMUS
HIPPOPOTAMUS AMPHIBIUS

So here's the thing to know about my sisters: They're close. To each other. Amelia, the eldest, is eight years older than me but only seventeen months older than Eleanor, whom everyone calls Lennie. They've always been as thick as thieves, and the idiom is apt because they've also been trouble since they were kids.

Before they were old enough for school, my sisters went everywhere with my parents, probably because it never occurred to them to leave the kids behind. They'd gone along on international shoots for the show, and my mom would hire someone local to take care of them. To this day, my sisters can go anywhere, be anywhere. They both speak several languages, and both chose work that keeps them traveling. I envy them their social fearlessness. Among other things.

However, it couldn't go on like that forever. School became a necessity, as my sisters were forty percent feral and Mom started to worry it was irreversible. Dad's career was taking off, and it was useful to be near the studios. They bought the Venice house, I came along, things settled down a bit . . . then fell apart completely. When I was born, my sisters were six and a half and eight, and I think my mom must have bribed them to stay in school by telling them I was theirs to play with. Certainly, that was how they viewed and treated me. I thrived and basked in their interest, letting them dress me up for hours and pull me around the neighborhood in a little wagon. My mom could not have been happier about this, and would frequently encourage them to "take the baby for a walk."

Lennie and Amelia look very similar to each other and were frequently mistaken for twins back then. I, on the other hand, was frequently mistaken for a cherub. This was an opportunity they were happy to exploit. One favorite swindle was as follows: They would park me and the wagon next to the candy store. They would both stand there looking concerned, sorting through their pockets and purses. They cut a very affecting scene. Lennie, in particular, was deeply gifted at flicking a glance at passing potential marks. As one such sucker would pass them, Lennie would mutter, worriedly, "But you *must* have another nickel," and literally, Amelia didn't even need to shake her head before the ~~mark~~ nice adult would offer to give them a nickel or (and this was a 70/30 chance) maybe even a dollar.

One time a lady walked out and simply handed my sisters a bag of candy. Like, three full-size candy bars and some gum. She'd also thrown in a book of matches and a scratch card that actually netted my sisters a further two dollars. It was almost like she'd seen children before and knew they liked candy, but beyond that was totally at sea. I like to think of her standing at the checkout, wondering if kids like lottery tickets, then grabbing a free book of matches as a last-minute addition. Could have been worse; she could have chosen condoms, which would have made for piss-poor balloon animals.

I felt myself getting lifted off the ground (did I happen to mention . . . yes, I did) and spun around. My oldest sister, Amelia, is a class A hugger. She fully embraces you, and even if you're taller than her (which would be hard; she's an easy six feet), she'll make you feel snuggled. She always times it right too, just exactly the perfect amount of hug, and if it weren't for her tendency to lift me off the ground, I would have zero complaints whatsoever.

Once she'd released me, I took a step back and grinned at her. She was as gorgeous as ever, her height combined with the same elegant features as Mom, but with an added muscularity that came with her work. She looks like the toughest player in a video game, which is funny, because she's a concert pianist.

"What's with your hair?" she said, reaching out to tousle it, a move I was able to block.

I shrugged. "I like it like this; it makes it easier for people to find me." It also goes with the tattoos and piercings to suggest I might be a badass . . . It's a basic tenet of camouflage: Look like something dangerous (an edgy chick who might mess you up) and no one will get close enough to see the truth (a nervous scientist who would rather be left in peace).

Lennie was, of course, right behind Amelia and now shouldered her aside to get her own hug. Lennie was almost as good a hugger as Amelia, but she could occasionally be bruising. She, however, was not a lifter, and I am grateful for small mercies.

As always, Lennie was dismissive. "Of course she has multi-colored hair. It goes with the weird tattoos and over-the-top body modifications." She shrugged. "Christa loves to be looked at." Actually, as I just stated, I hate being looked at, and the way I look is designed to keep people from looking too hard. But that's Lennie for you. She's always completely confident of her opinions, never hesitates to express them, and is ready to throw hands in their defense. She reminds me of that movie with the adorable creatures you weren't supposed to feed after midnight . . . She's small and cute, her features fine and regular. Her voice is mild and soft. She'll smile at you with great forbearance and shake her head in disappointment, then turn into a nightmare creature forged from rage and teeth and rip your throat out in one brutal, devastating move. After she spits the torn pieces of your neck onto the floor, she will explain why your necklessness is your fault, and why she'd had to separate your head from your shoulders. I love her just like I love Amelia, but it's not completely clear she loves me back.

I said evenly, "It's easier to say, *She's the one with colorful hair* than, *She's the brunette in shorts*, which describes a lot of people on the island."

"People could just say, *Oh, she's the very beautiful one . . .*" Amelia was smiling at me like I smile at dog reunion videos online. "Or, *You can't miss her, she's the sweetest snail scientist you ever saw.*"

"Funny," I said, shaking my head.

"I mean it," she said, because she probably did mean it in that moment. "You look fantastic. Island life must agree with you."

I relaxed a little, realizing how nervous I had been about reuniting with my family. The more time we spent apart, the harder it was to be together, do you know what I mean? I worried that they'd bring up the past, which they never did, or ask me about my love life, which they sometimes did, or be as disappointed in me as they had been, back in my teens. Right now we were being nice to one another, the suitcases of resentments still unpacked, the potential for peace still present. It seemed entirely possible we could navigate this bizarre situation without deepening any existing rifts or adding new ones. The possibility got more remote with every word uttered and every look exchanged, of course, but right then things looked peachy.

"She did nearly cause a riot at the airport," said Nate, who had managed to creep up behind me again. This time I stepped back onto his foot, so hopefully he'll stop doing that.

"As expected," said Lennie, turning at the sound of the oven door opening. "Leo, what are you up to now?"

Leo said nothing but removed a tray of baked savory . . . uh . . . pocket-pie-type things that made my mouth start to water. "These are too hot to eat right now, but in about ten minutes they'll be ready." He put the platter on the counter and turned to the fridge. "I'm going to make a sauce to go with them."

Nate had hopped over to one of the counter stools to take off his shoe and check I hadn't broken his toe (I hadn't, but I did say I would get him back) and reached out to snag one. "You'll burn yourself," said Leo, without turning around.

Mom took my arm. "Let me take you to your room, lovely," she said. "And you can have a quick shower and compose yourself."

I nodded, suddenly feeling tired and small and glad to be home. I hefted the backpack and followed Mom out of the room, with Marcel whisker-close on my heels. I hit the brakes a couple times to keep him on his toes, and will admit to some satisfaction in feeling his tiny, cold nose crunch into the back of my feet. He only fell for it once though, so not as dumb as he was cute. Behind us we could hear my sisters encouraging Leo to hurry up with the sauce and Nathan running cold water on his hand. It felt very much like home all of a sudden, like a familiar book released in a new edition.

Mom had obviously redecorated my room since I moved out, and it had become a light and friendly guest room. It actually reminded me of Violetta, but with the saturation turned down fifty percent. It was pale, creamy, with spangles of yellow light bouncing from ocean to beach to windows fringed with suncatchers. I'd been obsessed with them in seventh grade, filling the house with a vaguely noxious smell and ruining more than one of my mom's baking sheets. But she'd kept them all, it seemed, because here they all were. All different animals, not a good one among them, not one where the colors stayed in the lines, but all of them were pretty and I was happy to see them. She'd threaded them onto ribbon and hung them across the tops of the windows. I walked over and touched one or two, wondering why hippos were always depicted as such plump and friendly animals when in fact they're ridiculously bad-tempered and ready to stomp you to death given half a chance. Did you know they're actually more closely related to whales than they are to pigs or anything like that? Think of them as crabby, landlocked orcas, looking around at their hot surroundings and yearning for deep, cool water. No wonder they're cross.

I put my backpack down and looked at my mom. "So . . . how did you actually hear Dad was back?"

Mom sat on the edge of the bed and shrugged. "There I was, watching *The Great British Baking Show* with Leo and Marcel, when the phone rings and it's some cop in Alaska, some local cop whose name I never even caught, and he said, 'Your husband, Jasper Liddle, just walked into the station here in whatever-the-fuck-ville and he says to tell you he'll be in touch soon.'" She turned up her hands in exasperation. "What am I supposed to say to that? I called the lawyer, and he was as perplexed as I was. For the first three days, I kept literally looking out the window in case Jasper was walking down the street, but now I'm just really pissed off." Irritation covered the anxiety in her voice, but not very successfully.

I sat next to her. "Did you think he would just show up?"

Mom rubbed her hands against her thighs. "I don't know. I don't know anything, because even though he's supposedly still alive, he hasn't extended me the basic courtesy of a phone call. I'd go up there but . . . you know how that usually turns out."

I did. Periodically over the years people would "discover" my dad. More at the beginning, of course. He'd been spotted in Spain, in South Africa, and at Walmart. There was a man in Kenosha, Wisconsin, who looked so much like him that for the first year or two after Jasper disappeared the poor guy had to grow a beard because people kept rushing up to him in excitement. Once or twice these sightings had seemed credible, and Mom found it hard not to get her hopes up. After the second or third disappointed and lonely flight home, she decided not to go in person ever again.

Now she said, "You know who I have heard from? His agent. Davis Reed. He and I have exchanged holiday cards and maybe three words in the last twenty years, yet he was on the phone to me the day the news broke."

"Great, let's call him tomorrow and see what he knows."

Denny nodded. "Sure. He and I went out for dinner a few times the year after your father disappeared. He was very suave, very smart, not my type. Now he runs his own agency and is a pretty big fish. For all we know he still considers your dad a client and is putting together a movie deal as we speak." She sighed. "You didn't know your father, but he . . ."

There was a knock at the door, and after a second, Leo poked his head around.

"Denny, not sure how to say this, but your dead husband's on TV being interviewed by Oprah."

Denny turned and looked at me. "Like I said . . ."

8

COCKER SPANIEL
CANIS WINFREYUS

As always, Oprah was calm, compassionate and wearing a trouser suit. She was sitting in a garden somewhere, facing Jasper Liddle across a white wicker table, with a small dog who had no idea it was on television.

Lennie and Amelia were both on their feet in front of the screen, radiating anger and confusion. Leo went back into the kitchen and started mixing cocktails alongside Nathan, who'd also retreated to a safe distance. I didn't think I would get away with joining them, although believe me, I considered it.

"I'm sorry, did this just come on?" I asked, confused.

"Like, eight people texted me it was on," said Lennie. "I cannot *believe* he went on national TV before he came to see us." She was furious, but her voice broke a little bit.

Oprah took a deep breath and in her straightforward way said, "So, Jasper, it's been over twenty-five years since your airplane fell out of the sky—we all want to know, where have you been?" She leaned forward, and so did the six of us, metaphorically at least.

The camera swiveled to Jasper, and I looked at my father with a great deal of curiosity. Apparently, he'd spent his time hiding out at a spa, because he hadn't aged all that much, and if anything the angled planes of his face were just craggier and more interesting. He looked like the hot dad at graduation. So irritating.

I turned to my mom. "How is it possible he looks so great?"

"Maybe he was abducted by aliens after all and they had excellent skin care?" I could tell by the jumping of her eyelid that she was completely pissed off. "That's what bothers you? His complexion?"

"Yeah," said Lennie, who was also clearly ticked. "How about why is he talking to effing Oprah and not us? Why didn't he come straight here?"

"Well, Oprah," Jasper was saying, "it's a strange story."

"No shit," yelled Amelia suddenly, startling Marcel so much he growled at me even though I had nothing to do with it. She turned to Lennie and said, "Do you think they're doing this live? Isn't her house somewhere near here? Let's go!"

Lennie nodded and pulled out her phone. "I'll google her address."

"Calm down," said my mother suddenly. "Calm down, sit down, have a martini. Let's hear what he has to say before we get all bent out of shape."

Amelia and Lennie started to argue, but she raised her hand so they sat down. Pushing me off the sofa, I might add. Leo was heading toward us with a pitcher of martinis, and I started getting a headache in anticipation. I scrambled up and went to grab something else to drink. I could hear just fine from the kitchen, and now there was a marble-topped island between me and my pissed-off sisters.

Nate was still there, and I realized he was watching the show on a tablet. I leaned over to look and he scooched a little closer. Now his hip was touching my hip, which was distracting, but I needed to see the show, right? Don't judge.

"Well," said Oprah, "why don't you start with the accident. You were an accomplished pilot—what happened?"

"Bird strike," replied Jasper, looking serious. "A fairly large bird, maybe a goose, knocked out the starboard engine and I had to put down." He shook his head at the memory, a lock of graying hair falling attractively over his forehead. "It was pretty much solid forest below me, and the plane sustained a lot of damage." He looked ruefully up at his interviewer and flashed the smile *Hello!* magazine once referred to as "charmingly crooked." "I guess I'm not as good a pilot as I thought."

I realized he was wearing essentially what he used to wear presenting his show: weathered jeans, flannel shirt, canvas field jacket . . . as if he'd just walked onto a set, not out of the grave. I noticed a cane leaning against the chair, dark and simple. Hmm. I moved away from Nate and opened the fridge, looking for distraction. Ooh, an unexpected glass-bottle Coke. *Come to me, siren.*

Behind my back, Oprah reassured him, "It must have happened very fast."

He was so earnest. "It did. The plane broke apart, and I was thrown . . . When I came to, it was dark." I pulled open a kitchen drawer and hunted for the bottle opener. Nate made a noise and slid it across to me, having used it to open his beer. I popped the Coke and leaned against the counter to half watch, half listen to the show. Nate looked at me and smiled uncertainly.

"This is incredibly weird," he said quietly. "Are you OK?"

I wasn't sure, to be honest. I looked down at Jasper on the little screen. He was answering Oprah's question, and his features had settled into lines of discomfort as he remembered. You had to give it to him: He hadn't lost any of his ability to connect with an audience. I turned away again and drank my Coke, shrugging. I was hoping the caffeine would help me stay awake. And though I appreciated Nate's question, and I really wasn't OK, there was no way I was going to admit it anywhere near my sisters. Plus, Violetta is eleven hours ahead of Los Angeles, and the jet lag was starting to fuzz my brain around the edges.

Oprah frowned. "Were you badly hurt?"

I imagined Jasper shrugging just as I had. I could hear it in his voice. He said, "I was confused . . . I guess I had a concussion, but at the time all I knew was that I'd woken up in a forest in the middle of the night with the worst headache of my life and no idea at all of how I'd gotten there."

Oprah was incredulous. "You lost your memory?"

"Yes," replied Jasper, nodding. "I didn't know who I was, or what on earth was going on." He looked at Oprah, and you could see the intensity of his expression. "It was freezing cold and completely terrifying."

Oprah turned to the camera. "We have to go to a break, but we'll be right back to hear more of this incredible story."

As an ad for potato chips came on, my sisters erupted. I was glad I was in the kitchen, because both of them leaping and stomping is a lot to dodge.

"Is he out of his mind?" said Amelia, pacing. "He cannot possibly think anyone's going to believe him!"

Mom frowned and looked up at her. "Amelia, it happens." She took a deep breath and looked pale for a second. "Can you cool down a bit? You're giving me a headache."

Lennie looked at her. "You OK, Mom?"

Leo appeared with a glass of ice water, and Mom's color started to come back. "I'm sorry," she said. "It's really quite a shock to see the old bastard."

My sisters and I looked at one another and telepathically agreed that if Jasper's return to the living affected our mother too badly, we would simply return him to his previously assumed state. The Liddles protect their own, though we've never had to protect our own from . . . our own before.

Oprah's show came back from the break, and Jasper got on with his story. "That first night, there were periods where I think I was hallucinating, or unconscious, but what I do remember is trying to walk downhill. That was my one thought. Head down, find water, follow it."

He swallowed and closed his eyes briefly. "I wandered for what felt like days. It rained on and off, so I had water, thank God, but that was it. No food. No shelter. Eventually, I bumped a tree a bit too hard and went down. When I woke up, I wasn't alone; someone had rolled me onto a blanket and was dragging me along. Every so often they would stop and give me water, but then they would just keep going. I was delirious; the journey seemed to last forever. When I finally woke up, several days had passed and I was in a cabin fairly distant from the crash site. There was a woman there, the woman who'd rescued me. Her name was Lorna." He looked at Oprah and smiled. "She'd been out with her dog; it was a miracle."

The camera cut to Oprah, but as always, she was radiating non-judgment. "Of course . . . carry on," she said. I guess it wouldn't be on-brand for her to point at him and shout *bullshit* really loudly, which is what I would have done, in her place.

Jasper kept talking. "I was there for weeks, sometimes with a fever, sometimes better. At that point I had no idea who I was, or what had happened. And neither did she."

Oprah was politely incredulous. "How is that possible? It was the biggest news story at the time; everyone was looking for you."

Jasper shrugged. "Lorna didn't know me. I was just a regular guy to her, a guy who needed help."

"Why didn't she call an ambulance?"

Jasper laughed. "There was barely a track to her cabin; she'd lived out there alone for several years. She had no TV, just a radio she never listened to. The nearest hospital was a hundred kilometers away, maybe more. I'd wandered miles."

Oprah didn't look convinced, not yet. "And a quarter of a century later you remembered who you were?"

"No." Jasper dropped his head and there was a long silence. He looked up and his eyes were filled with tears. "I remembered a few months after the accident . . . that I had a wife and children, a whole life back in Los Angeles."

Oprah cocked her head, as she does so well. "And?"

He made a helpless gesture. "I panicked at first, trying to understand . . ." He shook his head. "Here's the thing." His eyes were still bright with tears, but his voice was clear. "I remembered it all. I remembered how tired I had been. I remembered my wife and I had been fighting and were separating." He blushed suddenly. "And Lorna and I fell in love."

Oprah was agog. "Before or after you remembered?"

Jasper leaned forward earnestly. "You have to understand, it just . . . happened. She was taking care of me, we were both alone . . . it was . . ." His voice faltered.

Oprah paused delicately. "You're using the past tense."

Jasper nodded. "Lorna died. Two years ago."

"And you were together that whole time?"

"Yes. Once I remembered, I told her, of course, immediately. We talked it over for weeks, and then it was winter, and then . . ." He looked at Oprah, troubled. "I don't really understand it myself, I'll be honest. Right now it sounds crazy as I say it. But I knew Denny and the girls would be fine without me; they had money, they had one another, they had my business partner, the show, the toys . . . and I had found something I didn't even know I needed— a totally different life." He looked at his hands as they sat curled in his lap. "We felt blessed, like it was a gift from the universe."

"Oh, for fuck's sake," said Amelia. "Is anyone else feeling nauseous?"

"I've felt better," said Lennie.

"Can a human get a fur ball?" asked Mom.

Oprah pushed a little. "Your children . . . You must have felt guilty."

He nodded earnestly. "I did. I do. I have no idea if my family will ever forgive me, or even see me." He looked up suddenly, straight into the camera. It was classic Jasper Liddle. "Denny, if you're watching, please know I'm sorry and I want to talk." He held the camera's gaze for a moment, the merest hint of a tearful dimple appearing on his chin and vanishing again. "Amelia, Eleanor, Christabel . . ." His voice broke completely and he buried his face in his hands. He lifted it for a moment to say, "I have a lot of apologizing to do."

"That's it," said Lennie. "I'm going to vomit." She got up and came into the kitchen, pulling open the freezer. "I'll obviously need to eat something first. Where's the ice cream?"

The interview ended not long after that, and Leo waved the remote control to turn off the screen. Nathan and I emerged from the kitchen, now that everyone seemed calm.

There was total silence for a moment. Then my mom spoke.

"Alright, folks," she said brightly, as though we were discussing paint colors for the kitchen. "Thoughts?" She was leaning back on the sofa, her arm along the back, her long legs crossed. She looked like a painting by Sargent, but her foot twitched like a dog dreaming of rabbits on roller skates.

I looked around, but no one said anything. I made a face and went first. "It's a ridiculous story. How could it possibly be true?"

Nathan raised his hand. "Because sometimes weird shit happens? Because what he's really saying is that he got a chance to walk away from an unhappy life into a happy one, and he did it." He must have realized how awkward that sounded, and he blushed. "I don't mean . . ."

"I get it," said my mom. "There's much less paperwork in abandonment."

I was playing catch-up. "Why was he unhappy? He was doing so well."

"Yeah," said Amelia bitterly. "And you know, a father of three and a husband and everything."

"Not that he was all that good at that," muttered Lennie. She chewed on her nails, caught herself, and said, "Sorry." I wasn't sure if she was apologizing for the nails or the criticism.

Mom frowned and was about to say something when her phone rang.

"Hello, Denny Liddle speaking." She listened for a moment. "Yes, Davis, we saw it, though a heads-up might have been considerate." She paused. "No, I realize it was kind of last-minute." She looked at us and rolled her eyes.

It's always a pleasure to look at my mom's face, and I enjoyed watching it go from irritation to skepticism and back to irritation. Her foot stopped twitching.

There was a long silence, then she said, "Not in a million years."

Another silence. Then, "Over my dead body."

Pause. "I'd rather slam my hand in a car door."

And finally, "Oh, sure, yeah, that's fine." She held the phone to her chest and said, "He wants to do a Zoom call."

For some reason this struck me as funny, and I giggled. "Sorry, is it just me or is it weird to come back from the dead and then leap on a Zoom call?"

Apparently, it was just me. Everyone stared at me silently until my giggles subsided. Then Mom turned back to the phone. "Yes, OK, when?" After settling the details, she hung up and cleared her throat.

"First of all," she said, "the Zoom call is with Davis Reed, the agent, not your father, who's apparently lost the ability to speak for himself." She looked at Lennie. "The reason he didn't come straight here is because they want to film the reunion."

Amelia frowned at her. "And that's when you said you'd rather slam your hand in a car door?"

Mom nodded. "It was an understatement."

Lennie sat down on the sofa, next to Mom. "Was it true you and Dad were separating?"

Mom looked at her lap, her lips tight. "It's true. It didn't come out at the time, but we'd been talking about it." She relaxed her mouth and smiled wryly. "That day, the day we saw him off at the airport? We'd had another row that morning." She made a face. "Every single time I see that dumb photograph, all I see is how we're not even looking at each other. I'd never been so glad to see a plane take off in my life." She made a noise. "Of course, I didn't realize at the time it wasn't coming back."

Lennie frowned. "Why are we just hearing this now?"

Mom looked defensive. "Because if you're about to burn down a building and it collapses on its own, why even light a match?" She turned up her palms. "I still loved him. He was your father. I didn't want him dead, and I didn't want anything to tarnish his memory." She twisted her mouth. "I know it sounds cheesy, but the Foundation has done amazing things."

I swayed a little where I was standing, and Nathan took a step toward me. I waved him away. "I get that this is a momentous, calamitous moment in our family history, but I am on my last calorie of energy, and if I don't eat soon, I'm going to fall down. I've been up for way too long, and this is all so weird and strange and upsetting and I'm toast." I looked around. "Sorry to be basic-needs lady, but I have basic needs."

"And I," said Leo from the kitchen, "have lasagna."

There was a small cheer of collective appreciation, and by mutual but unspoken consent we all headed to the kitchen. We had this huge issue to discuss, we had this family earthquake to deal with, but first we were going to eat lasagna and pretend everything was fine.

IN THE NEWS . . .

Trending on Twitter:

@funnyguy2222
Jasper Liddle walked out of the woods and revealed he's
spent the last twenty-five years . . . hiding from his wife
and avoiding his children. Relatable.

@juneaubroninety
Wait . . . can Alaska gets its money back for that search,
then? What's the statute of limitations on wasting state
resources?

@janthemanjannsen
Kinda bummed Jasper Liddle not mysterious nature hero
after all, but runaway scumbag. #anotheronebitesthedust

@catladywithcattitude
"I forgot, then I remembered, then I didn't care." Wow.
Can you divorce someone if you're already their widow?
Asking for a friend . . .

9

TIGER SHARK
GALEOCERDO CUVIER

For a long time, the only sound was forks.

I broke the silence. "Alex Dutton was at the airport."

My mother hissed between her teeth, like a goose. Lennie made a fur ball noise, and Amelia snorted *asshole* into her hand. Nathan burst out laughing, and Leo looked over from the kitchen, where he was taking garlic bread from the oven. "Who's Alex Dutton?"

Denny narrowed her eyes. "A journalist who has an obsession with Jasper. Oh my God, he's going to be insufferable." She looked at me. "You wanted to kill him. I apologize for stopping you."

I shook my head at Leo. "Dutton wrote a long article in the *New Yorker* a couple of years ago, talking to some aviation expert who said the crash site wasn't actually a crash site, per se, and relating it to some other missing-person cases and general aviation safety. It wasn't *specifically* about Jasper, and there was honestly a very interesting section about forensic metallurgy . . ." I caught Mom's eye and quickly course corrected. "It was a terrible article because other outlets picked it up and ran a load of 'Liddle Faked his Death' articles and there was a solid month of harassment and irritation." I looked at Leo. "The thing is that 'The Story'"—I made air quotes—"takes on a life of its own. Once people get an idea in their heads . . ." I trailed off. "Anyway, Mr. Dutton isn't very popular around here."

"Fair enough," said Leo. He gathered his stuff together and leaned over to kiss Mom goodbye. "Are you alright? I can stay . . . ?"

She shook her head and finger tapped him on the nose again. "Are you kidding? Look around."

He waved at the rest of us as he left. "I'll be back tomorrow before dinner."

The door closed behind him. I was surprised. "So wait, he doesn't actually live here?"

"You're so nosy," said Denny. "No, he often stays over, but he has his own place, other friends."

"Girlfriends?"

"Maybe, I don't ask. Don't be old-fashioned, Christa." Mom took her fork and carefully scraped any remaining molecules of lasagna from her plate. "Remind me to question you incessantly if you ever get around to having a boyfriend."

I looked at Nathan, unable to stop myself. "I've had boyfriends."

Amelia laughed. "None you've ever introduced us to."

I shrugged. "You weren't around at the time."

"What time was that?" asked Lennie.

I looked at her. "Anytime." There was a pause, then I added, "Look, I know it's going to be a shit show starting in the morning, but I'm really close to passing out. I'm going to go say good night to the ocean and go to bed."

Lennie raised her eyebrows at me. "You still do that?"

I nodded. It was an old habit. She'd made fun of it before.

"What would you do if you weren't living next to an ocean?"

I frowned at her. "Probably call the FBI and report my own kidnapping."

She opened her mouth to say something further but then, to my surprise, just laughed. "Funny," she said, and let it go.

I borrowed a coat from my mom, and when I came back into the living room, Nate was on his feet, tugging on his own jacket.

"I'll come with you," he said. He raised an eyebrow. "If that's OK?"

"Sure." I looked around. "Anyone else?"

Amelia and Lennie were still at the dinner table, leaning back in their chairs and getting ready to play cards. Mom had gone to get ready for bed. It was quiet.

"No, thanks," said Lennie. "Once I thrash Amelia at Go Fish, I'm going to turn in myself." Amelia shook her head too, so when Nate held the door open, it was just for me.

It's never completely dark by the ocean. The moonlight bounced bright off the breakers, and shifting silver circumflexes flickered at the horizon. The tide was in and high on the beach as we walked down to the ocean. It's such a human response, so basic, to walk to the edge of water and stare at it. Luckily for crocodiles.

The ocean around Violetta is filled to the brim with sharks. Lots and lots of sharks, sharks to the left of you, sharks to the right. I don't go in the water, and I use a pretty long net to fish out my snails.

It had gotten me out of the habit of wading in the ocean, so when Nathan rolled up his pants and walked straight in, I hung back.

"They're night feeders, you know," I said, referencing *Jaws*, one of my favorite movies and a definite stumbling block during my first attempt at scuba-diving certification. Thanks, Spielberg. I overcame it, obviously, but I still never went diving in the dark.

He laughed. "Not coming in?"

I shook my head and turned to walk a little ways back up the beach, to where the sand was soft. I could see giant ropes of kelp down the beach, and clouds of sand flies feasting on it in the moonlight. I looked up at the stars, so different here than on Violetta.

"What are you pondering?" asked Nate, arriving and sitting next to me on the sand. There were droplets of seawater on his legs, and he tossed his shoes a little way off. He started absentmindedly digging his toes into the sand.

"Decomposition," I replied.

If he was surprised, he didn't show it. "Lovely," he said. "Your own or other people's?"

I pointed to the kelp. "It's a never-ending cycle, like the shitstorm that's about to hit us."

He nodded. "I wasn't really part of it, the first time around."

I looked sideways at him. "You were there." I grinned. "I've seen you in pictures. I was only a baby; I don't remember any of it."

He nodded. "Yeah, but your sisters and I didn't get dragged into it like you did." He made a face. "Mind you, we weren't daft enough to get caught sniffing a butterfly." His hands picked through the sand, flipping aside pebbles and shells, sorting. He was putting round pebbles together, shells together, pieces of glass.

I giggled. "It wasn't like I trained it to do that. It just landed." I picked up a bigger seashell, turned it over in my hand, then added it to his pile of shells. "And Mom thought she was doing a good thing, taking me on TV with her." We'd never actually discussed it, but I was only ever prepared to ascribe positive motives to her. Anything else would be disloyal.

He looked at me, surprised. "I wasn't criticizing Denny. I forget how much you two were in the public eye."

I laughed. "I wish I could forget it." I picked out a couple of round pebbles and added them to his collection.

"And then of course you started going rogue." He chucked a pebble at me. "Causing trouble, dragging down the family name."

I threw a shell, hitting him neatly in the ear, despite his quick ducking. "Until you stepped in?"

He cackled softly. "I wasn't exactly riding in on a white horse."

This was suddenly uncomfortable. I wanted to change the subject, so I did. "I was thinking about the stars too. About how different they look from here." I gazed up at the sky, leaning back on my arms. "It's always amazing to me, to realize that here I'm above the equator, there I'm below, and that even though it's the same sky, I see a different half." I turned to him. "Do you know what I mean?"

He was facing me, and for a second he said nothing. Then he looked up and shook his head. "Is everything different?" He paused. "I mean, I don't know much about astronomy."

"Nor do I," I replied truthfully. "I just know I see different constellations." I grinned and pointed. "She's always the same though, Mrs. Moon."

"Mrs.? I didn't realize she was married."

I laughed. "Of course! She's married to the sun."

He made a face. "I guess they don't get along very well; they pretty much never see each other."

I lay back on the sand and closed my eyes. "I disagree. I've always had this idea that they love each other very much, but circumstances keep them apart. They get to see each other twice a day, at dawn and dusk, simply glimpsing each other over the curve of the earth. As one gets out of the bed, the other returns to it, the sheets still warm."

He was silent, then he said, "You're quite the romantic."

I turned my head. "You think? I have an alternative theory, that they both love the earth and battle every day for her affection. That's why sometimes you see the sun lingering as the moon rises, or see the moon hanging out in the later part of the dawn—they're keeping tabs on the competition."

He frowned quizzically at me. "You're very dreamy for a scientist. I think of you guys as practical and all about the facts, ma'am."

I laughed. "You're completely wrong. Scientists fall deeply in love with something and spend their lives obsessing over it." I turned my head to look at him. "Like when you first fall in love with someone, and want nothing more than to be with them all the time, learn everything you can, discover how they feel, what they think . . . that's science. Isn't love just an overwhelming desire to solve the mystery of another human being?" I shrugged. "Science is full of mysteries, and people trying to get to the bottom of them."

"Like?"

I sighed and thought for a moment. "Oh my God, so many. Spontaneous combustion, the nature of dark matter, how life actually began, quantum entanglement . . ."

He raised his eyebrows and started re-sorting his shells and sticks. "What's that? That sounds amusing."

"Quantum entanglement? Yes, that's a good one." I propped

myself up on my elbows. "It's not my field, so I might mess this up, but here's the gist. Physicists have observed that occasionally, on a subatomic level, particles influence each other, even though they're completely separate. They're in pairs, and they relate to and affect each other, despite being physically distant. If one spins up, the other spins down, that kind of thing." I pointed at him. "I've always liked the idea. I like inexplicable connections, like my various sun-and-moon theories, or why my mother always calls me ten minutes after I think of her."

He laughed. "You and your mother are quantumly entangled?" He made a face. "If I'm saying that right."

I shrugged. "Why not? Nobody really understands it, or what the purpose of it is, or even if it's real. But I like to think about it when I'm on the island and feeling very distant . . . that even as I sit thousands of miles away from the people I love, they still feel me, somehow. That we are still connected." I sighed, and then yawned. "I'm sure I'm mangling the theory . . . I should go to sleep." I sat up and shook myself, then turned back to him. He was still looking at me, his expression unreadable.

"Oh my God," I said, "will you stop staring?"

"Sorry." He smiled at me and turned away. "I'll do my best."

We turned and started walking back up the beach slowly, our swinging steps making us sway toward and away from each other. I was so tired, I could barely think straight.

We reached the paved bike path that separated the sand from my block. As I stepped up onto the path, I was so tired I wobbled, off-balance. Of course he reached out to steady me, because he's a good guy, and of course I avoided his hand, because I don't need anyone's help, and of course I fell on my ass, because I was tired, as anyone would be after being awake for more than a day. For a moment, I flailed like an upturned beetle, then suddenly, I lay back and gazed at the stars. The sand was cool and supportive.

"Fuck it," I said. "I'll sleep right here."

Nathan peered down at me, then suddenly turned, scattering sand across my face. I sat up, swiping.

"I have an idea," he said as he loped off toward the house. It wasn't that late, but many of the neighbors' places were dark. He disappeared.

I lay back down and stared at the stars. He'd deserted me. That's fine; I do better on my own. I closed my eyes and started to drift off. Then, distantly, I heard the kind of repetitive mechanical squeak that suggests the serial killer is approaching through the knife factory pulling the wood chipper.

I sat up immediately. It was Nate. Pulling the old kids' wagon that still lived in our garden. Less scary, just as squeaky.

I watched him approach and saw his grin through the gloom before I saw his face. He wheeled up in front of me and did a daring dirt-track swerve at the last minute, scattering sand again.

I glared at him and wiped my mouth. "You do understand the physics of sand, correct?"

He laughed. "Get in, Cinderella, your coach awaits." I peered into the wagon. He'd gone inside and gotten a blanket, bless his little socks.

I looked at him. "Doesn't that make you a rat?"

He turned his mouth down. "You're quite rude, aren't you?"

I ignored him and looked at the wagon. "You really think I'll fit?"

He nodded. "It won't be first class, but it's a short trip. Just sit on it and tuck your feet up." He helped me to my feet and watched me shake the sand from myself. "Sorry about that."

I sat down on the wagon and crisscrossed my legs. Holy crap, I did fit.

"Ready?" Nathan started pulling, silhouetted against the street-lights. There was a balance to his body I liked; the way he moved through space was . . . appealing.

I nodded and held on to the sides. The thin, sharp rustiness of it was familiar; the balance of it came back to me. We began trundling down the street, the occasional squeak really loud. I started giggling. Nate looked back at me and grinned.

"You're quite surprising too," I said, having reached the no-filter part of exhaustion.

He looked back at me. "How?" he said.

I folded over onto myself and rested my head on my knees. "You're very good-looking," I muttered, "and very nice." I was really getting sleepy now. "You're always saving me."

We rolled along in silence for a moment. "It was just that one time, Christa. You haven't been around to save ever since." Then he pulled in silence until he turned the wagon into our front gate. "You're really quite small, aren't you?"

"You're not so towering yourself," I muttered into my lap.

"Taller than you," he replied, trundling onward. I realized suddenly that the sound of the wheels had changed. I lifted my head.

"We're inside the house," I said.

"Not so tired you can't recognize entering a building; that's a positive sign." He wheeled into my old room and over to the bed. He did the big swerve again, but I was holding on and managed not to get tipped out. As I opened my mouth to complain, he bent down and scooped me up. After dropping me lightly on the bed, he saluted, turned around on his heels, and pulled the wagon out again.

"Good night, Christa." His voice drifted back slowly, the curls at the edge of it so soft, so gentle. "Thanks for letting me save you again."

"You're welcome," I muttered into the pillow. "The pleasure is all mine."

And then I fell asleep.

IN THE NEWS . . .

NYSE ONLINE: Stocks opened mixed today, with Donco (NYSE: DNCO) up sharply on news of Jasper Liddle's return. The toy manufacturer has been a steady performer since going public, but trading of the collectible toys on the secondary market showed a measurable uptick overnight.

DEADLINE.COM: Buzz over a potential Jasper Liddle biopic continues to grow today, with various studios expressing interest. Jasper Liddle is repped by Davis Reed at DRA.

@moviecat245
Dream casting for Jasper Liddle? Jason Momoa? John Krasinski?

@hothandedstranger
Kit Harington?

@naturegirlalison
Any of the Hemsworths?

10

RING-BILLED GULL
LARUS DELAWARENSIS

I opened my eyes to sunlight. The light through the curtains said morning, my body said middle of the afternoon and my brain said midnight. Not sure when my ability to leap time zones was rescinded, but my jet lag was definitely getting worse. I missed my island. I missed my snails. I needed coffee.

Having levered myself out of bed, I stood and stared at myself in the mirror. Please, God, let me age as well as the old man. I have his cheekbones, his wide jaw, his crooked smile. He was—is, I guess—a big smiler. I am not. Hopefully, that will mean fewer wrinkles, although . . . I leaned forward and looked really closely. Just when I started thinking, *Wow, I should buy some moisturizer*, I stopped giving a shit. Besides, look at my mom: Her face is lined by years of smiling, laughing and presumably crying, yet it only makes her more lovely. Maybe I should chill out a bit and crack a smile from time to time. I smiled at myself like a doofus, then switched it off like a light. Never forget: Looking approachable will encourage people to approach you. Think it through!

I pulled off last night's dirty clothes and put on a clean T-shirt and shorts and headed toward the kitchen. As normal service resumed in my head, the end of last night was coming back to me. I felt a little shy about Nate and was glad he didn't seem to be anywhere around. An enormous vat of coffee and something emphatically sugary would get me back on track. I looked around for my phone, feeling slightly disconnected without it. What does that say about Los Angeles—I'd only been here for a day and a half and it was already a necessity. As we've established, on the island I often leave home without it.

I do not want to get used to being here.

I do not want to get reconnected.

I finally spotted it on the kitchen counter, plugged in and fully charged. Someone was taking care of me. I was surprised to discover it was well after ten. I started opening cupboards, looking for coffee. I set up the coffee maker, turned on the radio and danced on the spot a little while I waited for it to finish. I started dreaming of Violetta, of sitting on the balcony every morning, sketching the volcano, slowly pushing down the press of the cafetière . . .

Someone coughed behind me.

I jumped like a hare and whipped around. Over on the sofa, both my sisters and my mom were watching me with their phones up and clearly filming. My mom was also looking at her watch.

"I win," said Mom. "I said it would be at least a full minute."

"I don't understand that level of obliviousness," said Lennie, with apparently genuine concern. "What if something crept up on her?"

Amelia laughed, clicking off her phone. "She'd punch first and ask questions later, which is why you have to make noise as you approach." She turned to my mom. "Do you remember when we seriously considered wearing bells?"

I leaned against the counter and regained my equilibrium. "I was just thinking," I said, defensively. "I'm always thinking."

They looked at me with identically furrowed brows.

"I simply don't believe your thoughts can be that compelling," said Lennie eventually. "Sorry."

Amelia nodded. "Plus, you've always been that way, and it's not like your thoughts were deep when you were a kid."

"In fact," added Lennie pointedly, "you had zero thoughts in high school and were still as jumpy as a froghopper." She held up her phone and took a quick snap of my frown. "Oh look, it's Butterfly Bitch, the face that launched a thousand embarrassing memes . . ."

I looked at her. "I had plenty of thoughts in high school. I graduated top of my class, remember?" For a moment I felt irritated, but as the coffee maker was done, I turned to get myself a mug instead. *Breathe, Christa*, I told myself. *Don't play this game. You'll get your ass handed to you on a platter.*

"Academic thoughts, sure," Amelia said, raising one eyebrow. "Outside of school, not so much."

"Not based on scientific evidence," said Lennie. "How much thought went into getting banned from Chateau Marmont?"

Amelia laughed. "Or getting so drunk you took your shirt off and ran down Wilshire Boulevard in your underwear?"

"At least she kept her bra on *that* time," said Lennie, with the teeny-tiniest edge to her voice. An edge that hinted at how much embarrassment I'd caused her. A hint so subtle we all caught it full in the face.

Then something weird and unexpected happened. "Wait . . . sorry," said Lennie contritely. "That was uncalled-for."

I stared at her, the mug still in my hand. Out of the corner of my eye, I caught Mom frowning and Amelia looking confused.

Lennie looked around. "Hey, I realize I can be a bitch from time to time, but I've been going to therapy and working on it." She looked at me. "Besides, it's not completely your fault you were a fuckup."

That was more normal. I turned back to fill my mug and added cream. I didn't know how to feel about Lennie being in therapy, apart from feeling sorry for her therapist. My sister had always been—until literally ten seconds earlier—one of the meanest people I'd ever known. It had peaked in my teenage years, but hadn't tailed off all that much, and although living thousands of miles away had led me to relax my guard a little, I'd noticed I was getting back into the swing of flinching whenever she opened her mouth. I was having difficulty processing her apology, so I looked out the kitchen window as a gull soared past; not a classic herring gull as you might expect, but a ring-billed gull (*Larus delawarensis*) for a change. Adorable. You see them at the shore, of course, but they also live inland, and many never glimpse the ocean their entire lives. (I mean . . . they might get postcards from other gulls, but they themselves . . . never mind.) I took a sip of coffee and burned my mouth. Dammit. Life was getting the upper hand already, and I'd been up for less than an hour.

"How long have you been going to therapy, and why didn't you tell me before?" Amelia asked Lennie, from behind me. "I've *also* been going to therapy."

I paused, and added sugar to my mug. I don't usually take sugar in my coffee, but something about the way this morning was going suggested extra calories might be necessary.

"Six months, and I *did* tell you," said Lennie. "We talked about it." She took a breath, clearly realizing she sounded cross. "Not that you're expected to remember every conversation we've ever had."

"We talked about it?" Amelia laughed. "Maybe that's why I started going." She shook her head. "I realized I was burying myself in work in order to avoid intimate relationships and personal growth."

I took a second sip of coffee and wondered if there was a way to retroactively increase the caffeine content. I turned back and leaned cautiously against the counter. Both my sisters and my mom were looking at me expectantly.

"What?" I said.

"Have *you* considered therapy?" asked Lennie. "You have all kinds of unresolved issues." She looked at me with an expression of sympathy mixed with the zeal of the newly self-reflective.

I raised my eyebrows. "I do?" I shrugged. "I went to therapy, remember?"

"When?" asked Lennie, slightly scornfully, and then caught a movement from Mom out of the corner of her eye. She colored. "Oh . . . yeah, sorry." She hesitated. "But that was one time." She looked at Mom. "Right? Didn't she go for, like, one session?"

Mom looked at me. "Well, it was three, to be fair. But that was her choice."

"I went," I said, "I talked through my experience, I processed it, I moved on. It was highly efficient, and I'm pretty sure I never need to go again. And as for my issues, I don't think they're unresolved." I blew on my coffee. "They're unacknowledged. Totally different."

Lennie looked at Amelia. "Classic deflection."

Amelia agreed. "Of course. It's normal for someone at her stage of emotional development. When she's ready, she'll do the work."

I opened my mouth to swing into battle but remembered deflection wasn't my only skill. I also had denial. I was going to think about gulls and pretend my sisters hadn't just called me emotionally immature. If I could have put my fingers in my ears and said *la la la*, I would have, but I was holding my coffee.

Let me be clear. I'm a young American in the first quarter of the twenty-first century. I'm fully aware that therapy is helpful, even essential. I'm not opposed to it, per se; I just couldn't be less interested in the workings of my own mind. *Workings* being a generous term for whatever went on in there that wasn't focused on snails, snail life cycles, or snail-related topics. Besides, I tried therapy, three times. It was helpful, insofar as it got Mom and my stepdad off my back. And then I went to boarding school and things got better on their own.

Amelia turned to our mom. "You've been in therapy, right, Mom?"

Mom made a face. "Of course. Who hasn't?" They all looked at me, then back at one another. Mom continued, "After Harry died, I started grief counseling and then segued into analysis and cognitive behavioral therapy." She looked over at me. "Christa, is there more coffee?"

"Sure," I said, glad of the request. Hunting for another mug and very slowly adding cream and sugar would provide plausible deniability for ignoring the therapy conversation.

Mom looked thoughtful for a moment, then added, "I learned a great deal about myself in therapy. With your father reappearing like this, it might be a good time to go back." She looked at my sisters. "What else have you dug up?"

"Well," said Lennie, "let's take my relationship with Christa, for example."

"Do we have to?" I said plaintively, but they ignored me. This one hundred percent tracked: I have many memories of being the subject of conversation while being very much *right there*.

Lennie folded her legs up under her, suggesting she'd taken up yoga alongside therapy. This was almost as surprising, as she'd been a compulsive marathon runner with hamstrings like piano wire. "Obviously, I had a great deal of jealousy in childhood because of her special role in the family."

Everyone nodded but me.

I paused to take a sip of my own coffee and raised my eyebrows over the rim of my coffee cup. "What special role was that?"

All three of them looked at me as though I'd opened a window and started competing with the gulls for French fries. I put down my cup and finished making Mom's coffee. Don't mind me, people, you carry right on talking about me like I'm not in the room.

"Well, after Dad died, you got promoted to superspecial baby Liddle, right?" Lennie turned to Mom. "To be fair, I would suggest you bear the responsibility for this. You definitely spent way more time with Christa than you did with us."

"That's true," added Amelia. "When we were little, you worked constantly, you and Dad. When you weren't fighting, of course."

My mom nodded. "I hear what you're saying, Lennie, but in my own defense, neither you nor Amelia was very easy to deal with after your dad disappeared, and Christa was a toddler. I couldn't exactly leave her on her own, could I?"

I brought the coffee over, placed it on the table, and stood there awkwardly.

"You could have left her with a babysitter," argued Lennie. "You were constantly leaving us with strangers when we were young. Constantly."

Huh. I guess that proves one person's thingy is another person's whatsit, as I'd always been jealous of exactly what Lennie was complaining about. I started to move back into the kitchen. Toast, possibly. Several pieces, toasted sequentially rather than in parallel, could easily keep me engaged and out of the conversation for ten minutes.

Amelia shook her head. "Not to pile on, but I will agree it felt painfully preferential." She turned to look at Lennie with a great deal of affection. "Not to speak for you, of course."

Lennie reached out and patted Amelia on the knee. "Of course not. And while I was acting out my rage and misdirected blame, as the eldest you were probably taking on a lot of inappropriate emotional labor."

Amelia put her hand on Lennie's hand. "While maintaining my own boundaries and bearing in mind I'm early in the process of working through my childhood parentification, I appreciate you bearing loving witness."

I felt my jaw opening slightly. The last time my sisters were in the same room, in my memory, they'd started the evening with shots of whiskey and ended it arm wrestling each other and hurling insults in several languages. I wasn't sure who these two well-balanced women were, but I couldn't decide if I liked them any better. However, at least they'd stopped talking about me, and so far nothing had been thrown.

Of course I spoke too soon.

"Staying on the subject of Christa," said Lennie, turning to me, "I owe you an apology. Once Mom began dragging you on TV and you got all famous, I started expressing my jealousy by breaking your toys. Do you remember that?"

I gaped at her. "Not at all. Like what?"

"I remember it," said Mom, shaking her head affectionately. "You pulled the heads off three Barbies before I realized it wasn't the dog who was doing it."

I frowned. "Did we even have a dog back then?"

There was a pause while Mom thought about that. "You know, I'm not sure, now you come to mention it."

"We did have a cat," said Amelia. "You got us kittens six months after Dad disappeared."

"Definite win, to be fair," added Lennie. "I barely remember Dad ever being around, but those kittens turned into amazing cats."

There was a moment while we all nodded in peaceful agreement. Most of the time, kittens are better than grown men; sorry, men, but that's the truth. Guys, try reducing yourself in size and covering yourself in fluff. It might make up for the patriarchy.[1]

"Anyway," continued Lennie, "I was a child myself, and therefore not really able to make super rational choices, but I am sorry."

I shrugged. "No big."

"Don't minimize, Christa," said Lennie. "You're allowed to be mad."

---

1. It won't, but it would be adorable.

I shrugged again, this time making it a bigger physical movement, in the hopes that would get it past the shrug censor. "I agree, and if I was mad, I'd let you know. Apology accepted." And if she wanted to apologize for breaking my toys and not even touch the things she'd said to me a decade or so later, fair enough. Baby steps, right?

Time to change the subject. I turned to Mom. "I assume we didn't hear from Jasper at all? I was thinking of going over to the university to make sure I still have a job."

Amelia frowned at me. "Is that a concern?"

"Because of your dad?" Mom looked confused.

I shook my head. "No, I meant mostly that my funding is getting low and I need a microscope." I took a sip of coffee. "Plus, I don't know if 'parent returned from dead' is a legally defensible reason for termination." I shifted my weight a little and took a deep breath. "I don't know how to feel about all this." I looked at Lennie. "Do you?"

She shrugged. "About Dad?"

I nodded. "Yeah. About the interview, about what he said, about the whole thing." I looked at them. "It's all completely weird, like it's happening to someone else."

Mom took a thoughtful sip of coffee, then rubbed a drip away with her thumb. "I'm going to go with nonplussed." She looked down at her shoes and her painted toenails. "I want to hug him because I used to love him, then I want to whack him with a stick because he broke our hearts." She looked at us. "I can forgive him for deserting me, but not you."

Amelia said, "I have no plans to forgive him for anything, and I'm parked comfortably in furious."

Lennie stretched. "I'm really pissed." She got up. "But also strangely hungry." She headed for the kitchen.

I stood up. "Wow, you guys are singularly unhelpful."

"Actually," said Mom, "we're collectively unhelpful."

As I was making a face at her, I remembered something else. "Oh, by the way, Mom? I should have rented a car. Can I borrow yours?"

"Of course," replied Mom. "Try not to run over any paparazzi if they find you, and if you drive past a department store, go in and buy an outfit that doesn't look like it's been lying in a pile of leaves for six months."

I shook my head again. "No."

"Or that isn't a sun-faded shade of tan, fawn, olive or khaki?"

"No, and I'm ignoring you. I don't think the press is going to show up at my work; they have no idea who I am. Remember, I'm Christa Barnet, scientist and spinster of this parish."

Mom shrugged. "We'll see, I guess. After that interview last night, I have a feeling they're going to find us any minute." She pointed toward the kitchen. "Car keys are in the ceramic chicken on the counter."

"Thanks. I might be right back. They haven't seen me for four years; they may have completely forgotten who I am."

My family looked at me, and Amelia was the first to speak.

"I doubt it, Christa. You're pretty memorable."

I fished the keys out of the chicken, not sure exactly what she meant by that. It almost certainly wasn't good.

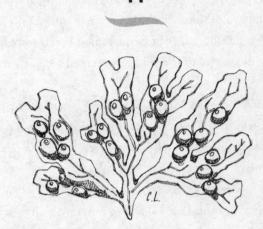

11

BLADDER WRACK
FUCUS VESICULOSUS

As always, I shouldn't have worried. Time is a relatively fluid construct in the zoology department,[1] and when Margaret, the department secretary, looked up as I came through the door, she stared at me for a second, then spoke as though she'd seen me the day before.

"Barnet, perfect person. Can you teach a seminar on bladder wrack?"

"Maybe?" I replied, remembering too late it was folly to enter the department through the office rather than the student common

1. The zoology department is actually called the Department of Ecology and Evolutionary Biology, but who the fuck has time for that? Everyone just calls it the zoology department, for obvious reasons.

room. In the common room, a student might try to bum twenty dollars, but in the office, you could find yourself scheduled. And while I could, in theory, talk about bladder wrack for hours (in fact, one short-lived relationship foundered for that very reason), I wasn't going to be around long enough to do much more than that.

"A week from next Thursday," said Margaret, looking at a chalkboard with her hands on her hips. The university is completely digital, of course, but the zoology department also had The Board. The Board was for the professors, and its chalk was law. If you were down for a 3 p.m. on brackish crustaceans, you'd better be there at 2:58 with your sloshing tank of shellfish, or Margaret would blow a gasket.

"Oh dear," I said vaguely, starting to back out the door. "I'm hoping to be back in the field by then." *God willing.*

"Fine. If you see Pelterman, ask him to come see me, will you?" Margaret put down her piece of chalk and wiped her hand on an already dusty skirt. It was gray, and the overlapping chalky handprints reminded me of Lascaux cave paintings.

"Definitely," I said firmly, having no idea who Pelterman was. "Is Professor Last here?"

Margaret looked at me incredulously.

"Sorry," I said, "I've been away."

It has long been rumored that Professor Murray Last literally lives in the attic of the zoology department. You would think that as he achieved the lofty heights of academic management, he would seek the largest office, which was on the ground floor, but he seemed to prefer his promotions literal as well as professional. His office was now on the top floor of the department, and years ago, before I even came to UCLA, someone started the idea that he'd never been seen either coming or going. Such was his dedication to his field, it was said, that he had forgone all semblance of a personal life, and the inevitable end was the annexation of the attic and the creation of a tiny apartment. Supposedly, Dr. Last entered his secret domain by way of a mechanism so brilliantly engineered that students gazing in vain at the ceiling were unable to see a seam or entryway of any kind. Then he apparently sat up there and did his work, subsisting on, what, book beetles crisped up in a toaster oven? This running joke never seemed to filter back to Professor Last, not that he would have cared if it had.

But anyway, that was why Margaret had given me such a look: Of course Dr. Last was in his office. He's upholstered in.

As I came through the door, Murray Last looked up and demanded I hand over a protractor.

I disappointed him. "Sorry, don't have one." I patted my pockets. "I do have a Leatherman multi-tool. Is that of any use?"

He regarded me hopefully. "Is it a math multi-tool?"

I shook my head. "Do you want me to go down and ask Margaret for a protractor?"

The old man shook his head. "Not worth it. Tell her on your way out; she'll send one up with the next student." He squinted at me. "You look familiar. You're not undergrad, are you?"

"Nope, I'm Christa Barnet, postdoc. I'm back very, very briefly from the field, and I came to see if you wanted an update."

He held up his finger, which had a Disney Princess Band-Aid on it, and gazed at me. What seemed like several minutes passed.

"Sea snails," he said suddenly. "Violetta, fourth year . . ."

I nodded. "That's right."

"What on earth have you been doing for four years?"

I felt myself going red. "I've been tabulating. Observing."

"How many seasons do you need?"

If it was possible for me to go a deeper shade of red, I did so. "I was thinking another year would do it." I coughed. "We had an anomalous algae bloom."

The old man narrowed his eyes at me. "Stay another twenty years and you'll be able to accurately say *anomalous.*" This is the problem with him; he lives in a bizarre world where a mathematics multi-tool seems plausible, but he's also so smart he'll see right through any lazy thinking you happen to demonstrate. I love and fear him in equal measure.

He was still holding up his finger, which he then pointed at me. "Wait. Aren't you Jasper Liddle's kid?"

Oh crap. Then I noticed there was a kitten asleep on his desk. It was black and white. It had no tail. It was distracting.

"Is he really back?" barked the professor.

I half shrugged and held my hands up in a classic "beats me" position. "I *think* so. I don't actually know any more than you do."

He laughed. "That sounds like your father."

"You knew him?"

"Know him, you mean?" Last made a face. "I did, at one time. Many years ago." He flapped both hands at me this time. "Go away. Come back next week and tell me about the work properly. No PowerPoint, no bullshit, just you." He started scrabbling around in his desk drawer. "It's time you came back anyway. Don't you want tenure? You'll need to get your tushy in gear." He pulled out a feather and poked the kitten with it. It was immediately on its feet. "You can't hide away forever, you know."

I'd been getting to my own feet when I suddenly processed what he'd just said.

"Wait, what do you mean?" I needed support, and reached for the back of the chair I'd been sitting on. "I'm not done with my research."

"Well, you are if I say you are," said my boss, who had engaged the kitten and was fighting a losing battle. "Funding's tight all over, Barnet. It's hard enough to argue for important things, let alone snails . . ."

I opened my mouth and frowned, hard, but he held up his hand (as though the feather was a gavel about to drop on my career). "I know, I know, snails are the future. But now that you're here, why don't you just stay? Pelterman is thinking of leaving; you can take his students and teach his classes."

"I'm at a crucial juncture," I said, which wasn't true. "I've been able to use pontoons to create a study population offshore." Also not true, but Dr. Last was not a crustacean guy.

He kept staring, the big wheels turning in his head. "Fine, go away," he said. "I'll pretend I never saw you on two conditions."

"Name them," I said.

"Start thinking seriously about your future," he said. "This is a university, not a travel agency for the antisocial and introverted." He scooped up the kitten and glared at it. It hissed like the world's smallest blowtorch, ready to throw paws, and Last switched his glare to me. "And tell your father he still owes me a charity dinner; twenty-five years ago, I guilted him into being a prize at an auction for the zoology department, and someone paid top dollar." He frowned. "I did wonder if he'd disappeared into thin air in order to avoid the dinner date, but the lady in question *must* be dead by now." He pointed the kitten. "Tell him to call me."

I grabbed my bag, double time. Dr. Last was nothing if not capricious. "I will, thanks so much," I said, and booked it out the door.

"Wait." His voice followed me down the hall. "Do you know anything about bladder wrack?"

"Nothing at all," I called back, and took the stairs two at a time.

12

BOUGAINVILLEA
BOUGAINVILLEA GLABRA

When I got to the bottom of the stairs, I checked my phone before venturing out. I had a message from my mother that didn't make any sense: **Don't come home. Go fetch Primo's. Wait for nuts.**

I frowned. I got the first part. I understood the second part, even, because Primo's was a fantastic donut place, and I appreciated the reminder. It was the third part that had me foxed.

I sighed. Might as well go get the donuts first and then I could eat one while calling for clarification.

As I left the department, I ran directly into some kind of event happening on campus. No idea what, but something that was causing a small crowd, most of whom were student-type folks staring at their phones and muttering to one another. If this was a protest, then it was the postmodern, decentralized kind where no one is in charge but things happen organically. I would love to be the sort of patient person who embraces frustration as a source of wisdom, but I'm not. I embrace frustration only when I'm getting ready to pick it up and chuck it, if you follow my drift.

I started stepping on toes, literally. Not to break, just to bend. Miraculously, the crowd made a path. When I stepped on someone's foot and they started to protest, I simply protested louder, which is a proven strategy used by pickpockets everywhere. Let me demonstrate.

First you step on someone's foot. Aim for the top outside corner. When they leap about and say *ouch*, or whatever, you simply say it louder and with more emphasis while shooting them a filthy look and hurrying past. Works every time. Eight times out of ten, they apologize to you. If you were a pickpocket, you might also hurry away with their wallet, whereas I was merely seeking a clear path. They really should have been thanking me.

However, just as I was achieving escape velocity and could see the sidewalk of Hilgard Avenue ahead of me, someone pointed directly at me and said, "That's her."

I literally looked behind myself. Just more young people, and now they were looking at me too. *Oh crap.*

"Aren't you Christabel Liddle?" said the first girl.

I shook my head. "No, I'm Christa Barnet." I started moving again, though now my toe-stomping technique was ruined. You can't accidentally-on-purpose step on someone's foot *while they're looking.* Seriously.

"That *is* her," confirmed another kid, a guy this time, looking at his phone. "Wikipedia says she uses her mother's name." He looked again. "She got fatter."

Ouch. I started to frown.

"Can I get a picture?" asked the first girl.

"Of what?" I asked, confused.

"Of us together!" said the girl, equally confused this wasn't clear.

"Why on earth would you want that?" I asked her, trying to move more quickly. "Do we know each other?"

"No, but you're famous," said the girl encouragingly. "Your dad just came back from the dead. That's pretty cool, right? And I saw you used to be a meme too. What a coincidence, right? I bet they make a movie. AND a limited series prestige streaming show. And a fact-based biopic!" She smiled at me suddenly, then whirled around to place herself alongside me, grinning into the phone she held up. "Chris Hemsworth is going to play your dad. You can play yourself."

I smiled reflexively, and the girl looked at the picture and hesitated. "Or they can find someone who looks like you, maybe?"

"You'll need to get back to your wiki weight," said the other guy, ever practical.

Half of me wanted to break into a run, but the other half was curious. "How did you know where I was? How did you know *who* I was?"

"You're on BuzzFeed," said yet another kid, with the air of telling someone they'd won big on a game show. I looked around at the growing crowd, all of whom were holding up their phones. There must have been two dozen people. I could not fathom why they were all here.

The first girl got chatty. "They have a whole article about your dad coming back, with a timeline, and there was a sidebar about his family—your family, right—and it said you taught *here* and I go *here* so I came to see if you were *here* and the lady in the office said you actually were *here right now*, so I posted about it and now I have a pic." She looked down at her phone. "Ooh, three hundred likes already, that's fast." I was semi-fascinated by her mode of speech, which had interesting emphasis with corresponding hand gestures, but I wasn't there to do fieldwork. Let alone kinesics; it wasn't even my field.

I looked around. The crowd was one giant compound eye, dozens of phones held up. And then, at the back, the larger, harder edges of an actual camera. The press had arrived.

Time to go.

"Christa? Sarah Pepperdine, ABC News . . ."

I turned to find a woman around my own age standing uncomfortably close. Like, touching shoe leather close. Who knew you could get a pantsuit, hair scrunchie and earrings all in a precisely matching shade of mulberry? This chick.

"Is it true you and your sisters have filed a lawsuit against your father for intentional emotional distress?" asked Ms. Pepperdine, misreading my expression. "It must be pretty shocking, discovering he left you on purpose."

"That's not actually what he said," I said, continuing to walk into her. She stood her ground longer than I would have thought, but eventually, I prevailed and she stepped aside. To try and positively reinforce this helpful behavior, I said politely, "I haven't had a chance to see him yet. I have no further comment." I kept moving, visualizing a glazed ring donut as motivation.

"Is it true he faked his death to avoid arrest?" She was still right in my ear as she said this, and I'll admit it, she startled me.

I turned around. "I'm sorry, what?"

Sarah Pepperdine was no doofus. An off-balance subject is far more likely to blurt out something newsworthy, so she doubled down. "Sources claim he was being sought for questioning by the IRS."

"Sources?" I noticed the camera operator was well-placed and catching everything. As were the forty-seven people around us who were also wasting their phone batteries on this utterly dumb conversation.

Pepperdine nodded. "It's also been said he faked his death to cover his involvement with another woman—do you have any comment?"

Well, that was just rude. I tipped my head to one side, frowned and opened my mouth.

"She has no comment," came a smooth, authoritative voice. An arm came around and grabbed my wrist, turning me and pulling me along.

So of course I planted my feet and resisted. "Hey," I yelled. "What the ever-loving fuck do you think you're doing?"

The guy turned around. He grinned that shit-eating grin he has. Alex Dutton.

"Oh no," I said, yanking my wrist out of his hand. "Are you literally kidding me?"

"Mr. Dutton," said Sarah Pepperdine, her eyebrows hitting her hairline. "Why are you here? Are you working on a piece? Are the rumors true? Has Liddle been arrested?"

Both Dutton and I turned and stared at her. I was impressed she'd recognized him at all—way to keep your eye on the competition—but I wasn't happy with either of them. They were both officially on my list, and not the list headed "Don't ever kick these people in the balls." I lost my temper a tiny bit, because, you know, freedom of expression.

"Are you just asking random questions to see if anything sticks?"

I asked. "I already told you I haven't seen my dad. I barely saw him the first time around. I have no idea where he is now, or what he's been doing. He could have been living it up in a former Soviet Republic, he could have been a popular leader on another planet, he could have been around the corner disguised as a fire hydrant. I know jack shit about anything and you can kiss my ass right now."

Judging by the silence, pierced only by a dozen people hitting the *stop recording* button, that had been a pretty good exit line.

So I exited. At a run.

IN THE NEWS . . .

@SarahPepperdine, tweeting live from UCLA
Christa Barnet, daughter of Jasper Liddle, refused to answer questions about the rumors of financial fraud and extramarital affairs swirling around her father's return. Clearly rattled and unprepared, Ms. Liddle became combative and verbally abusive before literally running away. Questions about Dr. Barnet's status at the university were curtly rebuffed, although sources indicate she has been absent a great deal in the last several years. Further details were unavailable.

@bruins4eva
Scored this selfie with @christabarnet secs before she blew up and took off. Stay on the right side of the Prof, amirite? #freechrista

TRENDING TIKTOK SOUNDCLIP: I know jack shit about anything and you can kiss my ass right now.

13

GLAZED DONUT
DONUTUS CIRCULUS

've already established that Nate is cute, but let me add that when I walked into Primo's, he was wearing a very well-cut deep navy suit with a crisp white shirt, sitting at a table looking like three or four million bucks *and* like the most comfortable guy in the place. In front of him on the table: two cups of coffee and a promisingly translucent paper bag. In his hand, half a glazed ring—the platonic ideal of donuts—the other half being already in his face. He was watching me come in the door, and as our eyes met, I swear to you my heart skipped a beat. Now, before you roll your eyes and feel your gorge rise, let me remind you I had just run for several blocks and I really do have a thing about glazed ring donuts. I was also, of course, surprised, but as I got closer and realized he was obviously waiting for me, it all became clear.

Firstly, whatever was in the bag was for me, and secondly, "You're nuts," I said as I sat down. I looked over my shoulder.

He very slowly tipped his head to one side. "I'm nuts?" he said. "You're the one who just sprinted into a donut shop."

I looked in the bag. A second glazed ring. *Be still my heart.*

I pulled it out and bit into the top. Primo's has that glaze where the sugar fractures into miniature ice floes that stick to your lips for an instant before melting. I closed my eyes to experience the full effect. When I opened them again, he was still looking at me.

All at once I smiled and leaned forward. "I am very glad to see you, thank you for the donut, it was my mom who said you were nuts."

He made a disbelieving noise and took another bite of his donut. Around it he said, "Why? She called me forty minutes ago—when I was in the Valley, I might add—and asked if I could come and pick you up here." He licked his fingertips. "She implied it was important."

"I think it was a typo." I showed him my screen and watched the increasingly familiar grin spread across his face as he read the message. He laughed and pushed one of the coffees toward me. He sat very casually in his seat, his forearm resting on the table, but like on the beach, I couldn't help noticing the effortless balance of his body. I frowned at myself. *Stop objectifying, Christa. So shallow.*

He said, "I believe the plan is for me to drive you back to the house, as no one knows who I am and I should be able to get into the garage relatively unmolested."

I finished my donut and took a sip of coffee. "What about Mom's car?"

"Leo's going to get it and take it to his place."

I shook my head. "How did Mom know things were going to go poorly?"

He frowned. "Things went poorly? She just said the press had shown up outside the house . . ." He looked at me and started to smile. "What did you do?"

I laughed. "Nothing, really. This reporter was saying deeply stupid things and then Alex Dutton showed up and I lost my temper a little bit and ran away." I sucked on my thumb to get the last of the sugar.

Nate looked at me. "A little bit?" He laughed. "I dread to think."

"You don't know me," I replied. "I was a model of decorum and reserve. It'll blow over like it always does." A thought occurred to me. "Mom's not going to be happy if it shows up online." I looked at him. "Do you think it will?"

He stared at me.

"Yeah, OK," I said, getting to my feet. "Where are you parked?"

This time I let him drive.

As we got closer to home, the traffic got even stickier than usual. TV trucks were double-parked on both sides of the street. There were many, and while those from the local stations held prime positions, I spotted logos from as far away as Japan and New Zealand.

"Shit," I said, straightening up to get a better look. "Was it like this last time?"

Nathan shook his head. "I was a kid—I wasn't paying too much attention to detail. But I don't think it was like this. Let's face it, people go missing all the time." He looked out at the mass of antenna

trucks, pools of well-lit TV hosts looking serious over their microphones, and said, "*This* is because someone came back."

He punched a button on the steering wheel and called my mom.
Her voice sounded as calm and relaxed as ever. "You know," she
said when she heard his voice, "it's just as well I sent you to collect
Christa, because once the paparazzi had staked their claim, the
legitimate press turned up, and we haven't been able to leave the
house since. What happened?"

I frowned. "I'm sorry, Mom, there was a crowd at the school
too." I didn't mention the BuzzFeed article or the possibility that I
was going viral as we spoke.

"Yes, I know," said Mom dryly. "I enjoyed the video of you being Professor Potty Mouth."

I closed my eyes. "Ah," I said. "You saw that?"

"Three different members of the Foundation board sent it to
me." She made me sweat for a moment, then said, "Oh well, what's
done is done. Can you get in here?"

"No," said Nathan, stopping at a red light. "Time for plan B."

I looked over at him just as Mom said, "Which is?"

"Go back to my place and make a new plan." He looked at the
traffic and got ready to make a U-turn. "We'll come up with something."

This struck me as silly. "Nate, just pull over anywhere and drop
me off. I don't care if there are cameras. I'll just walk right through."
I grinned at him. "I'm a big girl now, remember?"

Nate looked at me. He'd managed to make his turn, so we were
now stuck in barely moving traffic going in the other direction.
People on bicycles were passing us. Old people on bicycles.

"No," he said, "I want to think it through."

I looked in the wing mirror, then opened the door. Leaning

back in, I snagged a Dodgers hat from the seat well and said, "I already thought it through, but thanks for the ride."

"What are you doing?" he yelped, slamming on the brakes, which was overkill.

"I'm getting out of the car," I replied.

"Get back in. You'll get run over!" he said, his voice a full octave higher than usual.

I laughed, looking around. "Only if I lie down and tuck myself under someone's front fender. No one's going more than three miles an hour." I started threading my way through what was essentially a two-lane parking lot. "Thanks for caring, though!" I gave him a broad smile and pulled the baseball hat lower on my head.

By the time I reached the sidewalk, I couldn't hear his complaining at all.

IN THE NEWS . . .

ABC.NEWS: Live from Jasper Liddle's family home in Venice Beach, where reports are coming in that he is in Los Angeles, and is expected there at any moment.

BBC.CO.UK: Famed naturalist Jasper Liddle has been seen in Los Angeles and is expected to make a statement. Our reporter is now live in Southern California, at the home of Liddle's wife, Denise.

ABC.NET.AU: Liddle spotted in Los Angeles. Our reporter is standing by live at the scene.

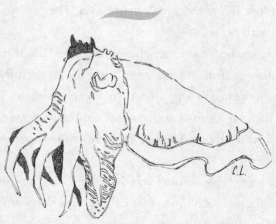

14

GIANT CUTTLEFISH
SEPIA APAMA

Having achieved the sidewalk, I paused for a moment to suss out the lay of the land. The alleyway entrance to the walk streets is relatively narrow, and the combined journalistic curiosity of the world was blocking the way very effectively. Cameras, people carrying sound equipment, people holding microphones and talking into them, you get the picture. I leaned against a nearby wall and looked for an opportunity. I decided, moreover, to take inspiration from one of my favorite creatures: the daring, brave and beautiful cuttlefish.

The cuttlefish—of whom there are over a hundred different species—are ocean marvels who don't get the credit they deserve (though Charlotte Cuttlefish was a big seller for Liddle's Liddles). Not only can they change color whenever they damn well feel like it, but male cuttlefish who are competing with another male for a female will creep past their rivals by changing one side of their bodies to look like another female, while keeping their hot male cuttlefish side facing the female in question. They are super sneaky bastards with nerves of steel.

So, channeling my inner cuttlefish (minus the three hearts), I pushed away from the wall and started purposefully walking through all the people who were there hoping to catch a glimpse of me, my dad, my mom or really any of us. *You do not see me*, I told them in my head. *I am blending invisibly into my surroundings and you see nothing.*

They spotted me before I was three steps into the crowd. To be fair, wearing a baseball hat pulled all the way down isn't really in the same league as employing a system of chromatophores that expand and contract in an instant. Still, as cuttlefish would be the first to say, you have to work with what you've got.

"Miss Liddle!"

"Christa!"

"Did you just see your father?"

"Are you on your way to see your father?"

"No comment," I said, putting my head down and pushing through. The space between the houses was filled with people and, I realized, cops trying to keep a pathway clear and prevent any kind of incident. I concluded my best bet was to hop the fences and walls that separate each garden from the next, making my way to the middle of the block that way. I'd grown up here; my neighbors probably wouldn't have me arrested for trespassing. Plus, I was planning to do it at a righteous clip.

One photographer was very close behind me when I reached

the first wall, and I decided to save him some trouble. I put my hands on the top of the chest-high masonry and smiled at him.

"Listen," I said, "there are seven of these between here and my house. I live and work on a very mountainous island with no cars and nothing to do. If I'm not running up and down the mountain for work, I am in the gym, bored and challenging myself. You probably drive a lot and are carrying a camera you don't want to drop. I'm going to jump these walls without breaking a sweat, and while I appreciate you're doing your job, I feel it's only fair to warn you that if you attempt to follow me, it will end in panting disappointment and possibly more than one skinned knee."

The cameraperson regarded me thoughtfully. His T-shirt had a cat pirate on it. We understood each other. "I probably won't get very far," he said.

I bounced and got one foot on top of the wall. "Probably not," I said, slithering over the top.

He stayed where he was. "There's no way I could catch up."

"It's doubtful," I called back, crossing the garden and getting ready to jump the other wall.

"I'll just wait here for a bit."

"OK then."

For all I know, he's waiting there still.

While it's true I'm in pretty good shape, after the fifth wall I started questioning the wisdom of my strategy. My legs were undeniably wobbly when I finally reached my garden, which was lucky for Sarah Pepperdine, committed journalist and bastion of the free press, who was standing by my front yard gate wielding a microphone. Honestly, she must have uploaded that video, then driven like an utter loon to beat me here. Ms. Pepperdine was not—if you'll remember—on my list of people whose balls I wasn't going to kick. But jumping all those walls meant I didn't have the legs for it, and this is how the devil protects his own.

I was also ever so slightly out of breath, so I didn't tell her to fuck off as loudly as I wanted to when she started yelling out questions. I just didn't have the puff.

When I went to open the front door, I found it was locked. I banged three times with a closed fist, and resisted the temptation to simply kick the door until it splintered.

The journalists outside our gate were calling my name repeatedly, but I tuned them out. Then I heard the gate latch click and turned; Sarah Pepperdine had decided my presence in the garden meant it was open season.

I glared at her, then turned back to the door. "'Sme," I said loudly, smacking the door with my palm for extra emphasis. "Let me in."

(Imagine the click-clack of high heels on the wooden floor.)

"Is that you?"

"Yes, Mom."

"Christa?"

I banged my head on the door. "No, Mom, the other me."

I heard her snort. "Nathan's very annoyed with you."

"Ask me if I care, Mom."

"Your sisters are very annoyed with you."

"Mom. Open the door."

Still silence. "Is that pushy lady still out there?"

I turned to look at Sarah Pepperdine, who opened her mouth to ask me a question. I held up my hand. "Save it." I kicked the door none too gently with my foot.

"Keep your pants on, sister." My mom unlocked various things and opened the door. She was fully made-up, gorgeous, and wearing jeans and a Rams sweatshirt. I rolled my eyes at her. She takes everything so casually.

I stepped inside, turned and revved up to slam the door in someone's face.

"Is it true," asked Sarah, her foot firmly across the doorway, "that you've been offered a show on National Geographic, and that Jasper Liddle plans to sue Nathan Donovan for his half of the Liddle toy company?"

On the one hand, I had to admire her take-no-prisoners approach to questioning—say something ludicrous and deliver it with conviction. Seeing as my appearing on TV was not in the cards and I had just seen Nathan Donovan not ten minutes earlier, I was confident she was running crap up the flagpole to see if anyone would salute. Just as I was about to open my mouth to call bullshit, Marcel, the little chocolate button of love, weaseled through our legs and made a snapping dart at Ms. Pepperdine's Balenciaga sneakers.

"He bit me!" she cried, pulling her foot back. "Let me in! I need medical attention!"

The dachshund was dancing around with a great deal of verve, and I suddenly remembered they were originally bred to flush badgers from their dens. I swept the little dog clear with my foot and finally slammed the door.

"He did not, and you do not," I yelled through the closed door, my hand still on the doorknob. "He never so much as touched you. If they swabbed your ugly-ass shoe right now, they'd find zero dog spit. Back off, lady, and don't forget to shut the gate."

I guess I must have given it a bit of brio, because when I turned away from the door, both Mom and Leo were giving me a look.

"What?"

"I thought you hated the dog?" asked my mom, bending to pick up the hero of the hour.

"Listen," I said, "I never said any such thing. I said he hated me. Totally different." I took a deep breath. "Where are Amelia and Lennie? I thought they were mad at me?"

"We're here," they called from down the hall. Lennie called out an additional clarification. "We're not mad at all; she made that up. You can make a tit of yourself on the Internet as much as you like." She stuck her head out of a room down the hall. "We're going through Mom's wardrobe to see if we can steal anything."

"In the middle of all this you're looking for clothes?" Honestly, they call me the weird one.

"Don't you want to tell your side of the story, Denny?" The reporter must have been pressing herself against the door; her voice was clear as a bell. "Before Jasper controls the narrative completely?" Her tone suggested we were all sisters together, facing down the patriarchy.

Mom shook her head, even though the reporter couldn't see her. She raised her voice a little. "No, thanks. He's welcome to the narrative; it's his story after all."

"I'm calling the police," I said loudly.

We heard footsteps receding and looked at one another.

"She's one hundred percent going to be back," said my mom, rubbing her nose against Marcel's smooth hazelnut-shell head.

"And if not her, someone else." I looked at the dog. Props to his tiny self, for sure. He still hated me, but he hated those sneakers more, and as ancient wisdom says, the enemy of my enemy is my friend.

Leo handed me a mug of coffee topped with foam, demerara

sugar sprinkled over the top. "Hazelnut latte," he said. "Want one, Denny?"

"What a genius you are," she said, taking a break from thanking Marcel to plant a kiss on Leo's cheek.

There was sudden loud banging on the door. A muffled voice called, "FedEx," but with a slightly questioning intonation. Like, *MaybeFedEx?*

"I sincerely doubt that's actually a delivery, and I'm not talking to that crazy woman again," said Mom exhaustedly. "You go, Leo."

"I'll go," called out Lennie. "I found a baseball bat in Mom's room. I'll go out swinging."

"It's OK, I'll go," I said, cracking my knuckles. "I'm still warmed up." I looked at Marcel. "If you hear things getting out of hand, go ahead and release the hound."

Leo held out his hand to my mom. "Come on, let Christa take care of it. I'll make you an almond hot chocolate."

My mom nodded. Then she turned to me. "Don't be rude, Christa, they're just doing their job. We need them when we're raising money for the Foundation, remember."

"Not me," I said. "I couldn't care less what they say about me."

She frowned at me. "Don't be a dick. It's not nice." The banging got louder and her expression became conflicted. She turned away and I marched to the door and flung it open.

15

PUMPKIN
CUCURBITA PEPO

Disappointingly, a FedEx guy stood outside.

"FedEx," he said, somewhat unnecessarily, as he was a) wearing a FedEx uniform, including the hat, and b) holding out a FedEx clipboard with a FedEx form on it. They still use clipboards? Old-school. I took it from him, and he handed me a Fed-Ex pen.

Behind the FedEx guy, literally right behind, like two kids sharing the same bike, was Sarah Pepperdine. Behind her was her photographer, along with half a dozen paparazzi. I was sorry I'd missed the moment when they all pushed through the gate; it must have been a classic clown car scene.

"Christa, you don't need to talk to me now," Sarah said, struggling to keep her tone even as the other journalists pushed and shoved her from behind, "but let's schedule a time to sit down. Your fans want to know you're OK." She shot the guy behind her a sharp look that suggested he may have applied pressure where he shouldn't have.

"I don't have any fans," I said, signing the FedEx slip with a flourish. "You're confusing me with my dad." I handed the clipboard back to the FedEx guy and took the flat cardboard envelope. I remembered what my mom said and added, "We have nothing to say, please go away, thank you very much."

You had to give Sarah credit; she kept trying. "How about we just take pictures? Two or three pictures of you and your mother, thirty seconds tops . . ." Delivered at an incredible rate of speed while she leaned steadily on the FedEx guy in the hopes of sliding past and getting into the house. Bless his heart, the FedEx guy had taken a wide stance and was keeping his head down and his shoulders braced. I appreciated his commitment to customer service, but it's a lot to expect. A couple of cops had shown up and were trying to persuade the other photographers to leave, but several of them were shoving to get an angle through the door. Flashes were going off, people were calling my name, and it was starting to seriously crumble my cookie.

"Alright," I said, trying to smile at the FedEx guy and frown at everyone else at the same time. "Thanks so much." Then I stepped back and started closing the door. Sarah Pepperdine looked like she was ready to throw in the towel, but the photographers behind her gave a final concerted surge, and the poor FedEx guy popped through the doorway like a pumpkin seed at a spitting contest. He tripped and sprawled, his clipboard spinning across the floor and scaring the dog, who started barking. Ms. Pepperdine and her photographer toppled over the FedEx guy, and there was a sad little glass-breaking noise as the guy's camera hit the floor. Several other photographers tripped over *them*, and for maybe fifteen seconds it was utter chaos.

I started yelling and pulling on random arms and legs to try and separate the pile. One of the cops came in and started yanking from the back. Mom and Leo sprinted from the living room to help, Lennie and Amelia thundered down the hallway, and Marcel doubled down on his barking work, which wasn't helpful *at all*. I saw the FedEx guy literally dragging himself out from under half a dozen members of the media, and Sarah Pepperdine doing her best to catch my mom's eye so she could ask her questions.

It wasn't a peaceful scene.

Eventually, we got everyone sorted out and on their feet, and then we had to chase them out of the house. Pepperdine had to be cornered in a bedroom, where she attempted to ask my mom about her sex life. A photographer locked himself in the bathroom and took pictures of the inside of Mom's medicine cabinet until Leo picked the lock. Suddenly, it was all over, and magically, my latte was still hot. I sighed deeply and sat on the sofa, closing my eyes.

"Wait," said Leo, "what happened to the FedEx guy?"

"He left, didn't he?" said Denny. "I never even got a chance to open the envelope." She spotted it on the coffee table and tore the little strip. She spread her thumb and index finger to open it, and looked up at me. "It's empty."

Wait. I hadn't actually seen the FedEx guy leave. *Dammit.*

I got up and looked around the partition into the kitchen. The FedEx guy was leaning against the sink, drinking a glass of water. He looked at me and smiled. There was a very long silence.

"Mom," I said loudly, "you better come here." Then I looked back at the FedEx guy.

"Hey, Dad," I said.

After a stunned silence, my mom leapt up to see her late husband for the first time in twenty-five years. After staring at him in total silence for a moment, she burst into tears, hugged him for about ten minutes, then got really mad at him with a great deal of profanity, then burst into tears again.

The rest of us just stood there like blocks of cheese until this touching yet highly conflicted scene was over. Finally, Jasper turned to us.

He looked around at all three of us for a tremulous minute. A tear overflowed and ran down his cheek. He held out his hands to my eldest sister.

"Amelia . . . my little pilot."

I watched my sister's profile and wondered if she was going to lead with a left or an uppercut. Maybe she'd go all in and kick him in the chest. Instead, she tottered forward and threw herself into his arms.

"Daddy . . ." She hugged him over and over again, crying like the ten-year-old she had been all those years ago. Now, as an adult, she stepped back eventually and said, "I'm incredibly mad at you."

"I'm so sorry," he said, holding her hands. "I messed up so badly. We'll take it slow; yell as much as you like." He reached into his canvas jacket pocket and pulled out a packet of tissues.

Amelia laughed through a snotty mess of tears, and Jasper turned to Lennie.

"Eleanor . . . my little politician."

Lennie hugged him too, all anger apparently dissipated under the rosy glow of his undeniable charisma. "Daddy, I missed you so much." She wasn't as tearful as Amelia, but she was also in no way giving him a hard time.

Finally, it was my turn. I wasn't really buying this whole scene, with its penitent yet princely central figure. Where was all the rage I'd been promised? Where were the recriminations and where on earth was the stomping? I knew Jasper the least, but at that moment I honestly think I saw him more clearly than anyone else. He turned to me and held out his hands.

"And Christabel, my little fighter."

I looked at him. We had the same eyes. The same bones. I must have gazed up at that face hundreds and hundreds of times, smiling toothless baby smiles, trusting implicitly, reaching up, all delight.

"Yeah, that's me," I said. "Fuck you, Jasper."

And then the front door opened and Nathan came through it.

16

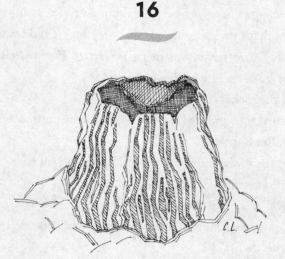

CALIFORNIA BARNACLE
MEGABALANUS CALIFORNICUS

Ten minutes later, I shot through the garden like a rocket, fully hoping someone would get in my way so I could forcibly move them out of it. I couldn't believe how fast everyone had folded.

Even Nathan.

He'd come in, recognized there was tension, immediately identified me as its source, and started trying to play peacekeeper. Marcel came to my rescue by scratching at the front door. Tiny little warrior needed to pee.

"I'm taking the dog for a walk," I huffed. "I'll be back."

Then I took way too long finding the leash, and it got really awkward because at one point Lennie confusedly asked Jasper if he knew where the leash was, which of course he didn't, *because he was pretending to be dead* when it was put away. I was angry, and I was angry that I was the only one who was angry, and I was angry that my big, angry exit was being thwarted. Fortunately, Mom found the leash and I was able to leave.

Thus the rocket.

I reached the sand and the smell of the ocean unmolested.

"Hey, Dr. Barnet!"

It was the nicest thing anyone had said to me all day.

I turned around. *Oh, for crying out loud.*

"Why?" I said to Alex Dutton, exasperated. "Why are you here?" I gestured around. "Everyone else went away. Why didn't you go with them?"

He grinned widely. "Because they didn't know Jasper Liddle was in there, talking to your mom and sisters. Along with Nathan Donovan, embattled current CEO of Liddle's Liddles." He shrugged. "Plus Leo Madrigal, your mother's boyfriend for the last ten months." He raised his eyebrows. "Was it awkward?"

I looked at him with interest. "Wait, Leo's last name is Madrigal? Like *Encanto*?"

He gave me a blank stare and then looked down at Marcel. "Shall we walk?"

"Are you asking him or me?" I said.

"Whoever's in charge," said Alex, turning and starting to saunter along the street that ran parallel to the beach. Marcel immediately followed him, and I followed Marcel. Alex kept talking. "In answer to your unspoken question, I know he's in there because I watched him leave the building where Davis Reed had him stashed, and tailed him to Studio City myself. He went into an apartment building and I nearly lost him, because he came out dressed as a delivery guy." Alex Dutton looked sideways and grinned at me. "I wouldn't even have looked at him except he was whistling, and I thought, wow, that FedEx guy really likes his job, and I looked more closely and . . ." He shrugged. "Then I tailed him here and watched him walk right through a crowd of photographers without anyone even noticing."

"Huh," I said. "Fucking cuttlefish."

There was a pause, then Alex said, "Sure, if you like."

We reached a crosswalk, and Marcel turned a neat little circle, then sat, lined up with my feet.

Alex looked down. "You've got her very well trained."

I smirked. "It's a he."

Alex looked up at me. "I was talking to the dog," he said.

The light changed and we crossed.

We didn't make it very far; as it turns out, Marcel prefers to be carried after he's completed his toilet. I managed to coax an additional half block out of him once I realized there was a coffee shop on the corner and a double shot of espresso was what I needed most in the world.

We got there and saw a line.

"Why don't you and the little chap take a seat out here, and I'll fetch us some coffee," said Alex, as if he and I were just, you know, old pals walking the dog. I looked at him and suddenly remembered another time when he'd brought me coffee. Alex Dutton had one of those faces that looks different in every light, and I'd seen it in many. He saw my expression change, and his mouth curled up. *Damn you, horny rat brain.*

"Hello there," he said more quietly. "I'd started to think friendly-you had gone away forever."

I rolled my eyes. "Go get the coffee, Alex. If I'm still here when you get back, we can talk."

He looked at me for a moment. "Or we can go straight to not talking. That works too." He grinned and disappeared indoors. Marcel made a little noise of resignation and curled into a kaiser roll under the table. I looked down at him and wished I could do the same.

So yes, maybe I didn't mention it earlier, but I had indeed slept with Mr. Dutton, in an uncharacteristic moment. To be clear, it's not uncharacteristic of me to sleep with people—I try to do it fairly regularly—but it's unusual for me to sleep with someone who is so irritatingly good-looking and full of themselves. But cut me some slack; unless you consider exchanging citations a form of foreplay, the researchers on the island aren't really all that appealing, and I'd been in a bit of a drought. Alex Dutton had emailed me several times, saying he was working on an article about my dad and would I care to comment. I didn't care to comment, and told him so. Then I went to a mollusk conference in London and he showed up on day one, specifically to talk to me. The aging journalist I'd imagined turned out to be young and very attractive, with a devastating accent and charm he laid on like a thick layer of caramel sauce. I deflected repeatedly, but he wore me down and eventually we met up so he could ask me questions, most of which I'd shrugged at, not being an expert in aviation. He was smart and interesting and did I mention the accent . . . ? We ended up in bed together for several days and—I'm a scientist, remember, and rigor is my watchword—established a new level of excellence in the field.

But then, a month or two later, he published an article that not only intimated there was something fishy about my dad's plane crash, but referred to me as *prickly and reclusive*. The article was about the science of forensic accident investigation, but he nailed us both. Now that my dad's available for questioning, I guess he could ask about those pesky anomalies in person. As for the prickly and reclusive thing, well, I was here now.

Alex reappeared with the coffee and took the seat across from me. Coffee with a handsome man twice in one day? The island was going to seem delightfully peaceful after this.

He looked at me, and smiled the smile I recognized as his first-thing-in-the-morning smile. It worked back then; I wasn't open to it working now.

"Would it be possible," he said in a gentle tone of voice, "for us to have a conversation as friends?"

I was still quite angry, I realized. "I doubt it, Alex." I sighed. "To be honest, it's not even about you. I'm just in a bad mood."

"Really?" He was teasing. "How surprising. Could it be because your father returned from the dead? Or could it be that it's much worse, that he returned from the 'fully alive and actively choosing to be somewhere else'?" He sipped his coffee. "Not a dead hero after all, but a living liar."

I frowned at him. "Now my bad mood *is* about you, Quippy McInsult. You don't know anything about my father."

"Neither do you."

"Well, I'm giving him the benefit of the doubt."

"Are you?" Alex raised his eyebrows. "Then why aren't you in there genuflecting with everyone else?" He leaned forward, at an angle he probably knew made him look sexy, and which brought him awfully close. I remembered very clearly the moment I realized I might end up sleeping with him. We were sitting in a pub, like you do in London, and I made a slightly racy joke about barnacle penises, and he gave me a look that suddenly revealed that this extremely polite British guy was actually going to be very, very rude later on. His inner devil liked to peek out to get a pregame look, so to speak, and he was giving me one of those looks now. My temper was cooling, but all that blood flow had to go somewhere . . .

"Don't even think about it," I said, thinking about it.

He reached out and drew a circle on my knee with his fingertip.

I didn't even look down. "Move that or I'll snap it."

He straightened back up. "Why aren't you with the rest of your family?"

"The dog needed to pee."

"No one else was available?"

"It was a bonding opportunity."

"Did your mother know your father was alive all along?" He threw that bombshell out as casually as his questions about the dog, so for a moment I didn't recognize it as the land mine it was.

I bit my tongue, literally. "I'm sorry, are you out of your fucking mind?"

He shook his head. "How was he surviving out there? What were they living on? I think someone knew."

"You think she funded his secret Alaskan love nest for a quarter of a century? Why?"

He shrugged. "You tell me. Do you think it's a coincidence that your dad reappears just as Donco has entered into merger talks? Are you watching the stock price? Since your dad came back it's through the roof."

I felt my rising attraction ebbing away and realized I had just dodged a sexual bullet. For a split second I'd been considering an angry distraction hookup, but he'd opened his mouth one time too many. Ah, the female body is a marvel.

I stood up. "Again, Mr. Dutton, you've managed to irritate me almost as quickly as someone who actually knows me. Thanks for the coffee."

"Does that mean you won't go out to dinner with me?"

"Again, your intuitive grasp of the situation makes you an effective journalist, but it's not making you any friends." I tugged on Marcel's leash.

"Tell me you didn't have a good time." He grinned a grin I'd seen several times from a slightly higher angle. "Every time."

I tried to give him a look that said, *Oh, I've had much better times*, but I don't think I pulled it off, because it wasn't incredibly true. So I added, "Whatever we had between us is over, and honestly, it wasn't all that memorable."

"Ouch," said someone else. "Little harsh, Christa."

Alex and I both looked up.

"Hi there," said Lennie, who was standing there carrying a cardigan. "Who are you and why are you harassing my sister?"

Once we'd clarified that no one was being harassed, Alex Dutton did his level best to ask Lennie some questions about the situation. He discovered that while Lennie looks like an ethereal creature of love and light, she is in fact an earthly queen of pain and anguish if you cross her, and after about sixty seconds, he literally put up his palms and made his goodbyes.

Lennie handed me the cardigan. "You went out the door pretty quickly," she said. "We thought maybe you'd forgotten how cold it gets in the evenings."

"Uh, thanks." I tugged it on, glad of the soft sleeves and grateful for the thought. We walked in silence for a few minutes, then by unspoken agreement we overshot the entrance to our street and kept walking. Marcel was in no way down for this, but neither was he willing to be left behind. Lennie had the leash, and he was getting yanked along exactly like a toy dog being tugged by a toddler: He'd pause, she'd tug, he'd resist, she'd tug, he'd scamper forward, repeat. All he needed was pleather ears and an orange bead on his tail and his Halloween costume would have been complete.

As we walked along, I shot Lennie a sideways look. Despite her recent ventures into therapy, Lennie has always been a tough relationship for me. She's closer to me in age than Amelia is but much further away in temperament. While Amelia, being a musician, can at least understand flights of passion, Lennie is all business. Presumably, she got it from Mom, who is one of the most competent people I've ever known. When I was a little kid, Lennie was always the one who leapt on every mistake, correcting me if she was in a good mood, mocking me and leaving me twisting in the wind if she wasn't. When I acted out in my teens, she was the one who pointed out how my behavior was embarrassing everyone else. As though I didn't already have the list carved in my conscience in deep, deep letters. I'd become comfortable with the way things were between us, even though their defining characteristic was discomfort. I wasn't sure how to deal with New Lennie. So I did the wise thing, and kept my mouth closed. First step for any scientist: Observe and gather data.

After a moment I ventured a question. "What happened after I left? Did everyone agree I was overreacting again?"

"No," she said, sedately enough that I knew she was lying. "We actually didn't talk about you at all." Subtext: *Don't get ahead of yourself, Christa. It's not all about you.*

"Is Dad . . . Jasper . . . still up there?"

She shook her head. "No. Mom decided we should table any discussion until we meet with the agency tomorrow." Lennie looked down at Marcel, who was flagging. "Dad left." She looked at me. "Nathan and Leo left too. It's just us."

I looked at her. "Why do *we* have to go to the agency? What does any of that have to do with us?" I felt a sudden twist in my gut, a sensation of vague panic I hadn't felt in a long time. I really missed the island.

Lennie sighed. "Apparently, Davis Reed is managing the whole thing. Dad says they're doing it to protect our privacy, but I don't know how plausible that is." She turned to head home, and the change in wind direction blew her hair back from her face. Her profile was just like my mother's, and for the first time, I saw the faintest signs of aging on my sister's face. She was only thirty-four, mostly single, childless, happy, busy doing what she loved, and the first cat whiskers of smile lines around her eyes softened a gaze I'd often found critical.

"About what? What is there to do?" I bent to pick up Marcel, who tolerated it. "I'm only planning on being here a couple of weeks."

Lennie nodded. "That's what Amelia and I thought too, but Mom says we might get stuck here longer."

I thought back to what Alex had suggested. "Do you think Mom knew Dad was alive?"

Lennie stopped and shook her head.

I was surprised. "You don't think that's a weird question?" I stopped too, holding the dog and shifting my weight from foot to foot, as if he were a sleeping child. His ears swung gently, like softly padded prayer flags.

"No. I thought the same thing at first, because she didn't freak out as much as I thought she would."

"Right. And?"

Lennie shrugged. "I realized the issue was my expectation, not her reaction. I called my therapist and she reminded me none of us were going to know how to deal with this because, let's face it, it doesn't happen very often."

"What doesn't?"

"Parents coming back from the dead."

"Does it happen at all?" I giggled, unable to help myself. "Does your therapist have a lot of clients among the undead?"

She laughed too. "Privacy regulations apply; she couldn't tell me if she did." She took a deep breath. "I don't know about you, but I felt very confused when I heard. I mean, genuinely, for probably half an hour, I literally didn't believe it. Then of course, I'm like, wait, has he been wandering around for the last twenty-five years trying to get home? No, of course not. So then I felt hurt and angry. I lost him when I was a child, so my feelings about it are from then, but filtered through twenty-five years of growing up, right? My inner eight-year-old is furious and hurt and conflicted, but my outer adult is amazed to get another chance to spend time with him." She grinned at me suddenly. "My therapist is fascinated, actually. I think she's going to write a piece for *Psychology Today*."

I shivered, despite the cardigan. "And how come you were all so nice to him? You were ready to kick his ass, until he dragged it through the door in a pair of FedEx shorts."

Lennie nodded thoughtfully. "I think it was the shorts that did it." She frowned at me. "I can't really explain it. I was genuinely furious, but then he showed up and I was just overwhelmed that he was there in front of me."

I frowned at her, but decided to let it go. "What about Mom?"

Lennie made a face. "I don't know. Either she's as surprised as we are, or our entire lives have been a lie, not only the huge, enormous part about our dad pretending to be dead."

I made a face. "It does seem unlikely. She can't even lie about who ate the ice cream; it would be an impressively long con for her."

Lennie started walking again, and I fell in alongside. Without looking at me, she said, "What's the deal with you and Nathan, by the way?"

I was glad she wasn't looking, because I definitely went pink. "There's no deal," I said. "He's just a friend, right? An old friend. An old family friend."

She said nothing, and after a second I looked at her. She was fighting a smile. "So . . . a friend, then?" She stopped fighting and grinned. "He was married until recently, you know."

I did *not* feel a little pinch in my stomach; that must be you. "Oh yeah? How recently?"

Lennie was watching my face. "He got divorced last year. They're still bickering. The company's doing really well, some big company wants to buy them out, and she wants her unfair share."

"Did you know her?"

Lennie shrugged. "Kind of. I was at the wedding; she seemed nice enough and certainly he was smitten." She held my gaze and smiled. "It didn't last very long."

I looked down at my feet as I walked along, wondering how Nathan had picked this woman in the first place. Lennie read my mind, which is a horrible new habit I hope she doesn't hold on to.

"She was deceptive. I mean, literally. She set her mind on having him, because she thought he was wealthy, which I guess he is, but she thought he lived like it, which he does not." She stopped and turned to look back down the way we came. "Within a few months, it was clear he'd made a terrible mistake, but he tried to make it work. She wasn't interested. She crushed him, carefully and thoroughly, and then filed for divorce and is trying to take half his company." She started walking back home. "He deserves a break; he's a good guy and always has been." She looked at me. "He's super into you. We can all see it."

"You had a conversation about it?" I frowned.

"Of course, it was right there in front of us." She shot me a look. "Don't get defensive, Christa. We love you, we talk about you."

I snapped back, "I'm not defensive, I just don't like being discussed."

She frowned, and for a moment I could see her anger growing, in traditional Lennie style. Then, literally in front of my eyes, she took a deep breath and pulled it back. "That's not unreasonable. For a long time we talked about you like you were a problem that needed to be solved, and that must have been really painful."

I stared at her. My throat prickled unexpectedly. I coughed. "No . . . it was fine."

"It wasn't fine, Christa. But that was then and this is now, and I think you and Nate could be good for each other."

"I'm leaving in two weeks."

"Why?"

"Because I need to get back to work."

"Snails running away, are they?"

I grinned at her suddenly. "Look, people underestimate their determination and commitment to freedom."

She turned back to head home. "Your violet sea snails don't even locomote."

"Is that a word?"

She nodded. "It is. I looked it up. You used it in a paper you published last year."

We'd reached the end of our street and I paused, my eyebrows up. "You read one of my papers?"

She nodded. "Of course. I read everything you publish."

I stared at her.

She shook her head at me. "I don't understand any of it, but I do read it. So does Amelia. So does Mom, I bet."

We'd reached the house.

"Why?" I asked. "If you don't understand it, why do you read it?" I put Marcel down on the ground, and he tap-danced a little, waiting to go into the house.

Lennie opened the gate, letting the dog go through. "Because how else would I keep your voice in my head?"

I turned away to close the gate, and so she wouldn't see the confused look on my face. But that mind-reading habit was apparently growing by the minute, because when I turned back to face her, she was looking at me and smiling.

"I miss you, Christa. We all do. I know the way we treated you was part of why you went so far away, but we wish you'd come back and see us sometimes."

My throat felt tight again, dammit. I'd been sent away for the last two years of high school and hadn't really lived in the same house as Lennie or Amelia ever since. When I'd left, it felt as though everyone was mad at me, and I'd been ashamed of myself. It seemed like every time I'd come home from school, for spring break or summer vacations, there'd be another reason my sisters weren't there.

They were in grad school. They were busy with work. They were in grad school *and* busy with work . . . My mom and stepdad would make excuses and look away, and gradually, I came to believe they simply weren't ever going to forgive me for causing them embarrassment.

I'd come back to Los Angeles this time knowing my dad was alive, that something very big had changed. I just hadn't also expected my sisters to have changed, and I wasn't sure yet how to feel about it. At least that was familiar: I've always found myself a little bit of a mystery.

IN THE NEWS . . .

PAGESIX.COM: Jasper Liddle seen partying in Vegas! Making up for lost time!

CATHOLICWORKER.COM: Jasper Liddle enters monastery, seeks enlightenment!

GOFUNDME: Raising money to send Jasper Liddle back to Alaska!

17

BLUEBERRIES
VACCINIUM CORYMBOSUM

I woke up very early the next morning, before traffic had really picked up. I could hear the ocean, and the daylight in the room was young and unsure of itself. On the island, the sound of the waves is inescapable, unless you head up the volcano and add vertical distance. In Los Angeles, the roaring and swishing of the traffic is usually louder, even at the edge of the shore. I thought about the island, about the swell lapping against the side of my little boat, the smell of the seaweed the snails enjoyed so much, the occasional nap taken under the trees that line the beach. I felt so much a part of the natural world there, as I noted and measured tides and generations and calendars. Here, not at all. Even the ocean sounded like a white noise machine instead of a body of water large enough to lick the coastlines of fifty-six countries.

My door nudged open. No one came in. Then Marcel's nose appeared at the edge of the bed. I rolled over and peered down at him. Apparently, the natural world was sending emissaries.

"Do you want to come up?" I asked him, reaching down. But no, he backed away and politely evaded my clutches. I let my arms dangle until he came closer again, and then I smoothed his little cranium. "You're not an evil little bratwurst after all, are you?" I said to him softly. He didn't reply, but his eyes became twin pools of soulful adoration, and I was overwhelmed by the urge to get up and feed him.

I hunted about for something to put on. Having gone to sleep still cross with Jasper, I'd woken up worried, fractious and out of sorts. I didn't want to go to the agency, didn't want to see Jasper again, didn't want to even be in Los Angeles.

When I walked into the kitchen, my mom was standing at the sink in her dressing gown, washing berries like someone in a health care commercial. I saw Marcel's dish on the ground, a few random kibbles still left from breakfast, and turned around to raise my eyebrows at him. He'd evaporated, of course, having been busted. Animals actually mastered teleportation years ago: Hear a crash in the kitchen and run in? No cat. Open bag of kibble spilled on the floor? No dogs within a quarter mile. They mastered the laws of physics; they're just wisely keeping it to themselves. There's probably a kitten somewhere who can explain quantum entanglement; she's just too busy chasing Ping-Pong balls.

"Hi, Mom," I said, not quite sure how to handle myself. She'd been asleep the night before when Lennie and I had returned.

She turned and smiled at me, her usual everything-is-alright-with-the-world smile, and thank goodness for that.

"Good morning, sweet pea!" she said. "I'm sorry I crashed out before you got back last night, but I was honestly so freaked out by Jasper appearing that I needed to crawl under the covers and hide." She shook her hands mostly dry, then finished them on her dressing gown, opening her arms to hug me. "I don't blame you for being mad at him, baby. I was mad at him too; the mad just got swept away by the surprised." She tipped the berries into a bowl, added a dollop of yogurt, and reached for the honey. "We'll go see what Davis Reed has to say and take it from there." She started pouring the honey and just kept going, covering everything in a healthy coating. I turned away and smiled because, right there, that was classic Mom. Excellent intentions, strong beginning, easily derailed in the homestretch.

Amelia came in, cracking her fingers. "Good morning, one and all." She came over to me right away and enfolded me in her freshly showered, Oil of Olay–scented hug. "You got good and mad last night. Are you feeling any better?"

Damn them both for being so irritatingly even-tempered and pleasant. And for knowing me better than I wanted them to.

I mumbled something and started poking about looking for toast. "I just, you know . . ."

"You were pissed off because we were all, *Oh, we're going to knock him into next week*, and then he shows up and we're like, *All is forgiven . . . ?*" Amelia settled herself on a stool and peeled a banana.

I stared at her.

She nodded. "Yeah, I can totally see why that would piss you off." She shrugged. "I felt so angry, but when I clapped eyes on him, he was just my dad and I was . . ." She ate some banana, and then waved it as she spoke. "I'm not enjoying any of it very much. I'm going to come right out and say it." She looked at Mom. "Are you happy about all this?"

Mom had wandered over to the sofa to eat her breakfast. "Not really, darling," she replied, "but what can I do? It's not like I can say to him, *Oh, go back, I was more used to you dead.*"

Amelia looked at her. "Do you think he knows about Harry?"

Mom shrugged. "Almost certainly." She ate a berry thoughtfully, having waited ten seconds for the honey to drip off. "Are you off to Mrs. Lobster's?"

Amelia nodded. "I'd be happy to skip a day, but she got the piano tuned specially." Mrs. Lobster (whose real name was Mrs. Lobesto; you do the math) was our old neighbor, and had been Amelia's first piano teacher, decades earlier. After a year or so, Mrs. Lobster had come to explain to Mom that Amelia needed a different teacher, one that could take her further, but she'd followed Amelia's subsequent education and career with delight. She still lived four doors down and had a Steinway concert grand, so Amelia practiced at her piano when she visited.

After Amelia left, Mom wandered back to her room. I padded after her and knocked on her door. She mumbled something I hoped was "Come in," and I did. She had all her clothes spread out on her bed and was standing there still in her dressing gown.

She turned her head and raised an eyebrow. "I'm having a crisis," she said.

"Existential or wardrobe?"

"Both, which is probably unsurprising." She turned to face me. "I'm ashamed to admit I'm feeling insecure about my appearance."

I went and sat on the floor by the wall. "I'm confused. Are you ashamed of your appearance, or ashamed that you're ashamed of your appearance?" I frowned. "Or ashamed of your admission?"

She gazed down at me. "You're actually supposed to say, *Why, Mom? You look amazing,* to which you could have added *for your age* if you really had to."

I have no idea what my face looked like, because I wasn't sure I'd ever heard my mom express anything but confidence and certainty before. It was her standard operating procedure and had always delighted me (*thank God someone's in charge*) and also dismayed me (*wait, adults are supposed to know what they're doing at all times? Fuuuuck . . .*). However, what I said was, "Well, I didn't say that because it was implied."

Mom sighed at this less-than-stellar answer, and turned back to her clothing. "That bastard comes waltzing back and literally puts on his old wardrobe without missing a beat. He looked exactly the same in that Oprah interview as he always did, and I hate that it bothers me so much." She sat down on the end of the bed and frowned at me. "Mind you," she said, "I'm glad he showed up now and not when I was still going through menopause. I would have throttled him on the spot."

"It made you murderous?"

She laughed. "You know how in hurricanes, sometimes the laws of physics are suspended? A piece of straw will go through an oak, or one house will be completely untouched while the one next door has been reduced to three bricks and a packet of Band-Aids?"

I wasn't sure where she was going with this, but she was certainly speaking my language. "Uh, sure, I'm a weather nerd, you know that."

"Right, well, menopause is the biological equivalent of that. Things you previously understood about your body are no longer true, and you go through this process of recalibration. It's like the reverse of puberty, where the storm of hormones is respected as a rite of passage with its own branding, literary genre and musical accompaniment. *This sucks, teens*, says the world, but a) you look really cool while doing it, and b) when it's over you get to be an adult. Menopause is similarly transformational, but whereas teenagers end up as adults with their lives ahead of them, menopausal women see nothing ahead but further atrophy, cultural irrelevance and death."

"Huh," I said. "You're not selling it."

She was just warming up, apparently. "It's like every shitty aspect of being a woman turned up to eleven. Always too hot or too cold? Welcome to hot flashes and night sweats. Somewhat tearful around your period? Try bursting into tears in the cereal aisle because Tony the Tiger reminds you of the cat you had in third grade. Familiar with your own libido? Say goodbye to that version and say hello to some kind of chemistry experiment where you become impossibly horny and pounce on your husband, only to find the smell behind his ear overwhelmingly repellent."

I was sitting there trying to process that when she turned around again and said, "You and your sisters missed most of it, of course. Harry dealt with it, and then just as things got better, he got sick." As always when she mentioned his name, she couldn't look at me. She couldn't look at any of us when she said my stepfather's name, because it still made her cry when she did.

She busied herself with sorting belts, and I got up to get more coffee.

I don't remember my mom dating at all when I was young. She may have, of course—a woman has her needs—but I'd never competed for my mother's attention, especially as we spent so much time together when I was little. My older sisters became teenagers not many years after Jasper disappeared, and there was a lot of door slamming, sulking and grounding. I was so much less trouble than they were, I got to feel pretty special.

When I was ten or eleven, she'd met Harry Fischer. He was a patron of the Foundation, and a charming, funny man who brought my mother to tears of laughter several times a day. He made her take time for herself, insisted she say no every now and again . . . He made her deeply, deeply happy. We all loved him, even though my sisters were both away at college when he and Mom got married. After more than a decade of happiness, Harry had gotten cancer and died while I was away, three years earlier. I'd offered to come back, over and over, but my mother (who is a very private woman) didn't want me to leave my work and insisted until the very end that Harry was going to be fine. Until he wasn't.

I came back for the funeral, shocked and angry I hadn't been able to say goodbye. I steamed into Los Angeles, devastated and furious with grief, but when I walked off the airplane and saw my mother standing in Arrivals, listing at an angle like the last reed in the field, my anger dissipated. Harry's death nearly killed her too.

Back then, my sisters had known no more than I did. Now, years later, I wonder if any of us know anything about my mom's private life. Leo's existence proves she hasn't been sitting at home in the evenings gathering dust, but for all I know, she could be throwing orgies and selling Tupperware. Possibly at the same time, though where would you keep your credit card?

"I assume you're not going to the agency in your pajamas?" My mom had tugged her competent face back on. Maybe thinking of my stepfather reminded her it didn't really matter what happened with Jasper. Maybe that's what real, lasting love does for you even after its subject is gone—it gives you a bright point of comparison. I miss him too. After things went badly for me, Harry and Mom set me on my feet again, with Harry urging gentleness.

Admittedly, they'd done it by sending me out of state, to an East Coast boarding school with a heavy emphasis on academics. I think my mom might have been in favor of a military academy, but fortunately, Harry tempered her. It had saved me, of course, and gotten me into zoology, but at the time it definitely felt like banishment. I was told to put my head down, keep my head down and get back on track. Harry had emailed me every day, the only one who kept talking to me. Mom was completely radio silent for weeks. I'd always assumed she was too mad to speak.

"Maybe after the meeting we can do a little shopping?" Mom was being hopeful. "You're such a pretty girl. Why do you hide it?" She pushed my hair back from my face and tucked it behind my ear. "I think you've gotten even prettier over the last two years."

I frowned. "It has not been two years since I've seen you."

"It has."

"No, I was home for the holidays."

She made a face. "Yes, two years ago. Last year there was some kind of algae thing . . ."

My eyes widened. "Oh, that's right, the bloom! I forgot that was at Christmas . . ." Oh my goodness, it had been so awesome and terrible at once. "It was really fascinating, the algae—"

"Wow," interrupted Mom. "That does sound . . . enthralling." She closed the closet. "The agency is right next to Bergdorf's. We could pop in after."

"Mom." My voice was firm.

"What?" replied Mom innocently. "You can't wander around Los Angeles dressed like Cranky David Attenborough."

"Why not? I bet David Attenborough does." I raised my eyebrows. "You seem to have forgotten what a lost cause I am." The subject of my "hidden" prettiness was as familiar and worn as a pebble, and far less interesting.

Mom shooed me out of the room. "I don't think you're a lost cause, but you do need to go get dressed. We will be presenting a united front. What do I always expect?" She looked at me.

"Exemplary behavior," I said. This was an in-joke, sort of. Whenever we had to go out as a family in public, or even when I was a little kid and it was just Mom and me, she would look around before she opened the door, and ask the same question. *Exemplary behavior* meant we were to do nothing that embarrassed her, ourselves, or the Foundation. It had been a reliable method of control for her until I'd hit my teens. Then it became something to throw in her face.

Mom nodded. "Right. Go get dressed."

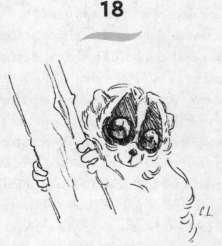

SLOW LORIS
NYCTICEBUS COUCANG

For most of the drive from Venice to Beverly Hills, the city was its usual hot and busy self, with thousands of people thinking of no one but themselves. But as we drew closer to the agency, I spotted someone wearing a *Liddle's Great Big World* vintage T-shirt, and then, as we turned the corner onto the correct block, there were crowd barriers and a corralled mass of press, photographers and presumably fans. Cops chewed gum and frowned. TV trucks clogged the street.

"What's going on?" asked Lennie, leaning forward to look out the window.

"Dad, I think," I said. "Look." I pointed.

There was the first sign: WELCOME HOME, JASPER! it said, and the middle-aged woman holding it looked thrilled to bits. She had a

T-shirt with his face on it, she had a baseball hat with his show logo on it, and she was going to be spitting mad when she saw how many other, bigger signs there were. Hers, however, did have flashing lights. I spent twenty seconds thinking about the effort someone had put into welcoming a total stranger. They'd decided to take time out of their life to stand on a Los Angeles street in case my dad showed up. They'd come up with a concept, shopped for their concept, built their sign in the privacy of their own home and then set out full of vim and vigor, ready to hold it up and exalt in my father's return. What had I done? I'd sort of half raised my hand and said, *Hey, Dad.*

For a moment, I felt bad about it, then I reminded myself this was the man who had abandoned me—by choice. I'm allowed to have mixed feelings about it, for crying out loud. I don't know about you, but it's pretty rare I have a single, clean emotion without various other feelings wanting to horn in around the edges. Happy to be eating ice cream? Sure, with guilt sprinkles. Admiration of someone's stellar achievement? Yeah, plus jealousy it wasn't me, relief it didn't have to be me, and sympathy for all the effort it had taken to be them. Lonely all on my own in Violetta? Yes, but also happy to not have to deal with people, wear clean clothes or reveal my personal hopes and fears. People talk about emotions as though they are stripes on a flag, distinct and tightly hemmed, but mine are always kind of a patchwork.

"How did they know he would be here?" asked Mom.

"Apparently, he's mastered social media faster than I have. He tweeted about it this morning." Lennie turned her phone around to show Mom.

Mom leaned forward and peered at it. Then she said, "Well, he's been practicing, then. He used to be a total Luddite."

The car turned off Wilshire onto one of the many alleys that

run between the enormous buildings lining that part of the boulevard. We pulled up alongside a nondescript side door, and two seconds later Jasper was in the car, and we were pulling away again.

I kid you not, he grinned around at all of us and said, "Hey, guys."
I'm not sure he got the reception he was expecting.

Lennie, who'd been closest to the door and therefore the most
startled when it suddenly opened, gaped at him and said, "What
the actual ever-living fuck are you doing?"

Mom had also apparently regrown her spine overnight, because
she followed up with, "Honestly, Jasper, you have to realize that
you've known for the last twenty-five years that you're alive, but
we've only known for a week. You must stop popping up unexpectedly, and this is my last warning." She gave him a gimlet eye. "I
will smite you next time, and you know I'm not kidding."

Amelia and I said nothing, because at that moment we pulled
up in front of the agency, which had one of those entrances designed for swooping in and out of. A whippet-thin young man appeared by magic and opened the car door. I looked at Lennie and
we were both like, *What on earth is happening???* I really hadn't had
enough coffee for this level of rapid-fire astonishment.

As Mom, Lennie and Amelia stepped out, the noise level went
through the roof and people just about lost their shit. They could
not possibly have recognized my sisters, unless there were classi-
cal piano fans or major polluters among them,[1] but they knew my

---

1. Amelia is a pianist, as I've mentioned, and Eleanor is an environmental activist.
    She doesn't consider it a day well spent unless she's rubbed an oil company's nose in
    their own effluent, or told a major international corporation that she'll sue them
    back to mom-and-pop status unless they clean up their act. She says it helps her
    sleep at night, but I also think she just enjoys random acts of vengeful reparation.

mom. The wave of noise made me duck, but as I did, I watched the expression on Jasper's face slowly change, and realized he must have missed that too. The people. The recognition.

Jasper turned to me and said, "Your turn, baby."

My turn.

I clambered out and heard my name rising up like a cheer. Apparently, I was the one thing the crowd needed to make this the single best day *ever*. No, but like, really. *Ever.*

"CHRISTA!!!!!!"

I'm not even kidding, people went berserk. It was so weird.

Then Jasper got out, and now I can say I've seen grown women burst into tears in large numbers, which wasn't something I actually had on my bucket list, but sure. People. Freaked. Out. There was applause that created an almost palpable sound wave, there was cheering, there was jumping up and down.

What did Jasper do? He smiled and waved and looked like a man who'd been locked in a closet might look upon seeing daylight. He soaked it in, and I swear to God I could see him swelling like one of those little foam dinosaurs I used to put in water. The rest of us just stood there like lemons.

After waiting a moment, presumably to let us soak in the worship, the slender young man started shepherding us politely to the entrance. The photographers felt there were still photos to be taken, and as they were closer to us than the public, they started calling out.

"Christa, smile!"

"Christa, why so grumpy, darling?"

"Cheer up, Christa!"

I think my face's regular expression must be set to "sad and underwhelmed," because even people who know how dangerous it is will occasionally tell me to cheer up. I'm fully cheerful, thanks, I'm just self-contained.

As we got closer to the door, the young man said, "My name is Jordan. I'm Davis Reed's assistant. Davis thought it would be a good idea to pose for a few family group shots here, seeing as you're all together." He looked beseechingly at us, as though used to being refused. "It will keep the press happy for a day or two."

Jasper smiled at him, Mom and my sisters smiled at him, and I frowned.

"Can't it just be Jasper? That's who they want to see."

"Oh no," said Jordan, startled. "They're interested in the whole family. People want to see Jasper made it all the way home."

All the way home. The phrase struck me strangely, as if Jasper had been a lost sheep bleatingly trying to get back. Which couldn't be further from the truth.

"I think it's fine," said Mom. "Come on, Christa, don't be difficult." She looked at Jasper, who was still waving at people in the crowd, grinning and thumbs-upping when someone caught his eye. She had her hand on his arm, and I noticed she was actually gripping it quite tightly. He wanted to go talk to the people, and she wasn't letting him. I also hadn't heard that particular tone of voice from her in over a decade; it was the voice she'd used when I was a teenager and trying to flex my independence muscle. She was such a generally kind woman that when she insisted on something, people tended to do it.

I'm no exception. I sighed. "Alright, no problem."

The five of us swung around, and Jordan rearranged us to his liking, with me in the middle, which emphasized that I didn't inherit the tall genes, thanks for that. For a moment, there was literally nothing but flashing lights and shouting, and my eyes started watering and I didn't enjoy it in the slightest. I tried to stay still and smile, doing my best not to look like an eighth grader taking an agonizing middle school photo. I was a confident, successful scientist, and several people had told me I was nice-looking, so I held on to that. When that wasn't enough, I thought about slow lorises, my never-fail escape mammal.[2]

After what felt like a long time, the young guy raised his hand and stopped the photographers.

"There will be a statement issued later with updates and information; there will not be another photo opportunity." He shone his smile around for precisely three seconds, then slammed it off again as he guided his little kittens into the building. The photographers kept shooting pictures and shouting our names, and I saw the young man giving one or two of them glares that would have curbed most. But paparazzi are thick-skinned and they kept snapping.

Now we were waiting for the elevator, the still-persistent flashes from the photographers reflecting and bouncing off the polished chrome doors.

"We're going to join the rest of your team upstairs. The caterers were just finishing their setup; we have plenty of yummy things." He gave the button a few more jabs, just in case he hadn't conveyed his impatience the first four times.

"How kind," murmured Denny. "Who doesn't like 'yummy'?"

Jordan looked at her nervously, but the elevator arrived and he

---

2. I heartily recommend everyone cultivate an animal they can focus on when the environment becomes too much to handle. Slow lorises are mine. You might choose a beetle or a bird; sometimes the weapon chooses the warrior, you know what I mean? The world is a wonderful playground, full of incredible creatures and amazements that help me deal with the fact that people are all over it and often want to talk to me.

graciously gestured for us to go ahead, casting one last glance at the press. I realized he was responsible for getting us upstairs in one piece, and I felt a little bad I hadn't been nicer about the photos. As we turned to face the closing doors, a random photographer broke through security and started sprinting across the lobby, chased by at least two guards. Jordan calmly watched him approach and then, as the photographer tried to hold the closing doors, pulled a fork from his pocket, leaned forward and pronged the poor guy repeatedly in the thumb until he let go and the doors bumped shut, cutting off his cries of pain and, let's face it, surprise. No one expects to get forked before ten in the morning.

The elevator began its graceful glide upward, and Jordan slid the fork back into his pocket.

"Like I said," he murmured to us, apparently thinking an explanation was in order, "the caterers were setting up."

I stopped feeling bad. This kid needed no sympathy.

19

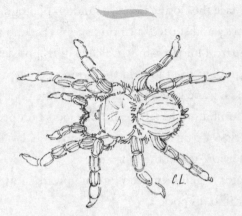

STRIPED-KNEE TARANTULA
APHONOPELMA SEEMANNI

The conference room was enormous. At one end there was an extensive buffet, and all over the walls were giant blown-up images from Jasper's show, old publicity shots and various images of his career. I looked around . . . Yup, there it was. The photo at the airport. Everyone loves that photo except the people in it.

Mom put her hand on my lower back and pushed.

"You're blocking the door," she muttered to me, and I realized I was. I had taken four steps into the room and stopped dead, gazing around. I muttered apologies and quickly found a chair.

"You don't have to say anything, remember," Mom said quietly. "Just smile and leave the talking to me."

I nodded, confident this wasn't going to be a problem. I was simply going to daydream about primates and eventually it would be over. It wasn't about me, anyway.

Jordan made sure we all had drinks and then disappeared. Apparently, he'd gone and rung some kind of bell, because the double doors at the other end of the room opened and an army of people came in.

Not an army. More than a squad, less than a platoon. I got to twenty before I stopped counting. They filed into the room, smiling at us and filling the seats around the table in some prearranged order that the younger members of the group were clearly more aware of than we were. There was one lady in a suit who paused to speak to Jasper before sitting, and about five younger people clearly couldn't sit before she did, so they pretended to be suddenly receiving important texts. Yes, all of them at once. I can't help enjoying these things; I'm a trained nature observer. The minute she sat down, the whole lot of them scrambled for the closest seats. I couldn't begin to imagine what all of them did, or why they were here, but I reminded myself I was just an incidental player in this story, and stopped thinking about it.

Once all the people were seated, Davis Reed swept in, alone and unaccompanied. Everyone turned to watch him take his seat, and I could feel the tension in the room ratchet up several notches.

Ah, I thought, *here was me, thinking we were the stars of the meeting.*

I'd never seen Davis Reed before, and I was surprised. He was tall and sharply dressed, with a barely suppressed vitality that crackled across the room. He was handsome enough to have been an actor, but as he took his place at the head of the table and looked around, I could see being a team player wasn't his bag. He was a king in every sense, aware of his power, happy to wield it, and comfortable that of all the people in whatever room he was in, he was the one most suited for leadership.

"Well," he said, "this is a situation none of us expected." He looked grave for a moment, and then smiled widely. "But what a wonderful situation it is." He looked at my mom. "Your husband is home!"

Mom didn't flicker. "Well, he's not actually my husband anymore, and where I live is not his home, but we're certainly happy to see him." She looked at Davis. "What I'm less sure of is why my daughters and I are here. We're not clients of the agency."

I looked at Jasper, but he was looking at the table. I was slowly realizing something I hadn't known before: My mom was the energy behind his career, not him.

Davis already knew this, because he answered my mom as an equal. "I understand, but many of the opportunities we're evaluating involve the whole family."

Amelia said, "Sorry, I'm onstage in Oslo in three weeks, so don't count on me for anything."

Lennie said, "Yeah, back in London week after next. Sorry."

Davis smiled gently. "I see." He didn't seem that bothered, but then he turned to me, and suddenly, I was reminded of that extra degree of stillness a cat employs just before it pounces. That held-breath of feline magic that halts the movement of air. "What about you, Christa?"

I shook my head. "Nope. I'm going back to the Indian Ocean in a couple of weeks."

Davis frowned without changing his facial expression at all, a miraculous gift. This guy was starting to freak me out. "Several potential projects involve you specifically. People are very excited about the father-daughter scientist angle." He very casually examined his cuffs, which were flawless. "It's commercially very compelling."

I tightened my lips. "It's not an *angle*; it's an actual career. I have a job to do. I can't just walk away." I shrugged. "Plus, being famous isn't something I'm interested in."

"You prefer studying marine mollusks?" Davis's tone was ninety-five percent polite and five percent wildly incredulous. Thanks to his mastery of intonation, however, the incredulous rang through.

"Yes," I replied calmly. "As you might have noticed, the environment is under threat, and sea snails are an excellent early warning system. Maybe you don't care about what happens after you're dead, but I do." Wow, who invited Miss Self-Righteous to the meeting? I felt myself blushing and looked at my hands. Which were shaking, but safely, to themselves, hidden in my lap.

Davis shrugged, politely ignoring the implied criticism. "You could have a big impact, you and your father together, entertaining and educating people about how they can help change the future."

I looked over at my mom very briefly, and she raised one eyebrow and half smiled. Did she want me to do it? Hadn't I given enough? I fell silent.

Davis moved his hand slightly, and Jordan appeared at his elbow. "Coffee, black, and something to eat." He smiled at us again, regaining control of the room. "Please, take a moment to get yourself some food. My team has been working very hard to prepare a presentation for you."

I looked around and realized how exhausted many of the people seemed. This meeting was the beginning of something for us and the end of a lot of work for them. We all got up and went to the buffet and did that thing where you talk about what's right in front of you in order to keep from either giggling or screaming.

Only me, then?

In case you wondered, I got some Caesar salad, a half sandwich I was probably not even going to attempt, and some berries. And by some I mean, like, seven. I immediately regretted each and every one of those choices, because once I sat down and looked around, I realized I was literally the only person to have gotten more than a cup of coffee. I shot my sisters a look, and Amelia had the goodness to get up again and get a donut. Then Jasper got up to get a donut. Then everyone else suddenly had to get up and get a donut and there weren't enough. If I tell you that the temptation to drop my napkin and duck under the table and never come out again was pretty damn strong, I trust you will understand.

Then we settled back in our seats and waited politely to see what they had for us.

Jordan dimmed the lights, and a screen whispered down from the ceiling. Touching music swelled from speakers concealed around the room. Clips of Jasper's old show started to play. Him on an elephant. Him with a classroom of children and a pair of quokkas. The whole family together, including baby me, footage I'd never even seen before. Lion cubs and baby bears and the infamous tarantula episode, where he'd misplaced the spider on an evening news show. (He hadn't really had a spider, just an empty family-size matchbox, but Barbara Walters hadn't seen the joke.)

A voice-over said, "Ever since Jasper Liddle started talking to the animals, the world has listened. For nearly a decade, Jasper's show led public television's crusade to create quality natural history programming. He traveled the world. He awakened a generation's love for the planet. And then . . . he left us."

The music changed, growing subtly more somber. Footage of the crash site. Coverage of his disappearance. Crying fans.

"Good Lord," muttered my mom to Jasper, so quietly only we could hear. "You were a TV presenter, not a damn brain surgeon." My mom hated the way Jasper got canonized simply because he disappeared. She felt it overshadowed the work living scientists and ecologists were doing.

"For years," the voice-over continued, "the world mourned, and his brave widow continued his important work." I heard Mom make a vomiting noise under her breath, as the screen showed clips of her over the years, digging tunnels for lizards, holding a lamb for reasons lost to history, laughing and covered in monarch butterflies in Mexico . . . Oh God, and then I showed up, six or seven, holding a hawk on my glove. Feeding a fish to a miserable imprisoned orca at SeaWorld. Holding a wolf cub, which I will never forget and never regret, and even if I'm emotionally a little closed off as a result of early overexposure, at least I got to hold a wolf cub and you didn't.[1] I started tuning out, thinking about the many animals I had held over the years.

"Until now . . ." the voice-over added, pausing elegantly to let the music swell and fill the room. The picture from the hospital, zooming in, then a smash cut to the interview with Oprah.

"I have so much explaining to do . . ." Jasper was saying.

The screen went black, then slowly, a title appeared: LIDDLE'S BRAND-NEW WORLD.

---

1. Maybe you do it every day, to be fair. I don't know your life.

A pause, and then a subtitle faded in: HOSTED BY THE LIDDLE FAMILY.

"No," said the Liddle family as one.

"Oh, we have other ideas," said Davis silkily. Somewhere a nervous junior finger pressed a button, because the presentation started again.

New voice-over. A woman this time, over a montage of footage of Amelia, Lennie and me. Not that there was very much, but they made the most of what there was.

"Three sisters, touched by tragedy. One turns to music, one to politics, the last to science. Three beautiful women, alone and unprotected, fighting for what they believe in."

Again, fade to black. Title text: THE LIDDLE SISTERS, A THREE-PART SPECIAL TELEVISION EVENT.

This time I beat everyone to it. "No way. Absolutely not. Plus, Lennie isn't in politics. She's a conservationist."

Davis cleared his throat. "Yes, but politics tested better and conservation was too close to the science one."

"You already ran focus groups?" I asked. "And just to clarify, I'm 'the science one'?"

"Yes, you're the family member with the highest name recognition, after your father, of course."

Amelia and Lennie burst out laughing, and I could tell this was going to be the hilarious takeaway from the meeting, for them. Fantastic.

"Mr. Reed, I realize you have a job to do, but I am not interested in becoming a celebrity in any way." I paused and waved my hands up and down in front of myself. "I did that. It was a disaster. I quit. Now I'm a research scientist who hasn't had her hair professionally cut in a decade. Look at me!"

There was a subtle shift in the air, and Davis's expression changed. "Actually, we had some thoughts about that." The screen came back to life, filled with a headshot of me. It was the one from the university directory and it was . . . unflattering.

I remembered that day like it was yesterday: I had overslept, I had grabbed the wrong pair of glasses, I'd lost a button on my shirt getting out of the car and spilled coffee on myself opening a desk drawer. And then, as I was sitting there holding the one clean T-shirt I could find in my office, which featured an underdressed toad and the line "Herpetologists do it in *and* out of the water," Margaret, the department secretary, had called to let me know a photographer was there to take faculty photos. I'd tried to get out of it, but she wasn't interested in my bullshit, so I was just opening my mouth to ask the guy if he was ready when he took the picture. As a result, I look like a flounder who'd been dragged from the ocean, dressed in a dirty shirt and given a bad piece of news. Not my best look.

The photo hadn't improved with age, but fortunately, the agency had more tools at hand than simple time. Before my eyes, the picture morphed into a far more attractive version of me. Same face, sure, but professionally made-up, hair bouncy and styled, a flattering neckline, no hint of a coffee-stained bottom-feeder.

My family betrayed me by all saying *awwww* at the same time. Loudly.

I stared and cleared my throat. "I assume you photoshopped that?"[2]

Davis nodded. "I hope you don't mind, but we had a hunch . . ."

---

2. Rather than, say, grew a clone? Honestly, sometimes I amaze even myself with my idiocy.

He smiled at me, unaware he was about to put his handmade shoe in his mouth. "You're extremely photogenic; you just need to let people see it."

My mom made a gurgling noise, indicating her cognitive distress at suddenly being on the same side as Davis. I was still staring at the photo. They'd given me subtle green and blue makeup that brought out my eyes, a rose lipstick . . . I didn't recognize myself, but a little voice in my head said, *Ooh, pretty* . . .

Davis Reed read the room, and decided to let that sit while he turned his attention back to Jasper. He took a breath and adjusted his cuffs to be precisely one quarter inch below the edges of his suit sleeves. "While obviously the Oprah interview broke the silence, the late-night hosts are currently in a bidding war over who gets to have you—and as many of your family as are interested—for a wider interview about your plans now you're back."

"Not it," said Lennie.

"Not it," said Amelia.

"Christa will do it," said Mom, "as long as you make sure to talk about the Foundation and she can hold something small and furry." She looked at Davis. "I assume you can arrange that?" She looked at Jasper. "Pick something fun to keep her busy so she doesn't need to talk."

I frowned a little. "Mom, I'm not eight anymore. You don't need to provide me with an animal companion." Then I thought for a moment more and raised my hands. "Actually, what am I saying, by all means give me something to hold."

Davis nodded. "Naturally. We'll need to move somewhat quickly, so not sure what will be available to us . . . I think next week is what we're shooting for."

I looked at my dad. He was looking back at me, clearly waiting to see if I was going to explode. When our eyes met, he rolled his and his mouth twitched. I felt a little better, though surprised he was the one who saw the funny side of the whole thing. I really didn't know him at all. Mom turned to me and smiled her most charming smile.

"It's just one interview, Christa, and you can leave all the talking to your dad. Donations to the Foundation are already up, people are paying attention and this is a fantastic opportunity to get our message across." She thought for a moment. "I'd join you myself, but then they'll want to ask about our marriage or whatever, and I want to keep the focus on the Foundation."

There was a pause, then Lennie said, "Yeah, Christa. Do it for the animals."

I looked over at her, but her expression was guileless. I realized I might as well give in. When Mom gets a bee in her bonnet, there's very little point in getting in the way. Lie down in the middle of the tracks and the train might roll over you; try to outrun it and you'll end up in slices.

Davis started speaking, pretending not to notice the tension. "Obviously, TV isn't the only option open to us. Several publishers have reached out—are you planning on writing a book?" He was looking at Jasper, but then switched attention to me again. "You could cowrite one. Nonfiction, possibly. Or a children's book. About fathers and daughters."

I opened my eyes very wide and started to say that it would be a cold day in hell before I wrote a kids' book unless it was titled *Violet the Shit-Kicking Sea Snail*, when Jasper shook his head.

"Davis, we went over this in Alaska. I don't know what I'm

going to do next." He shot my mom a sidelong glance. "I agreed to the one interview, we seem to be agreeing to one more, then I need some time with my family."

This was news to me, and apparently to all of us, based on my mom's expression. Amelia had started playing arpeggios on her knees, which was a really bad sign. I started disassembling my sandwich to give myself something to do, and rolled a cherry tomato to one side of the plate, in case I needed to throw something. I met Lennie's eye across the table, and she looked at the tomato and I looked at the tomato and there was a moment where I came *this close* to flicking it at her and she knew it . . .

Meanwhile, Davis rolled on. "You could also sit down with a major outlet and do a long-form article . . ." He looked around the room. "Rebecca, print media?"

Rebecca, who was the lady who stopped others from sitting, tapped on the tablet in front of her. "*Vanity Fair*, the *New Yorker*, *National Geographic*, *Hello!*, *Vogue*, *Outside* . . . editorial is extremely excited. An in-depth piece could be optioned as readily as a book."

"True," said Davis. "How do you feel about a profile? Much less effort than a book, quicker to market . . ."

Rebecca continued, "Individual journalists have reached out as well, of course. The *New York Times* has Alex Dutton ready to jump whenever we say so."

"No," said my mom. "Alex Dutton is a hard pass."

Rebecca was surprised. "He's a top feature writer."

"He's a muckraking bastard." My mom really doesn't like Alex Dutton.

Rebecca folded like origami. "Fair enough, no Mr. Dutton. I'll ask the *New Yorker* if Susan Orlean is available."

Good luck with that, I thought. Jasper rubbed the back of his head in what I was coming to realize was a characteristic way. "I'm not sure, Davis, I feel like I need to . . ."

"You need to get back to work," said Davis. "As you saw outside, you still have an audience. You have a moment here, a chance to do something important. *Liddle's Great Big World*—the show you started, don't forget—is still running, and PBS would love to have you back. They've suggested a special, based on you getting up to speed on what's happened ecologically in the last twenty-five years. Visiting places you visited with the show, years ago, using it as a platform for highlighting climate change." He shifted in his chair, flicking invisible lint from his pants. Like a cat feigning nonchalance on a mantelpiece while evaluating the stability of the valuables. "They've offered to fund a million-dollar Liddle endowment at UCLA . . ." He shot me a look. "It could fund years of valuable research."

My mom leaned forward. "And you would love to start earning commission again."

Davis leaned back. "We've been earning commission steadily the entire time Jasper has been in seclusion."

I felt the hairs on my forearms begin to rise. *In seclusion?* That's what we're calling it now?

Davis looked at his hands. "As you know, we set up a trust shortly after Jasper was declared dead, and the checks have been faithfully deposited." He extended his fingers and checked his nails. "I can provide you with a complete accounting, should you wish."

Mom opened her mouth to ask another question, but Davis spoke first. "Right now, we're simply having a conversation. You can choose to decline any of these opportunities, but some might be appealing. This is a whirlwind. Why not reap while you can?"

Mom paused, but the expression on her face told everyone to

hold their tongues, and they did. "Davis, this might be a whirl-wind, but if you remember your sources, the person who reaps is the one who sowed." She pointed at Jasper. "That guy. We just got caught in the storm."

Good Lord, who the hell is that? Honestly, my mom has always been a tough cookie, but she was one hundred percent velvet glove all the way. Elbow-length velvet gloves, in fact. But this woman was nothing like her. This woman had one fuck left and was un-willing to give it. Suddenly, my rough-edged interpersonal skills made more sense.

Davis was up to it, though. "Fair enough." He raised his finger and barked, "Darcy."

Darcy, who seemed a little more relaxed than Rebecca the book lady, said, "Movies. Three majors and four mini-majors have ap-proached us about tentpole biopics." She looked at us and smiled. "The biggest offer has Chris Hemsworth lined up to play you, Jasper."

Jasper laughed. "As the younger me, presumably." He looked at me and winked. I looked away. I started wondering what a mini-major was. I imagined tiny little soldiers.

Darcy looked excited. "Yes, and one studio also mentioned Anne Hathaway for the romantic lead. For Lorna." Then she made a tiny noise I honestly think was the sound of her trying to bite off her own tongue. Too late.

Every single head turned to look at my mom. Awkward.

Then Davis turned to look at Darcy, and if she didn't hear the wings of the angel of death hovering above her head, she was the only one in the room. She was made of stern stuff, though, and kept speaking as if she hadn't just insulted the wife of the client.

"There really isn't any reason all the movies can't be agreed to in theory; the journey between approved project and final movie is a long and tricky one. Anything could happen." She'd recovered, and would maybe survive the day.

Davis Reed nodded, and sipped his coffee. Apparently, it was subpar, because he made a face I thought only I noticed, but twenty seconds later, Jordan appeared at his elbow with a fresh cup of coffee, a new napkin and ice water. I don't think Davis even noticed, so smooth and flawless was the delivery and exchange. The offending cup of coffee was removed, presumably to be cast into outer darkness where its remaining dregs would eventually evaporate, leaving the failed cup empty and alone.

Darcy wasn't finished. "While my team has been fielding offers for movies and TV shows, the merchandising team has been busy too." She walked over to the side of the room and started flipping giant presentation boards. "Some are products who've already approached us for sponsorship; others are ideas we brainstormed internally."

- **Liddle Bugout Bags**—*When you're not sure how long you'll be gone.*
- **Liddle Backpacking Equipment**—*Survive and thrive in the wilderness.*
- **Liddle's Getaways**—*Remote cabins in Alaska.*

My mom raised her eyebrows. "Aren't some of these in pretty poor taste?" She turned to Davis. "What, no airline? No *Liddle's Travel—Surprising destinations since 1997?*"

Darcy looked uncomfortable.

I chimed in, "Or *Liddle's Family Therapy—Absence makes the heart grow fonder?*"

Lennie added, "Or an ad for Twinkies where he comes home and the ones in the cupboard are still good?"

We laughed, and Mom said, "Why would I have kept the Twinkies?"

"Sentimental reasons?" I asked.

"Maybe he'd opened the box just before he left," suggested Lennie. "It could have been like a shrine."

"A kitchen cupboard shrine?"

"It could totally take off on Pinterest."

There was a pause, and we realized everyone else in the room was a little bit horrified. This is why we don't get together in public very often. We can't be trusted.

After a moment for us all to wipe our memories, Darcy picked up the ball again. "Of course," she said, "there are also the Liddle's Liddles." She flipped another board to reveal a beauty shot of the stuffies in a happy child's arms—*Make coming home even sweeter.*

"Good Lord," I said. "You're all over this, aren't you?"

"It *is* our job," murmured Darcy. "The Liddles aren't actually under our control; that was just an idea we had for a tie-in to the current situation. I'm sure their people are already on it." She smiled. "Donco has managed to maintain market share despite stiff competition from larger companies." She turned to look down the table. "In fact, Chelsea has something . . ."

Chelsea looked as though she were on a school outing, some kind of "take your daughter to work day," because if she was over fifteen, I was a narwhal. Teenager or not, Chelsea had the confidence of . . . well, actually, a fifteen-year-old girl.

"Hi there, Mr. Liddle," she said, grinning at Jasper. "I cover animation rights, and Cartoon Network has approached us about doing a Liddle's Liddles animated show." She looked excited. "The *My Little Pony* team is interested."

Jasper looked at her and raised his eyebrows. "*My Little Pony* is still around?"

I gasped, Chelsea gasped, it's possible we all did. Chelsea said, "Mr. Liddle, *My Little Pony* and its associated products have generated billions of dollars in sales, four generations of successful animated shows, and toys that are both loved to death and preserved in museum collections. The brand celebrates the gentle arts of female friendship and cooperation and has weathered years of sexist criticism not equally applied to He-Man or any of the Marvel canon franchises." She huffed a little. "My girlfriend and I went to Comic-Con as Pinkie Pie and her sister Maud last year. *My Little Pony* is fire."

Jasper opened his eyes very wide and nodded. "Sorry, I didn't realize." He coughed. "I've been away."

Chelsea looked at him suspiciously. Her expression suggested that unless he'd been in a closet in a basement on the planet Krypton, there really wasn't any excuse for not appreciating *My Little Pony*. "Alright, well, I'm also running your social."

I could tell Jasper wasn't entirely sure what she meant by that, because for a moment his eyes met mine and I could see *My social what?* forming in his head. Then, still smarting over the shellacking he'd just received, he nodded and murmured his thanks.

Apparently, that was the end of the presentation, because the screens started sliding back into their housings, making the kind of non-sound only lots of money makes.

"Just think about it," replied Davis Reed, looking at Jasper. "This is an unprecedented opportunity, and the Foundation could benefit enormously." He coughed, and turned in my direction. "And I assure you, the head of zoology was quite excited about the publicity you could bring to his department, and the university in general."

I did that thing where you nearly choke on air, but I think I managed to cover it. "You talked to my boss?"

Jordan appeared at my elbow with ice water. Dammit.

"Of course," purred Davis smoothly, having kicked something valuable off the mantelpiece. "We like to consult all interested parties."

"Well," replied my mom, "we're somewhat interested, but I'm not convinced it's time to party." She stood up and pushed her chair in. My sisters and I got up, and Jasper pushed his chair back. Apparently, we were leaving. "Jasper is, of course, free to do whatever he wishes. Christa will do the late-night show with her father, assuming she continues to want to. Anything more than that is up to her."

There was a scramble as everyone tried to get up quickly but not before Davis, so that was fun to watch. Despite the fact that the meeting presumably hadn't gone as well as they'd expected, the agency people were all smiles. We made our way to the elevator, and once we got there, my mom turned and faced everyone.

"I know you're just doing your job," she said, mostly to Davis.

Davis made a head movement that looked like acquiescence at first but never actually made it into a nod.[3]

"Christa has a chance to do something important here."

"She already does something important, Mr. Davis," replied

---

3. Seriously, this guy's mastery of subtle body language would make an ethologist cream her pants.

my mother. "She pursues her passion. Nothing is more important than that."

Feeling a bit like a child who requires the understanding support of grown-ups, I reached out and pressed the button. See? Entirely capable of self-directed button pressing.

"You just pressed the up button," murmured Amelia. "We're going down."

She was right, but a car in the opposite bank of elevators opened, and I followed the others inside. Jasper was just joining us when Mom literally put her hand up. "It's fine, Jasper, we've got it from here."

"But I was going to come with you." He looked suddenly forlorn. "I got up when you did. I thought we were going together."

Mom sighed, and turned to look at me. Amelia and Lenny looked at me. I refused to meet anyone's eye, but I'm pretty certain the agency people were all looking at me. And they didn't even know how mad I'd been the night before.

I looked at my dad.

"Oh, come on, then," I said. "Get in."

20

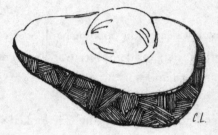

AVOCADO
PERSEA AMERICANA

Remaining in Beverly Hills . . .

Davis led the way back to the boardroom, or rather he stalked and the rest of the team followed, shedding assistants and juniors as they went. By the time Davis looked around the table at the team, there were only four of them: Rebecca, Darcy, Jordan and him. And Jordan was only there to take notes and keep his head down.

"Rebecca," started Davis, "reach out to Alex Dutton directly, not through the *Times*. Just feel around and find out why Denny hates him and Christa doesn't. Take calls from publishers, Big Five only. Call the New York office and get someone on the ground. Fly out yourself as soon as there's anything to discuss."

Rebecca frowned. "He just said he didn't want to do a book."

Davis shook his head. "Wrong. He basically said he didn't know. It is our job to know, and we know he should do a book."

"What if he chooses not to?" asked Rebecca. "I don't want to waste chips on him if he's a bad bet."

"He's not," said Davis in a dangerously mild tone. "I was there when it all got big for him. He loved it; I don't care what he says. It won't take him long to remember how good being adored feels." He looked around. "The mistress bewitched him. Now we have him back." He turned to Jordan. "I want everything you can get on Butterfly Baby. She always had lots more charisma than the others, despite how hard she's trying to hide it now. Why did she change her name? She was forever in the news for a while. Why is she called Christabel anyway, for crying out loud?"

"She's named after Christabel Pankhurst, a suffragette. All of them are named after badass women." Jordan looked quickly at his tablet, double-checking his sources. "BuzzFeed says so. It also says she's a Scorpio with Aquarius rising, which tracks." Silence fell, and he looked up to see Davis regarding him icily. "Sorry."

"Darcy, keep fielding offers. I want producer credit, script approval, and casting input." Darcy snorted, and Davis added, "Nothing less, Darcy. You have no idea how big this is going to get. Nail down the late-night show this week, and let's start brainstorming other shows and specials." He looked around. "Wait, where's Chelsea?"

On cue, the door flew open and Chelsea walked in. She was carrying a burrito the size of a fire log and singing along to something on her earbuds.

"Sorry, sorry, had to get food. I was getting all hypo." She threw the burrito on the table and sat. "Guac and chips, anyone?" She skidded a paper bag across the table and it fell over, scattering a few rattling triangles on the mahogany. "You get to my part yet?"

Davis watched her unwrap one end of her burrito, add enough hot sauce to make a whale cough, and take a bite. Jordan, Darcy and Rebecca waited nervously, as you could never be sure which way Davis was going to blow.

"Thank you so much for joining us, Chelsea."

"Oh, no worries."

"There was nothing in the buffet that appealed to you?" Davis's tone was soothing, concerned. Jordan's toes started to curl in his shoes. He was too young to witness a murder, and his next therapy session wasn't for another five days.

Chelsea tipped her head. "You mean instead of a burrito? Oh no, I like to watch my food being made, right? Who knows what's in those sandwiches." She held up the burrito. "This is one hundred percent organic, vegan and biodynamic and was assembled by a guy named Dario. I watched him do it."

"Fascinating," said Davis. "We were just about to discuss social media."

"Great," said Chelsea, chewing. "It's going to be massive. I'm already posting a lot, you know." She looked around and grinned. "Get this, we already had the accounts—I went back ages ago and took care of it for all the clients." She shrugged. "The old ones, of course. The new ones have it covered, obvi."

Davis was intrigued. "When and why did you do that?"

"I was bored one afternoon, so I got the complete list of clients and made sure everyone had TikTok, Twitter, Insta, a website that wasn't shit, you know, basic entry-level noise. Most did, some didn't, so I made accounts and parked them." She grinned. "Obviously, I get pinged when one of those ancient clients hits the news, and I make sure I tweet or whatever. When Jasper's name popped last week, I updated his website for him in an hour. Nothing fancy. Sign up for news, send your best wishes, yada yada." She dropped a clump of black beans onto the table and scooped it up and ate it. "Five-second rule, yeah?" She wiped the bean-smear away with her sleeve and laughed. "We already have three million followers and he hasn't done anything yet. Why do you think there was a crowd today? I tweeted last night, asked fans to tag pics, offered signed photos and merch for the best sign and/or cosplay, and while I was waiting for Dario to build this puppy, I posted arrival pics from an hour ago and teased the network interview." She looked around. "Who does merch, btw? I need half a dozen T-shirts by Friday."

Game recognizes game. The agency had over two thousand clients, and if even a tenth of them didn't have a complete suite of online presences, that was a lot of work. Davis picked up a pencil and made a note on his notepad. It was a little habit he had, when somebody did something he approved of. Rebecca and Darcy knew this, and kicked themselves. Chelsea had no idea, being only two months into the job, and not interested in what the old people did at work. She knew Davis was the boss, but for how much longer? The guy had to be sixty.

"Satisfactory. Carry on. Monitor anyone related too and try and keep physical tabs on the client, if possible. We gave him an agency phone. I'll text you the number so you can track him."

Chelsea was halfway through her burrito and started to rewrap it. "Anyone want the rest of this?" Strangely, no one did. "OK, boss dude, I got it."

There was a collective freeze around the room as the other employees waited to see how Davis was going to react to being called *boss dude*. Surprisingly, Davis simply nodded curtly, got up and left. This was also a habit of his, leaving the room as if he'd suddenly remembered he'd left the oven on. It was weird, but someone must have told him it was memorable, and he'd committed to it. As usual, the people left in the room kind of awkwardly got to their feet and dispersed. Except for Chelsea, who put her boots up on the conference table and pulled out her phone.

No rest for the wicked.

21

COLOMBIAN WHITE-FACED CAPUCHIN MONKEY
CEBUS CAPUCINUS

When the elevator doors opened in the lobby, we all had the same sudden realization. There was a crowd outside and we hadn't even called a Lyft.

"Go back up and ask that nice young man if he can get us a car." My mom watched the doors close nearly all the way and then jabbed the *open doors* button.

"Jordan," said Jasper. "He's Davis's assistant." But when he tried to press the button for that floor again, it wouldn't let him. "There must be a key card thing," he said.

The doors closed again, and again my mom waited until the last minute to poke the button. So incredibly annoying.

A security guard stepped into frame, so to speak. "Please stop doing that, and exit the elevator," he said. See? Not only me.

"We need to go back up," said Jasper.

"No," said the security guard firmly. "You need to get out of the elevator . . ." The doors began closing again, but we were all too scared to press the button. ". . . and call your building contact so they can escort you back upstairs." As he finished his sentence, perfectly timed, the doors reached where he was standing, and he literally raised a fist and extended it between them, exactly where they met, bouncing the doors open once again with the least possible effort. It was clear this man had prevented these doors from closing more times than we could ever comprehend, and that in his quest to empty his elevator bays quickly and efficiently, he was going to be dogged.

"Out," he said, and we all trooped out.

Chagrined, I suggested we just walk outside and see what happened. "Maybe Dad has to sign a few autographs. How bad can it be?"

"Great," said Mom, twirling around looking for somewhere to sit. "You two go out and do that, and the rest of us will call Jordan and wait here."

"I don't want to do it," I said.

"They want to see you too," said Lennie easily. "He's not the only famous Liddle."

"Focus groups don't lie," said Amelia. "You have the best name recognition."

I stared at them coldly, but they didn't care.

"Besides," said my mom, "you need to practice being friendly to your public."

The three of them headed to the front desk, and Jasper turned to me and smiled. "Shall we?" he said.

Somehow, there were still people outside with signs, though very few photographers. Jasper walked over to where the people were waiting, much to their excitement. I trickled along after him uncomfortably.

"Hey there," he said to the first lady, who promptly burst into tears.

"I'm so glad you're back," she said, holding out a shaking autograph book. "We love your shows. I watched them with all my children." She wiped her eyes with the back of her hand. She wasn't weeping so much as expressing happiness in liquid form. Tears as a by-product of the limbic system doing its job, bless its little hypothalamus.

"Thank you," he said, smiling at her, and posing for a picture. "I hope you'll watch our new one. This is my daughter, you know." He turned and pulled me closer, throwing his arm casually around my shoulder. "We're doing a show together."

We were? I was about to call him out when I realized there were people filming. I'd save it for later.

"Oh, you should!" said the lady, beaming. "We know Christa! We've watched you grow up, honey, while your dad was away."

I smiled at her; it was hard not to. She was filled with so much enthusiasm and was being so obviously kind about my "growing up."

Jasper moved along the line of people—there were maybe a couple dozen, not a huge crowd, but people who cared enough to leave the safety of their dens in the hopes of meeting him. He took pictures, he signed posters, he signed books, he listened to stories. As

I followed him, people naturally started talking to me once Jasper had moved on. It was very strange. I tried to emulate the way he so easily established a rapport with fans. I observed what he did and tried to do the same, but it was something that came easily to him and not at all to me. Here's an example:

SIGN-HOLDING FAN: You know, your episode with spider monkeys changed my life. I became an animal keeper at the zoo.

(Note: This is a completely fictional conversation, I'm just illustrating a point.)

JASPER: That's incredible! Have you been able to work much with primates?

FAN: Why yes, I've been able to successfully implement a breeding program among our capuchins.

JASPER: Incredible! I'm excited about that. They're such bitey little bastards, aren't they? And they smell like someone tucked a piece of bacon under a log and left it there.

FAN: Oh my goodness! I've been struggling for years to describe the smell, and that captures it perfectly. Thanks so much.

JASPER: Of course!

Same conversation with me:

FAN: Your dad changed my life. That episode with the spider monkeys made me want to be a zookeeper.

ME: Great. Good luck with that.

I'm just not good at small talk, probably because I generally don't find the human animal anywhere near as interesting as any of the others. I'd rather observe a caterpillar in a state of torpor than talk to someone about cars, for example. I once sat very still for forty-five minutes while a leaf bug sat on my arm munching a twig that could have been its aunt Alice. It was infinitely more interesting than any conversation I've ever had about TV shows. Or team sports. Or politics. Or even sex, because it was a very singular leaf bug.

A few more moments passed before a long, dark car swooped into the driveway, and we heard Mom calling us over. Jasper looked at the line of happy fans, and raised his voice.

"I can't tell you how much it means to see you, and to know the show carried on all this time." He looked genuinely moved. "And you've all supported the Foundation . . . it means a lot to me." Not a dry eye on the line, and even I felt the back of my throat start to prickle. Either I'm getting soft or the Jasper Liddle Reality Distortion Field is an actual thing.

We all got in the back of the car, which was even fancier than the one that had brought us. Jasper and I sat facing the others, and I couldn't help feeling we'd somehow been placed on the same team.

"Tell me, Jasper," said Mom, somewhat acerbically, "did you have a plan when you walked out of the forest?" She'd done her hair that morning in a low ballerina bun, and she was giving off a headmistress-in-a-Disney-movie vibe. She always did her hair, in buns or chignons or braids or some other fancy shapes I don't know the names of. I wanted to have the kind of hair that did that kind of thing, if you know what I mean, but it was never to be. Hardly the tragedy of my life, although there were evenings in eighth grade where it felt like it. God, eighth grade really had been subpar in every way. I looked at Jasper and tried to stay in the present. Approximately.

He closed his eyes and laid his head back for a minute. "Kind of. My plan was to come back to Los Angeles and see what happened."

I looked at him. "*See what happens* isn't really a plan."

"Why not?" He shrugged. "I didn't know how people were going to react." He started shrugging his jacket off. "I could have been turned away at the gate. It's been a long time." He looked out the window, still seeing the occasional fan walking away. "It's quite touching, really. I didn't expect people would care."

Mom's phone rang. "Hey," she said, "we're on our way home now." She listened for a moment, then said, "Good plan." She hung up, and said, "Nathan and Leo are at the house, and the press is still camping out. We definitely don't want them to see you going in. We'll never scrape them off the sidewalk." She paused. "That sounded harsh. I do appreciate they're simply doing their job."

Lennie frowned at her. "Mom, you don't have to be so nice all the time. It's super irritating to those of us who are less evolved."

Amelia nodded. "Generally, I appreciate your niceness, but occasionally it's pathological."

Jasper laughed. "This is clearly a new thing. No one would ever have accused you of being nice when I knew you."

All three of us kids turned to look at him, and the temperature in the car dropped about twenty degrees.

I said evenly, "Actually, she's been extremely nice my whole life. So that sounds like a you problem."

Mom laughed. "It's the truth. I didn't use to have much time for people; I just wanted to get the show done. If I'm nicer now, it's largely because I have more time." She looked at my dad. "I'm still really unclear about a lot of things, Jasper, and I have questions. However, we're nearly home, and you need to lie on the car floor so we can hide you under our feet. I, for one, am going to really lean into it. Fair warning."

"Ah," said Jasper, "there's the Denny I knew."

IN THE NEWS . . .

VARIETY.COM: Jasper Liddle meeting with movie studios and news outlets to sell story. Publishers reportedly bidding north of the current record $20 million book advance as media scrambles to capture rights.

NATGEO: As Jasper Liddle remains silent about details of his time in the wild, experts debate possible locations of his hideout.

COSMO.COM: Could you leave it all behind for love?

PLAYBOY.COM: Sex in the wilderness! Our favorite twins work on their wood crafts!

OUTSIDE.COM: How to survive a twin-engine plane crash!

MOTHERJONES.COM: Man abandons family and gets praised for it—again!

PROBATE AND PROPERTY NEWS: Holy resurrection, Batman! Liddle v. Liddle promises to be a nail-biter!

22

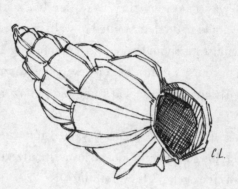

WENTLETRAP
EPITONIUM SCALARE

When we walked into the house, the first face I saw was Nathan's. I'd known he was there, I was ready, but he looked up at me as I came through the door, and our eyes met immediately, and held. The corners of his mouth turned up, the corners of my mouth turned up, and I felt a sensation in my body I can only describe as a swoon. I mean, genuinely, like a wave of lust cresting and breaking against the inside of my skin, hijacking my central nervous system with the ruthless efficiency of a neurotoxin. It was as though his body and my body had come to some kind of prior arrangement, and every time we were in the same room, they got super excited to put their plan into action, while our brains were still playing catch-up. Bearing in mind everything else that was happening at the time, it seemed like pretty poor planning on their part.

Mom walked over to Leo and bent her head to press the crown of it against his chest. He grinned and enfolded her in his arms; clearly, this was a position they were familiar with. My heart frowned; I wanted to do that, wanted to walk over to Nate and lay my cheek against his shoulder and pretend nothing else was happening. But of course I didn't, because everyone was watching and it would have been weird. But you know and I know, and we'll just leave it there.

He was still looking at me as I walked into the kitchen; he hadn't broken his gaze once. I looked away, finally, and he spoke.

"How was the agency? Is everything OK?"

I nodded and shrugged at the same time. "It was weird, but it's fine." I lowered my voice. "They really want me to go on TV, and I really don't want to."

He nodded. "You didn't like it last time."

I looked at him, grateful I didn't need to explain myself. He knew me. He'd been there. I shrugged again, and he reached out and touched my arm, resting his palm against my skin.

"You don't have to do anything you don't want to." He smiled, his voice low. "Want to go walk on the beach?"

I looked at him, feeling as though we were the only people in the room. My arm was tingling, and suddenly it was all too much. I was aching for him, a relative stranger, and it scared the crap out of me. I do so much better on my own. If you stand completely alone, no one gets close enough to knock you off your feet.

"I'm good, thanks," I said briskly. "I'll let you know if I need your help." Then I turned and walked away, down the hall and into my room. I closed the door and leaned against it, resting my head against the wood as I'd wanted to rest it on his shoulder. Tears were fighting to fall, but I wasn't having it.

Nothing to see here. Move the fuck along.

When I came out an hour or two later, Leo had left and Nate and Jasper were playing chess. Apparently, Jasper had originally taught Nate the game, and was gently ribbing him about not having improved all that much.

"What else have you let slide?" he asked. "Do you still sail?"

Nate nodded, and moved his piece. "When I can."

I couldn't help it; I kept watching him, the tilt of his head as he considered his next move, the little look up at my dad after he'd moved, the way his hand hovered above the board and his thumb and first two fingers pinched and wiggled as he tried to choose. My eyes wanted to rest on his face, and they were fighting every effort I made to look elsewhere.

"Do you still have your dad's boat?" Jasper smiled. "He loved that thing almost as much as he loved his car."

Nate shook his head. "Mom made him sell it in the divorce." He colored suddenly, and concentrated on the board.

"You sail, right, Christa?" Jasper looked at me, then frowned. "Or am I confusing you with Lennie? Sorry, baby."

I was leaning on the kitchen counter, scrolling idly through an article about wentletraps but not really reading it, and looked up. "No, it's OK, I do sail. Not as much as I used to, but I do. I have a little skiff I use for work on the island, largely not under sail, but sometimes . . ." I looked over at Nathan. "Your dad taught me, but you and Amelia were already at college and Lennie was half out the door as well." I looked back at Jasper. "You presumably didn't do a lot of sailing in the backwoods of Alaska?" Crap, I'd forgotten my mom was in the room, I'd been so focused on Nate. I shot her a look. "Sorry, Mom . . ."

She looked up from the book she was reading. "Why?"

I hesitated, and she took pity on me. "Because you're worried I'll be upset if we talk about him deserting me and choosing another woman?" The room got quiet, then she laughed. "Don't be. It was a long, long time ago. I got over him and fell in love with someone else, remember? I've done extensive therapy and worked it through." She looked serenely around the room. "No offense, Jasper, but you're more like an old college roommate than an exhusband." She frowned. "Or late husband?" There was a pause, and then she started laughing. "I may lose my shit with you later on, but for now I'm happy to see you. Eighteen different shades of surprised, but happy."

He looked back at her and beamed. "I'm happy to see you too, baby."

I frowned and looked at my sisters. They looked back, also frowning. Slow your roll there, Mr. Liddle. Don't get any ideas. The three of us would be going back to our separate corners of the world soon, and we'd happily take pieces of Jasper's body with us if necessary.

Returning to the game, Jasper moved his chess piece. "Checkmate."

Nathan frowned, then laughed. "Wow, that really didn't take you very long." He looked over at me and shrugged. I let myself smile at him, but looked away before he could smile back. Engaging with him felt . . . I don't know what exactly. Not dangerous, but something that shouldn't be done lightly. I had to resist whatever was going on between us, because there was zero way it could end in anything other than tears.

"I played a lot of chess in the intervening period," said Jasper. "Don't get mad at yourself."

"You played chess with Lorna?" I asked. Lennie made a noise, but I looked at her and shrugged. "Mom just said it was OK to talk about it."

Jasper waited until Lennie shrugged too, then answered. "Yes, I played with Lorna. She beat me a lot."

"What was she like?"

Jasper sighed, and pulled out his wallet. He Frisbee'd over an Alaska driver's license, and I very nearly caught it. Once I'd dexterously deployed some toast tongs and scrabbled it out from under the oven, I took a look.

"Lorna Wesson," I read. A sweet-faced woman, pale blue eyes in a face that spent most of its time outdoors. She looked like she should be running a bake sale, not inspiring perfidy.

"It's hard to talk about her." His face was tired suddenly. "I miss her all the time." He looked at my mom. "I'm sorry."

"Don't be sorry," Mom replied. She threw up her hands in a very characteristic gesture, her fingers spread. "Like I said, this situation is weird as hell, and I'm not entirely sure how I feel about it. But right this minute I'm OK, and definitely not in the mood for drama. Let's just forgive each other our past transgressions and start over like people who just met on a cruise." She held out her hand for the license, and I walked over and gave it to her. She looked at me and smiled, and I understood she was letting me know I hadn't hurt her with my question.

Jasper smiled briefly, and nodded. "I really did think you would be fine, Denny. You were always so independent, and . . . you know"—he looked down at the floor—"things weren't going all that well for us."

"You were right," said Mom. "We *were* fine. After a while." For a moment, we all saw irritation on her face again, but she made that gesture a second time. Just one hand, though. "Keep talking."

Jasper nodded. "I'm not really sure how to explain it. In the beginning, it was magical, which sounds ridiculous, but there isn't another way to describe it. It felt like another planet. I felt incredibly free."

"Plus," I added, "you did have that traumatic brain injury."

Jasper looked at me and grinned. "Funny. I do think I had a concussion. It's the most likely explanation for the memory loss." His face changed. "It's strange, having a memory of remembering. I'll never forget it. I was sitting at the kitchen table. I was peeling potatoes." He looked at his hands. "They were rough and I was getting soil all over my hands. I didn't care, and I was looking at my own dirty palm, just like I am now, and suddenly, I remembered everything."

He glanced up and around the room with tears in his eyes, his skin pale. No one had ever said Jasper Liddle was an actor. He didn't seem to be acting now, and for the first time I felt a twinge of sympathy for him.

"I started crying, and panicking." He shook his head in recollection. "It wasn't pretty. Lorna came running and we sat there and talked it out for hours." The corner of his mouth turned up. "It took most of that time to convince her I wasn't delirious. It sounds crazy, right? *Oh, my bad, I totally forgot, I'm a mildly famous naturalist with my own TV show, plus I'm married with three kids, sorry about that*." He shrugged. "It had been nearly three months. We'd . . ." He blushed and shrugged again. "I decided to stay."

"Wow," I said. "Can I ask the very obvious question?" Amelia handed me the license to give back to Jasper, and I took another long look at Lorna's very ordinary face. Ordinary, but with a strength that came through in that most unflattering of media, the DMV photo. I handed it back. "Why didn't you just let Mom know you were alive? She wouldn't have come after you. She wouldn't have told anyone." I looked at Mom. "Probably."

She shook her head. "No clue. The woman I am now barely remembers the woman I was then. From what I do remember, she was pretty uptight." She looked at Jasper. "Right?"

He smiled gently. "She was awesome, but yes, pretty driven. Davis said everyone would ask the same thing. I don't have a good answer. The longer I stayed with Lorna, the more my life here seemed like a dream someone else had told me about. I knew you would be fine. I knew Davis would take care of the money."

"How did you know that?" I asked. "He could have run off with the lot."

Jasper laughed. "Why run off with it when it kept on coming?"

Lennie finally started to get interested. "How did you know it would keep coming?"

"Because I knew you also had John Donovan. The toys were doing well. There was no reason to suppose your mother would run out and spend it all on cocaine and hookers."

We all laughed and looked at Mom, who shrugged. "Like he said, pretty driven."

Jasper looked around. "I don't want you to think it was an easy choice to make. But I was so overwhelmed with everything, with the show, with the pressure. At the time, it seemed impossible to go back to it, after the months I'd been with her. I couldn't face it." His face brightened. "Also, the natural world there was incredible. I was able to spend hours alone in the forest, observing and enjoying. No worrying about the light. No fretting over camera angles and hair."

Lennie had another question. "And you never thought of coming back?"

Jasper shook his head. "Not until Lorna got cancer, a few years ago. Then I wanted to come back, get the best treatment. She said no. She didn't want to fill herself with chemicals, and she didn't want to die in the public eye, or in a hospital. It was brutal. We fought about it over and over. Eventually, she got very weak and I thought the effort of standing up for herself was going to cut what little time she had left even shorter. I accepted her decision." The tears were back. He got up and shook himself. "And then she died." He walked into the kitchen, and we all watched him pour himself a glass of water.

I looked at my mom, who was looking at Jasper with a gentle expression. I realized they'd both lost their partners to cancer, at around the same time, and wondered if that's what she was thinking about. Or maybe she was just wondering what to have for dinner.

Suddenly, Lennie broke the silence. "Oh, wow," she said, looking at her phone.

"What?" Mom asked. "What on earth has happened now?"

"Nothing, really," said Lennie, giving me an unreadable glance. "Just pictures from the agency this morning." She looked over at Jasper, who was standing in the kitchen drinking his water. "Did you post these?"

"What's posting?"

Lennie shrugged. "Well, someone's posting for him, because there are several fan selfies from this morning."

Mom had pulled out her phone. "Oh . . . I found it. You look very nice in this one, Lennie." Then she gave me the same look Lennie had, and I got a weird feeling.

I pulled out my phone. I searched Jasper's name. I looked up; all of us had our phones out, which meant that when I saw the first picture of myself, I was three seconds behind Nathan, and he looked up and our eyes met.

His mouth twitched. My mouth twitched. We burst out laughing.

I swiped on the photos, and kept laughing. "I look like a bad-tempered forest elf," I said. "Why do I look so grumpy? Why are my shorts so deeply unflattering?" I looked at Nathan, who had stopped laughing. "They're very comfortable."

"Which is all that matters," he said pleasantly. "Honestly, they're just bad pictures, Christa."

Amelia nodded. "You don't look like this in person."

"Well," said Mom, "I mean . . ."

I looked around. "Guys, you're more upset about this than I am. I've never taken a good photo in my life." I turned to Nathan, who seemed to be the only one who got it. "You missed a classic terrible ID photo of me in the meeting today." I looked at the photos again and shook my head. "I don't know, Mom, you might be right. Maybe I should come up with a better LA uniform."

"We can go shopping tomorrow," she said.

I frowned. "I really hate shopping. Can we do it online?"

She shook her head. "No, you need to try things on. We can go in the morning. We can hit Nordstrom and then Rodeo Drive and then the mall . . ."

I started to shake my head. "I would rather be covered in jam and rolled in fire ants, Mom, you know that."

She frowned at me. "Well, you can't just . . ."

Nate spoke.

"I was actually hoping Christa might come out with me tomorrow."

Total silence in the room. Like, total. Then everyone's head swiveled to me.

"Um . . ." I said wittily.

"I have a tide pool beach I'd like to get your professional opinion on."

"Tide pools?" I said faintly. I fucking love tide pools.

He nodded. "There will be whelks. And anemones. And . . ." He paused, clearly struggling to remember. "Sea hares."

I raised my eyebrows at him.

"I googled," he said, smiling.

"Well, in that case," said Mom, "I'll just pick up some options for you in the morning and you can see what you like here. I'll return what you don't."

"Uh, OK then," I said, once again reaching heights of eloquence.

Jasper stood up and stretched. "I'm tired," he said. "I'm going to head out. Davis has me stashed near the agency. I'll call a cab."

"I'll take you back," said Nate. He went into the kitchen to grab his keys. "I'll see you in the morning, Christa." His cheeks were flushed, and when our eyes met, I realized asking me out had taken some balls, right there in front of every member of my family. Especially if you throw in one who was only recently resurrected. My earlier reticence melted under the warmth of his courage.

I smiled at him, and meant it. I smiled and hoped he could tell I was pleased, that I was with him in his desire to look at tide pools.

As we looked at each other, something changed, something subtle. Some kind of acceptance. Some kind of promise.

All of a sudden, Nate and Jasper were gone, and after a moment, I stopped looking at the door and turned back. Only to discover both my sisters, my mom and the dog all staring at me with an expression of knowing amusement.

"Oh, fuck off," I said, but they just laughed.

IN THE NEWS . . .

WWD.COM: The Liddle Effect: Safari shirts and khaki shorts fly off the shelves.

REI.COM: Classic nineties flannel workshirt, inspired by Jasper Liddle.

NATIONALENQUIRER.COM: Jasper Liddle uses alien tech to un-extinct the dodo!

ABC.COM: The original *Liddle's Great Big World* seasons 1 & 2 will be airing this weekend. Join us for a nature marathon in honor of Jasper Liddle's safe return. Starting at 10 a.m. EST.

23

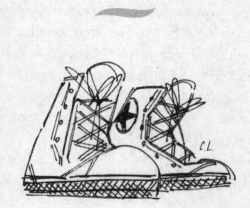

CHUCK TAYLOR HIGH-TOPS
CALCEAMENTA HIGHTOPUS

When I stumbled out of bed the next morning, Nathan was already there, eating toast and eggs at the kitchen counter. I'm sorry to continue being so shallow, but he was wearing yet another old T-shirt and jeans, with a pair of red Converse on his feet, and he looked gorgeous. I love a slightly scruffy guy, and when he turned and saw me walking out, his eyes—I'm not even slightly joking—got all twinkly. Honestly, I was barely awake, but there was something about the way our eyes met, an immediate flush of heat, a subconscious *holy crap* of arousal. It was on his face as much as I'm sure it was on mine, and he wasn't hiding it any more than I was. I swear to you my underpants got tight. An English friend of mine calls it a lady boner, and while it isn't poetic, it does capture the enlarging quality of sudden wholesale blood diversion. I'm looking at it purely from a scientific perspective, because I am really struggling to put words around this giddy, rapturous thing my body does every time I see him.

Christa, pull your shit together. I got myself a cup of coffee and huddled on a stool nearby. "Are you one of those horrible chipper-first-thing-in-the-morning people?" I asked, clutching my mug and resting my forehead on the counter. If I didn't look at him, it was much easier. Maybe I was developing a migraine and horniness was somehow related. Like visual disturbances or auditory hallucinations.

"I'm afraid so," he said. "But, to be fair, Christa, it is eleven a.m."

I looked up at the clock. "Crap. Sorry, didn't we say ten?"

He laughed. "We did, but it's fine. By the way, your mom hit the stores as soon as they opened." He tipped his head, and I turned to see maybe half a dozen bags from a variety of clothing stores on the sofa. "Then she and your dad went off to do something. Amelia's at Mrs. Lobster's, and Lennie went for a run. It's been me and Marcel, waiting patiently." We both looked down at Marcel, who was curled around the foot of Nate's stool, fast asleep.

"He does look unworried," I said.

"I'm trying to model myself after him. What would Marcel do? It's a question I ask myself once or twice a day." Nate gingerly extended his leg over Marcel onto the floor.

"And are we really going to visit some tide pools?"

Nathan nodded. "Well, we're going to the beach, and there are tide pools, but you don't have to look at them if you don't want to." He checked his watch, and I got a sudden memory of his dad's hand on the steering wheel of the Mercedes, the same watch glinting in the sun. I'd known this man my whole life. But I really didn't know him at all. He and I shared some of the same history, had been present for many of the same events, knew each other's lives . . . but who he was now was essentially a mystery.

I realized I had been staring. He had tilted his head very slightly to one side and smiled at me.

"Where did you go? You were here and then suddenly you weren't."

I laughed. "Not sure, sorry. I just kind of drifted off."

He nodded. "Very relatable. I do that all the time. I spend way too much time in my head." He pointed to the bags. "Go try on your clothes and see if there's something good for the beach."

I made a face. "Better than my fantastic shorts?" But I went and got the bags, and headed into my room to change.

I ended up walking out in jean shorts that somehow managed to be as comfortable as my quality shorts without making me look like a forest dweller, and a plain but incredibly soft white T-shirt. I'd also fallen in love with a navy blue cheesecloth shirt with bone buttons I never would have chosen for myself. I had been pleasantly surprised to see I looked much more like a regular human woman than a part-elf walking tree stump. When I'd opened the last box and saw bright yellow Chuck Taylors, I smiled. No Cinderella was ever happier with new shoes.

Thanks, Mom.

"Yay," said Nathan softly as he looked up and saw me. "That looks great. Does it feel good?"

The front door flew open and Lennie came in, sweaty from her run. "Those reporters are not very nice," she said, pausing at the door to toe off her running shoes. "They asked me if I had an exercise disorder. So rude." She looked up and saw me. "Oh my God,

Christa, you're wearing actual clothing." She looked at Nathan.
"Who knew you'd be a positive influence?"

He laughed. "All Denny's work." He turned to me. "Ready?"

"Where are you guys going?" asked Lennie, grabbing an apple
from the kitchen counter.

"I have no idea," I said. "It's a secret."

Lennie grinned and waved her apple. "Have fun, kids."

24

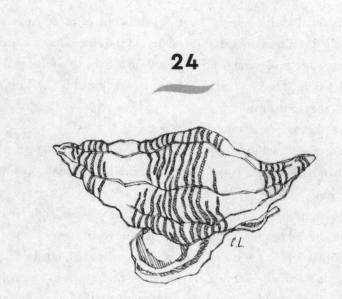

KELLET'S WHELK
KELLETIA KELLETII

The old Mercedes ate the miles with purring satisfaction as we headed north on the Pacific Coast Highway. Nate pulled over briefly in Santa Monica to pick up a large white bag he said contained lunch, with no further details offered. Any questions were met with an increasingly smug grin, and eventually I realized I was amusing him and frustrating myself, so I quit.

I looked out the window at the rocky coast that hugs the freeway. I can't count the number of times I've seen porpoises and dolphins just, you know, hanging out. California might be falling into the ocean, but it's doing it beautifully.

Nate said, "Lennie told me they wanted to do a TV special on the three of you? I wasn't clear if it was fact or fiction."

I nodded and laughed. "I think it was one of those ripped-from-the-headlines things. Mostly true, but improved. Lennie had to change her profession from conservation activist to politician."

"A job she'd be very bad at." Nate grinned. "But anyway, I hear it's you they're really after."

I turned to look at him. *They didn't.*

"You know, with your greater name recognition." Long pause, and then he shot me a look. "I bet you're tired of that one already, aren't you?"

I was smiling, but I nodded. "It's kind of an old idea, right, that I'm the one who wants to be famous? At any cost?"

"Is that how it feels?" He was watching the road, but I could tell he was actually listening. To be fair, if he'd taken his eyes off the Pacific Coast Highway, I would have demanded he pull over and let me drive.

I thought about it. "It feels confusing. When I was a kid, it was kind of fun and kind of not. It was definitely cool to play with all those animals, no question. But it's not cool to be the kid parents want to talk to in fourth grade. *Oh, I saw you on TV last night*, that kind of thing. They'd say, *You'll have to come over for a playdate*, but the kids never asked. I was shy as hell in elementary school." I laughed. "I don't think anyone ever physically bullied me over it, but there was a lot of sudden silence when I walked into rooms." I spotted a fin slicing up and down through a wave, and thought about dolphins for a moment or two. A little cetaceous self-soothing session. Try saying that three times fast. Nathan simply kept driving and didn't comment. Normally, I heard silence and felt judgment, but his silence felt more like patience.

After a moment, I got back on track. "Like, when new kids came, or visited the school. Teachers would often get me to show them around 'cause, you know, they thought I was good at being social. And every time it would go great and we'd hang out all day and get on. And I'd go home and tell Mom I made a friend, and I'd think about it all evening, and plan excellent conversation starters and interesting questions to ask them. But by recess the next day, the other kids would have told them I ate bugs or kissed bats or whatever, and then I was as weird to them as I was to everyone else." I shrugged. "It sounds a lot sadder telling it like that than it felt at the time." I laughed again, but fuck, my throat was suddenly getting tight. I knew how to do this. I turned away and stared at the ocean, starting to list the layers: epipelagic, mesopelagic, bathypelagic, abyssopelagic (my favorite to say) and hadalpelagic, or *here be sea serpents* territory. I started to feel better. I had this. I took a long, slow breath. Fourth grade was fine. No one likes fourth grade.

Nate didn't say anything for a moment. Then he took his right hand off the wheel and reached over to take my hand. He apparently echolocated it, which was my first thought, literally. One part of my brain was like, oh my God, he's holding my hand, and the other half was like, how did he know exactly where my hand was without looking?

He squeezed my hand and let it go. Then he looked at me (presumably to double-check he hadn't just reached over and palpated my boob) and said, "That sucks. We've still got a ways to go. Do you want to stop for coffee or something?" He smiled at me and I nodded. He pulled into the next gas station and parked, getting out of the car before the engine had even fully stopped.

I watched him lope across the forecourt, pausing to hold the door for someone coming out, and disappear inside. I realized I felt better. He wasn't going to ask me for more. When people know the circumstances of your life, they sometimes believe it entitles them to further clarification. Sometimes they poke until it hurts.

Not even a minute later, Nate was back in the car, handing me a frothy latte, a candy bar, a banana, and a bottle of water.

I laughed, peeling the banana and taking a huge bite. I realized I hadn't eaten anything. "Where's yours?"

"I'm saving myself for lunch." He looked at me and grinned and rubbed his hands together.

"Will you at least share the coffee?" I held out the cup and finished the banana.

He smiled. "I already drank some in the gas station."

"You sneaky bastard."

"I burned my mouth."

"Serves you right."

He looked at me for a second. "Feel better?"

I nodded at him and sipped my coffee. "Yes, thanks." I felt shy, but it was true. Blood sugar really does call the shots.

He smiled and turned around to reverse out of the spot. I looked at the shape of his head and shoulders as they were angled away from me. I suddenly imagined coming up behind him and putting my arms around his waist and resting my cheek against his broad back. Feeling protected, feeling safe.

Maybe I'm about to get my period.

We ended up driving much longer than I thought we would, and suddenly, Nate was slowing and looking for a turn, and then we were on an obviously private road.

I turned and looked at Nate. "Did we go wrong?"

He shook his head, and honestly, if he smiled any harder, he was going to snap a tendon. He was definitely tickled. The road was smoothly blacktopped and curved gently down a fairly steep set of switchbacks. I wound down the window and stuck my head out. We were very close to the ocean, and I couldn't hear any traffic at all.

We came to a gate. No number, no hardware, no name. A simple keypad on a stand.

I looked at Nate, who'd stopped smiling. I hadn't seen a lot of Serious Nate. He was generally kind of a smile-fest, and it turned out S. Nate was even sexier than regular Nate. He lowered his window and punched a code into the pad. Slowly, the gate began to swing open. I started looking at the trees instead. Coastal scrub oak. Black walnut. Lots of natives.

We rolled gently along, still in silence. As we came around a corner, the trees parted and the Pacific was in front of us. A small house sat on the lot, which continued to slope until it reached the beach. The Pacific Coast is a bumpy bugger, and this house was placed just perfectly between two bluffs, creating the illusion of total privacy.

The house itself seemed deserted, and Nate pulled up on an empty driveway.

"Nate," I said, lowering my voice for no reason at all. "Whose house is this?"

"A friend's," he replied, getting out of the car. He looked at his watch and said, "We arrived at the perfect time." He opened the back of the car and pulled out blankets and a cooler. "Can you grab the food? It's in the back seat."

I was still not quite getting it, but I grabbed the bag and followed Nate. I peered into the windows of the cottage as we passed.

"Nate?"

"Hmm?" He was a little way ahead of me.

"Is that an Academy Award?"

He didn't even look. "Possibly," he said. "Come on, we only have a couple of hours."

A bank of bamboo extending from the house prevented me from seeing the beach until we were almost on it, and when I did, I stopped immediately.

"You are kidding me."

The beach itself was quite narrow, maybe only a hundred feet of sand, with craggy rocks abutting higher, steeper bluffs. But because of the specific topography of the shoreline, at this point in high tide it was completely cut off from any other stretch of sand. I could see the tide pools, not a lot of them, but with a promising variety of depths. The beach was an inlet, sort of, but only temporarily, which might disqualify it from *being* an inlet, and in some senses it was a pocket beach, but only tidally, and as a constrained sedimentary system . . . It doesn't matter. The point is, the beach was small, pretty and completely empty. Next time, I'll bring an expert in beach morphology and we can really nail it down.

I looked at Nate. "This is incredible."

He smiled. "As the tide goes out, it obviously reconnects with the rest of the beach, then anyone can walk along. My friend told me about it once, and I thought you might like it."

"Your friend?"

He nodded at the house. "You meet a variety of people in the toy business, genuinely. Everyone from collectors to regular parents whose kids love Liddles and just happen to have a very special beach cottage."

I raised my eyebrows. "I find that very difficult to believe."

He laughed. He spread out the blanket and sat down to start unpacking the lunch. "Well, how else do you explain it?" He looked up at me. "The gate code was a lucky guess?"

I joined him on the blanket and considered the question. "You're a highly accomplished hacker, and you cracked his fancy automated house system and stole his gate code and calendar?" I looked at the food he was laying out. The man knows how to provision, I'll give him that. Crusty French rolls, soft Brie, pickles, mushroom pâté, strawberries. Some other things in little tubs.

Nate opened the cooler and pulled out whipped cream for the strawberries, and what looked like a tall, slim bottle of wine. He held it out to me, grinning.

I raised my eyebrows. "It's a little early, don't you think?"

He handed me the bottle. "Absolutely, plus I thought you might want to drive on the way back. It's grape juice made from wine grapes. It's insanely delicious and toddler approved. I just wanted you to have an hour or two of quiet ocean time without worrying that anyone's taking your photo." He shrugged thoughtfully. "Plus, the chances of getting to talk to you alone with all three other Liddles in the house seemed remote."

He handed me a glass, and I held it as he poured. The grape juice smelled like peaches or sunshine or the first bite of watermelon every summer. It tasted incredible.

I looked at the label. "Well, you just ruined Welch's."

"Unintentional, I promise. Nothing wrong with Welch's."

"Sugar content?"

"I promise you this juice has sugar."

I shrugged. "Fair enough. I'll try to forgive Welch's for not being this."

"Yeah, just let Welch's be Welch's. Not a contest."

We sat there for a few moments, just gazing out to sea. While it was beautiful, it was nothing like Violetta. This was a different ocean, different bird sounds, yet I got the same feeling of reassuring smallness. I turned and looked at Nate. "Thank you for this. The ocean makes me feel better. Not that I was feeling terrible; it's just been a lot." I hugged my knees. "And it's a luxury to feel totally unobserved."

"You're welcome. I've never taken her up on her offer before."

I raised my eyebrows. "A *female* celebrity invited you to her beach cottage?"

He looked at me. His eyes were such a distinctive blue, like his dad's had been. I didn't remember his dad's changing as much as Nate's did, though. Sometimes his eyes were the color of denim; sometimes they reminded me of cornflowers, or the sky above the ocean at noon on Violetta. I wondered what other shades might appear.

"No," he said evenly. "A well-known and highly respected actress, as a gesture of gratitude for a soft toy–related problem I'd been able to solve for her, offered it whenever she wasn't in town. Just the beach, not the house. I've never told anyone, and until today, I never took her up on it."

"So she's not going to walk in on us?"

He shook his head and poured me some more grape juice. "She and her family are in the Kingdom of Tonga, don't ask me why."

"Why?"

He laughed and rested back on his elbows, looking out to sea. "And you're not completely unobserved." He turned his head and grinned at me. "I'm looking."

I grinned back. "You, I can ignore."

He kept looking at me, and just as I was starting to feel that slow but steady flushing of my cheeks, he suddenly leapt up. "Let's go look at the tide pools," he said. "I googled 'what lives in California tide pools,' but then I stopped. I have so much to learn."

I looked up at him and laughed. "You're suddenly seized with curiosity about rocky intertidal habitats?"

He nodded. "Yes, now that I know their fancy name, even more so. And how often will I have a captive marine biologist?" He hesitated, then said, "Not often enough, it turns out."

I got to my feet, swiping sand from my legs and ignoring the implication of his words. I followed him across the beach, admiring the backs of his calves, the tendons and sinews that moved under his skin as he walked on the sand. I'd like to say I was studying anatomy, and reflecting on the differential deployment of musculature on soft surfaces versus hard, but what I was actually thinking was that he had nice legs, and not a lot more than that. He was bringing out my hidden shallows.

There were really only two or three pools, one of which was much deeper than the others. We stood next to it, and Nate looked at me expectantly.

I laughed. "Let's take a look, shall we?" I leaned over to study it and literally hopped up and down. Just once—don't imagine anything crazy. "Holy crap, a Kellet's whelk." I pointed to a much larger shell than most of the others. "You don't see them intertidal very often. That's supercool." I glanced around. "There's an elegant aeolid, and over there . . . that's *Aeolidia papillosa*, so named because it's hairy." I grinned, amused by the Latin names of things, as usual.

He smiled suddenly, as I was coming to realize was his way. His face was handsome enough at rest, but then he smiled like the sun emerging from a cloud and transformed into . . . maybe the most attractive man I'd ever seen. Time to stop pretending, Christa. He was gorgeous. "It looks very soft." He shrugged. "Although I'm not sure why the other one was elegant and this one isn't."

I turned away, trying to cover what must have been visible on my face. "Its common name is shag-rug nudibranch, or sometimes shaggy mouse."

He reached into the water and pointed. "What's that strangely pretty thing?"

I leaned over next to him, our arms touching (not that I was paying attention), and looked. "That, sir, is the ever-helpful opalescent nudibranch, or *Hermissenda opalescens*." I smiled at it fondly. "Bless its aggressive but interesting little self." I straightened up and turned to Nate, who was startlingly close. In the reflection of the ocean, his eyes had taken on a green tinge, and I tried not to stare. "It's a very common model organism, you know, for lab experiments."

"People study these things in the lab as well as in the ocean?" Nate asked.

I nodded. "Sure. This species tells us a lot about neurology, toxicology . . . lots of things."

"Huh." Nate looked out at the ocean. "Tide will start coming in soon. Shall we eat while we can?"

I nodded. "Exhausted by nudibranches? We haven't even started on the mollusks." I leaned closer to the water. "My favorite thing about tide pools is that they're never the same pool twice, do you know what I mean? Every tide changes them, brings new things in, takes other things out. When systems are healthy and thriving, they constantly change, right?"

He was still so close. "Will you be very surprised if I told you I wasn't all that interested in the tide pools?"

I raised my eyebrows. "Not very."

His smile was still there, gently tugging at the corners of his mouth. "It seemed as good an excuse as any to get you alone and to give you something to talk about." He took a step back, casually putting a little space between us. "I love hearing you explain things. You're charmingly enthusiastic."

I half frowned. "Not sure what to do with that, but OK."

There was a moment, just a moment, as we looked at each other when I thought he was going to kiss me. Then I thought maybe I was going to kiss him. But in the end, neither of us did anything but smile, and then he turned and headed back up the beach.

We returned to the blanket and I sat down, still half thinking about that Kellet's whelk. They really aren't all that common in tide pools.

Nate remained standing, and suddenly he said, "Shit, wait," and headed up the beach again. He has a lot of energy. Not sure yet if it's too much, or just right. I shrugged off my shirt and felt the sun immediately baking my shoulders.

Nate was back. He had a long umbrella, and sunscreen. He dug the beach umbrella in and opened it up. Then he plomped back onto the beach blanket.

"Turn around," he said. "I'll do your shoulders before you burn to a crisp."

I gave him a look. "I only just took my shirt off. And I'm tanned as hell from being on the island."

"The sun is a deadly foe," he said. "Never underestimate her power." The sunscreen was cold, and I squeaked. "Sorry," he said, "I'll rub it in." He started smoothing it into my skin with long, even strokes. I'll be honest with you, it felt incredible, and I rested my head on my folded knees and closed my eyes. He scooched a little closer behind me, and held out one of my arms.

"Now this one," he said, as if evaluating a chicken in a grocery store, "is a fine arm, seems to go all the way to the hand, yup." He was spraying as he was talking, and rubbing it in. "Yes, the consistency is excellent, not too hard, not too soft, yes, it's a Goldilocks arm, folks, we've got ourselves a classic beauty . . ." Then he transferred to the other arm and kept up the ridiculous patter the whole time. I started to giggle, not to mention it tickled. It felt almost transgressive, relaxing this easily. *Relaxing* is the wrong word, because I could feel myself getting increasingly turned on every time he touched me. I took a deep breath and tried to pump the brakes a bit. I've felt intense arousal before, don't get me wrong, but this was . . . visceral. My body was moving toward his as unconsciously as a vine twines toward the sun, through a fascinating process known as phototropism.[1] I was doing my level best not to lean back against his hands, not to angle my neck perfectly for his hands to reach, not to moan out loud. I took another long, slow breath, tried to calm the tingles in my fingers, and sat up.

"Your turn," I said, turning around. I just needed to get moving, keep the blood from settling in distracting places.

"I'm fine," he said. "I did my arms and legs this morning. California native, baby."

"What am I, a Gibraltar campion?" I scoffed. "Take your shirt off."

He hesitated. "I have no idea what you just said, but I got that last bit." He tugged his shirt over his head, making his hair go all crazy for a moment. "Be gentle."

---

1. The process for vines is phototropic; the process for me and Nate was almost certainly pure animal lust. In case you needed clarification.

I scrambled around behind him. He handed the spray bottle over his shoulder and I let him have it.

"Wow," he said a second later. "I've never heard myself make that noise before."

I was now laughing openly at him, and began to rub in the spray. I'd been a little generous, I'll admit, going for impact rather than frugality. It took me a while, and I settled into a rhythm, smoothing it across his shoulders and then down his sides in shorter strokes. I pride myself on my sunscreen application; no streaky bacon burns on my watch.

Once I was finished with his lower back, I moved up to his neck and found he had adopted the same position I had, with his head on his knees. His head was turned, though, and he was smiling a little pussycat smile of happiness that I couldn't help echoing. I remember watching him when I was a little kid, envying all of those older kids their freedom and confidence. The difference between nine and seventeen is a chasm that's hard to bridge. I couldn't quite believe either of us had turned into the people we had, or that we were here right now, but I've been accused of overthinking.

His back was gorgeous, did I mention that? I didn't lead with it, because I'm not objectifying him. But purely as reportage, ten out of ten for strong without being showy, broad at the top and narrow at the bottom, and doing a sterling job of supporting his lovely head. The way the back of his neck met his shoulders made me giddy. I wanted to be closer. I wanted to count the myriad freckles some biological painter had brush-spattered across his skin.

I stopped for a second to get more sunscreen on my fingertips, then knelt up to do the tops of his ears and the sides of his neck.

"I may not be as funny as you are," I said, leaning on his back for a second to check I'd gotten everything, "but I am way more thorough. Did you even think to do my ears?" I sat back and looked smug. *He did my arms. Would it be wrong to offer to do his?*

He twisted back toward me, and suddenly, our faces were incredibly close.

"Let me see," he said. "I would hate for you to be better at sun protection than I am." He looked stern. "Avert your gaze."

I looked down and away, so he could see the backs of my ears, and I started squirming as he got closer and closer.

"Obviously," he said, "it's been several minutes since I applied the sunscreen here."

"Allegedly applied the sunscreen," I said.

"Allegedly applied the sunscreen, hmm . . ." I could feel his breath on my ear. "It's very hard to tell for sure. I'm afraid I'm going to have to . . ." And then he stuck out his tongue and booped me on my ear.

I jumped a foot and burst out laughing. "Did you just lick my ear? I mean, actually?"

He was laughing really hard and pulling a terrible face. "Oh, yeah, definitely sunscreen. That's an unmistakable aftertaste." He held out his arms to me. "Come back, let me check the other one."

I shook my head and sat back on my heels, regarding him suspiciously.

He tried beseeching. "What if I missed your other ear, and on the way home you develop a sunburn on this tiny but very important area and it's all my fault?"

"I imagine you could live with yourself and I would recover." I held my hand out for the sunscreen. "I can do my own ear."

He laughed, and sprayed sunscreen into my hand.

25

STRAWBERRIES
FRAGARIA × ANANASSA

I don't think of myself as a big cheese person, per se, but we packed away that bread and Brie like France had been plucked from the planet and it was the end-times for baguettes.

Nate had opened one or two of the tubs, and I was dipping strawberries in the cream. We were employing a scattershot approach, but it was working.

"You make an excellent picnic," I said. "Thank you so much."

He smiled. "You're welcome. It's nice to have a reason to take a day off. I realized when your dad popped up that I hadn't thought about anything but work in way too long. I'd gotten in a rut." He turned over on his stomach and poured some water onto the sand. "Look," he said, "World's Smallest Sandcastle." He built a tiny pyramid.

I frowned. "That's a pyramid."

"Fine, but it's also a sandcastle." He was firm. "The two aren't mutually exclusive."

"A pyramid is not a type of castle. It's for burying, not ruling."

He ignored me and shaped it a bit more. He only needed one hand; it was very small. He removed his hand. "Ta-da!"

I said, "Um, now it's a sand cube."

He said, with suitable seriousness, "It's brutalist architecture."

I rolled over and squashed it. "Deconstructionism."

We were lying shoulder to shoulder now, both of us kicking our feet in the hot sun, our top halves shaded by the umbrella.

"Despite the fact you just crushed my sandcastle, you're much less scary once you're on your own and near the ocean," Nate said, reaching over to brush a little sand off my shoulder.

"Am I scary?"

"You're lots of things, actually. You're . . . forceful. In public, anyway." He looked at me. "You're different in private."

I looked back. "Isn't everyone? I feel like there are at least three or four versions of me, depending on context. Social camouflage."

"Maybe. I feel like I'm pretty much this." He shrugged. "Basic dude."

I laughed. "You're not very basic. You've got too much vim."

He was amused, which made his face crease all up on the sides. "No one has ever told me I had vim." He giggled. "What even is vim?"

"You know. Pep, energy . . ." I gave up. "It's a good thing."

"Well, as I mentioned earlier, you're a surprise." He looked down, stirring the rubble of his sand cube until it dried away. "It's not like we, you know, hung out when we were kids."

I rolled over onto my side, propping myself on my elbow. "Yeah,

I don't remember really connecting with you over our shared love of Elmo."

He smiled and looked at me. "I remember this weird little quiet kid lurking around the house. And obviously I remember you as a teenager." He laughed softly. "When you were this weird little noisy kid lurking around the club scene."

I sat up and pushed him over, which he didn't even try to fight, just laughed and rolled. I frowned at him, hard. But after a moment, I looked at him from under my lashes and said, "I don't think I ever got the chance to thank you."

He knew what I was talking about. "Not personally. They got you out of town pretty quickly. Your mom said thanks." He hesitated. "Lennie called me." He looked at his watch. "The tide is going out. We should go in the water while we can." He got up and held out his hand. "Come on, Butterfly Baby."

I frowned up at him. "Don't even."

He just grinned, and we wandered down to the surf. The Indian Ocean is deeper than the Pacific, but the water of the Pacific feels much colder to me. It's always a shock, the first foamy slide across your sun-heated feet, and this was no exception. We both did that little hop step you do, but it went from cold to delicious in a minute.

I could feel the beach caving away under my foot with every tug of the tide. I watched for sand crabs and sandpipers and tried to ignore the fact that Nate was still holding my hand. Whatever this was, it was clearly mutual, even if neither of us had actually come out and said anything yet. He'd gotten under my defenses because when I set them up, he was already inside. And now standing next to him in the surf was making me breathless. I wanted to kiss him so, so badly.

I decided what to say. Then I changed my mind. Then I really decided. Then I second-guessed myself.

"Here's the thing, Christa," said Nathan, dropping my hand. "I don't know the best way to say this except to just say it. I haven't seen you in, I don't know, ten years? More? But when you came around the corner at LAX, it was like, oh, look, *there's* that woman you've been searching for this whole time." He was blushing, and hesitating, but I was getting it. Nathan reached out and tucked my hair behind my ear. "I understand that the kid you were is nothing like the woman you are, and that I don't really know you, and I'm sorry this is so weird and sudden, and God knows it's terrible timing, but I find you startlingly attractive, and not just because you're beautiful." He took a deep breath. "You're just . . . so yourself. Such a force of nature. So smart and fierce and independent. You know so many things I know nothing about and when you talk about them you light up and all I want to do is watch your face move and listen to your voice. I just . . . Sorry."

"Why sorry?" I asked.

He shrugged, and suddenly looked less sure of himself. "I've been told I'm too much." His eyelid jumped barely perceptibly. "I don't mean to be. It's just . . ."

"That's how you feel?" I was staying pretty quiet, but I was impressed by his openness. He wasn't pretending to be cool. He wasn't holding back. He felt something and he was talking about it. I wished I could be that brave.

He nodded. "I can't take my eyes off you. The other day in the donut shop, you closed your eyes to lick sugar off your lips and I nearly had a coronary. You sucked the rest of it off your thumb and I had to start reciting the States in alphabetical order. You leaned against my back four minutes ago and I can still feel it. The curve of your cheek, the way you hold your pencil, the way you disappear into your thoughts so completely . . . all I want to do is be with you, touch you." He took a shaky breath. "I've never been so attracted to anyone."

I suddenly remembered what Lennie had said, that his ex-wife had been cruel to him.

I stepped closer. "I don't think you're too much. I think you're great. I think if we think about it too hard, we'll break it." I looked up and smiled, watched the creases at the corners of his eyes relax, laid the palm of my hand across his ribs and felt his breath quicken. "I'm only going to be here for a little while, so let's just . . . accept it." I smiled at him. "If we can keep it private, I'm one hundred percent in." I stretched up on my tiptoes, placing my hands on his arms to resist the gentle pull of the tide. I kissed him, finally; there's nothing else to say about it. I kissed him and it was simple and effortless and sexy. I bit his lip gently, leaning back into his arms and pressing against his hips. Heat flooded my body; everything ached with my pulse. I stepped back and took a somewhat shaky breath. "Let's just see what happens. Is that OK?" I turned, walking against the current. Once in the shallow surf, I reached back for his hand, drawing him close. I had zero inclination to play games, or to be unclear. "I want this," I said. "I want you."

He took a deep breath, and nodded. Then he lifted me up and I wrapped my legs around him as he carried me up the beach.

"I don't know why this is happening," I continued, pretty sure I was about to lose the power of speech, "but at least it's an interdependency."

He stopped and grinned at me suddenly. "A what now?"

I frowned. "Are you making fun of me?"

He shrugged. "I really couldn't tell you. I can barely think straight."

I laughed, not entirely convincingly. "Really?"

"Yeah." He drew in his breath. "Can I be clear, we're going to go ahead and do this? Even though it is almost certainly nuts?"

"Yes," I said. "And we better do it really soon, because the way you're pressing against me is making me light-headed."

We reached the blanket and he stopped, slowly lowering my legs to the ground. As I slid down against the length of him, I literally felt my head spin for a second with a distilled rush of dopamine. He steadied me, dipping his head to check in with me again, his eyes meeting mine in a smile. Now they were the color of the sea at sunset, the color of the shirt I'd shrugged off not ten minutes earlier. I wondered how dark they would get.

Slowly, he began kissing along my collarbone. I could feel him trembling, and the sudden knowledge that he was as overcome as I was made me shudder and arch up against him, my fingernails raking across the skin above his waistband. He moaned against my neck, then peeled my T-shirt up and over my head, his sharp inhalation at the sight of my breasts making me flush with heat again. He slid his mouth down to where the lace of my bra covered my nipple and took it between his teeth, gently but not too gently, making me catch my breath and tangle my fingers in his hair.

I don't want you to get the impression I haven't had hot sex before—I have, but this was different. I was all in. I'd always felt safer when I held something of myself back, kept a little distance. Sex was still sex, right? It was almost always good, and if I felt a little outside of myself, it was a small price to pay for emotional buffering. But this was different . . . My guard was down, and when he looked up and our eyes met, he made no effort whatsoever to hide how much he wanted me. Not some idea of me, not some concept he'd picked up somewhere, but me as I actually was right there in his arms, under his fingertips. He reached around and undid my bra, still watching me as he hooked his other hand over the waistband of my jeans, running the backs of his folded fingers across the soft skin of my belly. My body, having waited several days for the green light it so dearly wanted, became very goal oriented. I tugged him down onto the blanket next to me, then straddled him, pinning him down. As I settled, I could feel how hard he was, and the pressure between my legs was starting to affect my breathing. I haven't felt that much lust for someone since . . . well, I'm not entirely sure I've ever felt it.

I let him see it. I held his gaze while I took his hand and brought it to where my jeans buttoned, our hands undoing them together. "How much time do we have until we lose our seclusion?" I bent down and kissed him again, feeling him move and flex against me. This was definitely not part of my plan for this trip, but here's an observation: Other animals are really good at accepting good fortune when it's presented. Surprise fruit? Let's eat it all! A really safe abandoned den? Pack your snacks, kids, we're moving in! I decided I was going to see this intense connection as a counterbalance from the universe, for the gut punch that was Jasper. If the *universe* wanted me to sleep with Nate, and *Nate* wanted me to sleep with Nate, and my body and his body seemed to have been waiting forever to find each other, who was I to argue? Nate looked at his watch. "We have twenty minutes until people could conceivably walk by." He looked at me. "Theoretically, anyone could kayak by, swim by, boat by, paraglide by or parachute in from above." He raised his eyebrows. "At any minute."

I made a raspberry noise. "Oh, please. You can do a lot in twenty minutes." I grinned and started leaning down to kiss him again. He grinned back, but then lifted me off embarrassingly easily and laid me down, propping himself on his elbow alongside. He started kissing my neck, grinning against my cheek as my breathing got shallow, the shaking in his hands gone now as he tugged gently on my waistband. He pushed the rest of the buttons open wide, then lazily wrapped his hand around my hip bone.

"You *can* do a lot in twenty minutes," he said against my ear, "but *should* you do a lot in twenty minutes? That's the question." His hand squeezed the soft flesh of my hip and then moved gently up my ribs as he started kissing me again, making me squirm.

As I think you know by now, I am a rational woman. Mind over matter. But as his hand curved over my breast and the pad of his thumb stroked across my nipple, I couldn't stop myself from swearing. Sorry, I'm sure gentle sighs and trembling moans have their place, but give me *fuuuuuck* every single time.

He laughed gently. "I could happily spend twenty minutes just doing this, for example," he said, his tongue tracing the edges of my mouth. "Or this." His fingers walked across my stomach, sliding under my waistband, into my panties. He caught his breath against my mouth and whispered, "I could easily devote twenty minutes to this." He started kissing his way down my body, his hand moving lower, curving and cupping. "Why don't you just let me take my time?" He bit down very gently on the skin below my belly button as his hands scooped under me, lifting my hips, loosening and tugging down my shorts.

I swallowed, and said, shakily, "I don't think I'm going to be a very good timekeeper."

His mouth was lower on my belly now, and I felt my skin flutter as I pressed my hips down into the sand, against his hand. "That's OK," he muttered against my skin. "I'm paying attention."

And he really, really was.

26

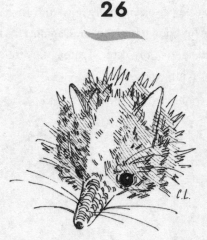

LOWLAND STREAKED TENREC
HEMICENTETES SEMISPINOSUS

On the way home, I suddenly remembered I had a phone and pulled it out. I was curled up in the passenger seat, feeling a little sleepy. It was late afternoon now, and the traffic was starting to pick up as we headed back toward Santa Monica.

Nate looked over. "Please tell me someone else is trending."

I shook my head. "No, Jasper is still pretty much the hot topic." I laughed. "Some of these memes are pretty funny."[1]

---

1. The speed with which the Internet collectively mocks the celebrity of the day is the thing that makes me optimistic about the future of humanity. Our ability to laugh at ourselves is incredibly adaptive: If we hadn't been able to giggle as we started to perfect bipedalism (oh my God, I've tripped *again*), we might never have made it out of the trees. Just a thought.

As the traffic slowed to a stop for a red light, Nate looked over and smiled at me, reaching for my hand. I leaned back in my seat and let myself look back. I was still warm and sandy, and I wanted to take a shower and pick up exactly where we'd just left off.

"I'm not going to lie," I said, "I really hope we're going straight to your place." I kissed his palm. "I don't like being in debt to anyone."

He laughed. "Well, I'm not going to lie either. It's all part of my fiendish plan to capture you and make you stay."

"Oh yeah." I sat up a little. "In two weeks?"

"I already started," he said, giving me a look. "I'm ahead—you just admitted it. Well, when we get to my place, I'm going to maintain that lead and keep on keeping on until you want to stay." He shrugged. "Early advantage, Donovan." He licked his finger and drew a line in the air.

Then he grinned and drew another. Keeping score.

I narrowed my eyes. "Oh yeah?" I turned away a little and extended my legs onto the dash. I saw him look, saw his hands tighten on the wheel, and said, "We'll see." I glanced down at my phone, opening my email and looking forward to playing this game. I also sat up because putting your feet on the dash is dangerous. Safety first, people.

Nate, for all his energy, is not a jumpy guy, not so far at least. Not a spooker, if you know what I mean. Which is why, when I suddenly yelled *crap!* at the top of my voice, he just raised one eyebrow and kept driving, waiting for me to elaborate.

I kept up a steady stream of curses as I read the email over again. It was from earlier that morning. I must have missed it when we left for our jaunt. "The department isn't going to fund my study anymore. Dammit, he *promised* me." I slammed the phone on the dashboard, which prompted a gentle *hey* from Nate. We hit another red light (welcome to Los Angeles), and he turned to look at me properly.

"No need to take it out on the old lady. It's not her fault." The light changed and we pulled away. "What does the email actually say?"

"It says *a decision has been made not to extend funding for an additional year.*"

"And?"

"No, that's it. That's the whole email." I gazed at the phone in my hands, and for a second I felt crushed—*wait . . . they don't like my snails?*—but shifted easily into guerilla combat mode, one of my favorites. "Well, I'm sorry, but that just can't happen. I've got snails to support." I turned to Nate. "I am so sorry, and I promise I hear you throwing down the gauntlet of friendly sexual competition, and normally, I am never one to shy away from a contest, but . . ." I stopped. "Why are you smiling at me like that?"

He turned back to watch the traffic. "Because I like the way you leap into action. It's adorable, because you're adorable . . ." He held up a hand. "Don't get pissy—I hadn't finished—but it's also terrifying because you're also terrifying. It's like a hamster suddenly pulled out a set of throwing stars and decimated the whole bar."

I turned and looked at him. "Why would a hamster be in a bar?"

"Where else is it going to get a drink?"

I stared at him.

He grinned, unfazed. "I assume you want to stop at home on your way to burn down the school. You know, to take a quick shower and put on your fighting shorts." He grinned. "I pity your poor professor."

I stared at him for a moment. "How did you know I call them my fighting shorts?"

He snorted. "Lucky guess. I'll drive you over, if you like." He shot me a look. "Will I need to park outside and keep the engine running?" He raised an eyebrow. "Here's where we find out if I make a good getaway driver."

"You're kind of a nice guy to be an accessory to crime, aren't you?" I'd said it lightly, even affectionately, but I could tell immediately it bothered him. "Not too nice," I added quickly. "You already cheated at our very first contest."

He smiled. "You should have lodged an official protest with the judges."

"The judges were distracted."

The traffic started to get a little challenging, and we fell silent for a few miles. I decided to change the subject.

"Do you still have all your Liddles?"

He laughed. "Yeah. Although I sold Frankie Fossa last year to pay my divorce lawyer." He shook his head. "I may need to liquidate Tommy Tenrec if Alison doesn't stop going after the company."

"Shut up. You sold Frankie?" All of the Liddle's Liddles were obscure animals overlooked by the global PR department. Frankie Fossa, Tommy Tenrec, Quentin Quokka and Angie Axolotl were the first Liddle's Liddles, and John Donovan and my dad had grossly underestimated the Beanie Babies–adjacent insanity, and made far too few of them. Any examples of the four original animals are now extremely rare and correspondingly valuable.

Obviously, the Liddle and Donovan kids had a huge advantage in the collectible Liddle's Liddles department. Every new model would be brought home in the prototype stage, for the valuable opinion of the kids. That's another memory I have and hold from my childhood: John Donovan's face as he sat us all down and showed us the latest imaginative effort. Of course, our opinions were not the only ones that mattered, but after a year or two, it became clear that Lennie, for some reason, was a very accurate and predictive focus group of one. She upvoted Shirley Sand Cat, for example, over Jenny Jerboa, and Shirley was *huge*.

Anyway, we all got the first of anything off the production line, sometimes missing tags, sometimes with weird anomalies that made them unsellable then and unique now. I was too small to care, so Mom put mine away for when I got older. Fortunately, she then promptly forgot where she'd put them, and we only found them when I was leaving for college. Pristine. Original tags, with *Christabel* written in my dad's hand on all of them. Although this would have been impossible to believe at the time, that collection of tiny beanbags paid for my education.

Nathan sighed. "I really didn't want to sell him, but that little guy took care of a pretty substantial bill, blessed be Frankie Fossa."

I repeated, "Blessed be Frankie Fossa."

"You know the one that really kills me?" Nathan said, and I was glad he seemed himself again. "Rebecca Rainbow Ring-Tailed Mongoose."

R3TM, as she's known in the trade, was a limited edition release mixed in randomly with the regular Liddles deliveries maybe three or four years into peak insanity. Rebecca showed up at mom-and-pop stores and gas stations and FAO Schwarz that summer, which means she still occasionally makes an appearance at swap meets, happy to make someone's year.

We were approaching the house, and Nathan edged past the smaller contingent of photographers outside the garage. He turned off the engine and we sat for a moment, listening to it tick and cool.

I undid my seat belt and leaned over to kiss him. "Between us for now, right?"

He twined his fingers in my hair and tugged it very gently, pulling me closer. "Yes, and after you've finished battling your nemesis, I plan to take you home and nurse you back to health."

"I'm sure you do," I replied, unclicking his seat belt and pushing it back across his lap. I let my hand rest on him for a moment, kissing him until I felt him get hard. Then I undid his top button and started to kiss my way down his chest. "I might die in the fight . . . I was thinking maybe something to remember me by . . . ?"

His head tipped back as I started on his zipper. Sadly, the sound broke my spell.

His head popped up. "No, no," he said, moving out from under me and getting out of the car. He did up his pants and literally hopped up and down on the spot. "Nope, nope, I see your game." He grinned and shook his head. "Not a fifteen-year-old boy anymore, actual self-control." I could tell from the way he was looking at me that it hadn't been an easy decision. Damn him and his mental toughness.

I was still leaning over the driver's seat, frowning at him. "Fine. Let's see how long that lasts."

I'll get him back later. Revenge is best served cold anyway.

27

KIRK'S DIK-DIK
MADOQUA KIRKII

We found everyone in the kitchen, where my mom was throwing a Ping-Pong ball for Marcel while Amelia and Lennie offered him encouragement. There was a ten-second silence while they stared at us.

Then Amelia said *dammit*, and pulled out her wallet. So did my mom.

Lennie was holding out her hand for their money. "I told you," she said. "You could see it in the way they walked out the door."

"What?" I said. "What's up?"

Lennie was counting money. "I bet you were going to declare your mutual attraction, sleep together, then try and pretend nothing was going on."

"To be fair," said Amelia, "I had no doubt of the first part; it was the last part I didn't believe. Why would you try and hide something so obvious?"

I walked into the kitchen and snatched the money from Lennie's hand. "We didn't sleep together."

"We would have, but we didn't have time," said Nathan behind me. I spun around to find him making the classic palms-up gesture. "Sorry," he said, "but it's the truth, and in the spirit of the wager . . ."

I rolled my eyes. "Fine. But it doesn't go beyond this room. Do NOT tell Jasper. We don't even know what's going on, really, and I'm going back in two weeks, so don't get carried away." I walked toward my bedroom. "Also, not that it's as interesting as speculating on my love life, but the university is shutting down my study."

Satisfyingly, they all burst out in howls of indignant protest.

"It's OK," I heard Nate say to them. "She's going to put on her fighting shorts."

Margaret, the department secretary, must have some kind of sixth sense for imminent chaos, because she appeared the minute Nathan and I walked into the department.

"Barnet!" she snapped. "He's in a meeting."

"Good to know," I said. "He's about to be in another one." I started up the stairs.

"With her," explained Nathan, who had paused at the bottom of the stairs.

"I got that," said Margaret dryly.

"She got that," I said, turning the corner at the top of the stairs and taking a breath before tackling the next flight. I leaned over the banister. "Wait down there. You don't need to come up."

"Alright," said Nate affably, sitting down on the bottom steps and smiling up at Margaret. "Are you a zoologist too?"

Margaret shook her head. "No, I don't really like animals."

"Huh," said Nathan, not sure how to respond to that.

I kept walking up the stairs, rehearsing what to say to Professor Last. *This is important work. These snails aren't going to track themselves. I can take a pay cut.* I was going to save that one till last, because I do like to get paid for my work, but if it meant giving up my top-floor bedroom in paradise, then I would sell Tommy Tenrec and never look back.

But as it happened, it wasn't necessary. I reached the top of the building, took a moment to catch my breath (I'm in great shape, but I'd been muttering the whole way up), and then knocked on the door.

"Come in!" boomed Professor Last in the most jovial tone I'd ever heard from him. I walked in, and guess who was sitting there drinking champagne at four in the afternoon?

I sighed. "Hi, Dad," I said, coming in and closing the door.

"I had a feeling you might show up," said Professor Last, winking at Jasper. "Lucky for you, your dad called me this morning just after I'd sent you that email about your study." He slapped his hand on the desk. "Why didn't you tell me about the special? The endowment? Not only will it fund your study, but it means I won't have to crush Pelterman's pink river dolphins either, which is such a relief." He nodded to Jasper. "Pelterman's a bit like Edwards the dik-dik guy, remember him?"

Jasper nodded his head. "Who could forget?"

I thought back through the ride to UCLA. Had Nate given me

mushrooms? Had I been hit in the head with a large cartoon mallet? No, so this was probably an actual conversation I was hearing. I sat down on the edge of a chair, in case they both went completely around whatever bend they were approaching. "The special?" I looked at Jasper, hoping for a clue.

"Yes, darling, the show." His expression was excited and guileless. "The show Davis was talking about the other day, the you-and-me show. The *special*!!"

I opened my mouth to remind him of our full and complete rejection of that idea at the time, but then he added, "We're also doing *The Really Late Show* on Friday night. Davis called me this morning and told me it's all set up." He looked at Professor Last, the light of science in his eyes. "I decided a bear cub would be a good start, don't you think?"

"Brown or black?" asked Professor Last.

Jasper shrugged. "Black, I think. Smallish. I had a friend back in the day . . . Anyway, Christa's going to hold the cub while we talk, and it's going to be so much fun." He turned to me. "Your mom says you were a fantastic animal handler."

I thought back to the time Mom had put a golden eagle on my head during a Letterman show, and chatted with him while the eagle—whose name was Dolores; you'd remember it too—casually but ruthlessly plucked out a square inch of my hair. I'd stayed quiet, I knew my job, but I'm not sure being a passive victim qualifies as "fantastic" animal handling. Fun fact: The golden eagle has a crushing strength of over 1,200 pounds per square inch in each feathery talon, and a deep and abiding affection for children's hair. I don't know what Dolores wanted with it; maybe she wanted to make herself a creepy friendship bracelet. She didn't say.

Jasper mistook my silent dissociation for acceptance. "The whole concept is to revisit many of the places we visited in the original show, illustrating how things have changed environmentally. Generational thingywhatsit." He mused. "It's a pity you don't have a child."

"It really isn't," I said. "Jasper, I do not want to be on television. I want to go back to work. My snails could be doing incredible things and I'm missing it." They both looked at me and raised their left eyebrows, which was surprisingly coordinated of them. "Fair enough, that's unlikely, but still."

The men looked at each other, then stood up. "Dr. Barnet," said my boss, "the department and the university at large would be grateful if you would take part in this project. I wouldn't want to suggest the continued funding of your research depends upon it, so let me be crystal clear: Your research definitely and entirely depends on it. Do the show and the endowment will fund another year of study for you and plentiful and more interesting work across the department."

I frowned at him. "Hey, my snails are plenty interesting."

He coughed. "Or don't do the show, return to Violetta, collect your belongings and release your snails." He shrugged. "In a week they will have oozed themselves to freedom."

I narrowed my eyes at him. I try and remember that he's a large mammal guy, whose original PhD (the first of three) was on tail variation in longhorn cattle. I guess if you spend four years standing behind a load of cows with a tape measure, you get a little bitter.

28

KELP
LAMINARIALES

An hour later, Nate and I were sitting on the boardwalk of the Santa Monica Pier, dangling our feet over the edge. I'd been silent in the car, trying to think of a way to get out of . . . everything. The special—assuming it happened—would be taped, so I could prepare. An interview would be live, and I was flipping out about it. I certainly wasn't paying attention to where we were going and jumped when we suddenly rumble-clattered our way onto the wooden slats of Santa Monica Pier. There's parking directly on it, and Nate picked a spot on the edge, facing Malibu.

"Come on," he'd said, turning off the engine and opening his door. "Let's go look at the water." He hadn't waited for an answer, and now we sat together, his legs alongside mine. I could feel the warmth of his body, and wanted to lean against him. I didn't, though. I can hold myself up.

"Listen," said Nathan. "It might not be so bad."

"I know," I said. "It's fine."

He was silent for a moment, then he said, "You talk a good game, Christa, but you're full of it."

I shrugged, gave up and leaned against him. "OK, yes, it's going to suck. When I was getting into trouble, it wasn't even as intrusive as it is now. They're already digging as hard as they can on Jasper; they'll just add a few shovels for me. Everything's going to get dragged up again, all the pictures, all the stupid shit I did." I held my hands out in front of me. Still steady, toughest cookie for the win. I breathed deep and slow, pulling myself together. Despite my best efforts, my voice was a bit strangled when I said, "There will be interviews and questions, and I just hate it." *I'm going to embarrass myself, and everyone else, all over again.*

"There aren't that many pictures, Christa. It's going to be fine." He reached over and took my hand. "That's not really it, is it?"

My throat gets tight when he's kind to me, I realized. I shook my head miserably. I turned to him and said the thing that really scared me, the thing I'd never said before. "What if they find out about the gala?" I swallowed and forced the words out. "What if they find out what happened?" A tear rolled down my cheek, and I reached to swipe it away.

Nate beat me to it, smoothing the tear away with his thumb. He looked at me for a long time without saying anything. Then he said, "Christa, Davis Reed took care of it, remember? I don't know him very well, obviously, but he didn't strike me as inefficient."

I looked down the coast toward the bluffs of Malibu. We'd been

there only hours before, when things had seemed more manage-
able. I shrugged. "No, he's pretty efficient."

He nodded. "You don't remember much about it?"

I shook my head.

Nathan sighed. "I'm so sorry, baby." He turned and put his hand
under my chin, tipping up until he could see my eyes. "It wasn't
your fault—you do know that, right?"

I pulled away from his hand and looked down. "Yeah, I do know
that. Not that it matters what I think." I looked up at him, feeling
my self-control starting to come back online. "If the Internet gets
hold of it, I'm sure I'll get abundant judgment." He frowned and
started to say something, but I interrupted him. "It's fine, Nate. It
was a long time ago. I'm over it."

"But what . . ."

I put my finger on his lips. "Seriously. It's fine." I sat up straighter.
"It's all good, baby."

Nate held my hand, swung his feet in time with mine, and for
a minute or two we just sat there. I carefully folded up my fear
until it was no bigger than a thumbnail and tucked it away.

Nate sighed and turned to look at me. "Do you want to go back
home? Alternatively, we could go back to my place and I could
make you a blanket fort to hide in." He waggled his eyebrows se-
ductively and grinned. "We can eat cookies and watch cartoons."

I started smiling. "I'll be honest, if we go back to your place, I'm
not going to be interested in hiding. On the contrary." I leaned forward and kissed him again. "I am still in debt from this morning . . ."

He looked at me quietly, smoothing his thumb over my eyebrow, tracing my cheekbone. "You don't owe me anything, ever.
Pleasing you was as much fun for me as it was for you."

I raised my eyebrows slowly and tilted my head. "Oh, you know that isn't true." I could feel the tremor of anxiety fading, warmed to vapor by the memory of all that mutual desire.

A tiny smile touched the corners of his mouth. He leaned forward and kissed me softly. "Let's call it a tie. You burn very bright, Christa. I can't wait to be inside you, surrounded by all your energy." He sat back. "But if next to you is what's available now, I'll take that and be more than happy." He stood up and dusted off his jeans. "I waited this long to find you, despite the fact I've known you all my life. I can wait a bit more." He leaned down and took my hand, lifting me easily to my feet. "I do want to point out, though, that we have deeply unfinished business we will eventually get to, over and over and over again. Agreed?"

I looked up at him. "Agreed." As we walked back to the car, I held on to his hand. One hand's worth of support was OK, right? I found myself praying we'd be able to keep this tiny, new relationship safe and unexposed. There aren't many secrets that survive the disinfecting properties of full sunlight, as I'd discovered far too many times before.

IN THE NEWS . . .

DEADLINE.COM: Davis Reed confirms client Jasper Liddle signed on to produce and star in several specials for PBS. Liddle's daughter, Christabel Liddle, will also appear.

PBS.COM: Coming soon: *Liddle's Landscape*, an exploration of California. Watch Jasper's daughter reacquaint her father with the Golden State.

ABC.COM: Jasper Liddle and his daughter Christa visit *The Really Late Show*, Friday at 10. Animals! Revelations! Don't miss it!

TOYBOOK.COM: Will Liddle's Liddles relaunch the original lineup to celebrate Jasper Liddle's return? Speculation about possible animation tie-in has retailers buzzing.

29

STRETCHING CAT
FELIS CATUS

When Jasper and I headed to the agency the next morning, Jasper was quiet and I was anxious. My fingers tingled; my stomach turned over. I hadn't been able to eat, and now I was hungry and my head hurt. But I made it all the way to the agency, and Jasper suspected nothing.

Jordan, Davis Reed's assistant, was magically waiting for us at the door. He'd probably had us microchipped by agency operatives, so he could track our movements and anticipate our every need. I like taking care of my own needs, thanks. This obviously started me thinking about the day before, and Nathan, and specifically his mouth and hands. In order to drag my attention back to the here and now, I started trying to spot natural materials (look, if you didn't know I was incredibly nerdy by now, I can't help you). Usually, office buildings have at least marble, but surprisingly enough, they'd covered the walls of this elevator in real leather. I leaned in close and scratched it to be sure. Huh. I straightened up and caught Jordan looking at me.

"It's real," he said, lowering his voice. "It was installed by special artisans who came all the way from Malta." He waited. "The island."

Once we got upstairs, Jordan paused like a tour guide and handed each of us a piece of paper. "These are your agendas for today. Christa, you'll see you're starting with a hair-and-makeup test and some pictures. Jasper, you're with Davis. Our plan is to have you totally ready for Friday night's interview."

I frowned and turned to Jasper. "Wait, this is a whole-day thing? I thought this was just a meeting."

His smile was apologetic and disarming. "Sorry, Chrissie, I didn't know either. You have plans?" He turned to Jordan. "We'll need to reschedule, sorry."

Jordan looked puzzled, and opened his mouth.

"Don't apologize," I said to Jasper, and to Jordan. "We might as well get it over with." I'd seen movie stars getting made up—they sat in chairs that essentially reclined. Sometimes they'd have their eyes closed. In my less-than-peppy state, leaning back and powering down sounded ideal. Maybe someone would put cucumber slices on my eyes and a rehydrating IV in my arm.

"Great," said Jasper, turning and walking away. Then he paused and looked back. "Jordan, you got my text, right? Christa's hungry and has a headache."

Jordan caught my eye and nodded. "I got it. We're all set."

I nodded and followed him down the nearest hallway. Now I

saw where Lennie got her telepathy from. Jasper hadn't been there for my life at all, but genetics is powerful stuff.

~~~~~

It was a different conference room from the other day, and the table was maybe half the size. It was still a large table, and a generous third of it was covered in makeup, hairpieces, mirrors and spray bottles filled with magical volumizers and flatteners, or curliness and wavifier, I don't know. A young woman smiled at us as we came in.

"Christabel Liddle?"

I opened my mouth to correct her, then suddenly changed my mind. "Yes," I said, taking the appealingly comfortable chair she indicated. "Nice to meet you." She looked harmless; I'd let it slide. Besides, maybe Christabel Liddle would be better at this stuff than Christa Barnet was. Jordan had disappeared but now reappeared with the following items: Gatorade, coffee, Tylenol, a pair of boiled eggs in eggcups, a side of well-buttered toast.

I looked up at him. "You had that waiting somewhere?"

He looked surprised. "Yes, we have a full kitchen. Your dad texted me from the car." He looked at the lady. "Jan, she needs to take a minute and eat something. Gently, gently, please."

Jan nodded, and Jordan left. Possibly to organize an international concert for world peace or maybe to order a sandwich; I really had no window into his life at all.

My head hurt. I opened the Gatorade and took the Tylenol and bit into the toast. I sat there and chewed doggedly, then I ate the eggs, drank the Gatorade, finished the coffee and went to pee. I washed my face, then shook myself like a dog getting out of the ocean, and normal service was restored.

When I came back and sat down, Jan wrapped some kind of headband thingy around my head and started brushing out my hair.

"Did you . . . Have you . . . What happened to your hair?" She was obviously uncomfortable asking so bluntly, but she had to. I understood.

"I cut it myself. I think I do a pretty good job, considering. I use trauma shears, like EMTs, firstly because they cut everything and secondly I have them with me, and I find if I just trim the bits that get in my way and then cut it along the bottom once it hits my shoulders, it works out fine. It's always kind of done its own thing anyway . . ." I tailed off because I swear I saw tears in her eyes. She was holding a hank of my hair, looking at the ends. It's strange what people find meaningful, isn't it? Hair and makeup were as blank a page for me as, say, 1980s video games, or the intricate footwork of the cha-cha danced to international standard. I closed my eyes and hoped the next part was going to involve nothing more taxing than sitting still.

Suddenly, the door flew open and another woman arrived as if fired from a cannon. I was startled, and opened my eyes to find her surveying me the same way I survey a snail's gender pore: comprehensively.

She was tall, with the bone structure of a Norse goddess. Her skin suggested she was no older than thirty, while her air of command and competence made her a decade or two older. When I first opened my eyes, she was frowning, but after a moment, her face smoothed out and she looked at the woman standing behind me. "Oh, that's not bad at all. The basic bones are great. Davis is worrying about nothing."

I stared at her. "I can hear what you're saying, you know." I held my smile, in case I needed it later. "I realize I'm sitting here with another woman brushing my hair as though I were a child, but I'm not, and you should feel free to address me directly."

"You're Christa Liddle."

"Yes."

"I'm Charlotte Young. I'm her boss. It's my job to evaluate your appearance. I'm sorry." She didn't look super sorry, but I was prepared to take her word for it. "You're a scientist, I hear."

"So they tell me," I said uneasily. Crapsticks. This cookie had turned out to be a scrapper.

Ms. Young walked halfway down the table and pulled out a chair, sitting and crossing her legs. She was wearing old jeans and biker boots, yet she reminded me of a cat extending its legs to check that its claws still worked. "What I do is kind of a science, and also an art." She paused and inclined her head 22 degrees to starboard. She expected a response.

"Oh . . . yeah?" Weak, I know. I needed more data to mount a response, give me a break.

"It's really all about refraction."

I held my breath. *Wait, what?*

"As light hits your face," she continued, "it bounces off a great many angles and planes." She leaned forward. "Are you following me?"

I nodded. A gorgeous woman was talking science to me; I could barely look away.

"The human brain is both highly preferential and easily confused. It likes balance, symmetry, and a hint of novelty. We use pigments and light-reflective substances to change the nature of what the eye sees, and therefore what the brain prefers." She shrugged. "You have very good bone structure. It's going to be very easy to make you appealing to the camera." She leaned forward suddenly. "The camera, of course, sees things differently, so then we're trying to make the unnatural look natural." She sat back again, and suddenly grinned. "Alright? Just relax and let Jan work her magic." She stood up and walked to the door. "I'll be back in an hour."

As the door sighed closed, I turned to look at Jan, who was standing behind me holding her brush.

"Wow," I said. "She's terrifying and wonderful all at once."

"She's my idol," sighed Jan. "She's the most powerful makeup artist in Hollywood."

"Huh," I said. "Is that a big deal?"

Jan stared at me. "You know they say the pen is mightier than the sword?"

"Sure."

Jan sniffed and started sorting through pots and tubes on the table. "Well, the pen's a total slacker compared to the sponge-tipped applicator."

"Really?" I breathed. This whole morning had taken a more positive turn, and I was all in.

"Oh, girl," she said. "I can tell you *stories*."

And she did.

When Charlotte Young returned, she brought Davis Reed and my dad.

Jasper burst out laughing, of course.

"Oh my Lord, you look like your mother." He slapped his thigh— no, literally, like a pirate. "Wait, no, you look like *my* mother." He went off into fits of laughter again.

I stared at him coldly, but he was the only one laughing.

Davis Reed was gaping; there really isn't another word for it. His jaw was slack.

"Jesus, Davis," I said, "it's just makeup." I made a face at his assistant. "Has he never seen social media?"

Jordan micro-shrugged. I looked pretty great—I'm not going to lie. Buoyed by her success with the hair part of my head, Jan had pushed the boat out and done my makeup. No fake nails or lashes, though, because who the hell has time for that? I loved my Hollywood hair and thought I looked gorgeous and it was totally insane, because I do *not* look like that. It was great fun, and I could not wait to take it off. I didn't like the way it felt on my skin and I didn't like the way it made people look at me differently. However, I wasn't blind to the effect it had on my confidence. It made this evaluation easier, because it wasn't even really me. *This* was Christabel Liddle.

Jasper threw himself into the makeup chair. He gazed up at Jan the makeup artist, and she blushed to the roots of her hair.

"Hi there," he said. "I don't think you can transform me the way you did Christa, but I'm willing to let you try." He smiled at her, and I thought she was going to have a conniption.

"You only need a little powder," she said, approaching him with a makeup puff apparently made of cloud. He murmured his thanks and created another lifelong fan. It's as easy as breathing for him.

Charlotte Young was the only person in the room who wasn't in any way afraid of Davis Reed. "I told you," she said pointedly. "She has the same bones. I knew it would be fine." She grinned at me. "You make an excellent light-reflective surface."

I laughed.

"Alright, Charlotte, I concede the point." Davis was magnanimous in defeat. "She looks great." He turned to Jordan. "Call Annie

Leibovitz. Alex Dutton's profile piece is going to have pictures—talk to the *Times* and let them know."

I frowned at him. "My mother won't talk to Alex Dutton."

Davis nodded. "She made that clear. But we've agreed to cooperate with Mr. Dutton, so we will be making our archives available, and giving him whatever information he needs. I suggest you talk to him yourself if you want accurate representation."

I looked at Jasper. "Are you going to talk to him?"

He nodded. "Of course. I want people to see I've got nothing to hide." He looked at Davis. "Right?"

"Exactly." Davis turned to head out, and Jordan altered the laws of physics so he could beat him to the door and hold it open. Davis paid no heed, and took a moment to give me one last look. "I appreciate this wasn't your first choice, Christabel, but I hope you'll soon realize we all share the same goal: to support your father as he makes this difficult transition."

I looked at Jasper. "A situation entirely of his own making, to be fair."

He smiled at me. "She's not wrong, Davis."

Davis barely hesitated. "She's not, but she's missing the point. The point is you're here now, and she can either climb aboard or get dragged." His voice floated back along the corridor. "Her choice."

30

LEAST SANDPIPER
CALIDRIS MINUTILLA

That day was filled with weird. I wasn't sure I would ever enjoy appearing on TV, but I did enjoy watching people run around engaging in antisocial behavior and getting away with it. It turned out TV was full of interesting interactions, if you were observationally minded. Eventually, it ended, and Dad and I got separate limos to go home in. That part I could get used to.

After the limo dropped me, I decided to walk a little on the beach while it was still warm. Making my way to the surf, I spotted a familiar outline walking toward me, a scarf over her hair. A small dog frisked about, chasing foam and harassing gulls. As we got closer, she spotted me too, and we both smiled. Having done a fairly wide reconnaissance loop to check me out, Marcel recognized me and came flying over the sand to guide me to my mom. Or to prevent me from getting closer, who knows? A miniature dachshund going wild with happiness looks very much like one that's about to take you out at the ankles. I assumed the best and got lucky.

We hugged while Marcel did victory laps around us. "How was the meeting?" she asked. "I honestly don't think I've seen you wear makeup since senior prom. You look amazing. Can I take a picture before you wash it off?"

"How do you know I'm going to take it off? Maybe I'm going out on the town." I laughed, pushing my hair behind my ears. "Dammit, the wind is already ruining it."

"It's hard to maintain perfection on the beach."

"Maybe that's why it's my favorite place," I replied. The wind was making my eyes water. "I'm not going to have to take it off at this rate; it's just going to wash away all over my face."

Mom pulled a tissue from her pocket and steadied my chin with her hand as she gently blotted my melting mascara. How many times had she tended to me, I wondered, beginning when she had to bend to cup my childhood chin and wipe my runny nose? She could see the changes in my face, I can only feel the changes in her hand, but we clicked together as well as ever.

She looked at me and smiled. "You didn't answer my question. How was the meeting?" She looked along the wavelets, keeping an eye on Marcel in case a hungry gull mistook him for an actual sausage.

I said, "It was fine." We walked in silence for a bit, and I watched the sandpipers pretending not to notice the surf until the last minute, skittering ahead in faux-panic. "Did you know," I said conversationally, "that sandpipers have a little cluster of cells at the end of their beak that detects differences in hydrodynamics, enabling them to stick their beaks into wet sand and sense objects that might be food?"

Mom slowed slightly and said, "You'll be horrified to hear I did *not* know that."

I looked at her. "Are you teasing me?"

She laughed. "Not really. I am interested, but this side of you is from your dad—you know that. There was nothing he didn't want to know more about. If no one else had climbed up it or down it or into it, he would. He was intensely curious about everything. All the time." She made a face. "It was exhausting."

"Are you glad he's back?" I looked at her. "That sounded weird. I mean, you're probably glad he's alive, right? But are you glad he's here?"

She sighed, fished a ball from her pocket and threw it for the dog. "Yes, of course, although it's complicated by the fact he could have been back the whole time. Well, most of it." She bent to take the ball back from Marcel and threw it again. "Not sure my therapist is going to have any experience to draw on for our next session." She laughed. "Plus it's making me feel old in a way I don't appreciate. He was thirty-five when he disappeared; I was thirty-three. In my head he's always been that age, and therefore so was I. He's back, he's older, I'm older, the whole thing is a bummer." She stopped walking and turned to face me. She reached out and put her hand on my arm and squeezed it. "For the last time, how was the meeting? 'It was fine' is not a real answer."

I decided I was old enough to tell the truth. "It was really weird. The whole thing is weird, and makes me anxious. I hated being on TV when I was a kid, do you know that?"

She looked at me for a moment, then nodded. "It was wrong of me, you know, to do that to you. I should have apologized to you a long time ago, but I'll do it now. I'm sorry, Christa. I pushed you to do things no little kid should have to do, to be well-behaved all the time, to be exposed constantly." She turned to start walking again. "And then, when things got bad for you in your teens, I wasn't there until way too late." Her voice got thick. "In therapy, I realized how much guilt and regret I have for that. When you needed me the most, I was busy with my new husband and didn't see you starting to walk off a cliff."

I took her hand. "You caught me, though."

She looked at me dubiously. "Yeah . . . and sent you away to school. At the time, I thought it was the right call, but . . ." Her eyebrows contracted, and tears welled up. "Was it? Do you hate me?"

I stopped, shocked. "No, Mom, I don't hate you. Jeez." I pulled her into a hug, and felt her relax onto me. "It saved me. Miss Lewis's biology class changed my life, woke up my brain, you know? I wouldn't have gone to college, or Princeton for grad school, wouldn't have come back home to UCLA . . . and I wouldn't have gone to Violetta, which is honestly the love of my life." Suddenly, Nate popped into my head, brought there by the phrase. I pushed the thought away. "I hate all this TV stuff, all this media, but Mom, I love what I do. I am so happy, and if you hadn't sent me away to school, none of it would have happened." I stepped back from her, so she could see my face, see that I meant it. "I'm so grateful."

Her eyes were filled with tears now. "I love you, Christa. I'm sorry I let you down."

I frowned at her. "Mom. I'm not a teenager anymore. I'm a grown woman, and you're going to have to take my word for it: We all make mistakes, but we have to let go of the past, right? We don't need to keep feeling pain for injuries we sustained a decade ago, or longer. We can choose to heal."

She raised her eyebrows at me. "I thought you said you hadn't gone to therapy. You sound ridiculously sane."

I laughed. "I'm not. I don't know what to tell you. I don't even know where that came from. I just . . ." I raised my arms in the air and opened my palms in an expression of everything I found mystifying. "I guess I realize I'm carrying a lot of old shit around and I don't need to. Lennie isn't going to eviscerate me, you're not mad at me, Amelia isn't . . ." I paused. "Amelia hasn't changed much, actually. She's just the same."

We both laughed.

"And Nate?" she asked. "Nate's different, right?"

I went red. "Nate's different, yes."

"And you," she said, "are you different?"

I laughed. "I don't know. I feel like the last few days have been a lot, and I'm not thrilled about the attention, but I'm trying not to be as bad-tempered about everything as usual. Look, if Lennie can change, anyone can."

We tacked right to head up the beach. There was a visible clump of people around the end of our block; not journalists, just people.

I said, "Jasper fans?"

Mom looked, and nodded. "Probably." She turned to me. "Jasper didn't come with you?"

I looked at her and shook my head. "No. You don't have to stay by his side, you know. No one would blame you if you wanted nothing to do with him."

She laughed, and pushed her hair back. "He's been gone such a long time. He feels more like an old childhood friend than . . ."

She frowned. "Whatever it is that he is. Not ex-husband . . . not late husband . . . whatever. I'm surprised how happy I am to see him." She turned and put her hand on my shoulder. "Don't forget, because of him I have you, I have Amelia and Lennie, I have Nate, I have the Foundation, I had a wonderful marriage to another man . . . I have a life I've really enjoyed, generally speaking. He missed out on all of that, so I can hardly be mad at him." She looked at the people waiting, and turned back to face the ocean. "Let's sit for a minute. I'm not quite ready to be charming to strangers yet."

We sat. Marcel was perplexed, then came and curled up in the space formed by my mother's folded legs.

"Besides," said Mom, "he's also changed a lot, of course. He's not the same guy at all."

I nodded. "That makes sense. None of us are who we were twenty-five years ago."

"Well, you were two and obsessed with eating sand, but sure. He's a lot nicer. He used to be a little . . . impatient at times, a little insensitive." She chuckled. "It could be age, it could be grief, it could be that Lorna was better for him than I was, it could be any number of things. People change; you have to let them." She looked at the backs of her hands. "I'm certainly not the same woman he left behind, and the outside is the least of it." She looked over at me, and assumed a bright expression. "So," she said conversationally, "what's going to happen with you and Nate when you go back to your island?"

"Jesus, that's a very personal question." I huffed and puffed for a moment, then admitted, "Honestly, I don't know what's going to happen with me and Nate when I go back to the house in five minutes, let alone the island. I wasn't looking for a relationship; I certainly wasn't looking for a relationship so . . ." I paused.

"Intense?" Mom grinned. "Don't worry, for once this isn't something I've discussed with your sisters. I just know your face very well, and when you look at him, it reminds me a little bit of the expression you used to have about dinosaurs."

I raised my eyebrows. "I'm sorry?"

She shrugged. "You would disappear into your own little world, just blissfully happy, learning about them, reading about them. Your face would get this light in it, of just complete . . . engagement." She smacked her knee. "Engagement is the word. You look at him as though you are all in, fully present, one hundred percent focused and completely head-over-heels stoked to be right where you are."

"Well," I said, hoping my face wasn't transparently showing the full extent of my physical desire, because that would be awkward. "It's not very convenient. I don't really have the time and space to be this attracted to someone. I'm leaving in two weeks." I picked up a handful of sand and tossed it down the beach sulkily.

She frowned at me. "So? That's two weeks to get to know him better. It's not surprising you find Nate attractive. He is attractive, objectively. He's also familiar, and familiar is appealing. But then he's also totally unknown, which is also appealing. Sure, our families have always been connected, but it's not like you hung out at all. Once he left for college, he never really came back, and in the last half dozen years, you've missed each other over and over again. You were with that extremely dull guy for a minute or two, then Nate was abroad, then you were abroad, then he was married for a while. Every time I saw either of you, you would both ask about the other. It was notable. He'd ask how you were, you'd ask how he was, you were just never in the same place at the same time. Now you've been brought together for the strangest possible reason, and maybe it's because now is the right time."

I frowned at her. "Are you saying Jasper returned from the dead so that Nate and I would get together?"

She shook her head. "Not *exclusively*." She looked thoughtful. "It was like you couldn't be in the same place at the same time until suddenly you had to be. Now you're stuck with each other." She paused and smiled at me. "But you know me—I'm always looking out for the nod from the universe."

This is true: She's the first to point out a rainbow, a humming-bird, a shared birthday with a stranger, a matching choice of scarf. She's a big believer in *meant to be*. I'm more of a *yeah, but probably not*.

Mom glanced over her shoulder at the crowd again and visibly started pulling herself together. "John Donovan was wonderful, one of the funniest and most honorable men I've ever known. Nate's the same. You might be good for each other."

"Or it could go terribly wrong and make it super awkward at Thanksgiving." I fake shuddered. "I'm not interested in being anyone's future ex-wife."

Mom laughed. "You haven't come home for Thanksgiving in years, and I'm not suggesting you get married." She smoothed Marcel's little head. "It's not a zero-sum game, baby. It doesn't have to be all or nothing. You are more than capable of having an intense romantic relationship, satisfying intellectual work and whatever else you want to put in your life. When everything's in balance, life just expands."

I stared at her. "Is that how it was with Harry?"

She nodded and looked down the beach. "Yeah. He had a big life, I had a big life, and then we had this awesome little life together, away from everyone else." She slapped her legs suddenly. "Let's run the gauntlet and go home. I need a nap before dinner."

I got to my feet and helped her up. "I love you, Mom. I'm sorry I'm away so much."

She brushed the sand off her pants. "I want you to be happy, and you're happiest when you're poking around, left in peace. You could call more often, but that's about it." She started walking up the beach. "Don't take this the wrong way, but people miss the point of the empty nest thing. The nest is empty because the poor bird who's been working her wings off gets to leave too. Otherwise they'd call it Exhausted Bird Sitting in Her Nest Syndrome, and they don't. As soon as the door hit you on your ass on the way out, I was already buying airline tickets and planning to do whatever the fuck I wanted. I gave you and your sisters the best years of my life very happily. The rest are for me." She smiled. "And although your dad reappearing is extremely inconvenient, you'll have to admit it does at least keep things interesting." She paused to cross the road, and one of the waiting fans spotted her. Cheering rang out, and I could see them all getting ready to collect autographs and take photos. Mom waved, and prepared to be friendly. "Besides," she said out of the corner of her mouth, "if he gets on my nerves, I can always move to Alaska myself."

"Good point," I replied, bending to pick up Marcel and carry him across the street. He has his own Instagram account these days, and his fans would want to see him up close.

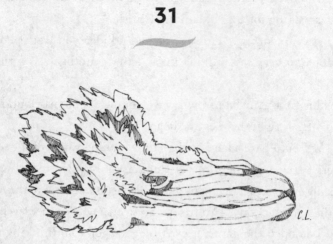

31

CELERY
APIUM GRAVEOLENS

When we got back to the house, Lennie and Amelia were playing Scrabble, and Nate was walking up and down the hallway, on the phone. Mostly listening, it seemed.

"What's up with him?" asked Mom, raising her eyebrow at Lennie.

She shrugged. "Some work thing." She pointed to a third rack. "He was going to play but then he got a call."

I leaned over to look at his letters. "Probably just as well; he's got the Q and the X but no vowels at all."

Both of my sisters simultaneously flipped their racks, spilling the letters across the board.

"For crying out loud," said Lennie.

"My God, why did you do that?" I said.

"Because you ruined the game!" Amelia frowned at me.

Lennie was muttering and gathering the tiles back into the bag. "I was waiting for the X, dammit, Christa."

I was apologetic. "I'm sorry, I had no idea you were playing Scrabble *strategically*. I didn't know letter counting was a thing, even."

This time Amelia's frown was genuine. "The distribution of the letters is right there on the board."

"Yes, but I have a hard enough time making words of the seven letters I have in front of me. If I understand you correctly, you're actually evaluating how many and which letters are still in the bag." I sighed and sat down. "You're operating on a whole other level. I'm glad I stopped the game; it can't be good for you, thinking that hard."

Lennie laughed.

Mom had headed into the kitchen to grab a drink, and now turned to address us. "Isn't Leo here?"

Amelia shook her head. "No, he has class."

"He takes a class?" I asked. I could easily believe it. LA is full of strivers.

"No," said Lennie, "teaches it."

Oh. "A cooking class?"

"Eighteenth-century French literature."

Mom chimed in. "He picked up the cooking as a hobby. Literature is his passion." She clapped her hands together. "Enough chitter-chatter, I'm starving. Let's order in."

Nate finally finished his call, but his face was still tight when he walked over to join the conversation.

"What's up?" he said, smiling at everyone, but his eyes came to rest on me. I wondered what the call had been about. Then I wondered if he would tell me or not. Then I wondered if it would always feel like that when he smiled at me.

"We were just pondering dinner," said Lennie, "because Leo isn't here and you know Mom doesn't believe in cooking."

"That's not true at all," protested Mom. "I fully believe in cooking. I watch Leo do it all the time."

"I'll make dinner," said Nate. "I need a distraction."

Lennie frowned. "The last time you cooked for me you burned hot dogs."

Nate laughed. "That was in college. I've improved somewhat." He paused and raised his hands. "I was just going to make, you know, pasta with meat sauce or something. Garlic bread. Nothing fancy."

My mouth started to water. "I am so down for simple and delicious right now. Are you going to the store?"

He started to grin at me. "Sure, want to come?"

"One hundred percent." For some reason, there was suddenly nothing in the world I wanted to do more than go to the grocery store with Nate. "I'll grab my sweater; it's freezing in the store."

"Wait!" My sister held up her hand. "Can I be emphatic for a moment? I am hungry. Now that you said *pasta with meat sauce and garlic bread*, that is all I want to eat." She pointed at us, though I felt her finger lingered on me for longer. "You two cannot waste time canoodling in the frozen section. Shop, return, cook, feed. That is the mission."

I pointed back at her. "There will be no canoodling in the store, jeez."

She narrowed her eyes at me. "Or in the car. Efficiency is your guiding principle."

I rolled my eyes. "Or in the car."

"Or in the garage on the way to the car."

"Wait," interrupted Nate, "we're wasting valuable time. I'm hungry too. Let's step it up."

We pulled the interior garage door shut behind us and immediately turned to face each other.

"It seems to me," said Nate conversationally, "that we can make up for a quick canoodle by dividing and conquering as soon as we get to the store."

I nodded. "I'll get the pasta, you get the meat, we'll meet in the bread aisle."

"You're a genius," he said. "Now stop talking."

~

"Cart or basket?" I asked as we walked into the store. Nate had grabbed my hand when we got out of the car, and was still holding it. I was starting to wonder anew if I'd maybe had an accident and was dreaming all this. Was I in a coma somewhere? Were we both in a coma?

"Cart," he said, "in case I get inspired."

I raised my eyebrows at him, but pulled out a cart and started pushing it. "Go on, then, Gordon Ramsay, do your thing."

It was one of those fancy, healthy Santa Monica–type grocery stores, where you can get spelt noodles and bee pollen as readily as bread and butter. Nate clearly knew his way around. He grabbed carrots, celery and onions. He got fresh tomatoes and canned tomatoes and ground beef from cows who'd been sunning themselves happily until killed unexpectedly by blow dart. I'm joking; it was just regular beef, but they claimed the cows were at least cheerful most of the time. He got cream, fresh Parmesan and red wine, and then we ended up at the bakery.

I could tell he was happy, but every so often I noticed him drift away into his thoughts, just briefly.

"You OK? You seem a little distracted."

Nate stopped in front of a freezer containing eighteen thousand varieties of ice cream made with everything but cream. Almond milk ice cream. Macadamia milk ice cream. Celery milk ice cream.[1] He turned to look at me. "Yeah? Sorry." He suddenly said, "Wait, none of this is what I want," and then moved down the row of freezers, looking for something familiar. "I'm partially distracted by my desire to stop shopping and start kissing, but I'm also stressed about work."

The phone call.

"Yeah? What's going on?"

He shook his head. "It doesn't matter."

I poked his arm. "Don't be silly, just tell me. I chattered on about tide pool creatures and snails and God knows what else. I want to hear you talk about what you care about too."

He gave me a strange look. "Those are things you love. This is just work."

"You don't love your work?"

He shook his head. "No. Not at all. But it's the family business. It's what I do."

I was surprised. "It doesn't have to be. You can do whatever you want, right?"

"No," he replied, reaching into the freezer for actual ice cream. "When Dad died, I became CEO without really thinking about it. But it was never something I loved." He flashed me a grin. "Don't

---

1. No, not really. Celery doesn't even have nipples.

take it personally—Liddle's Liddles are adorable but not super interesting to me. I'd much rather be sailing, or building boats."

"Really?"

He nodded. "Yeah, but I loved working with my dad. When he was alive, it was different, because everything we did was together." He paused, and took a deep breath. "I miss him every day. It's a lot, running it on my own. He was so much better at it than I am."

I reached up and kissed him gently. "He was amazing."

He tucked my hair behind my ear. "I know. I love that you knew him too." He paused. "Alison, my ex-wife, would have made a much better CEO than me, something she pointed out regularly."

"She's a business person?"

He nodded. "Yeah, that's how we met. The board wanted me to expand overseas, move production elsewhere, all that good cost-cutting stuff. They brought in an expert to do analysis and that was her."

"Huh," I said. "And then you married her."

"Yup." We were in the bakery section. "Cake or pie person?" he asked, turning to me.

"Mostly cake, some specific pies. You?"

"Ice cream with either. Nothing sour. A pox on rhubarb, for example."

I laughed. "Seems harsh, but I get it. So what was that call about?"

He shot me a look. "Another company wants to buy us. I don't want to sell. That was my ex trying to persuade me."

"What does she have to do with it?"

"They'll make her the CEO. Probably. If not immediately, then after they've made it so uncomfortable for me to stay that I leave."

"And would you?"

He shook his head. "I can't. Everyone is relying on me."

"But you don't like it, they would have control . . . Why wouldn't you leave?"

He stopped pushing the cart. "I don't know. Because my dad would never quit." His face changed a little, and he sighed again. "I don't want to talk about work. Tell me something about your island. About you."

"You sure?"

He nodded.

I thought a moment. "Let's see," I said. "Last year I won the Violetta Annual Coast to Cone Race, beating out forty other international experts and several dozen assorted locals."

Nate carefully examined a bag of shallots, put them in the cart, then turned to look at me.

"Coast to cone?" he asked calmly.

"Yeah, you run from the beach to the top of the volcano." I made a face. "It's pretty much straight up for a mile and a half, so it's not the distance that kills you. It's the elevation gain."[2]

Nate sighed. "That is impressive, but I hear your volcano race and raise you the Liddle Lobbing League, at the factory, where I am the reigning champion."

My turn to gape. "I'm sorry?"

He was cool as a cucumber, I had to give it to him. Not the slightest hint of a smile as he explained it to me.

"It's a simple contest of strength, much like your hill climb."

I smacked him on the arm. "It's a nine-thousand-foot volcano."

---

2. Plus the ever-present possibility of molten rock and superheated gases, but that would really be super unlucky, am I right?

He shrugged. "Sure. Each contestant gets to choose a Liddle, and—if the name wasn't a total giveaway—has to throw it as far as they can. You must remain within the marked contest area; an out-of-bounds throw results in no points that round."

"There are rounds?" I asked. Nate started walking again, heading toward the checkout. I looked into the cart. "We didn't get pasta."

Smoothly, Nate changed direction. "Bucatini?" he said. "Tagliatelle?"

"Chef's choice," I replied. "Don't change the subject. You're trying to tell me that in a competition between you, the owner, and them, the employees, you somehow came out the victor?" I looked guilelessly at him. "How incredibly unpredictable."

He stopped immediately. "Wash out your mouth," he said. "My employees would be only too pleased to triumph over me; they frequently do." Again, his face was completely neutral as he said, "In the construction contest, I get creamed every time." He pulled a couple boxes of bucatini off the shelf. "We have an employee named Edith who can make Sharon Sunfish in seven minutes thread to tag."

I was surprised. "It's not all done by machines?"

He shook his head. "No, there's a lot of fiddly handwork in soft toys—you'd be surprised."

I was quiet for a moment as we made our way to the checkout. "To be fair," I said eventually, "a sunfish is a pretty easy stuffie to make. I mean, they're essentially a giant disk with an apprehensive expression and a weirdly lumpy body. Marcel the dog could probably make a pretty good sunfish."

Nate regarded me coldly. "Hey, back off the gentle sunfish. I feel a lot of kinship with Sharon; she was one of the first Liddles we made after Dad . . . after I took over. She's sold out twice, despite the fact one focus group participant said she looked like a shark who'd been run over by a Zamboni."

I made a face. "And how exactly would that have happened?"

"No clue," he said, unloading the cart onto the conveyor belt. "We didn't press her for details."

Then he started talking to the cashier and I watched him. I wish I could explain how it felt to be with him, but I can't because I'm not sure. It felt happy. But it also felt a little blue, a little sad. I had discovered something unexpected in the middle of something unexpected, and I couldn't sort out which feeling was attached to what. Nate turned his head to check that we got everything, and smiled at me.

"All good?" he said.

"All good," I said firmly.

"Have a good evening," said the cashier, smiling at Nate, and then as he turned away, she caught my eye and gave me that look we give each other. You know the one. "Bye now," she said, grinning.

IN THE NEWS . . .

ABC.COM: See Jasper Liddle and his daughter live on *The Really Late Show* tonight.

TRAVELOCITY: Hide out in the woods—vacationing Liddle style!!

VOGUE.COM: Denise Liddle goes from widow to wow overnight!

32

BLACK BEAR CUB
URSUS AMERICANUS

The *Really Late Show* is taped in Los Angeles, right next to the Farmers Market. I'd been to this studio many times as a child, when a different host had sat in the chair and peppered my mother with flirtatious questions. Mostly, what I remember is being offered red-and-white-striped peppermints at every turn, while people fell all over themselves to tell me how much I looked like my dad. That and the raptor hair ripping we've previously discussed. All TV studios are the same inside anyway: cables all over the floor, the smell of dry shampoo and gaffer's tape, and doorknob-carpet combinations that create buffalo-stunning static shocks. I guess if you work there all the time, you get used to the occasional zap and scream.

The host was famously good-humored and was clearly tickled pink to be the first late-night show to present Jasper to the world.

"So exciting, so exciting, can't wait to get started," he said, pumping Jasper's hand and grinning at me. "I heard they brought a bear? Is that right, a bear?" He laughed as if we'd all made a fantastic joke, possibly the best joke ever, and the word *bear* had been the punch line. It was the single greatest day of his life and the greatest honor in the world to meet Jasper and me, and I realized as he walked away after ninety seconds that he'd said literally nothing meaningful and yet had made me feel like entertainment royalty. And that, ladies and germs, is why he is a late-night TV show host and I am a marine biologist who hides on an island and hopes no one wants to talk to her.

The bear was only a cub, but still, at around four months it was no bunny rabbit. The bear wrangler handed me a bag of treats and regarded me unfavorably.

"I googled you," she said. "You do snails."

I wasn't sure where she was going with this. "Your point?"

"They're not the toughest animal in the yard, are they?"

I raised my eyebrows. "I wouldn't suggest stepping on one in your bare feet, but no, not aggressive, if that's what you mean." (To be honest, we don't know that for sure, do we? I mean, all the snails in the world could be advancing on us in a crowded mass of frustrated rage, painstakingly raising their single feet in the hopes of smothering us all, but by the time they get there we're miles away. Poor bastards. They can't even slam their door.)

"They're not gonna try and run out on ya, are they?" She scrunched up her face in a rictus of skepticism. "I mean, you could stick 'em to yourself if you had to."

I didn't bother explaining the difference between sea snails and the regular garden snails she was clearly imagining, because I didn't see how her ignorance was ever going to hurt her and, frankly, it's not my job. However, she wasn't getting any pushback from me over their speed, despite the fact that your average garden snail can clock a hair-blowing millimeter per second, if it thinks the bars are about to close.

She continued, "This here bear cub has escaped three times in the last month alone."

We all looked at the cub, who was dreamily eating peanut butter out of half an acorn squash.

"Maybe she's not suited for a life in entertainment, then," I replied. "Do you have one who finds this fulfilling?"

She regarded me with some distaste. I was a coward who chose to work with mollusks, I was apparently being sarcastic, and I was almost certainly going to drop her bear.

Jasper stepped in. "I assure you, Miss . . ."

"Abernathy. Iris Abernathy."

Jasper looked delighted. "Any relation to Jackson Abernathy the Third?"

She gasped. "He was my grandpappy!"

I was looking right at them, so I couldn't roll my eyes, but trust me, I wanted to.

Jasper beamed and turned to me. "Jackson Abernathy was the greatest bear trainer of all time." He turned back to the woman. "Your grandfather appeared on the second season of my show with a Kodiak bear he was raising from a cub."

"He died five years ago," said the wrangler, who had transformed from the crazy prospector in a *Scooby-Doo* cartoon to a sweetly tremulous fan-for-life. "We miss him all the time." She wiped away a tear. "In the last year of his life, I had to feed him by hand."

Jasper looked sympathetic. "I'm sure he appreciated your care."

"Well, it's hard to tell, of course," she replied, "but he never lost his appetite. On his very last day, he ate three pumpkins, forty pounds of salmon and two jars of peanut butter."

Oh my God, we're talking about the bear. I hope.

A producer stuck her head around the door. "Let's get out there, people. We're going to have you guys settled before the monologue so we don't have to manage an entrance."

The bear lady was all smiles now and basically chucked the cub at me and followed Jasper out into the studio.

"Her name is Dorothy," she said, walking away. "She may pee on you."

I looked at the bear. "You may have heard that as *permission* to pee on me," I said gravely, "but it isn't."

I looked around and spotted Miss Abernathy's bear supply kit, and picked it up to take with me. Then I grabbed myself a handful of peppermints. I'd learned early on that sucking on a hard candy helps with dry mouth, and there was every chance the host was going to ask me a question. Some people might dismiss me as just a snail scientist, but this was in no way my first rodeo. Not that snails take part in rodeos. You know what I mean.

***

While the host was famous for his geniality, as I've said, he had a history of sharper questioning, so I kept one eye on the bear and one on him. The set normally had his desk and then a chair or sofa for the guests. Tonight, as there were two and a half of us (I'm counting Dorothy as a lap-bear), we got the sofa.

During the monologue, the host introduces his guests, obviously, and this is what he said about Jasper and me:

"Tonight we have the pleasure of welcoming both Jasper Liddle and the liddlest Liddle herself, Christabel. Jasper's the one we haven't seen in twenty-five years, and Christabel's the one we all saw so much of . . ." I looked at the monitors and saw they were showing a montage of images, my dad doing various interesting things (climbing a tree, descending a rope ladder) and me doing various stupid things (falling out of a taxi, getting arrested). I took a very deep breath and plastered a smile on my face. I looked over at Dad, who was frowning at the monitors. He lowered his voice.

"That sucks, Chrissie, I'm sorry."

I shrugged. "He's just doing his job." I sighed. "As Mom once said, all they do is take the picture; I'm the one who did the stupid."

Dad raised an eyebrow. "That's not very supportive."

The bear cub shifted on my lap and seemed to notice me for the first time.

"Hi," I said.

The bear said nothing, but looked pointedly into her squash half, which was now one hundred percent devoid of peanut butter. Hmm. I looked over to check that the host was still embarrassing me publicly, then opened up the treat bag.

Which was completely empty.

The studio audience burst into applause, scaring both Dorothy and me, and while I worried she was about to make a run for it, what she actually did was throw her little arms around me and squeeze. Without even thinking about it, I took the peppermint out of my mouth and handed it to her. She took it as readily as a human toddler, and was examining it with interest when the host arrived behind his desk.

I looked into the wings, where Iris Abernathy could be seen . . . talking to the musical guest. Crap. I looked over at Jasper, but he was smiling at the host. I looked back at Dorothy, who had the peppermint in her mouth and was clearly having her little bear cub mind well and truly blown. As I watched, she exhaled carefully and then shook her head. If I had to put a speech bubble above her head, it would have read, "Dude . . . trippy." (She's from California—what do you expect?)

"So," said the host, rubbing his hands together and looking at me, "on a scale from one to ten, how pissed are you that your dad's been avoiding you your whole life?"

(cue audience laughter)

Ouch.

(cue internal conflict)

Dorothy was sniffing my face, looking for more peppermints. *Focus on the bear*, I thought to myself. *Tolerate the people*.

"Uh," I replied wittily, "you know, like, probably a twelve."

He laughed as though I were a genius, and turned to Jasper. "And now that you're back, how are you planning on making it up to her?"

Jasper smiled. "I'm going to start by pointing out that whatever trouble she got up to in her teens was probably no better or worse than what you did at that age; it's just that people took pictures." His smile was still absolutely in place, his body language was entirely friendly, but he was calling the talk show host out in front of a nationwide audience and I was flabbergasted. "You know she was a minor in those photos. You really shouldn't show them at all."

There was a brief awkward silence, then someone in the audience started clapping and then they all were, and up on their feet as well.

Great. Fantastic. Now everyone feels sorry for me.

The host was both a professional and a parent, and he had the grace to look abashed. "You are so right, Jasper. Apologies, Christabel."

"No problem," I muttered, reaching in my pocket for another peppermint. Dorothy—who could smell the socks of a dead mouse from twenty miles away—was getting squirmy. I smiled at the host, prayed he'd move on quickly, and tried to subtly unwrap the peppermint with one hand before Dorothy lost patience.

Too late. Dorothy reached out her paw and I handed her the mint. The wrapper wouldn't kill her. Probably. While everyone watched, she put one end of the wrapper between her teeth, and without really thinking about it—honestly, I was panicking—I reached over and pulled the other end. Dorothy held on to her end and, physics being what it is, we unwrapped it together. The peppermint fell from the wrapper into her paw, and she tossed it into her mouth. Then she tipped up her head and bumped noses with me. Her breath, needless to say, was minty fresh.

Obviously, she hadn't been trained to do it. Almost certainly she was just looking for more candy, but once she'd done it, there was a sound from the crowd unlike anything I've ever heard. They were already feeling sorry for me, *thanks, Dad,* and now I had accidentally created a surfeit of dopamine by overstimulating the orbitofrontal cortex, which (not that you asked) reacts to "cute" in about a seventh of a second.

It started out as a collective inhalation, followed by a sound I might spell *aww-ooo-gasp-awwww,* and then there was applause that shook the rafters, if a TV show can be said to have rafters.

As I looked out past the lights, I saw something I wasn't expecting. Friendly people, and lots of them. Hundreds of people smiling broadly and looking completely stoked to have seen Dorothy doing her beary best. Not laughing at me. Not pointing and taking photographs. Just interested.

I turned to the host. "This is Dorothy, she's four months old and this is her first experience with peppermint."

He laughed. "She seems to like it."

I grinned. "I think she loves it."

I looked at Dad, who reached over and scratched Dorothy on the head. "The last California grizzly was killed in 1924, and the species was listed as officially extinct, but there's every chance we could reintroduce the species here." He looked at the host. "Christa and I are going to be exploring California in our new show, you know. A lot has changed since I ran off to hide in the woods, but Dr. Liddle has been paying attention." The host laughed, the audience laughed, and as Dad continued talking about the science behind de-extinction, I looked out past the lights and spotted a row of young women, all of whom were smiling. One raised her hand and waved as she caught my eye, and I waved Dorothy's paw back at her. Laughter rolled around the crowd, and I got a very strange feeling in my stomach. It was . . . enjoyment.

Well, shit.

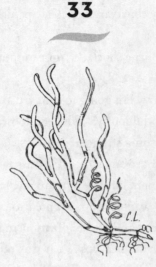

33

EELGRASS
ZOSTERA CAPENSIS

I wasn't entirely sure why Nate's was where I wanted to be after the taping, but I found myself texting him afterward and knocking on his door within the hour.

He opened the door and looked at me, his smile widening.

"Huh," he said, stepping back to let me in. "I'm not sure I've ever seen you looking this energized. You've looked happy, sure, but you are glowing."

"It wasn't terrible!" I said, walking into his living room and looking around. So. Many. Boats. Model boats and wooden ships crowded surfaces, some still under construction, others complete and gleaming. Large blueprints and construction plans were framed on the walls. The house was about ten minutes away from my mom's, nearer the heart of Venice. Hidden behind high walls and through a shady courtyard, a classic Spanish. "It was fun! People were nice!"

He laughed. "What a shock . . . Your misanthropy is really taking a beating lately."

I nodded. "I know. I'm going to start trusting the press next."

"Well," he said dubiously, "don't go too far. Do you want a drink? Beer? Something stronger?"

"Uh . . . do you have any scotch?" I wasn't sure this was a wise call, but at that moment it made sense to me. I suddenly realized I was here because I wanted him. Wanted to continue what we'd started on the beach, and the realization made me nervous. It wasn't that *he* made me nervous . . . It was the way I felt around him that made me nervous. I was scared by how much I had come to want him, to care about him, from what felt like nothing.

He nodded. "Sure. Ice? Soda?"

I shook my head. "Neat is fine."

I walked around the living room and paused in front of the bookcases. I frowned as he came up behind me and handed me my drink. I could smell him, feel the warmth of his hand as I took the glass. I sipped the scotch, felt the heat on my tongue. Why was everything about heat right now? *For crying out loud, Christa, hold it together.*

"Not what you expected?" he said, looking at my face.

I frowned. "The scotch?"

He grinned, and shook his head. "No, the books."

I turned back to look, tilting my head to read the titles. After a moment, I looked back at him. "No, not really."

The grin was still there, and as he looked down at me, I noticed the faintest dimples on his cheeks, deeper on the left side. Dimples are the result of a bifurcation of facial . . . You don't need to know that. I often reach for science in situations where science doesn't really apply. There was nothing clinical or scientific about the way his dimples made me feel, I promise.

"I guess I didn't realize how into sailing you are. I mean, you used to sail . . ." I turned back to the bookcase. Books on sailing generally, sure, but also manuals from specific boats, books of plans, maps and route guides. And not just one or two. Shelves of them. It was reassuring to see some Lee Child mixed in, some Wode-house, some Piers Anthony. I smiled and tapped one of the spines.

"Fantasy?"

He'd turned away and was heading to the sofa. "Why not? I read those as a teen, and they stuck around because sometimes I need a little levity, right?"

I leaned back against the shelves, not quite ready to join him on the sofa. "Sure. I'm more of an Ursula K. Le Guin fan myself."

He shrugged. "It's all good. I love her too."

I pushed off from the shelves and went to sit down. I curled my feet up under me and drank a little more scotch. It wasn't hitting me yet, but I knew it would. Another old friend. "Nothing for you?"

He wasn't drinking, and shook his head. "No, I'm good." He leaned forward suddenly, and touched my forearm. "What's this one? Is it an eel?"

I jumped, which wasn't awkward at all, and looked down at the tattoo he was pointing to. "Uh." *Oh my God, Christa, take a breath.* "That's a hagfish. It's not an eel, although, you know, it kind of looks like one."

He moved closer and frowned, taking my hand. His finger traced the tattoo, which ran around my arm. He turned my arm over, following the tattoo down the soft skin of my inner arm.

I shivered. I couldn't help it, and he looked up at me, his eyes dancing. "And why the hagfish?" He paused. "It's not very . . ."

I frowned, and debated whether to pull my arm away. "If you're about to say *pretty*, don't. The hagfish might be a long tube with a mouth on one end, but if you grab it, it exudes an incredibly fibrous slime that will completely immobilize you and then, while you're floundering around unable to breathe or see, it will tie itself into a knot, clear itself of its own slime and disappear."

He raised his eyebrows. "Huh." He hesitated . . . "No, I have absolutely no response to that." He turned my arm again, walking his fingers up to another tattoo, just above my elbow. "And this guy?" He ran his finger around the shape of the stonefish, carefully tracing each spine.

My God, I was getting so turned on. He was literally just touching me. Barely even that, just the whisper of a fingertip against my skin. I've said it before, and I'll say it again: I am officially losing my mind.

"That's a stonefish. The most venomous fish in the ocean. Step on one of these guys and you may or may not live to regret it."

His eyebrows had gone down, but now they went up again and he let go of my arm and sat back. Still close. Still very close. "Are all your tattoos of deadly animals?" He looked quickly at my other arm. "I see a snail. That's presumably harmless."

I laughed. "That one is, yes. That's just one of my little bubble guys." I leaned forward and tilted to show him the back of my shoulder. "But that one there is a cone snail. They're also pretty badass. They have a harpoon-like tooth that injects a powerful neurotoxin."

He laughed. "At least that one's pretty."

"Sure." I straightened up. "But pretty is as pretty does, right? And if you're a little fish, pottering around, minding your own business, it's not something you want to catch sight of."

He was still very close. "Now all I can think of is the dad in *Finding Nemo*."

"Why?"

He shrugged. "He's the poster child for nervous fish, right?"

I stared at him. "Uh . . . isn't he essentially the only one?"

He shrugged. "I guess." He reached over to my collarbone and tapped the top of a tattoo that was only just visible over the collar of my shirt. "What's this one? I saw it on the beach but . . ." He looked at me. "I was distracted."

I blushed. Twenty-seven years old, blushing.

"That's eelgrass . . . Zostera . . . super important marine plant."

He used his fingertip to pull down the collar of my shirt a little, and smiled. "I seem to remember it goes all the way . . ."

I looked down to where his finger was hooked around my shirt. "It's . . ." I swallowed. "A promising source of carbon sequestration."

He leaned forward and kissed me. "Is it?" he asked, pulling back a little, then leaning in again. "Tell me more."

I felt my breath catch in my throat as he closed his teeth very, very gently on my bottom lip, tugging for a split second before his hand left my shirt collar and threaded itself into my hair, cupping the back of my head behind my ear and pulling me close, his lips firm and warm on mine.

"Well," I said shakily, "the process of . . ." His mouth was on the move, traveling down my neck, across my shoulder. I stopped talking. There was no point, as my mind had completely emptied of all scientific information, filled instead with the scent of his hair,

the sensation of his lips on my collarbone. I could feel my back starting to arch as I pressed against him, wanting to get closer. I gave
up and reached for him, curving my hand across his ribs, feeling
him take a sharp inhale just as he had in the surf.

"Christa," he said softly, "I want . . ." His voice tailed off and I
kissed him, hard, suddenly understanding this was about to happen, that I was going to get what I wanted. I'd known on the beach
that it was foreplay, that there was going to be a next step, and now
the moment was here.

"Nate," I whispered against his mouth, "I want too . . ." I
straightened on the sofa, tipping myself up onto my knees in front
of him. I put both my hands on his head, pulling his mouth tightly
against mine as we kissed, and I felt my body start to flush, a heat
that began between my legs and spread outward.

He reached for the hem of my T-shirt, but I beat him to it,
crossing my arms and tugging the shirt off in one easy movement.
I watched his eyes darkening, his pupils dilating. He bent his head
and started kissing along the lace of my bra, one hand resting on
the curve of my waist, the other grazing the underside of my breast.
I gasped, my head falling back, as he moved to take my nipple in
his mouth, biting gently. I felt dizzy, my breath catching in my
throat, my words lost. Then I reached behind and undid my bra,
tossing it to one side, keeping my eyes on his face as he took me in,
sighing, then bent his head again to slowly trace my nipples with
his tongue. As they hardened in his mouth, I heard him groan,
then he nipped the very tip of them with his teeth, exquisitely, then
immediately sucked away the pain. I gasped, so aroused, feeling
myself growing hotter with every movement of his mouth.

Nate wrapped his arms around my waist, then slid them down,

cupping my ass and pulling me against his hips, the shape of him making it very clear he was as turned on as I was. For a moment he looked into my face, his skin flushed, his desire as open in his eyes as it was in his body, then he bent his head and bit me gently where my neck curved into my shoulder. It hurt a little, it tickled a little, and I moaned as I felt a pulse of hot and wet between my legs. He lifted me so I could unfold my legs, then laid me down on the sofa, propping himself above me. His hands slid up and over my breasts, turning me to liquid, making me close my eyes as the ache deepened, becoming insistent. He stroked one of my breasts with the flat of his hand, while he curved his hand around the other, pinching and squeezing tightly, making me cry out as pleasure rippled through my body.

He moved again, looking into my face. "Can I take you to my bedroom?" he asked. "I'd like to . . ."

I couldn't speak, but nodded.

He stood, picking me up easily, then carried me down the hallway, kicking open a doorway and moving quickly to lay me on his bed. While I enjoy a show of strength as much as the next woman, I sat up and reached for him, tugging him close until he was between my legs at the side of the bed.

I looked up at him, unbuckling his belt, pushing his jeans open, pulling him free of his underwear. I won't go into it, but oh my God . . . he was so hard, so delicious. I licked up the length of him, taking him in my mouth as I sat on the side of the bed, feeling his thigh muscles jumping as he tried to stay standing, smiling around him as I pulled him tightly into my mouth, taking as much of him as I could, sucking and circling him with my tongue, then pulling away, for the moment. I stood up and started undoing my own jeans, but he pushed my hands away, and when I looked up into his face, I could see he was feeling the same urgency I was.

He tugged my jeans off, then my panties, and as I lay down on the bed, he tossed his own clothes away and came to join me. He paused, smiled at me, then moved down to kiss me just above my knees, licking along the soft, smooth skin of my inner thighs. I wanted to watch him, but I was overwhelmed by the sensation of his tongue and closed my eyes, feeling the tickling of his stubble against the inner crease of my thigh, the softness of his breath against me. I rested my hands on his head as he pushed my legs wide and licked and sucked until I moaned his name, and started wordlessly pulling on his shoulders, his hair, trying to tug him up so I could feel him inside. He looked up and grinned at me, then moved to kiss me. I could taste myself on his skin, in his mouth, the heat of his tongue against mine, and I was moaning against his lips, almost beside myself, going mad with longing.

"*Please,*" I moaned. "*Please, Nate . . .*"

He started gently, slowly, but then with one thrust he was all the way in, so hard and deep I cried out, wrapping my legs around him, pulling him even tighter inside. The sensation was overwhelming, his every stroke moving through me like a wave that started everywhere at once. I looked up into his face and could see he was as overtaken as I was, the connection between us even deeper than I had anticipated.

His mouth was on mine, both of us kissing and biting and licking and panting as he pushed into me over and over and harder and harder . . . I was so close, so fast, the waiting of the last week forgotten in the face of such intense pleasure. I could feel myself starting to peak, and then just as I couldn't hold it any longer, I heard his breathing start to change, and realized he was close too.

"Don't stop, baby," I whispered, ". . . please don't wait . . ."

He groaned, pushing so deep into me, and I felt myself letting go just as I felt his heat inside me growing, the sound of him saying my name over and over the only thing I could hear over the beating of my own heart. I wrapped myself so tightly around him and felt the ache finally start to subside.

As he relaxed and settled against my breasts, his breathing slowing against my neck, I realized something.

Now I was really in trouble. Now I was going to want to stay. And that was simply not an option.

IN THE NEWS . . .

ABC.COM: See Christa Liddle and Dorothy the Bear doing tricks!

TMZ.COM: Christa Liddle keeps her clothes on—and still impresses!!

ALLABOUTBEARS.COM: The history of the grizzly—and why Dorothy loves mints!

DEADLINE.COM: Rumors of Christa Liddle biopic start to swirl.

HOLLYWOODREPORTER.COM: Christa Liddle signs with DRA, first-look deal at Netflix.

NATIONALGEOGRAPHIC.COM: VIDEO: Christa Liddle explains de-extinction, with some help from Dorothy!

34

ELEGANT TERN
THALASSEUS ELEGANS

I left Nate sleeping and went home to sleep in my own bed. (I left him a note; it's not like I left money on the bedside table, people, I just sleep better alone.) I was exhausted physically, and more than exhausted emotionally. I'd been nervous about the show, and it had gone so well. I'd been nervous about sleeping with Nate, and it had gone incredibly well. I was so confused on so many levels for so many reasons that I fully expected to sleep for several days. However, I woke up at the usual early hour and, after lying in bed gazing at the ceiling for a while, decided to give in and let the day go where it wanted. I got dressed, fed Marcel (he'd adapted quickly to another potential feeder in the house and was waiting in the kitchen when I got there) and headed out for my morning walk by the ocean, my nature journal tucked under my arm.

I was just starting to muse pleasantly on my time with Nate (his eyes, his hands, the way his eyes looked when he was using his hands . . .) when I realized someone was sitting on the ground by our gate, fast asleep. It was Alex Dutton.

I closed the gate quietly and pondered my options. There was a giant cup of coffee on the ground, but clearly it hadn't worked. I slid down the wall and sat next to him. Nothing. I nudged him with my shoulder.

He turned his head without lifting it from the wall and opened one eye. Seeing it was me, he smiled and closed it again.

"I was waiting for you," he said. His English accent was thicker than ever, his voice sleepy. "You were on the TV. I saw it." He smiled, still with his eyes closed. "You were very pretty."

I smiled too, not that he could see me. "Why are you here so early?" I said.

"Because I didn't go to bed yet. It's *not* early, it's very, very late last night." I suddenly realized he wasn't one hundred percent sober.

I gazed at him and waited. After a minute I said, "Are you going to tell me why, or am I supposed to guess?"

"You know, Christa," he replied, opening his eyes, "you're very often exasperated with me, and I want you to know it's not attractive."

"Excellent," I replied. "Best news I've heard all day." I gave him a stern look. "Are you going to spit it out, or are you just dancing with your own mortality by getting this close to my mother?"

Alex Dutton had a pleasing laugh, and he laughed now. "Oh, dancing with mortality, definitely," he shot back, then grinned. "You always come out swinging, don't you, Christa?" He eyed me, and again, there was that little frisson, dammit. Why is it you crawl

across a flirtation desert for months and then suddenly you're surrounded on all sides by appealing people?

"Listen," he continued, all business again, "I need to show you
something."

I shrugged. "Knock yourself out."

He lifted his butt a little and slid out a large envelope he'd been
sitting on. "I was up all night going over agency archives, and I
found this." He handed it over and watched as I pinched together
the little metal wings.

I raised my eyebrows at him. "Does it need this big reveal? Can't
you just tell me?"

"My God, woman, will you do as you're fucking told for once?"
he said.

I paused and raised my eyebrow at him. He put up his palms
immediately, and after staring at him coolly for a moment, I emptied the envelope onto my lap. Half a dozen xeroxed sheets, with
photos and text. I looked up at Alex again. "Please cut to the chase.
I don't have time for scrapbooking."

He said, "Those are company newsletters, from when the Davis
Reed Agency was starting. Party pictures, babies and anniversaries, that kind of thing." I must have been looking confused, because he did that sarcastic head tip thing he does. "I realize you're
a professional recluse, but you must have heard of these things?"

"Babies and anniversaries? Yes, I've heard of them."

"Then look . . ." He pointed to one of the sheets and I looked
closely. Holiday party, 1994. Costumes, gaiety, mirth.

I was starting to get irritated. "You're killing me. What am I
supposed to be seeing?"

He sighed and sat up straighter against the wall. He shook himself and prodded the newsletter again. "*That.*"

I looked. A woman, blond, sweet-faced, wearing a Santa hat. She was familiar, but I couldn't place her.

Alex slid his finger down to the caption and read it out loud: *"Account services manager Lorna Wesson celebrates the season with colleagues Sid Meltzer and Aurelio Saiz."*

I frowned. "Why do I know that name?"

Alex Dutton sounded genuinely disappointed. "You're being remarkably obtuse, Christa."

"Hey," I snapped back, "I'm not at my best first thing in the morning."

He looked at me. "I have personal evidence to the contrary, but let me spell this out. That's Lorna, the woman who rescued your father in the Alaskan wilderness and spent the rest of her life with him. That's her, working for Davis Reed three years before your father disappeared."

I looked at the face again. Sweet. Gentle. Normal. Not a face to launch a thousand lies, and yet . . .

Plot twist.

I sat there for about twenty seconds, shaking the snow globe that is my brain and letting it settle. "So," I said, tentatively, "are we saying the woman in the wilderness was not a stranger?"

"Yes." Alex Dutton handed me his coffee and I took a healthy swig. As I'd suspected, it was at least a quarter scotch. Bless his hardened British liver. "That's what we're saying."

I'm really not sparky first thing, but I was getting there. I said, "She worked at the agency the whole time he was doing the show. They would have interacted frequently."

Alex nodded, offering me the cup again.

I took another sip. "His mistress, then?"

Alex barely shrugged, but I got it.

"So now what do we do?" I looked around. "If he lied about that, what else did he lie about? Everything? Why, for crying out loud?" I felt a mixture of disappointment and self-recrimination. I knew I shouldn't have let my guard down. I should have gone with my first impression, dammit.

Alex shrugged. "I'm still digging. I don't want to say anything yet."

I rubbed my hands together. "I've got a better idea. Let's go find him right now and ask him." I stood up. "Let's do that." I started bouncing from foot to foot. I couldn't believe I had nearly hugged Jasper.

Alex shook his head. "No, Christa, we have to be sure."

I looked at him for a moment, confused. But then I got it.

"Oh my God, you're scared of Davis Reed," I said. "You're working for him. You don't want to piss him off."

Alex Dutton might have been drunk, but the look he gave me would have sobered anyone. A major problem with English people—in my limited experience—is that they're generally mellow as long as you don't accuse them of either cowardice or hypocrisy, at which point they turn into stalactites of bitter reproof. It's like a hidden extra gear.

My turn to raise my palms. "You're right. I'm sorry." I was contrite. "What's the plan?"

Alex Dutton regarded me coldly for a moment more, then relaxed and said, "It's a simple plan: You do nothing. There's something going on beyond the obvious."

I frowned. "Sorry, which part is obvious?"

"That he faked his death."

"Right," I said. "That main part."

"But that's just one piece of it, I think." He frowned at me. "Can you give me a day or two and keep your lips buttoned?"

I nodded. "Can I tell my sisters?"

"No." He looked scornful at the suggestion.

"My mother?"

"Definitely not."

I thought about it. "Yeah, probably wise. They might push him out a window."

"Agreed." Alex gave me a look. "I'm sorry, Christa." He got to his feet and wobbled a little.

I stood up and steadied him, ignoring his apology. "Too much coffee?" I said jokingly. "You're not driving, are you?"

He grinned. "No, I'll sober up in the cab, eat in the airport, sleep on the plane and arrive in Alaska ready to roll."

"I'm tempted to say good luck, but I don't know why. I'd much rather you found nothing."

He gave me a straight look. "You think maybe it's just a coincidence? That he crashed a plane in the middle of a hundred million miles of forested wilderness and happened to land next to an old work colleague from another state?"

I sighed. "Doesn't sound deeply plausible, does it?"

"I'll call you as soon as I know anything," said Alex. "I really am sorry he's lying. I don't know why he is, but promise me you won't blow your stack until I get back?"

I nodded.

He paused. "Promise," he said firmly.

I nodded again, and he tipped his head and sighed.

"OK," I said, "I promise. I won't do anything till you get back."

He narrowed his eyes at me, but let it go. We parted, him to go find a cab and me to the beach. I was surprised to find myself close to tears . . . of what? Disappointment? Anger?

No . . . it was my old friend grief.

I texted Nate to meet me on the beach and started walking in that direction, trying to calm myself. I took slow, steady steps just above the surf line, where the sand was packed and cool. My favorite slice of any beach; the perfect ratio of silica to salt water.

Epipelagic

Mesopelagic

Bathypelagic

Abyssopelagic

Hadalpelagic

Nate hadn't really asked any questions. When I'd said it was urgent, he said he'd leave right away. But when I spotted him walking toward me, he didn't look particularly hurried. He was walking steadily, sure, but he was also gazing out to sea and watching birds and generally looking . . . engaged. I have to acknowledge that my earlier concerns about how his energy would sit with me were misplaced. His energy sits with me just fine.

We came within hailing distance eventually, and I could see his smile as clearly as I wanted to. There's no point in pretending I don't find him profoundly attractive. Having slept with him, I now found him not only attractive, but deeply compelling. I wanted more. More sex, definitely, but also more driving his car, more walking on the beach, more discussion of his books, more . . . him. You know it, I know it, I just don't know what to do about it apart from the short-term and obvious. The night before had been incredible, I'd thoroughly enjoyed every second, but surely, sexual attraction that intense couldn't last and didn't necessarily mean we were going to have, you know, an actual relationship. Besides, I was leaving in two weeks. Slightly less, actually.

Nate wrapped his arms tightly around me, bending his head to kiss me as deeply as if we'd been separated for weeks, rather than hours. I let him hold me up for a moment as I twined around him in return, as pleased to say hello as he was. But then I put my feet back under me and stepped apart.

"Hi there," I said inadequately.

"Dammit, Christa, you're overwhelmingly pretty." Nate was looking a little windswept, and obviously exerting a great deal of self-control. "I know you have something to tell me, but can you tell me while we walk back to my place so I can take your clothes off and spend the day in bed?" He kissed me again, his hands tight around my hips. "I've been thinking about that little sound you make, and I want to hear it again." He kissed my neck, and when I didn't respond, he paused, and angled his head to see me better.

"Shit," he said, stepping back. "Not going to lie, I was watching you walk toward me and I kept thinking about last night . . . your skin and your eyes and your wrists . . ." He made a grumbling noise in his throat. "And I completely forgot you called this meeting." He turned and walked up to where the sand was dry, sat, and patted the sand next to him. "I'm sorry, you have my full attention."

I walked up and joined him.

"One question," I said, wiggling my butt to make a sand chair, "before I tell you the latest ridiculous piece of news. My wrists?" I raised an eyebrow.

He blushed a little, but grinned. "You have beautiful wrists. Actually, all your points of articulation are lovely."

I tightened my lips. "Points of articulation?" I asked. I could feel the side of his body against mine as we sat and realized from the minute I'd seen him ahead of me in silhouette, I'd felt better. Easier in my skin. Less worried that disaster was about to ensue. Having said that, this comforting thing he does wasn't going to stop me from making fun of him.

He coughed. "Yes, wrists, elbows, shoulders, neck, ankles . . . hips." He was fully red now. "It's a toy-manufacturing term."

I laughed out loud. "Like an action figure? You like my bendable parts?" I'd walked onto this beach angry and confused, and after two minutes with Nate, I was amused and slightly turned on. "No one has ever commented on my joints before. I really have no good comeback."

Nate smiled. "For once. Go on, tell me your thing."

I pulled out the xeroxed sheet I'd taken from Alex's little sheaf. I handed it to him. "Look at the picture at the bottom, and the caption."

There was a short pause as he took it in. I was assuming he'd be as lost as I had been, but irritatingly, he said, "Holy crap, that's the woman." He looked up at me. "The woman from Alaska, right? When was this taken?"

"Years before he disappeared." Maybe I needed to get my eyes examined. Right after my head.

He sat for a while in silence, organizing his thoughts or screaming internally, who knows? Finally, he said, "What the actual fuck."

I leaned against him. "Dude." I tipped my head up against his shoulder so I could see him. "Why would he lie about one part, when he's already admitting so much? I'm finding it all kind of mystifying."

"No shit," he said lightly, kissing me on the forehead. "Do you want to make a run for it?" He looked at his watch. "It's not even ten—we could wake up tomorrow in Paris, or we could jump in the car right now and hit the freeway. Tijuana for lunch and a long siesta." He smiled and looked at me the way he'd looked at me the night before. He took my hand and hooked his over mine, tracing the edges of my fingers. His hair was a little messy, blowing in the stiff breeze, and I wondered if he'd literally gotten out of bed to walk to meet me. The sheets would still be warm. Tempting. Oh, so tempting.

I shook my head. "Can't leave Mom. Definitely not without telling Lennie and Amelia."

He grinned. "Isn't that like hanging the guy before the trial? They'll tear him apart."

I didn't want to think about my sisters getting angry. I watched the seagulls swoop and bully the pipers. A few elegant terns (that's their name; I'm not commenting on their deportment) were watching nearby, and I wondered as always whether or not animals discuss one another the way we do.[1]

Nate continued. "Wait and see what the journalist finds." He paused. "What was his name again?"

"Alex Dutton."

"Why did he tell you?" He looked at me. "I thought you hated him."

I knew this was coming. "No, that's Mom. I don't hate him, but

---

1. "Oh my GOD, did you see her feathers???"

I wouldn't call us friends." There was no point in not telling the truth. "We had a brief fling years ago, then he wrote that irritating article and I hadn't laid eyes on him for years until the other day at the airport."

"How brief?" He was frowning, but not very hard.

"Brief. Days."

"Huh." He half shrugged. "I was married at that point, so I can hardly complain. What do you think he's going to discover in Alaska?"

"No idea. Not sure anything he finds is going to make a difference."

"No?" He looked at me. "Doesn't intention make a difference? It does in law."

I nodded, but said, "This isn't law; it's just people. Jasper might have had problematic intentions twenty-five years ago. But if he's ready to make amends, who are we to stand in judgment?" The seagulls were now harassing a small child farther up the beach, and she couldn't decide if it was funny or terrifying, her cries veering wildly between giggles and gibbering fear. *Baby, you and me both.* I was also abruptly aware I was arguing a position I wasn't certain I agreed with. Why *was* I siding with Jasper? Because we both like animals? Because he'd defended me on national television?

"I don't know." Nate frowned. "Isn't it wrong to lie? If he had a mistress, why didn't he simply file for divorce?" He shook his head. "It's not like people don't do it every day. Choosing instead to fake your death and hide in the Alaskan wilderness for twenty-five years seems like overkill." He snorted. "It's pathological. It's weird. It's not normal."

I understand my dad disappeared when Nate was ten, an age

when Jasper probably represented peak coolness. He was on TV. He got to hold spiders. I get it. But Nate had his own dad, and it abruptly started to annoy me that he was so pissed off with mine.

I said firmly, "No one's pretending it's normal. Nothing about any of this is normal. Including whatever it is you think *this* is." I waved my hands between us and recognized I was losing my temper. I'd expended a lot of calories the night before. I really should have eaten. "Listen, a week ago I would have considered it an interesting day if the single store on the island started carrying a new soda, and I was OK with that. Ever since I left the island, it's been one ridiculous thing after another. To start with, of course, we've got dead dad walking. Then you show up all sexy as fuck and hot to get in my pants, Lennie and Amelia want me to address my suppressed rage or whatever, and it's really only Mom who's got anything good to say at all."

Now, before you get all up in my beak, I understand none of that was completely true. I mean, sure, some of it was true, but mostly, I think I was finally cracking under the strain of not cracking under the strain. Nate opened his mouth to reply, but before he could say a word, I added, "I'm not saying he's a hero. I'm just saying give Alex a day or two to do his thing."

He snapped back, "Like you did?"

There was a moment, right then, where we could have backed it up and started over. The sun was starting to come out, it was early in the day, he was probably as hungry as I was. He could have said, *I'm sorry, that was out of line*, and I could have said, *I know this is upsetting for you too*, but instead what I said was this.

"Fuck. You." I stood up. "Look, Nate, I'm just going to call this now. It's been fun, but now we're done. This is way too much drama for a fling." The minute I said it, I wanted to take it back. It wasn't too much. It wasn't even just a fling, whether I wanted to consciously admit it or not.

He stayed sitting, leaning back to look up at me. "Ouch. That's what you think this is? Just sex?"

Being me, I doubled down. "What else could it possibly be, Nate? We barely know each other and we don't live in the same city. I can't handle this along with everything else. Maybe next summer? Maybe a year from now? Maybe never."

He got to his feet, slowly, brushing off the sand and taking a beat to think. An interesting approach. I should consider it.

He looked at me, and I could see I'd hurt him. "I'm sorry, Christa. I don't know exactly what this is, but I'm certain it's not just a fling. We've known each other our whole lives. Sure, there's a lot of chemistry, but there's also a lot of everything else. I think you're brilliant, and funny, and a little bit terrifying and a lot unpredictable . . . I care about you."

"Well, don't." I turned to walk away.

"Christa . . ." He called after me. "Please, can you just . . ."

I turned back, suddenly feeling the most terrible wave of regret. I wanted to walk right back into his arms and put my cheek against his chest and listen to his heart. I felt safe with him, but it couldn't be real, this fast. It was confusing and it hurt, so I did what I always do.

I swung, and I swung hard.

"Why do you even give a shit, Nate? How can any of this really matter to you?" I was struggling with myself, fighting to keep my temper because I knew my anger was stepping in to protect me from a growing tightness in my chest. "I'll be leaving soon, and we probably won't see each other any more frequently than we have for the last decade."

Nate ran his fingers through his hair, clearly annoyed. "Why do you say that? What have I done that suggests this doesn't matter to me, that it's not just as disruptive and overwhelming for me as it is for you?" He raised his eyebrows. "Because I didn't have to get dragged off an island? Because my dad didn't come back from the dead? You're right, I was here all along, not hiding away and pretending."

"Pretending what?"

"Pretending you're not lonely. That you don't need anyone, or anything."

"I don't."

"And as for your dad, don't you think I'd love it if my dad came back, for even a fucking minute?"

"Yeah, because your dad was awesome and mine is a big, lying coward."

Nate stopped. "You think he was a coward? For giving everything up for the woman he loved?"

"No, for not doing it honestly, publicly."

He looked incredulous. "Really? After everything you've said about the media, about what the press did to you? Maybe he loved her so much he wanted to protect her from that." He hesitated. "I would want to protect you."

I frowned at him. "Maybe it was easier for him to hide. Maybe it was as simple as that."

"Is that why you do it?"

I glared at him. "I'm not hiding from anything. I'm working."

"You're literally as far away from here as it's possible to be."

I looked at his face, so handsome, so kind, so openhearted and affectionate. Already so dear to me. And then I said, "Well, right now it doesn't feel anything like far enough."

I started walking down the beach, knowing I had just been cruel, knowing I had hurt someone who'd done nothing but be nice to me. He hadn't said my name again; he was letting me go. So I walked and let the breeze blow the tears from my eyes before they even had a chance to fall.

I'd like to say the day improved from there, but sadly, it did nothing of the kind.

35

COCA-COLA BOTTLE
POTUM COKUM

As I approached my block again, I realized Jordan, Davis's assistant, was standing at the end of the street. I frowned and quickened my pace.

"Hi there," I said as I got close. "What's up?"

Jordan smiled at me politely. "Mr. Reed would like to talk to you, if you're available."

I frowned. "Uh, sure." I looked at him. "He sent you here to tell me that in person? Does he want me to call or come to the office?"

Jordan shook his head. "Neither. He wanted to talk to you privately, so he's here."

I looked around. I really didn't have the patience for whatever this was. I turned up my palms. "Where, exactly?"

Jordan turned and pointed. A long, low limousine was illegally parked a little way down the street. I turned back to Jordan and made a face.

"We're having a conversation in the back of a limo? That's a little dramatic, isn't it?"

Jordan looked mildly taken aback. "Everything Mr. Reed does is dramatic. This is Hollywood."

And people wonder why I prefer an island in the middle of nowhere.

I sighed. "Let's do this thing." I walked over and knocked on the window, which, of course, smoothly and slowly lowered. "You wanted to talk to me, Mr. Reed?"

He was sitting on the back seat in the opposite corner, elegant and sophisticated and clearly waiting for me. "Please join me, Miss Liddle."

Internally reviewing all the advice I'd been given about not getting into cars with strange men, I got into the car.

Davis Reed gazed at me for a moment and then smiled broadly. "Last night was a triumph."

Last night? There was no way he could be referring to me and Nate, which was the only thing I could think . . .

Wait. Last night. *The Really Late Show.* Jesus, was that only last night? Things move fast around here.

I smiled a little. "Thanks, but I think the credit goes to Dorothy."

He nodded. "Yes, the bear was the biggest hit, but sadly, she's not an agency client. You, however, also did very well, and there was a whole reaction to your mistreatment as a younger woman that I think we could definitely work with."

I thought about that for a second, but needed more. "Uh, how do you mean?"

"Well, the whole Time's Up, Me Too, Britney thing. There's a definite reckoning over how the media treated women in the past, and I think the audience reaction last night indicates people are ready to reframe you as a victim."

"I'm not a victim," I replied.

"Yes, of course you are," he said. "The press made sport of you for a couple of years and then you were sent away to boarding school."

At first I was like, *Wait, how does he know that?* And then I remembered that he knows everything. Jordan probably looked it up. Jordan, for what it's worth, was standing outside the car, checking his phone. Doubtless coordinating an airlift of some sort.

"So the point is, we've received multiple calls this morning already asking about your interest and availability. Netflix would like to offer you a solo show on an issue that matters to you, National Geographic offered a three-part miniseries on a topic of your choosing, and Amazon suggested a podcast-livestream combo on something that concerns you."

I was surprised. "Why? I don't know anything about making content or TV shows or anything like that."

"Of course not," replied Davis, "but there are plenty of people who do, but who nobody would recognize on the street. We'll pair you up, don't worry."

I frowned. "I'm not sure, Davis. Maybe you should just stick with Jasper."

He frowned back at me. "Your father's career trajectory is limited by his age and narrative failures. You, on the other hand . . . The agency would love to represent you and build a career."

"Like you built Jasper's?"

"Sure." He nodded.

"And will you cover up for me if I run away?"

Davis looked at me and went silent and still for a second, as though running a diagnostic. "I'm not sure what you mean."

I hesitated. I couldn't believe I'd just blurted it out like that. Honestly, Alex Dutton was going to be so pissed with me if I ruined his scoop. But at the same time, fuck it.

"I mean that Lorna, the woman my dad ran off with, worked at your company," I said calmly. "Alex Dutton found pictures of her in the company archive." I looked at him and realized something. "You knew he would."

He raised his right index finger half an inch, his equivalent of a shrug. "I knew it was a possibility."

"A possibility you could have avoided, presumably?"

Davis looked out the window for the moment, watching people pass by. His suit, I noticed, was some marginal shade between blue and black that perfectly set off the oyster shell cream of his shirt. He might be an evil serpent in human form, but damn, the man could dress. He sighed, as if having to explain something simple to a child.

"In order to keep a story alive and fresh, one must continually provide new details. By inviting Alex Dutton into the archives, I was rolling the dice. It could have taken him weeks to work it out, or even longer, but I had a pretty good sense he would find it eventually."

"But why?" I asked. "Why not let the lie stand?"

Davis shrugged. "Well, for one, it will make Alex Dutton's profile piece far more explosive, which will create a bidding war. Secondly, the weakness in Jasper's narrative is an abandoned wife and children left to fend for themselves. Nobody wants to play that guy. A much stronger character arc is a man who gave up everything for the woman he loved, bravely risking his life in the process." He snapped his fingers. "They'll be lining up to play that one."

I stared at him. "You do know you're talking about my actual life, right? It's not simply storyboards for a movie."

He looked pityingly at me. "I'm afraid you're missing the point. The *story* is what we tell people to believe about your life. Your *life* is what you actually live, and generally, you try and keep that away from the public. And finally, the gap between the two is where people like me can get creative. A little bit of fact, a little bit of fiction, and suddenly you have a Narrative."

I laughed in his face. "Here's your problem, Mr. Reed. Do you want to know the real Achilles' heel of Jasper's story right now? Me. I'm going to tell my family the truth the minute I see them. Good luck finessing the timing on that. You'll see it on the ten o'clock news tonight, as an explanation for why my mother beat my father to death with her shoes."

Davis considered that. "May I make a suggestion? Why not let your mother continue to believe what is essentially the truth: Her husband went away for twenty-five years, and now he's back."

"Because it's not actually true?"

Davis laughed. "But what is truth, really? I mean, genuinely." He reached for his bottle of water. (I assume it was water. It could have been the spinal fluid of orphaned pandas; he really isn't a very nice person.) "Here's the thing, Christa. These additional revelations aren't supposed to come out just yet. Right now the story is very much about your dad's return, and for now I want to keep it that way." He undid the bottle and took a sip. "I would hate to see anything change my timeline, and I'm willing to take steps to protect it."

I looked at him and said nothing. I could hear another shoe being loosened, ready to drop.

I bit. I couldn't help it. "What kind of steps?"

Davis recapped the bottle and replaced it in the walnut-lined cupholder. "Well, everyone is focused on your dad right now, which makes sense, he's the main story. However, you're also having a moment, especially after last night, and if there was breaking news about *you*, I'm pretty sure the world would be happy to pick it up and run with it. At least for an uncomfortable amount of time."

I held my tongue. Fortunately, Davis loved to hear himself threaten.

"Do you remember, Christa, the night of the gala?"

I nodded silently.

"What an unfortunate evening that was." He shook his head sadly. "Those young men, so ill-advised. You were lucky Mr. Donovan noticed you leaving and I happened to be paying attention." He raised his eyebrows. "I always had my eye on you, Christa. You had star quality even then. I understand you and Nathan Donovan have reconnected on this visit—that's something else the press would enjoy, a little romance to go with the drama." He held up his hand and sketched an imaginary headline. "*He saved her once . . . now his love saves her again.*"

I raised my eyebrows at him, and was pleased to hear my voice was still steady. "Davis, you're being somewhat opaque. If you have a threat to make, please go ahead and make it."

"I have the footage from that night," he said calmly. "The video taken on that kid's phone."

"I thought you destroyed it. My mom said you had destroyed it." I could hear my heart suddenly.

"No, what I actually said at the time was that I had disposed of it. I did. I disposed of it right into a safe-deposit box where it sits to this day."

My chest was getting tight. "You just said yourself that people don't want to see me victimized again."

He smiled. "Nice people, sure, but there are a lot of people who would enjoy watching you . . . in trouble . . . and then click their tongues over the villainy of men. Then hit the *play* button again, just in case they missed something the first time." He shrugged. "Hypocrisy goes very nicely with privacy—have you noticed? In the light of the computer screen, you can indulge in any of the sins you criticize in daylight, including prurient interest in the lives of the young and famous."

I swallowed. "I was a minor when that incident took place, Davis."

He turned up his elegant hands. "Well then, we can turn the recording over to the police. Once it's in their hands, if pieces leak onto the Internet, we can just blame them." He shrugged. "Your parents decided to send you away to safety rather than press charges, but it's not too late for a flashy court case."

I was starting to feel light-headed, and suddenly, Davis leaned across the car and pulled a bottle of Coke from, apparently, a secret magical refrigerated vending machine. He popped the top and handed it to me.

"Drink this," he said. "You look a little faint. Sugar and caffeine will help."

I took it and drank, because I never turn down a bottle of Coke.

Sorry, I know it will dissolve a human tooth overnight, but have you had one lately?

Davis watched me and smiled faintly. "It's really up to you, Christa. All I ask is your silence, at least for a while. Let the story about your father come out at the right time, under my guidance. In return, I will destroy the footage from the gala and give you more money and fame than you know what to do with. Not interested in money and fame? Fair enough, then I will make sure your department head is very happy with whatever you choose to do, and I'm sure tenure can be arranged. You're a very intelligent woman. Be smart."

I burped semi-politely, to show my opinion, and opened the car door.

"Goodbye, Mr. Reed."

"Don't be hasty, Christa."

"I won't," I replied, and left the car.

I slammed the door and looked around. People were walking. Looking at their phones. Living their lives.

Time to *run*.

*T*he day of the Foundation Gala started poorly and went swiftly downhill.

I didn't wake up until four that afternoon, and when I did, I wasn't entirely sure I'd made it back to the corporeal world. I was in a foul mood, hungover from booze and a variety of pills, none of which should have been taken with alcohol, let alone with one another. I was also very much in the doghouse, having come home at 4 a.m. only to discover I'd left my key somewhere. I'd knocked on the front door as quietly as I could considering my advanced state of inebriation, but when Lennie had yanked it open, she'd wasted no time telling me what a piece of crap I was.

"You are so fucking selfish, Christa," she'd hissed at me as I pushed past her on the stairs. "You only care about yourself."

"Someone has to," I'd said, and then slammed the bedroom door so she couldn't hear me throwing up. What a bitch. She used to be cool,

but college has made her so fucking judgy. I looked up at my wall of posters. Jack Sparrow wouldn't judge me.

Now it was sometime after six in the evening and we were in the living room waiting for Mom to make her entrance. My head was killing me despite the four painkillers I'd taken. The Foundation threw two or three big parties a year, and we were expected to attend and be charming, because Mom took these events very seriously. Amelia was in cream satin, Lennie in blue velvet. I was wearing a red dress made of tulle that I really liked a lot, and I was curled around my phone on the sofa looking like a small, cranky raspberry.

"That's a pretty dress, Christa," said Mom, walking in quickly and looking around. "Little bit short, maybe?" The smell of Chanel No. 5, the swish of formal clothing, the scent of face powder—these things make me anxious.

"I like it," I muttered, scrolling. She ignored me, but I felt my sisters look at each other. Such a fucking disappointment, I thought to myself. Damn, it's exhausting, letting people down so hard.

"Are we all ready?" Mom continued. "Is the car here?" She looked around at Harry, who was beaming at her from across the room, his tuxedo immaculate, his gently handsome face one of the few that never looked at me with anything other than affection.

"Yes, my darling," he said, walking across to take her hand and kiss her. "You look incredible, as does everyone." He winked at me. "I happen to think Christa's dress is adorable."

"Hmm," Mom replied. She looked at me sharply. "Seriously, Christa, at least bring a wrap."

"Don't worry, Mom," said Lennie, "if she gets cold, she'll just find a group of guys to lie under."

Mom frowned at her, but Amelia added, "Or she'll steal something warm."

Accidentally, someone else's coat. One time.

"Plus," said Lennie, getting into it, "if she maintains her usual blood alcohol level, she won't physically be able to freeze."

"Ladies," said my mom disapprovingly. But not very loudly. I could never tell if she was scared of my sisters or simply amused by how funny they could be at my expense. I had gotten used to it, but tonight I was feeling a little fragile.

I stood up and stretched. My sisters had been my heroes when I was little, my most fervent wish being simply that they would notice me. All I wanted was their admiration, but these days, I got nothing but criticism, and was well on my way to believing I didn't care what they thought of me at all.

"All done?" I said, shaking out my dress. "Let's go."

Nothing to see here, people. Let's move this thing along.

The Beverly Hilton was a paradise of lights and flowers, and the warm evening air was filled with the competing scents of perfume, champagne and buckets and buckets of money. There was a red carpet area beside the entrance, and we were expected to walk it and pose for the press.

I hate it. Anytime you see pictures of the whole family, I'm the one on the edge, slightly excluded from the well-orchestrated pose of the others. My mom and sisters balance one another beautifully, Mom in the center, my sisters on either side, a triumvirate of beauty and elegance. Then there was me. As the car pulled up and the press surged forward, Mom turned to me. "Christa, please try and behave tonight. There are lots of people watching."

"There always are," I replied, but she wasn't listening anymore.

My stepfather, Harry, got out of the car first, in order to escort my mother in. Then my sisters, and finally me. As I was left alone in the car, I turned to the limo driver and said, "How much to peel out of here and head to Mexico?"

He looked at me and grinned. "Have a nice evening, miss."

I took a deep breath, wished I'd thought to bring a flask, and stepped out of the car.

Flashes. Shouting. My name.

"Hey, Christa! Exciting plans for tonight?" The paparazzi were mostly there for bigger fish, but some of the guys knew me from the club circuit, and were always poised to catch me making a fool of myself.

I shook my head. "Sorry, ladies, planning to keep it quiet this evening."

One of the photographers I knew well laughed out loud. "That's always the plan, Butterfly, right?"

I opened my mouth to respond, but suddenly someone took my elbow. I looked up to see John Donovan, and just behind him, Nathan, his son. Nate was friends with my sisters, but he knew me too. He didn't know I thought he was good-looking and charming and what I was increasingly recognizing as sexy. He probably didn't even think of me at all. I'm seventeen. He's twenty-four. I smiled at John.

"Hi there," I said. "Going in?"

John nodded. "How are you tonight, Christa? Everything good?" He smiled around at the photographers, but kept moving. John Donovan always makes me feel better; he's one of those people who don't take any crap, not now, not tomorrow, not anytime. Nate was right behind us, and I looked over my shoulder at him. He wasn't looking at me. It's fine.

In the main ballroom, John Donovan stayed by my side at first, but soon he was drawn away to glad-hand and chatter. I drifted around the edge of the room, smiling politely and avoiding conversation.

"Hey, Chrissie . . ." A low, vaguely familiar voice made me turn. "What's up, baby?"

A guy with a smoothly self-satisfied face had walked up and was holding out a glass of champagne. Damn, what was his name? Jack? Jake? Jim? One of those. We didn't really know each other, but I saw him all the time in the clubs; he was one of those smiley guys who always has plenty of coke. I had another flash of memory of possibly kissing this guy . . . or was it another guy who looked like him . . . but it wasn't exactly crystal clear.

"Hey there," I replied. "Nothing much, you know." Nope, really can't remember his name. I took the glass of champagne and drank off half of it in one swallow. It was really a very dry evening, and a little hair of the dog would probably settle my nerves.

"Did you want to . . . party at all?" He lowered his voice even further. "My cousin's here from New York. We were going to go clubbing after this."

I shook my head. "Sorry, have to stay straight tonight. This is kind of my family's thing, right?"

He raised his eyebrows. "Oh yeah, that's right. No worries." He grinned at where my nipples would be visible, if he'd had X-ray vision. "I like your dress."

I smiled, despite feeling the familiar ripple of anxiety at being stared at. "Thanks." I should have worn a wrap. I should have worn a fucking coat that went to my ankles and tied over my head. I finished the rest of the champagne.

Jason. His name is Jason. Thank you, brain.

"You finished your drink," he said, still staring at my chest. "Let me get you another."

"I'm fine," I replied, but he was gone. Having remembered his name, I would have called after him, but the crowd had swallowed him up immediately. Great, maybe I could make my escape.

I looked around and spotted Lennie and Amelia. I headed in their direction, hoping for a little safety in numbers. Maybe I could hang out with them and when they left I would go with them and it would all be fine. They stopped talking as I approached.

"Hi, guys," I said as I joined them. "How's it going?" I kept my tone light, neutral. This is me making peace . . . please let me stay with you . . .

"Fine," said Lennie, looking me up and down. "Drunk yet?"

I shook my head.

"High?" asked Amelia, raising her eyebrows. Neither of them had cracked a smile.

"No," I said, "I've had one glass of champagne and nothing else."

Of course that was the moment that Jason reappeared, handing over another glass and grinning tipsily at my sisters. Lennie snorted and turned away, and Amelia went with her. Great. Back on my own. Fuck them.

I was starting to feel more relaxed. If my sisters didn't want to be friendly, at least Jason was. I sipped my drink and tried to remember where I'd last seen him.

"Were you at Ginny's party last weekend?" It was good I hadn't brought a wrap, actually. The room was getting hotter and hotter.

He nodded. He was sweating, I noticed, and kept wiping his hands on his pants. "I was, don't you remember?" He leaned closer and I smelled scotch and weed and something else . . . "We made out." He literally licked his lips. "Do you want to go outside?"

So I had kissed him. And yeah, that was the smell: rising despera-tion. I took another sip of my drink. "No, thanks. I'm supposed to min-gle and talk about the Foundation, you know." I tried to walk away, dismissing him politely with a smile, but he stayed close.

"No one cares," he said persuasively. "Come smoke a little weed; no one will notice." He put his hand around my upper arm, and tugged.

"*Come on, Chrissie, let's go have a little fun.*" *He looked over my shoulder and grinned. "Hey . . ."*

I looked. Another guy our age was smiling at me, high-fiving Jason. His cousin, presumably.

"*Hey, babe, check this out . . .*" *He pulled a phone out of his pocket, having apparently mistaken me for someone who gave a shit about technology.*

I looked back at Jason and raised my eyebrows. He was cuter than I'd first thought. I can see why I'd . . . I shook myself. Maybe it would be OK to blow off this dumb party. No one cared I was here. My mom hadn't even looked at me since we'd arrived.

"*See?*" *the cousin was saying. "Up to nineteen hours of high-quality video . . ."*

"*Fascinating,*" *I said, but didn't sound all that convincing even to myself. I looked around for my sisters again, for anyone I knew. I could see Nate Donovan on the far side of the patio, my mom and Harry were holding court in the middle of the ballroom, and John Donovan was talking to Davis Reed, that guy from my dad's old agency. Which direction to pick? I took a step and felt wobbly, the room suddenly very hot, the lights confusing. I laughed out loud, disbelievingly: Crap, I was drunker than I wanted to be. What is my problem?*

I looked at my sisters, both of whom had heard my laugh and were staring at me. I waved giddily and grinned. They looked away, and I could see my name on Lennie's lips, the twist of her scorn visible across the room. Oh, fuck you, I thought. I don't need your dumb help anyway. As I turned back to Jason and his cousin, the only other person to meet my eye was Nate Donovan, who raised one eyebrow as our eyes met. Not in judgment. In a question—you OK? For a split second I looked at him and wished I had the guts to shake my head and go talk to him instead. But the moment passed.

Damn. Well, at least I was feeling so much better. I turned back to Jason, who was both very good-looking and actually pleased to see me. I grinned widely at him, and let him take my hand.

I said, "Let's go party."

—

The air was much cooler outside, and for a second I felt better, *my head clearing. How had two glasses of wine gotten me so tanked? The hotel gardens stretched out on either side of the large driveway, rosebushes and hedges forming paths and squares. I'd heard there was a hedge maze somewhere . . . I'm probably confused enough.*

Jason was holding my hand, and I noticed his cousin was trailing behind us, still playing with his stupid phone.

"Where are we going?" I asked, but Jason just smiled at me. I slowed down, but he tugged me, and after resisting a second, I gave up and followed. Feeling all kinds of tired. Maybe there was a bench somewhere.

"This is good," said Jason, coming to a halt in what I realized was a small . . . what do you call those little shelters with flowers growing on them . . . pergola? No . . . like a little summerhouse thing. I don't know what it's called. But there was a bench and I headed for it.

"I need to sit down," I said, feeling a little woozy. "I think maybe . . ."

Jason sat next to me. "Let's smoke. You'll feel better . . ." He pulled a joint out of his pocket, and I giggled.

"Magician," I said, grinning at him. He wasn't very in focus, and we hadn't even smoked yet. It was all very funny.

We smoked the weed, the three of us. The cousin, whose name I never got, pulled out his phone yet again and started filming us.

"My plans to run for president are screwed now," I said, exhaling into the lens. "Oh well, not a very solid plan anyway . . ."

I really felt very fucked-up, and decided to give standing a try. "She sings, she dances, she walks . . . oops, not so well . . ." I was up, but as I stumbled across the uneven wooden floor, Jason intercepted me.

"Steady there, sweet stuff," he said, taking me by the arm. "Where are you off to?"

"Well," I said carefully, "I think I should go back to the party now."

"No way," he said, turning me around. "We're just getting started."

"Yeah," said his nameless cousin. "Let the games begin, right?" He shot Jason a look. "Jason tells me you're a very friendly girl."

I'd let Jason guide me back to the bench, but I didn't want to sit on it. I stood there, irresolute, not entirely sure why my brain wasn't cooperating with me. I hadn't realized how wobbly I was until Jason gave me a very small push and I sat down, hard.

"It's OK, Chrissie," he said, sitting down next to me. "We're all friends, right? It's all good?"

"Sure," I said, "it's all good." I frowned. "But I should go back." I tipped my head to one side, which made me feel slightly unwell. Shit. No. This isn't right. I tried to stand up again, but Jason wouldn't let me. I looked at him and frowned. "I don't feel so good."

"She's not going to puke on us, is she?" said his cousin, who was still holding up his phone. "That's no fucking fun at all."

I turned to him. "Hey, I'm not going to puke on you." I'm the cool girl, the one who drinks everyone under the table, the one who does all the drugs. My head was starting to spin for real now. "At least I don't think so." I looked at Jason. "What's going on?"

"Nothing, we're just going to have a good time."

I shrugged, starting to feel that maybe I was losing the plot a bit. How had I gotten here again? Wasn't I supposed to be somewhere else?

"No," I said, firmly, "I'm going back in now. I don't feel well." I was way more messed up than I should have been, and for a moment I

wondered if Jason had dosed my drink. Why would he do that, when I could reliably be counted on to get drunk all on my own?

I put my palms on the bench and tried to stand. I was suddenly so confused, everything was very choppy and I really, really wanted to leave. But I couldn't make my legs work, and when Jason started kissing me and put his hand on my thigh, I wasn't even entirely clear what was going on.

"Wait, sorry," I said, apologizing reflexively. "No . . ."

He started pushing me down on the bench, realized he didn't have enough room and suddenly stood and dragged me off the bench and onto the hard floor of the . . . whatever you call it.

"Hey," I said loudly, startled and hurt. "What the fuck . . ."

Suddenly, he was on me, so heavy, so angry for reasons I didn't understand, yanking at my dress, his arm across my neck, holding me down. He was hurting me. It was hurting.

"No," I said. "Stop . . ." But it was pointless; he wasn't listening. I could feel gravel digging into my back, the hard wooden floor scattered with tiny stones, could hear the distant noises of the party; suddenly, everything was very vivid and fuzzy at the same time, like a rapid-cut nightmare.

"You getting this?" he muttered, and somewhere in my head I realized the cousin was still there. I turned to see if he was going to stop Jason and help me, but all I could see were his shoes, a little way off. He wasn't going to help. No one was going to help.

Jason was fumbling at his fly now, and suddenly I realized I was in real trouble. I tried to pull myself out from under him, but he was so heavy, so much stronger than me. He started pulling up my dress. He was going to tear it. He was going to ruin it. My mom was going to be so mad at me.

"Please don't . . ." I said desperately, breaking my nails trying to get

purchase on the painted wood, the scent of roses heavy in the air, the sound of traffic in the street, the rapid panting of the man on top of me.

"Shh, Chrissie, shh . . ." His arm was still across my throat, and I couldn't breathe. I should have felt rage, should have fought, but I could barely breathe and I was so, so scared. I felt myself starting to slip into unconsciousness, the fight strangled out of me.

And suddenly, it was over. He was gone, lifted off me. I rolled over and curled up into a ball, sobbing, trying to cover myself with the torn strips of my dress. I could hear breathing, fast footsteps, anger.

And then I heard Davis Reed, probably the last voice I was expecting.

"Mr. Donovan," he said calmly, "why don't you take Christa somewhere quiet and help her get herself together. I'll deal with these two, alright?"

John Donovan was there? He came to help me. I started to sit up and suddenly threw up all over myself. I started to shake, to cry, too ashamed to open my eyes. I'd really messed up this time. I'd ruined everything.

Strong arms gathered me up and lifted me, and I tried to close my eyes and curl into an even smaller ball. John would take care of me, but it was all going to come out, and my mom was going to be furious with me.

"It's OK, Christa," said a voice in my ear. "I got you, it's over now. You're safe, I promise."

Oh my God.

Not John Donovan.

Nathan.

36

ROMANTIC GIFT
DONUM DOLOSUS

I came through the front door of Mom's house at about thirty miles an hour and startled Marcel and both of my sisters. Marcel barked sharply; my sisters paused their game of Go Fish and looked at me in consternation.

"What the hell happened now?" said Lennie, taking one look at my face and putting down her cards. She turned to Amelia. "Did we have money on them breaking up?"

Amelia shook her head. "No, we had the original hookup bet, then Mom has a wager on . . ."

"Stop talking," I said. "We have a problem." I looked down the hall. "Where's Mom?"

Lennie answered, "She went to the pier with Dad, for lunch."

They both giggled strangely, and I gave them a look.

Lennie added, "He showed up with flowers and her favorite candy."

I raised my eyebrows. "The toffee from the Farmers Market?"

They nodded, looking back down at their cards.

"Wait, like a date?"

Amelia shook her head. "No, I think they're just talking. But he's laying on the charm, as well he might."

I turned to my other sister. "He's going to need more than toffee and roses."

"Why?" asked Lennie, looking up at my tone. "What's going on, Christa?"

"We need to go get Mom right now." I was starting to panic. I could feel it coming up my spine like running horses.

She looked over at me, hearing a familiar note in my voice. "Try not to get triggered, Christa. Take a deep breath and center yourself." She looked at Amelia. "Perhaps we should all do a quick meditation?" She pulled out her phone. "I have an app . . ."

I said nothing, just handed her the xeroxed printout. Then I waited. Let's see how long it takes this pair of smart alecks.

"Holy shit," said Lennie approximately three seconds later. She stood up and handed Amelia the piece of paper. *Why does everyone get it quicker than me?* "Dad lied about Lorna. He worked with her, for crying out loud."

"When is this from?" asked Amelia calmly, smoothing out the wrinkles.

"It's from 1994. Three years before he disappeared." I looked at them. "She was his mistress. The whole thing was planned. I have no idea why, but if the shit's going to hit the fan, if we're going to tell Mom and the world is going to find out, I have to go pack. Can you guys go rescue Mom?"

"Why are you packing?" Amelia asked.

"In order to be able to carry my belongings all the way back to Violetta without dropping any of them."

Lennie frowned. "Why are *you* leaving? He's the one who should be leaving."

Amelia was looking under the table for her shoes. "We're definitely telling Mom," she said firmly. "And she'll decide whether to blow him sky-high or simply retire to a safe distance and hire a sniper."

I started walking toward my room, thinking about what needed to be packed. I suddenly thought of my new blue shirt, which I'd left in Nate's car. Dammit, I love that shirt.

"Christa!" Lennie's voice was sharp. "I asked you a question. Why are you leaving?"

"Davis Reed has video from the gala," I replied calmly. Having completely freaked out in the car and speed-walked over here, I realized I had reached the acceptance-of-imminent-disaster stage of the process. "He wants the truth about Dad to stay hidden, at least for a while. He said if I told anyone, he'd release the tape." I shrugged. "I can't stop it from happening. I just want to get away before it does."

"Davis said that?" Amelia's voice was still cool, and when I turned, she was folding the xeroxed paper in half. Then in half again, and again.

"Yes," I said. "And of course he has the fucking footage. He probably has Amelia Earhart stashed in a conference room somewhere."

Lennie cocked her head and stared at me. "Well, that seems unlikely," she said, "for several reasons."

Amelia stood up. She'd folded the paper small enough to tuck into the front pocket of her jeans. She kicked down her cuffs, made herself comfortable. "Alright, ladies. Let's roll."

"Where are we going?" I asked, looking at the time. "I really need to book a flight."

"You don't," said Amelia. "You're not leaving. We're going to go get Mom away from Jasper, and then we're going to the agency to talk to Davis."

I shook my head. "Ammy, if the truth about Dad comes out before Davis wants it to, he's going to release the footage. He's held on to it for a decade, and kept Dad's secret more than twice as long as that . . . He plays a very, very long game, and I really don't think we should even attempt to tackle him." I swallowed and tried not to cry. "I don't want to even think about that night, let alone deal with the world seeing footage. I want to go home."

"Christa, you are home. And I'm not telling you how to process your trauma, but that was a long time ago, was in no way your fault, and no one is going to use it as a tool to keep you quiet, hold you down, or drive you out of town, not on our watch," said Lennie, also getting up. "And as for Davis, I don't care if he's a Bond villain with a fluffy white cat and a sliding bridge with sharks under it; we are going to go make him keep his curling lip buttoned." She came up to me, and for a second I got ready to flinch.

She touched my cheek. "We let you down so badly that night. But not this time." She walked toward the door, then turned back. "Come on, Liddle Sisters," she said. "Time to boogie."

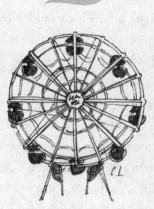

37

FERRIS WHEEL
ROTA FERRISSIA

The Santa Monica Pier boasts many things, including an arcade that was among the first in the United States to feature *Dance Dance Revolution*. If that isn't a reason for a moment of respect, I don't know what is.

One of its current claims to fame is a solar-powered Ferris wheel. I'm not entirely sure what that says about the state of either energy or entertainment in California, but it is what it is. When we reached the fun park end of the pier, which is actually in the middle, we trifurcated, which is one advantage of having two sisters. Better search-and-rescue coverage.

"Look out for Nate," Lennie called as we separated.

"Why?" I asked.

"Because I called him when we left. He might already be here.

His place is much closer." Her phone must have buzzed, because she turned it over and looked at it. "Huh, he must have been standing at the front door when he got my text. He's here already and they're at the Ferris wheel."

Nate was here. Fantastic. That wouldn't be awkward at all.

Even without the tip, it wouldn't have taken us long, because the crowd was headed in that direction. From fifty feet away it was clear something was going on.

There was a ramp going up to the Ferris wheel, which was where you lined up to get on the ride. When we spotted Jasper and Mom, they were at the top of the ramp, surrounded by people taking pictures and getting things signed. Why would anyone sign a hot dog bun? No clue. Ask Jasper, I just saw him do it.

Amelia had started calling Mom's phone repeatedly when we left the house but hadn't gotten an answer. Mom's not a huge phone person; it could as easily be in her bedside drawer as in her handbag.

"You're small," Amelia said, turning to me. "Push your way through the crowd and get close enough for Mom to hear you."

"No," I said crossly. "You're tall—you push. If I push in, I won't be able to see a thing. How is that a good plan?" I was trying to catch Mom's eye, but she was talking to people and being nice, damn her. I could tell just looking at her face that she was having a good time, and I felt a wave of guilt that I was about to rain on her latest parade. I like to divide my mental energy between not caring about other people and caring way too much, that way I can be damned if I do and damned if I don't.

"Nate!" Lennie yelled his name two or three times until the lady in front of her turned around. "Sorry," said Lennie, "I'm just really trying to reach that guy right there . . ." She pointed.

The lady tapped the guy in front, explained, and so on, and

eventually, some distant person tapped Nate on the shoulder and he turned around and immediately spotted me. He made the universal facial expression for *God, I'm glad to see you and I'm sorry we argued*, but this really wasn't the time. I was sorry we argued too, but as whatever I said to him next was going to end with *and now I'm catching the next flight to Paris*, I doubted I was going to be able to make things much better between us.

It's fine, it's just a fling. We'll both get over it soon enough. I had a brief flash of the previous night, the connection I had felt—and feel—with him. I shoved it down because this girl has no time for love. Who even mentioned love?

Lennie waved and pointed to the side, and Nate got it. He and I both headed to the far right of the crowd, where the shooting games were. Lennie and Amelia went to the other side. Nate was going to be the first to get close, but by the time he reached hailing distance, Jasper and Denny were already on the wheel.

Rather than face Nate, I started to make my way through the crowd, hoping to get to the point where the exiting passengers would get off. I wasn't completely sure where it was, and as soon as I was in among the people, I couldn't see. As I'd predicted this myself, you would think I'd remember.

Suddenly, phones started pinging all around me. The temple bell, the chirp, the gong—it was a club-dub medley of alert sounds. People did as they were told and looked.

I became aware of it passing around me like a large snake moving through dry grass: *Jasper Liddle's mistress . . . it wasn't an accident . . . all lies . . .*

Above us, Jasper and Mom were revolving, smiling and waving at the crowd below. Maybe they were too high up to make out the changing facial expressions beneath them, or maybe the people clustered right at the bottom didn't care what Jasper did. But by the time the ride ended, it seemed like everyone in the crowd had heard the news and the vibe had changed from genial celebration to *let's all you townspeople get torches and meet in the woods*. Lennie and Amelia had found the exit to the ride, and I could see them intercepting Mom as the crowd surged a little. For a second, a split second, I was lifted off my feet and carried forward. The feeling of being trapped made me panic for a moment, but another second passed and the crowd moved again, dropping me on my feet.

Over the heads of the crowd, I heard an irritatingly familiar voice. "Jasper, why did you do it?"

How was it possible Sarah Pepperdine was here? She'd gone for mustard in a big way, and I suddenly recognized the purple printout in her hand. She had the original. She had the newsletter. How the fuck did she get that, and oh my God, Alex Dutton was going to plotz when he discovered he'd been scooped by Miss Co-ordination. He was probably still on the flight to Alaska and would discover it when he landed. I was glad I was going to be on another plane at the time.

It was then I decided to flee the scene. Turning, I started to push my way to the edge of the crowd again. As I did, I saw Jordan from the agency, pushing back in the other direction, his eyes laser focused on—presumably—Jasper.

Great. The cavalry had arrived. I'm outta here.

38

CAROUSEL HORSE
EQUUS UPANDDOWNUS

As I hope you know by now, while I generally don't hesitate to make my presence or opinion known, when it comes to fight or flight, I am flight all the way. Difficult situation? Painful emotion? That's me out the door before anyone's even had time to say, *Hey, where's Christa*? I have excellent acceleration, and a sense of self-preservation so developed I will hide in a sock drawer if I have to. When the crowd surged forward to ask a million questions of poor old Dad, I was already on the move in the opposite direction. I'm sorry, but he'd made this particular bed and was going to have to hide under it alone.

I heard someone call my name, and shifted up a gear. Christa Liddle would not be available for questions or photographs today or any other day. All of Davis Reed's plans were going tits up, and whose fault was that?

I could see the arch at the end of the pier ahead, by the historic rotunda that houses the carousel, but the boardwalk narrowed and the crowd thickened at that point and I'd be trapped. But this had been my playground, literally. My sisters and I spent days and weeks and summers pottering around on the pier. Time for a good hiding spot. I hit the gas, cut through a narrow alley behind a fish restaurant, popped through a door marked STAFF ONLY and was climbing onto an inner-circle carousel horse before my pursuer even entered the rotunda. There's a seven-second hitch between the music starting and the ride moving, during which all the attendants are looking somewhere else. Local kids knew about it, and the attendants knew the local kids and it was all cool. I haven't paid for a carousel ride since 2002, which is admittedly a strange flex.

I ducked my head down as I buckled the narrow leather belt around my waist, the only safety measure the antique carousel offers. *Good luck getting a photo of me now, sucker.* I was surrounded on all sides by tween-age girls, or maybe they were teens; it was hard to tell. They were wearing a variety of small clothes but also carrying armfuls of stuffed toys they'd clearly won that day. They teetered on the edge of adolescence, giddy with the freedom and promise of simply being out under their own steam, the possibility that something new might happen. It was like hiding in a flock of canaries; their enthusiastic chirping and waving of hands was the perfect cover. They paid me no attention whatsoever.

I risked a quick peep to see which journalist had pursued me. Please, God, let it not be Sarah Pepperdine, the color-coordinated cobra. Nope, it was a guy. He came to a stop and started scanning the room. His face was flushed, and as the attendant rang the bell and the carousel began to turn, I realized it was Nate. I opened my mouth to call his name, but found myself hesitating. I was too tired to fight anymore, and I regretted so many of the things I'd said to him. Why do I always act so fast and push away so hard? Oh my God, my sisters are right: I need therapy.

My horse began to slowly rise and fall, and as we circled for the first time, I could see Nate moving through the crowd, looking for me. He didn't look angry. He looked desperate, and I felt my heart lurch as I lost sight of him.

You're probably familiar with carousel music, but if not, imagine music made by throwing hundreds of bells against a wall. It was very loud, and I knew if I called Nate's name, there was every chance he wouldn't hear me. The carousel was picking up speed, so a few seconds later I was around again, and this time he was nowhere to be seen.

Then I spotted him, heading toward the exit. He was nearly there, he was going to leave, and I was stuck on a wooden horse on the other side of a very large room. Without thinking about it for even a single second, I stood up in my stirrups and yelled as loudly as I could, "Nate! Nathan Donovan!"

He turned around. The carousel carried me out of sight, and for a moment I shared his desperation. Until that second, I hadn't realized how much it would hurt to watch him walk away.

I slowly sat back down on the horse, my eyes prickling. I took a deep breath and got ready to yell his name again. And keep yelling, if necessary.

All the tweens nearby had whipped around in surprise when I yelled, having not noticed me among them. Young girls don't *see* adult women; their eyes just slide over our faces with their occasional wrinkles and regular, unadorned features. We're like cutlery, or maybe a nonflowering shrub. They were amazed I had infiltrated their group, and concerned I might be a total lunatic who'd just yelled for no reason at all.

"Hey!" barked the carousel attendant, scuttling around the central support, her reflection leaping from mirror to mirror. "No standing on the ride!" She glared at me, but the minute I was out of her eyeline, I stood up again. As I came around the circle, I got ready to yell again, this time with even more emphasis.

But he'd heard me the first time.

He was standing by the fence that surrounded the carousel, his hands holding tight to the top rail, scanning the riders' faces.

He spotted me, and I saw his eyes widen and color flood his skin before he dialed it back, trying hard to appear as if he chatted with women on carousels every day. "Hey there," he called out as I swung past. He raised his hand a little and waved it. So casual, like he hadn't just chased me down a pier.

"Hey there," I called back, like I hadn't just screamed his name across the void.

The carousel's spin separated us again.

A girl seated on a rabbit nearby said, "Is that your boyfriend?"

I shrugged. "Kind of? Maybe? Not sure."

"Ooh," she said. "Tea."

The Santa Monica Pier Carousel turns at a fleet four and a half miles an hour and takes around thirteen seconds to make a rotation. Two breaths later, Nate was there again.

"Are you OK?" he called out as I glided by, going up and down in a stately manner. "That was . . . a lot."

"Yeah, I'm OK," I called back. I wasn't OK at all, but now wasn't the time to get into it. "You?" He was nodding as we revolved away.

Bunny Girl said, "He's very cute." Her eyes were wide and encouraging.

Her friend, who was on a nearby horse, shook her head. "He's alright, but he looks too much like Spider-Man."

Bunny Girl frowned. "The actor or the actual Spider-Man?"

Horse Girl: "The actor, of course. Spider-Man doesn't have a face."

Bunny Girl: "Well, of course he has a face."

Horse Girl: "No, he wears a mask."

Bunny Girl: "Yeah, but with a face under it, doofus." She suddenly seemed annoyed. "Otherwise it would just be all saggy." She rolled her eyes.

This silenced her friend, and I couldn't argue with it either.

Nate came around again. Or rather, we came around; he stayed still. You know how carousels work, sorry.

"I'm sorry about earlier," he called. I noticed several people openly enjoying this back-and-forth. I guess I don't care so much about privacy after all.

"Me too," I called back, then added, "I'm leaving . . . I have to go back to Violetta." I lost sight of him.

"Who's Violetta?" asked Bunny Girl, deeply interested. "You have a girlfriend as well?"

"Are you cheating on Violetta with that guy?" said Horse Girl, who clearly enjoyed cutting to the chase.

"No," I said to both questions. "Violetta isn't a person."

For some reason, Horse Girl took umbrage. "Hey, don't diminish her agency."

I let it lie. Just no point.

We swung around again, and Nate started yelling as soon as he saw me.

"No, don't go back, stay here with me." He was doing that thing where he bounces on his feet, like a cat getting ready to jump. "I know it's all surreal," he called, "but you and me is the realest thing about it."

"No, I gotta go," I called back. "Why don't you come with *me*?" We revolved out of sight.

Horse Girl was scandalized. "You just said you weren't sure he was your boyfriend and now you're ready to move in with him? How well do you know this guy?"

I shrugged. "I've known him my whole life."

Bunny Girl narrowed her eyes. She'd been paying attention. "Wait . . . so he's your friend with benefits? I appreciate your rejection of labels and limitations, but are you friends or lovers? I mean, literally?"

"Well, both, but it's . . ." I stopped, struck by an incredible realization. The blood rushed to my head as I shakily grabbed the golden pole in front of me. I had been a very bad scientist. I had ignored plentiful evidence. I hadn't drawn the obvious inference. If I was my own boss, I would have fired myself.

As Nate came into view, I knew to my marrow that it was always going to be this way for me. I would always be waiting to see him again, even as I happily lived a life that kept us apart a lot. Once more, and to the deep disappointment of the carousel attendant, I stood up in my stirrups so there would be no miscommunication.

"I'm falling in love with you," I yelled (that was the realization). "I don't know what that means, exactly, but I'm here for it. As long as I don't have to literally be here for it."

Nate went pale and his jaw dropped. This reaction was more than I expected from Mr. Blasé, and I felt a wave of relief that—I'll be honest—I'm still feeling to this day. I'd pulled an emotional splinter, and it felt great to get it out.

Bunny Girl was simply agape. There's no other way to say it.

Horse Girl, on the other hand, was frowning. "I didn't get that," she said. "Are you here or not here?"

"She's here metaphorically," explained her friend, "but not necessarily physically." She looked apologetically at me. "Sorry, she's a Virgo."

As we came around again, I could see there was some kind of . . . something . . . going on. The carousel attendants were both crouching with their arms out, advancing on Nate, who had jumped the fence around the ride and was apparently intent on leaping onto the moving carousel. There was no way that was a good idea.

"What on earth are you doing?" I yelled as I galloped around the curve.

"Coming to kiss you," he yelled back. "They won't let me."

I twisted over my shoulder to watch for as long as I could. To be honest, only one of the attendants was really making an effort; the other was shuffling sideways while using his phone to call the Carousel Cops. I got the impression working at the historic Santa Monica Pier Carousel was not his passion project. Nate suddenly feinted left and broke through the (two-man) security cordon. He started running to the carousel, the attendants in startled pursuit.

"Wait," I called, "I'm coming!" I started fumbling with the belt buckle. Almost immediately, the ride attendant was three millimeters away from my face. She had trained for this, dreamed of it, and today was her day.

"Ma'am," she said firmly, "you may not remove your safety belt while the ride is in motion."

I could still hear shouting from the other side of the rotunda, and in the distance, the sound of sirens. I had the belt undone and gave the attendant a firm look. "I understand you have a job to do, but I'm getting off this ride right now."

She placed her hand firmly on the painted mane of my trusty steed. "Ma'am, dismount from this horse and you will be violating city safety codes and committing a criminal offense."

We'd come around to the crowded side again, and I saw it had turned into a classic Los Angeles scenario: Filming in Progress. Maybe a dozen people had taken out their phones in a serious way, and were attempting to capture whatever the heck this was. No one was intervening; they were too busy trying to get the framing right. Nate was dodging what had become four attendants and a random person dressed as a clown. No, wait, the clown was on his side. No idea how that happened.

"Oh my goodness," I said, pointing over the attendant's shoulder. "Is that a clown??"

She looked, I leapt, and two seconds later, I was discovering that it was much harder than I'd expected to run between moving wooden horses on a wide platform that rotated at speed. Centrifugal force is a bitch.

Nate, meanwhile, saw me trying to get to him and redoubled his efforts. Sprinting between two guys, he ran in the direction of the carousel and leapt with—no shit—the elegance and power of a deer, grabbing one of the golden poles and swinging around it like Gene Kelly dancing in the rain. Landing easily, he caught my hand and pulled me to him.

As spontaneous applause filled the rotunda, we kissed and

clung on tight, while the attendant turned off the music in a fit of pique.

"Please remain seated until the ride comes to a full and complete stop," she shouted, "and the attendant rings THE BELL." Over Nate's shoulder, I saw cops coming through the door.

I looked up at him. "Something tells me we're not going to get to spend much time together tonight."

He looked at the cops, and shook his head. "Ready to make a run for it?"

"Always."

I took his hand, and when we reached the furthest point of the circle, where the cops couldn't see us, we let go of the carousel—which had in no way come to a complete stop—and jumped off. Yes, I immediately fell to the ground and bruised my pride, but Nate pulled me up and we were out the door and gone before the cops even got past the clown.

39

POCKET UNIVERSE
KOSMOS MARSUPIUM

We made it past the building supplies and security tape, creeping between parked cars to one of the rusty cement staircases leading down to the sand. A few people came spilling out of the carousel rotunda behind us, but we were under the pier before they could work out where we went.

"Shit," said Nate suddenly. "Drop." As if we were a pair of marines who'd been training together for months, we both hit the sand.

I heard voices for a second or two before I placed them. I turned my head to look at Nate, who had his finger on his lips. Our faces were inches apart. In the midst of all this chaos and disaster, I couldn't help feeling one of the clenching inhalations of pure desire that I got every time we were together. Followed by the crushing recollection that I was going back to Violetta and leaving him behind.

Up ahead of us, Jordan was talking to Jasper. Somehow he'd worked his client free of the crowd, and now it looked and sounded like he was taking control of the situation, rising to the moment in a way that would have made Davis proud. Above us, the crowd was very loud, thousands of sneakers echoing on old wood, but thanks to the magic of acoustics, we could hear.[1]

"Davis made it extremely clear, Jasper," Jordan was saying. His tone was firm, but not mean. "Come with me to the agency and we'll make a plan. He'll come up with something; he always does."

Jasper laughed bitterly. "I wish I had the same faith in him that you do, but I guess it's better than turning and walking into the ocean until it closes over my head, which is my best idea currently."

Jordan patted my dad on the arm, like you might a horse, or a dog you didn't know very well, and they turned and started trudging up the sand. Jordan handed Jasper one of those dumb wigs where the baseball hat has hair in it—I mean, genuinely Halloween costume–level bad. But that and a pair of sunglasses made him completely unrecognizable. I guess if you're not looking that closely, anything works. Nate and I sat up and watched them walk up the beach and away without anyone even approaching them.

He turned and looked at me. "What on earth is going on?"

I leaned over and kissed him as hard and deep as I wanted to. It was possible this might be my last chance, and I wasn't going to

---

1. I imagine the hard underside of the pier and the soft absorptive qualities of the sand made for an interesting ray diagram of acoustical analysis, especially when you factor in the Pacific Ocean rumbling in the background, but it's not really my field. OK, not at all my field, but I bet it would be cool.

miss it. He was right there with me, his hand curving around my head, holding me close while his arm went around my waist, pulling me against him.

"I'm sorry about earlier," he said. "I've barely been able to think straight. I was walking up and down the beach for an hour trying to decide what to say to you, then Lennie texted."

"I'm sorry too," I said. "I get cranky too fast. I'm . . . going to work on it." I kissed him again, then said, "But I have to leave." I felt my throat getting tight and tried to pull myself together. "I can't stay."

"Because of Jasper?" Nate looked confused. "I really feel like I missed the memo here. What happened? Why?"

I couldn't look at him. "It's not just my dad. There's video. From that night at the gala. Davis Reed has it. He said if I told about Jasper, he would release it." I stood and started brushing the sand off my shirt. "And now the story about Jasper is out, and even though it wasn't my fault it got out, I think I need to go."

"But wait . . . you just said you were falling in love with me." He stood and reached for my hands. "Stay with me. We can hole up in my place until it all blows over." He smiled. "We'll hide out in bed."

I smiled back at him, but shook my head. "I *am* falling in love with you. It's confusing as fuck, I don't understand it. I've never felt like this about anyone, with anyone. But I don't think hiding out is going to work." I thought about that for a second and laughed at myself. "I mean hiding out here. Hiding out on the island will be fine."

"Why not hide here? Or even just face it down? The media will lose interest eventually, especially as now they're going to be all over Jasper and his ridiculousness."

I frowned. "No way, there's just too much appetite for content, they'll want it all. They're going to cut that video up into hundreds of stills that are going to follow me everywhere I go. Someone will work out who designed my dress, and that will trend for a minute. There will be discussions of teenage drinking. Teen sex. Sexual assault. Date rape. Roofies. All related to my story, even though no one will ask my opinion of any of it. Every dumb, drunken thing I did as a teenager will be paraded across the public square, and if they can tie it to my dad being a cheat and a liar, they'll do that too and call it thematic. If I press charges, there'll be a court case they can salivate over. If I don't press charges, I'll be a sad cautionary tale about how the legal system revictimizes victims with no acknowledgment that the media raises the hammer higher and harder than anyone else. That night will get attached to my name just like the butterfly, the dead father, the drugs and the drinking all got attached." I shook my head. "The lies just build up like the layers of a pearl . . ." I paused, something striking me. "Although slightly less stochastically, I guess, because at least there's a timeline."

Nate raised his eyebrows. "What, now?"

I nodded. "Well, surprisingly, the process of nacreous accretion seems like it would be somewhat systematic, but there's really a lot of random . . ." I stopped because of his face. "Sorry. Sidetrack." I sighed. "When I get anxious I get fact-y."

Nate took a deep breath. "Well, not sure how pearls came into it, and there were several words there I have no idea the meaning of, but I get that it's scary to have people talk about you as if they know you when they don't, and when the lies keep on building and there's nothing you can do about it."

I nodded.

"That's totally reasonable, but your family knows the real you. I know the real you."

My turn to raise my eyebrows. "You do? After what, a few days? A week?"

"A few days and a lifetime, yes, I think so. And you know the real me, because for some reason the real me is who I am when I'm with you. I feel so . . . myself with you. It's just so easy." He frowned. "You don't feel that way?"

My anxiety made me want to say no, to pretend I was impervious. But I didn't. "Yes, I feel the same way." I looked down. "However, I'm not completely sure I know who the real me is right now. Everything feels very . . . transient and weird." I giggled unexpectedly; honestly, my emotions were all over the place. "*Weird* not being a very accurate term, but you know what I mean." I looked at him suddenly, wanting to hear what he thought. "Who is the real Christa Liddle, then? I mean, the one you think you know."

Nate shifted his weight on the sand, looking thoughtful. "Well, to start with, and maybe most of all, you're a massive pain in the ass. I mean, really. You're prickly as fuck, you won't take help of any kind, God forbid anyone should see you have human emotions or needs, and you fly off the handle at the drop of a hat."

I opened my mouth to respond, but he wasn't having it.

"You're also an incredibly tough motherfucker who won't take any shit from anyone, and is ready to fight for what matters to you. No hesitation. No uncertainty. Those two aspects alone make for a pretty scary experience, and maybe if there wasn't anything else, I wouldn't be saying all this. I'd just be running for my life." He smiled. "But there's so much more."

I narrowed my eyes at him, but he kept rolling on.

"Let's not forget Professor Barnet, zoologist and super nerd. I could listen to you talk for hours, and have literally zero idea what you're talking about. You said the word *wentletrap* the other day and I pretended to know what it was. I was willing to bet it was alive in some way, probably some drippy little ocean dweller, but it could just as easily have been a restaurant, a clothing label or a tropical disease. It didn't matter; I just like hearing you think out loud, and God knows I could stand to pick up some new vocabulary." He stroked my cheek with the back of his finger. "So brilliant. So curious. So quick-witted."

I pulled out my phone and looked at the time. As soon as Davis knew the story had broken, he would release the tape.

"Nate, I realize I asked, but I forgot I have to pack." I smiled and started to pull my hands away. "I'm happy you like . . ."

His face got serious. "No, Christa, hear me out." He tightened his grip on my hands. "Then there's the you I've only just gotten to know. The private you, the woman I . . ." His voice changed, his tone dropping. "The woman I was with last night." He bent his head to kiss me, and I stopped pulling away and leaned up on my toes, letting gravity help me press against him, wanting to soak in as much of him as I could.

He stepped back a little, catching me as I tipped and curling his hands around my waist. "The intoxicating, overwhelmingly sexy woman who wants me as much as I want her." His cheeks flushed. "The one I crave. But here's the thing, Christa. *All* those different women are the real you. There is no single, one-sided Christa. There are many, all of them part of the complex pocket universe that is you. And all your sides fit up against all my sides and we tessellate, baby . . ." He grinned and waggled his eyebrows. "Note the fancy word." He repeated it. "We tessellate, Christa. We fit like a glove and I'm here for all of it. I'm here for all of you." He kissed me, and he was completely correct: We fit good. (Technical term.)

"Stay here, Christa," he said against my lips. "Stay with me."

For a moment, I considered it. Then I remembered the footage, the embarrassment I was about to face. The media that was going to descend now that my dad's bullshit had come out. The cameras, the upheld phones, the interviews, the speculation . . . It would be too much, even with two of us. And there was my work, not that the snails were slowly counting the days till I returned, but it was still my work, and I wanted to get back to it. Why was life so complicated?

"Sorry," I said, "I have to go back to Violetta. And it's not even just the footage, or my dad, or my family or the show or the media . . . If I stay here, I'll be happy with you but I'll miss the island, and if I let myself fall deeply in love with you, I won't be happy there either because we won't be together." I shrugged. "I can't be in two places at once."

"Lovers are separated all the time," he said, putting his hand on my arm. "You won't be there forever. You'll finish your work and come home."

"Maybe." I thought about Dr. Last, and his offer of tenure.

"When is there ever more than maybe?" he said, tugging me close. "For any of us? Nothing is certain. The world could end tomorrow. All I know for sure is whatever this is, I'm here for it. I accept it. I'll take whatever time we have together now and make the most of it, and putting thousands of miles between us isn't going to change how I feel. It's that thing you said on the beach . . . the thing with the entangling."

I raised my eyebrows. "Quantum entanglement?"

He laughed. "Yes, that thing. We're connected somehow. There's no point pretending we're not. When you're happy, I'll smile; when you get cold, I'll shiver. I'm not scared of distance, Christa. I'm scared of disconnection."

I gazed at him, and for a moment I wanted nothing more than to accept it, the love he was offering so wholeheartedly. It was a tiny bit terrifying, not going to lie, his readiness to dive into whatever this was between us, this depth. I wasn't as fearless as he was. I wasn't as ready.

"I can't do this now," I said, suddenly restless and uncomfortable. "Maybe I should be a stronger person or something, but all I want to do now is hide."

Nate looked at me, clearly thinking. Then suddenly, he stepped back and let go of my hands.

"Christa," he said, smiling, "you do you. Go do whatever you need to, and I will be right behind you, or right next to you, or standing in front of you, or living my life waiting for my next chance to be inside you." He hesitated, then stepped close one more time and kissed me, his hands finding my waist, bending his fingers over the edge of my jeans, tugging me close. I felt my body responding as it always did, my nerve endings firing, my back arching. This I was certain of, the physical part of us. For some reason we *were* connected, like a single form that had been broken in two and thrown out into the universe separately. We'd found each other. What we were going to do about it, I didn't know. But maybe he was right; maybe nobody knows.

Nate pulled away a little and angled his head so he could see me clearly. "Go fight your fight, Christa," he said. "Until you tell me otherwise, we're together. I am here for you." He stepped back and swept his arm around, taking in the beach, the pier, the city, the state, maybe even the entire continent, I wasn't sure. "Wherever here is, and wherever you are, it won't matter. We're together now. Entangled."

I raised my eyebrows. "You really like that whole quantum entanglement thing, huh?"

He grinned. "Well, I'm no physicist, but if it explains why I feel this way, then I'm all in. Plus I like the way it sounds." He laughed and suddenly I laughed too, because he was right. Everything was a little unbalanced, a little surreal. This whole day had been a trip and a half, and maybe it was time to just go with the flow and see what happened.

"I have to go now," I said. "I have to go talk to Mom and Lennie and Amelia and work out what to do."

He turned me around and gave me a little push. "Go, baby. Go do your thing. You know where I am when you need me."

I turned and looked at him. "Wait, where are you going?"

He grinned. "I was going to give you a head start and then kind of trail after you . . . You seem to have a full head of steam. I didn't want to ruin your dramatic exit."

I giggled. "That seems unnecessary. You can come with me."

He grinned. "You sure? You're somewhat . . . unpredictable. I didn't want to get in your way."

"In case I run you over?"

He picked me up and held me very close. "There is always that danger. You're a force of nature."

I nodded, dropping a kiss on the end of his nose. "You've mentioned that before."

"I wasn't wrong." He put me on my feet and smiled. "Lead on, baby. I'm right behind you."

40

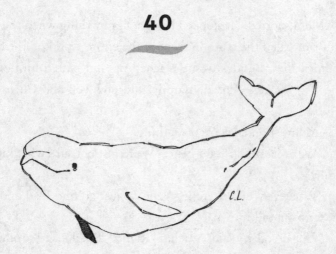

BELUGA WHALE
DELPHINAPTERUS LEUCAS

When we got back to the house, everyone was impatiently waiting for me.

"Where the hell have you been?" asked Lennie, who was pacing back and forth. "We've been calling."

"I've been ignoring you," I said. "Sorry."

"Let's go," said Mom. "We're going to the agency right now."

I looked at her. "They told you?"

She looked at me and nodded. "They did." For a moment, she frowned, then she added, "Honestly, what a dickhead."

Then she wiped her hands on her lap, stood up, whistled to Marcel, and said, "Let's go kick some ass." Then she looked at Nate. "I assume you're coming too?"

He hesitated. "Uh . . . maybe I shouldn't. It's kind of a family thing."

Mom snorted. "It stopped being a family thing when the journalist revealed the truth in front of the entire world on the Santa Monica Pier. Besides"—she reached up and patted him on the cheek—"you're essentially family, and now you and Christa are a thing."

"Mom," I said, "we're not a thing."

"We are a thing," said Nate. "We're just not sure what kind of thing."

"Whatever," said Lennie. "Can we just go find Dad and beat the crap out of him?"

"Not literally," said Amelia. "Right?" She looked around. "I mean, sure, we're all mad, and it definitely is subpar behavior and I get it, but at the same time, wouldn't it be better if we all just honored our feelings without resorting to violence?"

There was a pause and then Lennie said, "It's possible to have too much therapy, Amelia. How about we honor our feelings by punching him in the throat?"

"How about we stop talking and start moving," said Mom, leashing up the dog. "We can always set Marcel on him." She looked down at her dog. "World's cutest avenging angel."

It is said that Davis Reed was once taken by surprise and disliked it so intensely it became his professional white whale. He is never unprepared, or never appears to be. When the entire Liddle clan walked through the doors of the conference room where he and Jordan were working, he merely looked up and blinked at us like a cat in a sunbeam. Jordan at least had the decency to look alarmed.

"Hello, Denny," Davis said to my mom. "I thought you might come and see me."

She looked back at him unsmilingly. "You're lucky I'm coming from the front, Davis. It seems you've been messing with my family for far longer than I thought." She walked around the table and sat where she could see everyone. "Where's Jasper?"

Davis looked at me. "I thought we had an agreement, Christa?"

"It wasn't me that broke the story," I said. "It was Sarah Pepperdine." I paused. "How did she get hold of it?"

Davis shrugged. "I'm actually not sure." He looked at Jordan, who, for the very first time, seemed slightly pissed off. "Somebody messed up."

Jordan opened his mouth and closed it again. I noticed his toe was tapping, and wondered if the worm was getting ready to turn.

"And where is Jasper now?" asked Amelia.

"Packing, presumably," said Davis. "We spoke briefly, agreed on a plan, and he left."

"He *left*?" Lennie's voice was a squeak. "He just walked away . . . *again*?" She looked around the table. "Mother. Fucker."

Suddenly, the doors to the conference room burst open and a young woman came flying in, a tablet in one hand and a phone in the other. I knew her from somewhere, but couldn't immediately place her.

"This is fucking genius," she said loudly, waving the tablet. "Was this your idea?"

She'd been in the meeting. The social media guru. Chelsea.

She gazed at Davis with a mixture of awe and surprise. "I mean,

no offense, but you're older than time and this is just brilliant—
perfect location without feeling staged, a very now sense of Being
Real, and so fucking streamtastic." She looked at her phone. "If I
can ironically paraphrase, when I left you, you were but the learner,
now you are the master . . . This stream has over two million in the
chat right now, and they are popping OFF . . ." She giggled. "I
gotta hand it to you, it's epic."

Lennie looked at me. "Remind me who she is again, because I
can't understand anything she's saying and she's making me forget
the tools I learned in anger management."

I opened my mouth to answer, but Davis Reed beat me to it.

"Chelsea, what are you talking about?"

"You sent him there and let the media know, right? Dude, they
caught up to him so fast and now they've got him literally cornered, surrounded by vipers." She looked at her phone, then over
at the tablet. "Dozens of new streams every minute, and"—she
laughed out loud—"and now the old-school media is there. This is
fantastic." She frowned suddenly. "Though if you'd let me know, I
could have sold sponsorship. We'll talk about it for next time." She
pointed at her boss, the head of a multibillion-dollar agency who
regularly put the fear of God into studio heads and media moguls
alike. "I'm telling you, dude, you are *catching on.*"

"Chelsea!" said Jordan, snapping his fingers. "FOCUS. What.
Are. You. Talking. About?"

"Jasper Liddle," she said incredulously. "Trapped like a rat.
Surrounded by fans and nonfans. Photographers. Streamers. Jour-
nos. It's a whole scene. I thought you must have set it up."

"Why would you think that?" Davis looked as rattled as I'd
ever seen him, which is to say, extremely mildly.

"Well, because of where he is. I mean, it's almost too much . . ."

She looked around at all of us, clearly wondering if we were in any way on top of our games. "He's at the LA Zoo, of course. In the reptile house." She raised her eyebrows in delight. "Where else would you find a snake?" She shook her head and turned to walk away. "Honestly, you guys need to up your Ritalin."

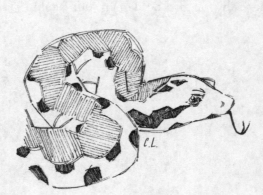

41

ARMENIAN VIPER
MONTIVIPERA RADDEI

After discussing various configurations, we ended up taking two cars. Nate and I went ahead in the Mercedes,
with my mom and sisters shoehorned and bickering in the back.
Davis Reed, Jordan and the redoubtable Chelsea, who was fascinated by the concept of experiencing things in real life as well as
online, followed in a limo. It was clear by the speed with which
Jordan mobilized transportation that the agency folks were keen to
beat us to Jasper. Control the story. Direct the narrative. Have him
killed, I don't know. The whole thing was getting a little fucking
silly at this point.

My family argued the entire way about whether or not to inter-
vene if Jasper was, indeed, surrounded by irritated fans and pushy
journalists.

Lennie was pretty clear. "I say we let the mob take him."

Amelia shook her head gently and said, "He made some very questionable life choices, but isn't being torn apart by strangers kind of overkill?"

They both looked at me.

I shrugged. "I didn't enjoy it at all when I was a teenager, but he's a fully grown adult male who had an affair and faked his death rather than admit it, so . . . this feels like a Mom question."

Mom was looking out the window of the car and saying nothing. She heard our silence and turned around.

"Sorry, what?"

"We were debating whether or not to let the crowd rip Dad apart . . ." Lennie raised her eyebrows. "Thoughts?"

Mom shrugged. "Wanting to think of yourself as a good person while facing undeniable evidence to the contrary is probably punishment enough. Your dad made decisions in the heat of passion and has to suffer the consequences in the chill wind of hindsight." She sighed. "There's nothing we can do to him that karmic retribution isn't already serving up by the bucketful."

We all stared at her, and I, for one, felt a cold shudder go over me. Like I said, she's a spiritual gangster: Take no prisoners, kick ass and tell the truth. King Solomon in a Hermès headscarf, Yoda with a Prada bag. I suddenly wondered if Dad might not prefer an angry mob to a one-on-one with Mom.

The LA Zoo has had its ups and downs over the years, but the Living Amphibians, Invertebrates, and Reptiles house (the LAIR, for those among you who enjoy a fortuitous and appropriate acronym) is a brilliant example of a creature-focused natural habitat exhibit. Dad, of course, hadn't been around for its opening, but I wasn't surprised he'd found his way there. He's always had a soft spot for the scaly. It contains several large rooms featuring a variety of creatures in their preferred habitats, ranging from rainforest to desert to ponds filled with crocodilians (to be fair, that one largely featured only crocodilians, as the other creatures were like, *Wait, no offense, but that water's filled with things that eat us, we're good over here, thanks*). It's a cracking exhibit—you should check it out next time you're in LA. Beats the Hollywood Walk of Fame any day.[1]

When we pushed our way through the crowd, Dad had his back up against the Armenian viper, or at least up against its glass-walled habitat. No doubt the viper was curled into the smallest, darkest corner it could find in order to avoid staring at the pressed, dressed ham that was my dad's ass.[2] And if my dad's butt wasn't enough to scare it off, then the hundred or so random people holding up their phones, cameras and microphones about two arm's lengths away from the front of the habitat would have done the trick.

Dad looked pretty upset, but when he saw us coming at him, he definitely started evaluating plan B: Break glass, tackle viper. Which I guess answers the question of how scared he was of Mom.

The media and assorted folks in front of him followed his widened gaze and turned to see what he was looking at, like a crowd at a very strange sporting event. And who was right there in front,

---

1. I've been told some people come to Los Angeles because of the movie business, and might therefore prefer their history Hollywood rather than Natural, but that can't possibly be right.

2. It's surprisingly easy to embarrass a viper, not just the Armenian ones. I'm joking. Have you ever seen a snake blush? Right, then.

dressed in an outfit that paired puce with turquoise and left both colors wishing they'd stayed in bed that morning? You guessed it.

Sarah Pepperdine could not have been happier to see us. You would have been forgiven for thinking we were there to hand her a Peabody, she greeted us with such enthusiasm. Of course, any shark gets toothy when it smells blood in the water.

"Denny Liddle!" It's possible Sarah Pepperdine was wasted in journalism and would have been better suited to the stage. Certainly, she could project, and when her voice rang across the Damp Forest area of the LAIR, it bounced off all the glass surfaces and made it into the ears of everyone present. "Any comment on the breaking news that your husband faked his death in order to run away with his mistress?"

Everyone fell silent and swiveled back to Jasper, again with a degree of coordination that in any other context would have suggested extensive rehearsal, but in this case merely reflected the crowd's awareness that history was being made. Albeit extremely unimportant history, historically speaking. Their silent concentration was helpful, because it meant when Dad opened his mouth and coughed, everyone could hear how dry his throat was.

"Don't say a word!" Davis Reed and his team had arrived. Jordan had paused to get a balloon at the gift shop, which was inexplicable, but did lend a festive air to what was otherwise shaping up to be a total shit show.

"Miss Pepperdine," said my mom, turning to the journalist. "Here's someone who can answer all your questions. Davis Reed is my husband's agent, and the one who came up with the plan to fake his death in the first place. He's been profiting from my family's sorrow ever since, and I'm sure he'd love to tell you all about it."

"Actually," said Davis smoothly, "you'll have to hear it from Oprah. We just signed an exclusive deal in the car. She'll be doing another interview tomorrow night." He made a tiny hand gesture, and Jordan glided forward, tying the balloon on my father's wrist. "My client will not be answering any more questions."

"I'm not your client," I said. "I don't mind answering questions." I turned to look at Ms. Pepperdine. "Fire away, I've got nothing to hide."

"Actually," said Davis, "you do. Or have you forgotten?"

"Are you threatening my daughter, Mr. Reed?"

"Threatening her with what?" asked Sarah Pepperdine, stepping closer. She raised her eyebrows at me, and I shrugged.

"When I was a teenager, I was assaulted at a party. My drink was drugged, and it was a traumatic and embarrassing experience." I swallowed. "Mr. Reed claims to have footage of the assault and is using it to make sure I don't tell you what I know about my father's disappearance." I looked at Davis Reed. "That's about the size of it, right?"

A ripple of firm disapproval went through the crowd, and those folks who hadn't been recording decided to stop being too cool for school and hit the button. Beeps aplenty. They weren't entirely sure who this guy was, but he was clearly an asshole.

My mother leaned forward, and I don't think I've ever seen a colder expression on her face. "My daughter was a minor and the victim of a crime. If you release any footage whatsoever, or spread any stories, or in any way steal her control over her own experience, I will use every single brain cell, every nerve, every connection and every single penny I own to crush you, your agency, your friends, your dogs, your apartment, your future and your fucking past. I will make you regret your great-grandfather didn't wear a condom.

I will pursue you to the ends of the earth and you will need to dig your own grave with your fingernails because you won't have a teaspoon to your fucking name."

There was a pause, and then someone in the crowd said, "Preach, queen."

Everyone was staring at Davis, but I was looking at my mom. She wasn't going to let them hurt me again. She was going to protect me. Despite the fact I was a fully adult woman, that felt really good. Sure, about fucking time. But still, better late than never.

And here's the really strange thing. As I watched her step up to the plate for me, and looked around at my sisters—and Nate—all of whom were united in their commitment to taking care of me, to protecting me, I realized I didn't need it. Not that I didn't need their help—*that* I would take quite happily—but . . .

"Besides," I said to Davis, "if you decide to be a dick and release the footage, I don't care. Let the world see me getting hurt. Let them see me in trouble. All the better to make it clear that I recovered from that experience and am fully ready to take on whatever further bullshit the world has to throw. I've spent the last decade hiding away—at school, in college, on a flipping island in the middle of the ocean—but enough is enough. Everybody goes through something, Davis, maybe even you. Everybody struggles, and most of us, if we're lucky, make it to the other side with a story to tell and new muscles to flex." I shrugged. "Write a press release, run it on the evening news, stream it on whatever platform your team says is popping right now and make the headline really big: *Christa Liddle got hurt and scared, then got back up and is ready to kick your ass*." I laughed. "No more hiding. Show the footage, Davis. Break the news. I couldn't care less."

There was a brief silence as everyone stopped staring at Davis and started staring at me. I looked at Nate, who was grinning. For a split second he poked his tongue out at me, a flash of sexy at the corner of his mouth. I grinned and poked right back.

Jordan spoke. "There is no footage."

Again, a ripple through the crowd, possibly even louder. They were really getting their money's worth this afternoon, here at the LA Zoo.[3]

Davis made a choking noise, presumably at having to tell the truth about something.

Jordan continued, "There never was. The kid never filmed anything. He was too scared to hit the button."

"For crying out loud," said Lennie, throwing up her hands. "Do you just lie out of habit, or do you actually think about it?"

Jordan looked at his boss. "Sorry, but if you can't read the room, I can."

Davis looked at his possibly ex-employee and decided to cut his losses. "Fair enough," he said. "Now, come on, Jasper, let's go. We have an exclusive interview to prepare for."

I said, "I bet Oprah was excited about that exclusive, huh?" I turned to Sarah Pepperdine and the other journalists standing around. "What a pity the entire story is about to get blown wide open on the Internet." I grinned. "Who's got questions?"

---

3. I later discovered there was a party of knitting enthusiasts visiting from a small town in Maine who had no idea what was going on and thought the whole thing was being filmed for a movie. They kept shimmying through the crowd to get a better look and possibly appear on camera, then getting shouldered aside by the press. Eventually, they took their knitting needles out, and if you look at YouTube and search "Jasper Liddle gets OWNED," you can see several of them triumphantly standing in the front row.

"Me!" Miss Pepperdine deserved the first question. She knew it, and she was ready for it. "Is it true your father faked his death?"

"Yes," answered my mother, "my husband faked his death in order to cover up an affair he was having." She looked at my dad, who was paler than the Armenian viper's belly. "What a total loser."

My father swallowed. "Denny," he said with an affecting break in his voice, "I'm so sorry you had to find out this way."

The crowd looked at one another, then pivoted to see my mom's response. Someone's phone went off and was swiftly silenced. (*Not now, Grandma!*)

My mom had spent many years in the public eye, and had clearly reached a place of acceptance about the way this was going to go down, because rather than attempting to move the conversation elsewhere, or not have it at all, she just waded in.

"Yes, Jasper," she said acerbically, "that's the issue here, the *way* I found out. Not the cheating itself, not the shock of the plane crash, not the weeks of waiting for first *good* then *bad* then *any* news, not the months of grieving, not the years of loneliness, not the decades of raising children alone, none of that." She sighed. "You could have just told me. It would have been messy, but I would have gotten over it much faster."

The crowd waited a moment to see if she had anything to add, then swiveled back to look at Dad. The same phone rang again, and this time a long and muffled beep suggested the phone had been completely turned off, and the next step would be sleeping with the crocodilians.

Dad looked like a guy waiting for the hangman to come out of the bathroom and start getting his ropes together. He cleared his throat and said, "I honestly thought—"

"Nope," interrupted Mom. "Try again. Whatever you did, neither honesty nor thought had anything to do with it."

Jasper frowned at his shoes. "I'm sorry, Denny, you're right. There's not a lot I can say in my own defense."

"No," said Mom, "and it's too late for apologies anyway."

"And yet," said Sarah Pepperdine, "America would like to hear what you have to say."

Jasper opened his mouth, but Davis was ready. "My client has signed a nondisclosure agreement that prevents him from answering any questions." Apparently, America was going to have to wait.

"No, Davis," said my father. "Enough secrets. It's too late." He smiled, a pale ghost of his usual high-wattage charmer. "Go ahead, Denny. I'll tell you everything."

Pings came from across the room as people double-checked their phones were working. Sarah Pepperdine glared at her camera operator, who nodded and took a wider stance. She wasn't going to miss any of it, low light conditions be damned.

My mom said, "This affair was going on for a while before you hatched your stupid plan?"

He nodded.

Mom narrowed her eyes at him. "Jasper, if you were already with Lorna, then why even try to fix our marriage? We weren't getting along, we had problems, but we could have separated civilly." She ran her hands through her hair, not that it needed any adjusting. "I didn't need to be your wife to be happy, Jasper. I've never needed anyone else to be happy."

Jasper's smile got a tiny bit bigger. "I know, Denny."

Mom said, "To be fair, Jasper, you did more for me by leaving than you could have done by staying. I pulled myself together because I had to. What was up until then the worst thing that ever happened to me turned out to be the reason I met Harry, who was the love of my life." Her eyes were clear. "I had thought it was you."

Jasper nodded. "And I thought it was you." There was silence for a while. The crowd held their breath. The journalists tried not to make cheering noises at the plethora of quotes and meme-able moments. My sisters and I just stood there.

It was, like, super awkward.

"I have a question," said Amelia. "This plan . . . I mean, no of-fense, Dad, but it's a little complicated for you, isn't it?"

A pause. Then we all turned to look at Davis.

Davis shrugged and smiled without the slightest hint of apol-ogy. "Sorry. I was just doing my job."

"Playing God?" My mother really could put a lot of ice into her tone. It's just as well the environment was temperature controlled, because some of those reptiles are very sensitive to cold.

Davis laughed. "Protecting my client." He sighed, looked around to see if any of the big networks had shown up, spotted a cam-era crew from ABC and turned his better side in their direction. "Twenty-five years ago, Jasper Liddle was at the height of his fame. The toys had taken off. The show was doing well, selling overseas in a record number of markets. Then Jasper came to me and said he wanted to quit." He looked at Jasper. "Because he was *in love.*"

"With a woman who worked for you," added Amelia.

"Indeed," agreed Davis. "Lorna Wesson. Jasper wanted to get a divorce and marry her." He straightened his cuffs. "I talked him out of it. I suggested an alternative plan, one that would keep his fortune intact, protect his family from scandal, and preserve his legacy."

Sarah Pepperdine: "It was your idea to fake his death?" She flipped to a different screen on her phone. "How do you spell your name?"

I was determined to get to the bottom of this. "But why did he come back now? I mean, why did he agree to it?"

Suddenly, Jordan spoke up. "Because he had to." Apparently, the toe tapping back in the office had been the start of a major rebellion. "When Lorna got sick, Jasper reached out to Davis and did a deal."

Davis spoke. "Jordan, this is not germane to the conversation."

"No, but it's germane to her question." He looked at me. "The deal was very simple. Davis paid for Lorna to get the best possible treatment, and Jasper agreed to work off the debt by returning when Davis asked him to." He looked around the room. "When Davis was ready, he called in the chit."

We all looked at Davis, who was looking at Jordan in some confusion, like a bird who showed up early for the worm but got a brick in the back of the head for his trouble.

"You blackmailed him to return?" Mom's tone was incredulous. "What is with you and the blackmail?"

"I wouldn't use that term," said Davis. "I merely reminded him of his debt."

I stared at Davis Reed. "You're shameless."

"No, I'm peerless." He checked his camera angle and emphasized every word, his elegant voice dropping half an octave and ringing across the room. "The Liddle Foundation has built three elephant sanctuaries, two gorilla habitats, and protected more acres of rainforest than almost any other charity. They fund animal shelters and community gardens and retraining for animals used in dogfighting. They raise millions of dollars every year and put it to excellent use. Would it have been better for the world if I'd let Jasper simply torpedo his career?" He turned up his hands, their long fingers sketching possibilities in the air. I was reminded again of the few movie stars I'd ever seen in the flesh. So. Much. Charisma.

He lowered his voice a little and looked around at the people, drawing them in.

"The natural world is in trouble. Every day fifteen species go extinct. Forty thousand acres of wetland are lost. Irreplaceable, magical animals stumble to their deaths, unable to find food or water, their habitat destroyed.[4] And why? Because we don't have enough heroes to fight for what matters. We need people willing to go to any lengths to save the planet, battle the big polluters, drag truth out into the daylight. We need people like . . . Jasper Liddle." He held up Jasper's hand, and the crowd shifted on their feet, wanting to see. "You all know him. You grew up watching his show, learning about the world through him, through his brilliance and commitment. Now is the time for him to come back and fight once more." He started raising his voice, passion in every syllable. "He'll fight for what matters. He'll fight for the planet! He'll fight for the baby animals, orphaned and alone!" He paused and I swear there was a tear in his eye. "He'll fight for your future!"

This time the crowd didn't just ripple. They erupted. Applause rang out. People cheered. Jasper looked shocked for a second, but then smiled and raised his hands in the air.

Jasper! Jasper! Jasper!

I looked around. I looked at Nate. I looked at my mom and my sisters. And then I looked at Davis Reed.

He grinned at me, and lowered his voice. "The people don't

---

4. None of these numbers are accurate; he was just winging it. Nobody cared.

want the truth, Christa. They want a story. They want a hero. They want distraction from their boring little lives. And that, my dear, is what we give them."

I gazed around at everyone pushing forward to get to my dad. Reaching out to take selfies. It was as if they hadn't been standing there for the last twenty minutes, as if they'd all been in a trance. "They're *idiots*."

"No," said Davis Reed firmly, "they are *the audience*." He turned to Jordan and pointed his finger. "You're promoted. Get Oprah on the phone. We need a new direction."

As my family turned and made our way out of the LAIR, I took one look back. The crowd was surrounding my father, buzzing happily. I couldn't see him at all, but I knew he was there because of the fucking balloon Jordan had tied around his wrist. I shook my head: Davis Reed had walked into that room knowing *exactly* what was going to go down. He knew he'd turn it around. He knew Jasper would end up surrounded by an admiring crowd of people and that Jordan would need a simple way to keep an eye on him. So they'd taken thirty seconds to buy a balloon. Never be unprepared.

I laughed.

Los Angeles is insane.

Time to go home.

42

OVERSIZED BACKPACK
BACKPACKUS GIGANTICUS

L AX is no better to leave from than arrive at. I stood at the check-in desk, watching the baggage people argue over my backpack. Was it oversized? Was it checkable? Most importantly, was it likely to explode?

Nate was standing right behind me, his hand on the curve of my hip. I could have told you exactly where it was to the millimeter, because for several weeks we'd spent an inordinate amount of time mapping the surface of each other's skin. I loved him. I don't know how or why, but I loved him with every piece of myself, and I'd given all the pieces to him over and over.

Don't get ahead of yourself. I'm still going back to work. I'm going to finish my study and then I'm coming back to UCLA, as-suming the river dolphin guy decides to move on. I already heard from Margaret about teaching a class on marine mollusks a year from now. Damn, that woman is organized.

I'd also gone with my family (sans Jasper) to a therapy session that turned into one of the best parties I'd ever gone to, if you like the kind of party where everyone ends up in tears, telling everyone else how much they love them and why. Usually, there's a lot of booze involved at that kind of event, and we were all stone-cold sober. But it was good, and if I can find a therapist on Violetta who isn't related to everyone else on Violetta and won't gossip about me, I'll carry on. And yes, I know therapists don't gossip, but one, you don't know what it's like on the island, and two, I'm still a little shy about being known. I'm working on it, but it takes time. Don't push me.

"Here's your baggage claim ticket," said the desk agent. "If for some reason it doesn't show up with the regular luggage, you might want to check oversized." She lowered her voice. "The baggage handlers in Paris are highly unionized. They get pissy."

Nate walked me to the security line and hugged me silently for a minute. Then he pulled back and looked at me.

"It hasn't even been a month since I picked you up here, but in that time everything has changed. You walked up that ramp and every cell in my body reoriented itself, do you know what I mean?"

I nodded, because I knew exactly what he meant.

He ran his finger down my jaw, and smiled at me. "You have such energy, Christa, such unique energy. I love the way you move through the world . . ." He paused and grinned wickedly. "The way you *move*, like you're about to start dancing any minute. And when you get excited, your voice sounds like it's on the verge of laughter, like you can barely contain yourself. And here's the thing, baby. I don't want to contain you, I don't want to hold you back or keep you by my side if you need to be somewhere else. Even though watching you want to leave is killing me." He took my hand and threaded his fingers through mine, speaking quietly. "But it's OK, because now that we've found each other, there's no un-finding." He grinned suddenly, and I could see he'd hit on something that worked for him. "You know when you're surfing and you wipe out at speed and get caught and driven down by the current?"

I nodded. *Of course.*

"Well, this feels like that to me."

I couldn't stop myself. "Like you're drowning?"

He laughed. "No, like I'm caught in a swell that started a hundred miles away and won't stop until it hits the beach. I'm as powerless in the face of this . . . whatever this is . . . as I am in the Pacific. I just have to go with it." He stroked my cheek. "*Trust* it." He shrugged. "I could get anxious, I could worry you'll never come back, but actually, you're not really leaving me. You're just stretching the connection . . ." He kissed me again. "I'll come visit you as soon as I sort out things at the company." He gave me a little push. "Don't miss your flight. Those snails are probably impatient to see you, although I'm not sure how you'd be able to tell."

I watched him walk away, the back of his head so achingly familiar, so beloved already. I couldn't believe I was making this choice. Maybe I should stay here? Maybe I should force him to come with me?

He stopped suddenly and turned back. He looked at me, seeing inside my head as clearly as he saw everything else about me. "You're spinning out," he said. "Stop overthinking it. You're going back to the place you love, to do the work you love. I'm going to spend the rest of my life with you, and when we look back at this, we'll simply say, *Yeah, we were apart a bit at the beginning, but then we were together forever.*" He waggled his fingers at me. "Go, take care of your marine mollusks." He waved his phone. "I'll text you."

I frowned at him. "I'll text *you*," I said.

He grinned at me, and my phone tinged.

He licked his finger and drew a line in the air.

Fine. I see how it is.

43

VIOLET SEA SNAIL
JANTHINA JANTHINA

N,

Got back in one piece, if you don't count the part
where I got into a fight with a lady in the Paris airport
and ended up having to wait for my flight in the
security office. She recognized me, knew all about Dad,
and wanted to tell me how having a mistress and a wife
at the same time was super French and chic. It went
downhill fast. Oh well.

I miss you already. They say the first forty-eight hours
are the hardest.

C

C,

Who are they that say such stupid things? It's not getting any easier over here. Can't bring myself to change the sheets because they still smell of you. Keep thinking about your skin, about the way your hips move as you turn over in bed, the color of your eyes when you reach for me in the morning . . .

Sorry about the French. I saw your mom this morning and she didn't look like she was wasting a lot of sleep over Jasper, not going to lie. Leo's been staying there to keep the press from the door, and the biggest problem is Marcel getting peevish. Lennie and Amelia both leave for Europe tomorrow.

I miss you. Send photos.

N

....

N,

See attached photos.

C

....

C,

These are adorable, but I meant pictures of you, not the snails.

N

N,

OK, see new attached photos. Things here are settling down now. It's been a few days and the jet lag is almost gone. They repainted my room while I was away, and I cannot wait to see how you look in it. I miss you more than I'd anticipated. I guess I'd gotten used to feeling very detached while I was here, very separate. But now I just feel . . . incomplete. Does that make sense?

In other news, my snails are cooperating and data gathering is going really well. Might be able to speed up the conclusion of the study, not sure yet. We have typhoon warnings every day right now, and that disconcerts the wildlife.

C

. . . .

C,

Very funny. Pictures of your hand holding the snails is still not what I was looking for.

Typhoons? Like, highly destructive storms that could wipe you off the face of the earth? Maybe you should come home after all. Losing you completely is not acceptable to me.

I told the board today I was going to transition away from running the company. I'm embarrassed to say they took it very well. As I suspected, Alison stepped forward and offered to take over, and if anyone objected, I didn't notice it. I feel enormously relieved.

Now all I have to do is work out what to do with the rest of my life.

Apart from spending it with you.

N

. . . .

N,

Congrats on quitting. I love a quitter.

We had a huge tropical storm last week, thus the radio silence. Sorry about that. When the weather gets bad (which it does a lot, prepare yourself) we lose the Internet and someone has to literally climb up the volcano and stick the transmitter back up. It's digital but also very analog over here, if you get my drift.

This being-apart thing is not working for me as well as I had hoped. Last night I woke up all tangled in my bedsheets, in what was clearly the middle of a dream about you, because I could feel your hands on my skin and my mind was filled with your face and the weight of your body on top of me, the pressure of you between my legs, the sensation of your skin against my inner thighs, your hair twisted in my fingers, your mouth on mine and the taste of you everywhere. I am eleven thousand miles from you and utterly wrecked.

What the actual fuck.

C

. . . .

C,

OK, you might need to keep your dreams to yourself because hearing that one ruined my morning. I miss you so much—not just having you in my bed, although that looms pretty large right now. Just standing next to you. Just being close. I remember that day in the kitchen, watching Jasper getting interviewed by Oprah. At one point, your hip touched mine, and from that second on, I was so aware of how you were standing, the angle of your head, where your hands were, what your mouth and eyes were doing, where your body was relative to mine. I wanted to touch you so badly. I wanted to put my hands on your skin, trace the edges of your body, take your clothes off and just look . . . I felt myself leaning toward you from the inside out. And now that I've seen you, been with you, I miss so much more. I miss your voice (I'm buying a satellite phone, by the way; that week of silence nearly killed me), the tones and shades it gets when I'm moving closer to you, the sounds you make when I'm pleasing you.

I have to stop thinking about it. I have to go to work, finish up handing everything over.

But I keep thinking about your face . . . so beautiful, so sexy, so entirely, uniquely your face. Your intelligence,

your whimsy, your fierceness . . . The way your
character dances across your features is endlessly
charming to me, constantly changing and drawing me
in. The way you look, the way you look at me, the way
you watch me watch you . . . your eyes and the way
they sparkle and darken. The even, balanced fullness of
your lips, the way they curve, the way you smile . . . at
me, at yourself, at the world. I miss you so much,
Christa.

N

. . . .

N,

OK, the only—ONLY—good thing about being
separated from you is the emails you write. You're
killing me, Smalls.

I love you. See attached photos.

C

. . . .

C,

Damn, woman.

N

44

SOUTHERN CASSOWARY
CASUARIUS CASUARIUS

I sat on the Violettan mountainside, high above the town, and watched the ferry disembarking its twice-weekly load of passengers and packages. Dotted outside the harbor were sailboats and smaller vessels; the ferry dwarfed them all. From this vantage point, they were pastel smudges of people, a bright hat, a patterned dress, their faces too far away for me to make out detail. One passenger carefully lifted a bike onto the jetty, another had two small dogs on leashes, others were clearly locals, striding away from the dock and hurrying home. I shuddered a little as I watched the ferry guys unloading freight by basically tossing it from one end of the boat. I was still waiting for my microscope, and if it didn't come in one piece, it might be months before I could get another.

I lay back on the grass, the smell of the slightly sulfurous breeze familiar and warm. At first I was worried I'd brought too much modern media and Los Angeles scheming with me, but the subsequent weeks had wiped me down and set me back on my feet. Maybe it's unusual to grow up in one place but feel more at home in another, yet that's how it was for me and Violetta. Missing Nate was making it harder to be completely at home here, but I was managing it. Mostly. At first we'd struggled a little, but now we had a routine: We FaceTimed when the satellites allowed, and wrote to each other every day. It turned out he loved to write and I loved to read what he wrote, so that was a win.

I rolled over onto my tummy and looked down at the town again. I could see Simon whizzing along on his scooter, the small family dog keeping up and threatening to cause an accident at any moment. I'd nearly bailed on bringing it for him, because the last thing you want when trying to blow out of town incognito is a large, strangely shaped box that seems to poke anyone who comes near. However, Simon was thrilled and had stepped onto it two months ago and hadn't stepped off yet except for meals. It had definitely pleased his mom, Miranda, and I felt like my tenancy was pretty solid now. Just in time for me to leave, but I certainly wasn't telling her that. Not until I'd picked a worthy successor for my room.

Things had settled down at home too. Davis Reed had underestimated the general public—despite the crowd at the zoo getting carried away by the actual presence of celebrity, the rest of the world was still pretty pissed off with Dad. Netflix et al. all withdrew their deals, and for a minute it looked like Davis himself was going to get canceled. But he announced his resignation (which was actually just a title change from CEO to president) and issued a statement of elegant contrition. As he wasn't in any way famous, that story died in a week. You have to hand it to the man, he's a genius of manipulation. Someone should do a study.[1] Alex Dutton is in London, feverishly working on his book, and at last count, Davis Reed is entertaining options from two major studios, one minor, and three streaming services.[2]

Jasper's career required a little more finessing. He disappeared for a couple of months, while Davis leaked photos of him crying in various forested locations, eventually with a dog he seemed to have acquired (when in doubt, add a dog; it never fails to humanize the villain). News of movies in the works and the attachment of Chris Hemsworth warmed the public up a bit, and eventually Jasper re-emerged. He did a second interview with Oprah (who basically represented a forgiveness proxy for the rest of the world). It was a work of apology art, expressing deep contrition while at the same time making it clear he'd risked his life to be with the woman he loved.

I'm still not quite sure how I feel about him, to be honest. But my therapist on the island says I don't need to reach any conclusions until I'm good and ready, and that feelings take time to settle. When I find myself going around in circles at the weirdness of his behavior and the mixed bag of feelings it causes in me, I think about the naked mole rat, who is able to operate each of its front teeth individually, like chopsticks. This reminds me that nature is weird, and people are just nature, after all.

---

1. Not me.

2. Which will hopefully take some of the sting out of my blowing his exclusive live, to the entire Internet, from a highly meme-able reptile house. I still have the expletive-filled voice mail he left me twenty minutes after he arrived in Alaska, and I didn't blame him at all.

When Jasper was underground, and my sisters and I had left the city, Mom and Leo were even more besieged by the press than before. After a few days of being trapped in the house, they'd dropped Marcel at a high-end Beverly Hills dog hotel where he'd receive daily massages and have his energy cleansed by breed-appropriate crystals. Then they'd hopped on a friend's private plane (it really does help to have wealthy friends at times like these) and flown to Papua New Guinea. It was very far away, the Foundation had a cassowary sanctuary there, and it seemed like a pretty safe spot. If anyone did bother to track her down, Mom could always threaten to set the giant birds on them. (An empty threat: Cassowaries are quite shy and only get stabby if you come between them and something they feel particular about, but most journalists probably don't know that.) She and Leo had sent me a postcard that was currently on my bathroom mirror: *Glad you're not here,* said the card, *as you'd probably rather be there. Hope to swing by on our way back to say hi.*

As I was thinking about her, my phone buzzed, and of course it was a text from her. I'm telling you, the quantum entanglement thing is very real in my family.

The text said: **Arriving in Reunion next week, nuts idea!**

I frowned, and typed back, **Great, why nuts?**

I waited. Nothing.

I looked back down toward the harbor, and watched as a lovely little sailboat tacked in neatly and tied up. From up here I could only see one sailor, a man who leapt from the prow onto the dock . . . landing like a cat.

I frowned. I pulled out my phone. I sent a text.

The man paused in tying up the boat, and pulled his phone from his pocket.

Mother. Fucker.

Nuts idea.

I scrambled to my feet and started running down the mountain. My Coast to Cone record was fifteen minutes. I was pretty sure I could beat that.

ACKNOWLEDGMENTS

So, I'm a novelist and inveterate curious person, but I am not a marine biologist. And while I've been a snail lover since childhood (garden-variety), I am not a sea snail expert. Luckily for me, Celia Churchill, who was one of the authors of a seminal paper about violet sea snails, was kind enough to answer my questions about being a malacologist, and has my eternal thanks. She is not, however, responsible for any mistakes that crept in; that's all me. I also got some help from Dr. Douglas Fudge, who has the distinction—in my house and, I suspect, wherever he goes—of being known as Handsome Hagfish Guy. Hagfish don't get the respect they deserve, whereas violet sea snails are at least recognized for their beauty. The ocean contains wonders hiding just beneath the surface and so does the marine biology community; thank you both.

This book was a lot of work and took longer than it should have. It would never have made it to the finish line were it not for the efforts of my editor at Berkley, Kate Seaver. She never gave up on either me or Christa, and any success the book enjoys is equally hers to share. Similarly, my agent, Alexandra Machinist, was patience personified as I plowed through draft after draft. Never has an author had a more wonderful agent with more incredible hair. I bow before thee.

Christa
Comes
Out
of Her
Shell

Abbi Waxman

DISCUSSION QUESTIONS

1. Christa has retreated—literally—to an island in the middle of nowhere to focus on her work. She also avoids her family and her past. What lengths have you gone to in order to avoid difficult things?

2. When Christa returns to Los Angeles, she is greeted by Nate, a man whom she had a crush on as a teenager. As a grown woman, she finds herself still deeply attracted to him. How have your romantic tastes and approaches changed as you've aged, and what lessons have you learned that changed the way you look at past relationships?

3. Christa has had rocky relationships with her sisters and mother in the past, although she loves them. When she returns to Los Angeles, she finds them quite changed, as a result of therapy (and simply getting older and wiser). She struggles to reconcile

the new people they have become with the person she still is. In what ways has therapy (or the lack of it) changed the people you know?

4. Christa was exploited by the media as a teenager and is wary and somewhat shamefaced as a result. What do you think is the worst impact of this kind of public shaming on a person? Is Christa's response reasonable?

5. When Jasper Liddle returns, he is greeted in a variety of ways. Discuss the differences in the ways the three sisters respond, and compare their reactions with the way the "public" responds.

6. Denny's grief for her "late" husband is complicated, as most grief is. They were about to separate when he disappeared, and a long time has passed. His return brings up difficult feelings for her. Talk about the changing nature of grief, the way time alters your perception of a relationship, and how you might handle the sudden reappearance of someone you considered long gone.

7. Jasper made a challenging choice in order to be with the woman he loved. Discuss the morality of his decision.

8. The connection between past and present is a consistent theme in the novel, particularly in terms of relationships. How does the history of a relationship affect its current and future nature? Is it possible to "start over" in a relationship, or is the past always going to be part of it?

9. We often feel we "know" a celebrity because we read a lot about them in the media. Think about how your own life could be reduced to a series of headlines. How would that feel, and would you struggle to let go of controlling "the story"?

10. Christa cares a great deal about her work and has sacrificed a personal life in order to pursue it. Is it possible to achieve a balance between work and play, and what are the pros and cons of following a career that demands a lot of your time?

Photo by Leanna Creel

Abbi Waxman, the *USA Today* bestselling author of *Adult Assembly Required, I Was Told It Would Get Easier, The Bookish Life of Nina Hill, Other People's Houses,* and *The Garden of Small Beginnings,* is a chocolate-loving, dog-loving woman who lives in Los Angeles and lies down as much as possible. She worked in advertising for many years, which is how she learned to write fiction. She has three daughters, three dogs, three cats, and one very patient husband.

Ready to find
your next great read?

Let us help.

Visit prh.com/nextread

Penguin
Random
House